HUSH LITTLE

BY JANE ISAAC

The DC Beth Chamberlain series
The Other Woman
For Better, For Worse
Hush Little Baby

HUSH LITTLE BABY

Jane Isaac

An Aria Book

This edition first published in the United Kingdom in 2020 by Aria,
an imprint of Head of Zeus Ltd

Copyright © Jane Isaac, 2020

The moral right of Jane Isaac to be identified as the author
of this work has been asserted in accordance with the Copyright,
Designs and Patents Act of 1988.

A CIP catalogue record for this book is available from the
British Library.

ISBN 9781838934736

Typeset by Siliconchips Services Ltd UK

Cover design © Charlotte Abrams-Simpson

Aria
c/o Head of Zeus
First Floor East
5–8 Hardwick Street
London EC1R 4RG

www.ariafiction.com

To the late DC John Thorogood, who was full of knowledge and good humour and taken far too early.

1

The heels of Jordan's shoes scraped the pavement as she stepped off the bus.

She was already late; she didn't care.

It was a clear winter's day, the sky a cornflower-blue, but the wind was cruel, nipping at every inch of bare skin. She zipped her coat up to her chin, dawdled down the street.

A car passed, and another, followed by a lorry; a woman battled with a pushchair against the wind, her free hand dragging a toddler behind. Jordan didn't hear them, the sounds smothered by the baseline beat of Ariana Grande blasting through her earphones. Jordan's head rocked gently to the music as she searched the ground, widening her gait to avoid the gaps between the paving slabs, a game she'd played since she was a kid. Although she wasn't a kid anymore. In a less than a week, she'd be sixteen. Old enough to make her own decisions. Old enough to stop playing children's games.

The traffic thinned. She stretched her stride, defiantly planting a foot squarely on the next crack.

School started ten minutes ago. Her phone buzzed in her pocket with messages from her friends, wondering where she was. She pictured Lucy and Georgia sitting in form, listening to the crisp timbre of Mr Gosforth's Welsh accent as he took the register while texting her from beneath their desks. There was no point in hurrying, she'd have missed registration by the time she reached the school gates, she'd have to sign in at the main office.

She continued down the road and paused beside the school entrance where a hairline crack forked through the middle of a slab, a legacy of years of boots and shoes turning to traipse through the gates. The school loomed in front of her, the car park heaving. She stared at it a moment, then moved on, past the entrance and out of town.

Further down the road, banners advertising *New executive homes for modern families* blocked off a construction site. The enlarged photo of a man and a woman with perfect teeth, grinning, arms folded around the shoulders of two children, repeated again and again across the barrier. Jordan checked over her shoulder and turned off the main road, taking a narrow pathway between the building site and the old shoe factory beside. She stopped twenty yards down to search for a gap, the place where the railings met, and found it at the edge of the mother's smile, slipping in behind. A few puffs were what she needed right now, a little calmness to get her through the day.

She had to be careful. Chunks of broken rubble mingled with the upturned soil, making the ground uneven. But apart from concrete and debris she was alone in this desolate corner. A smell she couldn't place curled her nose.

Jordan found her footing, pulled a packet of Lambert and Butler from her pocket and lit up, taking a long drag. She exhaled slowly, watching the smoke swirl around her and trying to ignore the smell. A crow cawed overhead.

It was warmer in this spot, the covered railings providing a welcome barrier to the cutting wind. She unzipped the top of her coat and was idly kicking at the loose stones and lumps of concrete beneath her feet when something caught her eye. She pulled the plugs from her ears and bent forward. Tiny fingers curled into the stone. Still, unmoving. She peered closer, pointed a toe and hesitantly scraped back the nearby rubble with her boot – to reveal a bluish hand, a bony wrist laced with a bangle.

Her jaw dropped. The cigarette slipped to the ground as she scrambled back and lost her footing. Fell. Needles of pain spiked her lower back. Was it real? Edges of brick dug into her skin, snagging at her trousers as she wriggled back further.

A voice in the distance, muffled as if underwater. Her eyes didn't leave the tiny hand. The call grew louder. A pair of Rigger boots entered her line of vision. She looked up to see a builder, barely ten yards away, his ruddy face contorted beneath a yellow hard hat.

Jordan cast one last gaze at the tiny hand, hitched a breath, jumped to her feet and scarpered.

2

The water caressed her body as she glided along, legs propelling her forward, revelling in the endorphins that slowly slipped into her system.

Another lap. And another. The smell of the chlorine sharpened her senses, cleansing her mind.

On the next turn, she felt a nudge from behind. A hand tugged at her foot. She quickened her pace. Another grab, this time momentarily pulling her below the surface. She gasped a quick breath before the water engulfed her face. She kicked the hand away and worked her arms faster, quickening to a sprint.

Her vision blurred through her goggles. She whipped out a hand for the end rail, and missed. Fingers grasped her foot again, taking a hold this time. She was pulled down, underwater. Another kick, resisting the tension. The hand released its grip and she shot to the surface.

Water droplets trickled down Beth's face as she grabbed the rail, lifted her goggles and laughed at her niece, Lily, who was now beside her. 'You almost got me there!' she said. 'You're getting so fast.'

The child wiped her eyes and beamed at her aunt. 'Can we go again?'

Beth glanced at the clock. 'Maybe next time.' The child grimaced. 'We've almost had our hour. Don't want to miss out on your ice cream.'

The words performed their magic and the seven-year-old hauled herself out of the pool. It was rare that a day off for Lily – the village school had closed to be used as a polling station for the national elections – coincided with Beth's rest day and she wanted to make the most of their time together. They entered the changing room, skirted around a line of women gathering for an aqua-aerobics class, and made a play of opening lockers and getting themselves changed.

Minutes later, rivulets of water trickled between Beth's shoulder blades as she tied back her curls into a loose ponytail on the way to the cafe. She spotted the familiar sporty stance of DS Nick Geary leaning over a table, flicking through a newspaper an earlier customer had left. The sharp contours of his back were visible beneath his fitted white shirt. He looked strong, vital and as attractive as hell.

Beth allowed herself a wry smile. Six weeks had passed since they'd got back together and he'd moved into her home – to lodge until he found a flat closer to Force Headquarters. The move would be temporary, 'a couple of weeks at best,' he'd said. But he showed no sign of leaving anytime soon. While there was something uncomfortable about having a relationship with her sergeant, she couldn't deny he was good company. She enjoyed having him around, even if, after careful consideration, she still resisted his pleas to share their relationship with colleagues. A lodger was one thing, a lover quite another and since they were both deployed on the Homicide and Serious Crime Squad and she'd recently applied for promotion, she didn't want colleagues to think she was sleeping her way to the top. No. For now, they were lovers in secret, friends and work colleagues to the rest of the world.

Nick had whiled away his time in the gym while they swam, his dark hair still slick from his shower. Lily rushed towards him and encased him in a hug from behind. She certainly relished having him around more, friend or not. He teased her by gasping, feigning surprise. 'Good swim?' he said, his Northern Irish accent filling the area.

'Fab!' Beth said. 'Lily almost beat me at the crawl.' She widened her eyes at the child. 'Until she cheated.'

'I did not!' Lily's mock indignance melted into a musical chuckle.

'It's all about the winning,' Nick said. He winked at Lily and tilted his head towards the nearby freezer. 'Ready to choose?'

Beth watched her scamper across the room, marvelling at the child's enthusiasm for ice cream, despite the fact that Christmas was only two weeks away and outdoor temperatures struggled to rise above single figures.

'DC Beth Chamberlain,' Nick said, raising a brow. 'I was going to send for you.'

Beth's stomach dropped. The mention of her job title on her day off meant work. 'What is it?'

'I've just taken a call from the DCI. A body part has been discovered, looks like that of a small child, on a building site in Northampton.'

'Where?'

'Boughton Green Road. On the edge of Kingsthorpe.'

Beth knew the area well. She'd been raised in Kingsthorpe. Boughton Green Road was a long winding road that ran from the heart of the suburb's main shopping area through a plethora of housing estates and out to open countryside. She'd read somewhere that some of the farmers' fields at the bottom had recently been purchased to make way for much-needed residential housing, a controversial move many locals had petitioned against. 'The site at the end, near the shoe factory?' she checked.

'That's the one.'

3

An hour later, Beth stood beside Nick at the front of the conference room in Northamptonshire's Homicide and Major Incident suite and sipped her coffee. After a bright start, clouds had drifted in and conjoined, blocking out the sun, and the murkiness seeping in from the windows combined with the fluorescent lighting inside the room made it feel more like evening than late morning.

'A child's arm was discovered on the building site at the end of Boughton Green Road at 8.43 a.m. this morning.' DCI Lee Freeman stepped forward and tapped the board twice, drawing their attention to an abundance of photographs of the crime scene. 'Given the size, it's believed the limb belonged to an infant, possibly a young baby.' By the time they'd dropped Lily off and made their way across town, Freeman had already carried out the emergency staff briefing and deployed the rest of the team on initial enquiries and the room felt oddly quiet with just the three of them present.

Beth moved down the line, scrutinising the pictures of the greying limb, taken at a variety of angles. Only the top surface of an arm and hand were visible; palm down, fingers curled, the rest looked like it was set in stone. Railings in the background indicated it was found close to the edge of the site. She leaned in close. The skin was taut and mottled.

'I take it the arm is still attached to a body?'

'We think so. Dr Hunter was already there when I arrived at the scene this morning.'

Beth gave a short sigh of relief. Out of the two pathologists that covered their area, Susan Hunter was the most enthusiastic and, with a wealth of experience behind her, she also prioritised cases, bumping them up the post-mortem list if the police needed quick results. A small mercy to be grateful for.

Nick's face twisted. 'Looks like it's been dead a while, poor little mite.'

Freeman lifted a folder from the side table. 'They've been working on it under a tent in situ this morning. Hunter emailed these across.' He opened the folder, pulled out two sheets of A4, and passed them around. More photos, taken at various stages as they uncovered the area around the limb. In the first picture, the hand and arm were all that were exposed, the rest of the baby's body covered by what appeared to be a sheet of concrete. Beth passed it to Nick and examined the second. A trench of rubble and soil had been removed around the edges of the sheet, showing the clear lines of a concrete rectangle.

'From initial analysis, Hunter thinks the child might have been set into some kind of concrete block and buried underground,' Freeman said. 'The block's plenty large enough to house a young baby. It was probably unearthed and broken by the recent construction work.'

Beth recoiled. She'd seen many bodies over the years: stab victims, tortured remains, suicide train casualties that were virtually unrecognisable. Every one left its mark, but the idea of a tiny baby buried in concrete plucked a heartstring. So young. Innocent and defenceless.

'Who would kill a young child and entomb them in concrete?' Nick said.

'Someone that didn't want the remains to be found,' Beth said. 'If the concrete hadn't been disturbed, it might never have been discovered.' The action implied planning and the thought that somebody had gone to such meticulous lengths to dispose of a child's body was gut-wrenching. She switched from one photo to another, her gaze resting on a tarnished bracelet on its wrist.

'Who owned the land before it was sold?' she asked.

'It was part of Moreton's farm. Pete's gone straight out to see the farmer this morning.'

Beth nodded approvingly. DC Pete Winston was the youngest officer on the team and what he lacked in experience, he made up for with abundant enthusiasm. He'd ask the right questions.

'Hunter's called in a specialist forensic anthropologist/archaeologist to be sure,' Freeman said, 'but the concrete isn't pitted or weathered which we might expect if it had been exposed to the elements. She believes the body could have buried for some time.'

'So, we're looking at an historical case,' Nick said.

'It's possible. Hunter reckons it could have been there a number of years.'

Beth stared at the remains. 'Surely it would be dust and bones by now.'

'Without further tests it's difficult to say how long the child's been there or how it died. Hunter dealt with a case when she worked in the Met – a man's head found in concrete. It was discovered at the bottom of a reservoir, eight years after he was reported missing, and preserved. The water hadn't penetrated the concrete. Given the state of the limbs on show and the smell emitting from the body – I'm told rapid decomposition starts as soon as it's exposed to the air – Hunter thinks this body may have been preserved in a similar way.'

'Babies and young infants don't disappear,' Nick said. 'Not without a fuss.'

Freeman passed him a knowing look. 'We've only got one outstanding case listed in our area.' He pointed at the bangle. 'And this does give me cause for concern.'

He pulled out another photo. 'We've enlarged the bangle to show the detail.'

Beth peered in closer at the tarnished silver, noting a tiny rabbit symbol on the edge.

'You're not suggesting it's Alicia Owen?' Nick said, incredulous.

Shocked faces looked back at the board. Three-month-old Alicia Owen disappeared from her pram outside a supermarket, fifteen years earlier. She was believed to have been abducted, although no ransom note was ever forthcoming, and she was never found. The story rocked the residents of Northamptonshire to the core and when the days after her disappearance stretched into weeks and months, panicky parents set up a 'Keep our children safe' poster campaign urging people to be extra vigilant around infants. Beth had only been sixteen at the time, but she still remembered the black and white photos of Alicia's discarded pram plastered across the newspapers.

'Without further tests on the body and the surrounding area, we can't be sure of anything,' Freeman said. 'We've pulled the old case; Baby Alicia was wearing a silver christening bangle with similar markings when she was taken. She was kidnapped in August 2002, less than two miles from the location, and her parents lived nearby. But fifteen years is a long time, we can't make any assumptions. I imagine there are plenty of these bracelets in circulation.' The buzz of his mobile interrupted the conversation. He excused himself and moved away to take the call.

Beth's gaze wandered to another board, standing on its own at the far end of the room; the remnants of an old investigation. Her eyes unwittingly met those of Dale Yates, the serial killer who'd systematically executed his victims in his twisted efforts to avenge the death of his late partner. The murderer who'd scrutinised the police case as it unfolded, led them on a cat and mouse chase; he'd placed photos of Beth on his murder wall and later broken into her home in an attempt to hamper the enquiry. Six weeks had passed since he'd escaped police custody. Six weeks in which he'd disappeared into thin air. A shiver rushed through her. Unsolved cases, with a murderer running free, were challenging enough, but a known serial killer who'd tortured his victims before he brutally killed them, still on the loose, filled her with disquiet. What made it worse was that every time she entered the conference room, she felt his eyes on her.

'Right.' Freeman cut the call and pocketed his phone. 'That was the super. The officers guarding the building site where the child's remains were found have requested additional assistance, there's already a crowd of reporters gathering at the cordon.'

Nick rubbed his forehead. 'They didn't waste their time.'

'Could the body have been dumped there during the demolition process?' Beth asked.

'Maybe,' Freeman said. 'Although I'm guessing it would take some muscle to move a concrete block that size. Considering the cracks in the block and the smell emitting from the body, Hunter thinks it's more likely it was disturbed by the early diggers this morning. The builders were taking a tea break when it was discovered. I'm hoping the forensic anthropologist/archaeologist will be able to confirm more details. In the meantime, we're contacting GP surgeries and health visitors for any unusual activity: babies or young children in the vicinity who suddenly moved away or dropped off the radar, and any pregnant mothers who skirted the system before they gave birth. We also need to speak with the Owen family and prepare them for any links that might be made.'

Beth examined the bangle. 'Why would someone go to such lengths to dispose of a body, yet leave a bracelet on them?'

'Maybe it's a copycat,' Nick said. 'Made to look like Alicia.'

'Again, that's possible,' Freeman said. 'Alicia Owen is the only reported missing baby in our area in the past twenty years. We are taking steps to check with other forces nationwide. In the meantime, we deal with what we have. The Owens divorced a few years after Alicia's disappearance. Marie Owen remarried and is now Marie Russell. I sent an officer out to her address an hour ago, when I called you,' he said to Nick, 'but she wasn't home. The next-door neighbour said she was at work and gave us the address of Mrs Russell's workplace. Which is where you guys come in.'

He placed his hands on his hips. 'Marie Russell works at Weldon's Soft Furnishings in town. I want you to go straight out there. Obviously, the bracelet gives us cause for concern. We'll need to get a sample of DNA from both parents to test against the child.' He turned to Beth. 'Set yourself up as the family's point of contact. It's early days. If this is Alicia, I'm going to need you to act as their family liaison officer. Warren Hill's away, sunning himself in Tenerife, so you'll need to shoulder the burden until I can get someone else to assist.'

Beth gave a sombre nod. Family liaison officers usually worked in pairs and, with less than twelve months in the role, she'd certainly miss Warren's experience and support here.

'I was away on a review team when Alicia's case broke,' Freeman said. 'The senior investigating officer was DCI Mark Tanner, now retired. If the forensics suggest this is Alicia, I'll get in touch with him and see if he can pass on any thoughts.'

'I was a rookie on probation at the time,' Nick said. 'Didn't work the case, but still remember it. It was the biggest enquiry Northamptonshire Police had faced in years. It was also the biggest disappointment when she wasn't found.'

'What do we know about Alicia's father?' Beth asked.

'Daniel Owen? That's proving tricky. I sent an officer out to the last address DWP hold and it's out of date. The current residents claim he moved years ago. He works for Hiltons, the hauliers just outside town. We've asked them for his contact details and they're being a pain in the arse, want all the paperwork before they'll part with any personal information. I'll let you know as soon as I have a current address.' Freeman raised a hand and scratched the wispy hairs around his balding crown. 'The Owen case made national news fifteen years ago. We need to keep an open mind, but if our Baby Doe is Alicia, when this comes out, the media will go into overdrive. I've persuaded the superintendent to keep the finer details to ourselves for now. We're putting out a general statement to the press, announcing the discovery of a child's remains, and keeping the bangle and a potential historic link confidential until we know more.'

He checked his watch. 'Right, I'm heading off to the post-mortem. We've had to get the fire service out to move the concrete block and call in environmental cleaners to sanitise one of the police garages to create a sterile environment for the examination. It's a bloody nightmare.' He heaved a sigh. 'Once we break into the concrete, we'll have more of an idea what we're dealing with.'

Beth looked back at the photo. 'I take it none of the site workers have seen anyone coming and going?'

'They say not. And there are no cameras. The informant was a builder working on the site. What drew his attention to the area where the child lay, was a sudden shriek. When he investigated, he found a teenage girl close to the body, between fourteen and sixteen, he reckoned. She ran off before he could speak with her, but he's given a good description. Long ginger hair – the tie she wore belonged to the nearby secondary school.'

'St George's?'

'That's the one. The child was found after registration. They're currently checking their absentee register for any girls missing or late today. I should have the details shortly.'

4

Marie Russell was staring at her computer screen, fingers rippling across the keyboard, desperately trying to feed figures into a spreadsheet before the sales review meeting at 12 p.m., when her mobile buzzed. She cast the phone an annoyed glance, pressed backtrack and deleted the last two digits, then double-checked her figures.

A voicemail message flashed up on her phone from her elderly neighbour, Elsie, back home. She paused a second. For the past twelve months, as Elsie's health deteriorated, she'd occasionally picked up shopping for her. Elsie was a family friend, she'd babysat Marie's son, Zac, in his early years and Marie was happy to support her. But Elsie didn't have any concept of work. Marie tossed the phone aside. She'd listen to it later. It was probably something simple like a request for her to pick up a bottle of milk on the way home.

The figures lured her back to the screen. Sales were down almost twenty-five per cent over the past quarter and they'd failed to hit all bar one target. There was no doubt about it, soft furnishing sales were waning. The footfall in the store hadn't declined; it seemed the people of Northamptonshire were visiting the shop, trying out their wares, then going home and ordering them cheaper elsewhere online, from warehouses with smaller overheads. This coupled with the fact they'd recently been taken over by a large corporation who'd increased their targets meant the figures made for bleak reading. Her eyes flitted to the clock. 11.51 a.m.

The skinny frame of Tim Brookes, the new assistant manager, appeared around the doorway. Brown hair, blow-dried at an angle, flopped over his forehead. Freshly out of university, he was almost young enough to be her son.

'Nearly ready,' Marie said in her cheeriest voice.

'The police are here to see you.' He looked harried as he stepped aside and ushered a man and a woman, both in dark suits, into Marie's office.

'DC Beth Chamberlain,' the woman said holding up her identity card. 'And this is DS Nick Geary,' she pointed at her colleague.

Marie felt like she'd been plunged into icy water. She shot out of her chair, pressed a hand to her chest. 'Has something happened to Vic, or Zac?'

'Please don't be alarmed,' Beth said. 'Your family are well, as far as I'm aware.'

'What then?' She switched from one detective to another.

The male detective turned to Tim. 'If you could give us a few minutes, please?' he said. 'We'd like to speak with Mrs Russell in private.'

The door latch sounded like a clock chime as it closed. Marie's chest tightened.

'May we?' Beth said, pointing at the chairs in front of Marie's desk.

She nodded.

'I'm sorry to bother you at work, Mrs Russell,' Beth continued when they were settled. 'It's a sensitive matter.'

'What is it?'

'Please forgive my bluntness, there's no easy way to say this. The remains of a young child were discovered on a building site on Boughton Green Road this morning.'

Confusion whirlpooled inside Marie. They'd said Zac, her son, was alright. 'That's awful. I don't see what it has to do with me though.'

'It's early days, there are more tests to be done, but it looks like the child may have been dead for some time. Maybe even years. There is a chance it could be your daughter, Alicia. I'm so sorry.'

Every muscle in Marie's body tensed. 'That's absurd. Alicia was taken fifteen years ago.'

'I understand Alicia was wearing a bracelet when she disappeared?'

'Y-yes.'

'Can you describe it?'

'A Peter Rabbit christening bangle. Silver. With a rabbit symbol.' She pointed at the side of her own bare wrist. 'It was mine when I was young. You guys already know that, I made a statement, several statements, when—'

'This child was wearing a similar bracelet.'

The whirr of the photocopier fan in the corridor outside penetrated the room.

'We can't be completely sure,' the detective continued, 'not until we've had time to investigate thoroughly. We wanted to let you know it's a line of enquiry we're pursuing.'

Marie opened her mouth to speak and closed it again, a fish out of water.

'There is always the possibility it's another child,' Beth said gently. 'But we wanted to let you know a child's remains have been found, before we release the details to the press. And we'll need your help.'

5

The swab slid down the inside of Marie Russell's cheek. The detective moved to the other side of her mouth and repeated the action before pulling it out and dropping it into a plastic tube. The green top squeaked, plastic against plastic, as she screwed it firmly closed.

'How long will the results take?' Marie asked.

'It's difficult to say until we know more,' the detective said. 'We're hopeful for a reasonably quick turnaround. I'll keep you informed.'

Marie gave a single nod. Since they'd visited her at work earlier, her mind had been awash. Was it or wasn't it, Alicia? The answer to that simple question was all she wanted to know. The detective said the quickest way to be certain was a DNA test. She wanted to ask what was left, what had happened to the child, but her tongue swelled in her mouth at the very thought. An hour ago, she'd been at work, preparing for the monthly performance meeting. Thinking about calling her neighbour and picking up some shopping on the way home. Now she was back in her kitchen having her mouth swabbed. It was surreal. Almost as if she was floating on the edge of reality. After all this time...

'You okay, love?' Vic said. He placed his hand at the small of her back, the heat of his skin sinking through her shirt. As soon as the detectives delivered the news that morning, she'd phoned him and asked him to meet her back at the house. He was her husband; he should be there.

She passed him a sideways glance, her gaze slipping past him and out into the back garden. The washing she'd hung out first thing hung limply on the line, a kaleidoscope of colours.

She should be relieved. They might have found her baby, her little girl; she could finally lay her to rest. Though, if it was Alicia, it raised so many ugly questions: What had she been through? How had she died?

Spiky memories of the frantic hours and days after Alicia's disappearance resurfaced. The question mark over who'd taken her, the uncertainty... The news appearances, the appeals for her baby's return that, as the months and years passed, she'd been forced to bury in the depths of her mind.

The very idea of reliving all that anxiety was suffocating.

All those years in which she'd buried the past deep in the filing cabinets of her mind, forcing herself to rebuild her life. But the longing remained, a warning finger. Just in case she ever relaxed enough to consider happiness. The longing that one day she'd get her child back.

'I understand Alicia had a twin?' the detective asked.

Vic jerked his head back. 'Is that relevant?'

'I'm trying to build up a picture and understand—'

'Your people have been trying to understand for fifteen years. It hasn't brought Alicia back.'

Marie pressed a hand on his forearm to silence him. She

had no energy for arguments. 'Yes. Her brother, Liam. He was stillborn.'

'I'm sorry.'

'Twins run in Daniel's family. He has a twin sister himself.'

The detective pressed her lips together. She had a kind face with petite dark features. Pretty. 'Do you have an address for your first husband, Mrs Russell?'

'Surely you can find that yourself,' Vic said, his eyebrows knitting together.

'We are trying to trace him, Mr Russell.' She turned back to Marie, her tone lighter. 'If you have contact details, obviously it'll speed things up. We need to reach him urgently.'

'I haven't spoken to Daniel for...' Marie shook her head, a desperate attempt to settle her jumbled thoughts. 'At least twelve years. I have no idea where he's living now.'

The detective thanked her and asked them both for discretion; they wanted to avoid speculation, control the flow of information to the press, until they knew more. She explained how the next few days would roll out. If they confirmed the identity as Alicia, her remains gave them new evidence; the case would be looked at afresh.

The words merged together, a dull ramble in the background. Marie caught the title, 'family liaison officer'. They'd had family liaison officers fifteen years ago, a middle-aged woman called Julie who wore wrap-around skirts and loose tops, and a young man in a sharp suit whose name escaped her. Visiting their home, updating them on the investigation, offering support. Both good detectives, no doubt, unobtrusive even. But they hadn't brought Alicia back. And the notion of going through all that questioning, subjecting her new family to all the hopes, fears and wishes, only to have them dashed again, made sick pool in her mouth.

Her gaze rested on the fridge. On a photo of Zac, her happy-go-lucky six-year-old, sitting on a beach. He was holding an ice cream, one eye closed in the sunshine. While he knew about his brother, Liam, they'd never spoken with him about Alicia, not wishing to scare him.

The chair leg squeaked against the floor as she pushed it back. 'I can't do this.'

She felt Vic's hand brush her arm, heard his footsteps behind her up the hallway. At the bottom of the stairs he moved in front, blocking her path. His grey-blue eyes were soft, beseeching. 'We *can* do this,' he said. 'If we stick together.'

He was right, of course. They needed to be strong, to comfort and console each other. She'd retreated into herself after Alicia's disappearance, watched from afar as it ripped apart her last marriage, tearing it into tiny pieces. Pieces that bowed and mangled until they no longer fitted together. So many years had passed; so much grief. She knew Vic was right, but she couldn't be there for him, or consider his feelings right now because her mind was brimming with her own and the possibilities that lay ahead.

'Please,' she said. 'I need a moment.'

She scooted around him and up the stairs, not daring to look back. In her bedroom she was alone, away from the head tilts, the sorry eyes, the questions. She lowered herself onto the edge of the bed. It couldn't be Alicia, could it? Not after all this time. No. No way. Though as much as she tried to block them, the detective's words wriggled back into her head, 'a young child wearing a bracelet similar to Alicia's...' They must have had reason to think it was Alicia, otherwise they wouldn't have taken steps to visit her at work and home.

She lay on her side, dragged a pillow down and wrapped her arms around it.

She could still feel baby Liam in her arms on the day of their birth. His skinny cold body, lips tinged with blue. Perfect nails, eyelashes; a bush of chestnut hair just like his sister. With his eyes gently closed, he looked like he was sleeping. A short hold, they'd said, to say goodbye. It had been a difficult birth. Through Alicia's delivery he'd become increasingly distressed in the womb and was pronounced dead on arrival, the cord wrapped around his neck. A rare tragedy these days.

The bed squeaked as Marie drew up her knees, coiling them around the pillow. The memories inducing a familiar rush of guilt. If she hadn't been so wrapped up in the foggy grief of losing Liam, she wouldn't have left Alicia alone outside the shop on that fateful day. Her baby wouldn't have disappeared.

If only... How those words had plagued her.

The not knowing was the hardest part to bear. But it was also soft and easy, like hiding behind a cushion. After all this time, finding Alicia uncovered harsh truths and she wasn't sure she was strong enough to face them.

The building site on Boughton Green Road, the detective had said. Marie knew it well. She'd attended the secondary school nearby when she was growing up. It had been farmers' fields, greenbelt, until recently when the diggers moved in. An icy shiver showered her shoulders.

So nearby.

Thoughts of Liam, swaddled in a blue and green fleece blanket with a teddy inside his tiny coffin, the shiny headstone she'd lovingly polished over the years were bad enough. But his sibling, the baby he'd shared womb space with, grown with, nestled beside... his own twin buried alone beneath the ground where nobody could visit her was too much for any mother. She opened her mouth and the scream that emitted pushed up from the pit of her stomach. Please, no. Don't let the baby at the building site be her Alicia. She couldn't imagine anything worse.

6

Back at the office, Beth slumped into her chair. It was awful delivering 'might be' news to Marie Russell, when there was still the chance this baby wasn't Alicia.

During her nine years in the police Beth had worked many missing person cases. Some were found and brought back home safely, much to the relief of carers and families. Others vanished, never to be seen again. It was a harsh reality of the job that some disappearances remained unexplained, and the unsolved always left her uneasy. The families left in limbo with no closure, no explanation; constantly aware that at any time a knock at the door or the ring of a phone might bring some news.

And in the case of an alleged abduction, this was even more poignant.

With the missing there was always the fragile hope that loved ones were still out there, their hearts still beating. Hope that they might show up, return one day. As time passed, the hope sank, deep down into the depths of loved ones' bones. But it never disappeared, and she'd seen that earlier look in Marie Russell's eyes before, many a time. The look that harboured the faint longing that the now grown baby Alicia might discover the truth, track her roots, search for her biological family and they would be reunited. The more evidence Beth found to support the findings that the body was Alicia, the more she was erasing that thread of hope and it didn't feel good.

The incident room hummed around her. Colleagues tapped keyboards and chatted into phone receivers, speaking with GP surgeries, carrying out searches. A liaison officer was deployed to get close to the family, sit in the background and watch for odd expressions, unusual comments, behaviour that may be construed inconsistent or out of keeping with the apparent situation. Most people were killed by someone close to them, someone they knew and while Beth supported families, she was also there to quietly investigate them. Before she could do that, she needed to familiarise herself with Alicia's enquiry and she pored over the digital case file from Alicia's disappearance: reading witness statements, checking alibis, working out where everybody had been in the hours leading up to the abduction.

She opened her day book, turned to a blank page, wrote Alicia's name in the middle and circled it. Beside it, she drew a line and wrote *Liam, (twin) deceased*, and above *Daniel and Marie Owen (parents – now divorced)*. Marie and Daniel were both now thirty-seven, twenty-two when Alicia was born. Reports indicated Marie's family emigrated to Australia when she was nineteen. Her mother came over for a couple of weeks, soon after the twins were born, but essentially Marie had no other family nearby, not that she was in contact with. Daniel had a brother, Scott, who was three years younger than him, and a twin sister, Cara.

Apart from Marie's mother, they had all been in contact

with Alicia in the days before her abduction, given statements after the abduction and presented substantiated alibis. Daniel's mother, Alicia's grandma, had given a statement too, and died a little over a year afterwards.

Beth worked each of the names through the Police National Computer, more in hope than expectation. Even though these checks had already been completed during the original investigation, it was important to her to start from scratch and not only familiarise herself with the current family setup, but also that of the time. None of them held a police record, apart from Scott Owen who'd been convicted of a couple of counts of shoplifting and theft of motor vehicles in his late teens and received two hundred hours of community service. He was at work, at Burston's Garage, on the other side of town, the day Alicia was kidnapped.

Marie divorced Daniel Owen twelve years ago, then married Vic Russell four months later. Beth added Vic to her family tree, along with their six-year-old son, Zac. Daniel Owen hadn't re-married.

Beth tapped her pen against the book. Vic's name was familiar. She reached for her keyboard, clicked a few keys and scrolled down. Yes, he'd given a statement as part of the case. He was the last person to visit Marie on the morning of the abduction. In his statement he referred to himself as a close friend of the family. So, he knew them before…

Was she having an affair with Vic while she was still with Daniel? It would have muddied the waters, but surely not enough to result in the abduction of her child?

She switched to Google, typed in 'Alicia Owen'. Numerous old press articles flashed up, all showing similar pictures: the photo of the empty pram the police had released when appealing for witnesses, another photo of sleeping Alicia with a pink hat on. She looked restful, angelic, like any other baby. A distressed photo of Marie Russell, the blonde Mallen streak weaving through the right side of her long dark hair like a beacon. Marie's hair was shorter now, cut into a long bob, but the thick streak remained. Beth remembered reading about those streaks. Something to do with lack of pigment; hair that was difficult to dye. It must have been tough to have such a distinguishing feature, be so easily recognisable, when the eyes of the country were on you during a police hunt.

Images of her visit to the Russells' home earlier popped into Beth's head. The spacious kitchen, the photos of Zac beside his splodgy paintings and drawings on the fridge. Vic placing his arm protectively around his wife. They appeared to have put the past behind them.

She glanced at her chart; these people were all cleared in the original investigation. Alicia was sleeping in her pram outside a supermarket when she was abducted. The supermarket was located within a small bank of shops on the Acre Lane housing estate, on the other side of Kingsthorpe to Boughton Green Road.

Marie had been scrutinised at the time, her mental health questioned as speculation grew over whether she'd killed her own child. Her conduct examined during public appeals where experts watched her body language from afar, searching for signs of latent guilt. And all they'd found was anxiety and sadness.

Marie Russell had said she was no longer in touch with Daniel Owen. Beth Googled Vic Russell and immediately found a personal piece about Marie marrying her husband's best friend. No wonder they weren't still in contact. Vic wasn't just a family friend. He had been Daniel Owen's best friend.

A hand on Beth's shoulder interrupted her.

'You ready?' Nick said. 'Freeman's waiting for us all in the conference room.'

Nobody noticed the cleanly shaven man standing close to the police cordon on Boughton Green Road that morning. Baseball cap pulled down low over his eyes, tightly packed between residents and reporters, he was just another face in the crowd. Another bystander, filling the pavement.

Two women jostled beside him. One blonde, one dark-haired. Rubbing their hands together to keep warm, talking in excited whispers. Holding up their phones, clicking their cameras. He did his best to ignore them, instead inhaling the sharp December air, dragging the scent deep into his lungs. Nothing like the pungent smell of a dead body to bring out the rubberneckers.

A group of CSIs carrying cases wandered along a thin channel reserved for scene officials. The officer guarding the cordon lifted the canopy behind the police tape to allow them through, exposing a narrow view of the building site beyond.

'Look,' blonde hair said, nudging her friend, pointing at the gap. Dark hair stood on her tiptoes, craning her neck to spy through the opening before the canopy flapped back into place.

'I think I saw a forensic tent,' dark hair whispered, so close her breath touched his ear. 'Must be serious.'

A head turned in front of them. 'No shit. They don't bring this lot out for a dead fox.'

The two women sniggered.

Shoulders jostled as more onlookers joined the burgeoning crowd.

A voice called out to the officer at the cordon. 'Can you confirm whether the injured party is male or female?'

The officer responded with a headshake, his remit clearly to guard the scene, not impart information. Another question followed from the back. And another. Their voices merging with the engines of the slow-moving traffic behind them, rising to a din. The officer fixed his gaze ahead, unfazed.

Time to go. He tipped the peak of the baseball cap lower, kept his head down as he squeezed his way out. The air was icy away from the horde of warm bodies; he pulled his jacket across his chest and twisted his head to the side until the cartilage cracked.

The putrid aroma hung, lingering like a dust cloud. He looked back at the crowd, pressed earphones into his ears and waited for the crisp sounds of Wagner to tickle his senses. He'd waited so long for this moment. They had no idea what was coming next.

7

Freeman stood at the front of the conference room and stretched out his back, an action that made his rotund stomach extend further than usual. 'Okay everyone, gather around.' He straightened as the last few officers shuffled forward. 'Hunter brought in a specialist forensic anthropologist/archaeologist to make a start on breaking open the concrete block this afternoon.' He crossed to a screen at the side of the room and angled it towards his audience. DC Pete Winston sat at a table nearby with his laptop open, poised.

'The process of removing the child from the concrete is likely to take a couple of days. They're filming it as they go along and sending us stills. We'll get the stills printed out in due course.' He nodded at Pete who clicked a button. The screen immediately filled with a child laid on its back in a sleeping pose, its trunk and legs covered in a dirty cream shawl. Only a blue-grey arm and face were visible. The eyes were closed and sunken, the skin around them shrivelled. A bush of hair stuck up from the head above a slightly distorted face, with mottled, greying skin that caved in beneath the cheekbones.

Barely two foot long. Who could do something like this? Beth thought. To a child. So small. So fragile.

'Hunter was able to confirm the child was a baby girl, possibly only a few months old, and she's certainly been there a while,' Freeman said.

'Do we know how long?' Nick asked.

'No, not until further tests have been carried out, but the forensic anthropologist/archaeologist is pretty sure we are looking at an historical case,' Freeman said. 'Sealing the child in concrete prevented oxygen from reaching the body, retarding the decomposition process.'

He gave Pete a nod and the screen changed. In the next shot the shawl had been pulled back, exposing a mottled trunk in a towelling vest. The remnants of a nappy poking out the sides. It was a pitiful sight.

A loose window rattling in the wind was the only sound to be heard.

'Soil samples have been taken from the scene to compare with what is on the block,' Freeman said, 'to see if we can determine how long she has been buried and whether she's been moved at any stage, but none of this is a quick process. It'll be weeks before we get any firm results.' A low-bellied murmur travelled around the room. 'I know, I know.' He lifted his hands to hush them. 'There is one piece of positive news. They'll be extracting DNA from the body today. Hunter is pretty confident there's enough soft tissue for a fast-track trace.'

Beth's shoulders slackened. Generally, in historic cases where bodies had been dead for long periods, DNA was taken from the bones, a lengthy process, often taking weeks to yield results. Fast-track traces were usually back in a matter of days. At least she would be able to confirm with the family soon.

The detective chief inspector tapped the screen. 'In the description given at the time, Alicia's mother said the child was wearing a towelling vest and a nappy. The contents of her changing bag, also taken with her, included a cream shawl, similar to the one this child was wrapped in. The burial site, if we can call it that, is less than two miles from the Owens' home at the time, and not far from where Alicia went missing.'

'Could it have been as long as fifteen years?' Nick asked.

'They can't be completely sure before they run tests, but potentially, yes.'

'So, we think it is her?'

'From what we've uncovered so far, it seems likely. Pete's been out to see the farmer who owns the land.'

DC Pete Winston approached the front of the room. He was a tall man, with short dark hair and soft brown eyes. The buttons on his shirt gaped slightly over an overhanging paunch. 'The land was owned by the Moreton family before it was sold for development,' he said. 'Old man Moreton must be in his seventies now. He ran the farm with his only son, it had been in their family over a hundred years. He claims he had no idea how the body came to be on his land.' Pete lifted a hand and circled an area on the map, indicating the location of the farm and the land attached to it. A purple-headed pin close to the edge marked the area where the remains were found.

'Moreton was quite clear that this particular field—' Pete tapped the crime scene twice '—has been used solely for crops for the last thirty years. It's several acres away from the farmhouse and not overlooked. There are no bridle ways or walkways that run through, or close by, and it was edged with high hawthorn hedging along the roadside, until recently when the developers cut it back.'

'How did they access the field?' Nick asked.

'Through a locked gate at the bottom of the road.'

'So, he's saying nobody else had access apart from farm workers?'

'Not legitimately. He did admit there were a few breaks in the hedging back in the day, caused by badgers and other animals, where someone may have climbed through.'

Nick's face crumpled. 'Surely the farmer or a labourer working the land would have noticed something freshly buried, or that the soil was disturbed.'

'Yeah, I mentioned that. Moreton wasn't convinced.' Pete glanced down and sifted through his notebook until he found what he was looking for. 'This was one field in a farm of over 700 acres. They combine crop and cattle. The work is constant. They harvest, cultivate and sow the crops. Often fields aren't touched for months in between. If the block was buried at the right time, the soil could have had plenty of weeks or months to settle afterwards.'

Beth narrowed her eyes. Once again, it indicated a level of knowledge and planning. To know when the seeds would be sown. Although it would have been cumbersome to transport a concrete lump that size into the field. The killer would have had to dig quite a hole to conceal it. 'How far does their machinery penetrate the soil?' she asked.

Pete shot Beth a knowing smile. 'Down to a maximum of thirty centimetres.'

Which meant if the block was buried deeper than thirty centimetres it could have sat there for years, undisturbed. Beth gave an appreciative nod. 'What about the builder working the digger this morning?' she asked. 'How come they didn't notice they'd hit the concrete block? Especially if they were working through soil.'

'They'd been breaking up the foundations of a dilapidated barn nearby. Some of the remains were mixed in with the soil in that part of the field. They probably didn't give it a second thought.' Pete snapped his notebook shut. 'The farmer's putting together a list of labourers he's used. They'd know the area, be aware it was remote.'

Freeman thanked Pete and sunk his hands deep in his pockets. 'As I said, if this is Alicia, the quickest way to confirm identity would be through a DNA check against her parents. Depending on how busy the labs are, we'd hopefully know within two to three days.'

'I've already taken a sample from the mother,' Beth said. 'It was couriered to the lab this afternoon.'

'Okay. How did the Russell family receive the news?'

'Stunned, bewildered.' The consternation in Marie's face filled her mind. 'I'll give them time to digest today's news, update them on the clothing tomorrow morning.'

'Good idea,' Freeman said. 'We need to tread carefully. Make sure they are well supported.'

'Do we know how the child died?' Beth asked.

'Not as yet. The body is still partially encased.'

'I've been searching news coverage about the Owens,' she added. 'Marie Owen married Vic Russell three years after Alicia disappeared, less than a year after her divorce with Daniel.'

'And?'

'Vic Russell was Daniel's best friend. One of the articles talks about him comforting her in her hour of need. The family are no longer in touch with Daniel.'

'Yes, I remember that,' Freeman said. 'Although it's not a crime to marry your ex-husband's best friend.' He turned back to the main room. 'I know none of us here worked on the case, so I've been in touch with Mark Tanner, the original SIO. He's agreed to help us in any way he can.'

'Any news on the schoolgirl who found the body?' Nick asked.

'Yes, there were very few absentees at St George's this morning, certainly in her age group. Only one with ginger hair. She's been identified as Jordan Quinn.'

'Is she known to us?'

'No. Her mother's bringing her in at 4 p.m. this afternoon for interview.'

'Do we know what she was doing on the construction site?'

'Not yet.' He switched to Beth. 'Can you set up an interview? Take an account, see if she knows anything about the body, or has seen anyone nearby?'

Beth nodded.

'Okay,' Freeman scanned the room. 'Where are we with tracing Daniel Owen?'

'We've got an address in Kingsthorpe,' Pete said. 'He's in Lancashire, delivering a load today. Won't be back until after 6 p.m. this evening. I did manage to speak to him briefly, but the signal was poor. I told him we'd visit him at home this evening. He'd asked his employer to be extra discreet with his personal details. Apparently, he's had problems with reporters. Even took out an injunction against one journalist who kept pestering him, a few years back.'

Beth sighed, recalling the newspaper article she'd read about Marie Owen marrying her husband's best friend. The disappearance of Alicia afforded the family little privacy in the eyes of the media. 'Which reporter did he get an injunction against?' she asked.

Pete checked his notes. 'Pip Edwards. Used to work for *Northants News*.'

'Ah,' Beth said knowingly. *Northants News* was headed by Mike Carter, an editor known for focusing on sensational headlines and civil liberties, rather than working together with the police to help solve crimes. Beth had rubbed shoulders with him a couple of months earlier when his wayward son was arrested for perverting the course of justice. Since the charge, Mike Carter had stepped away from the limelight 'to spend time with his family' but if Edwards had worked closely with him, he likely followed a similar line. 'One to watch out for.'

'You can say that again. Pip's freelance now and still shows a lot of interest in Alicia's case. He wanted to write a book about the Owens but the family refused to assist him and I don't think it ever came to fruition.'

Freeman scratched the back of his neck. 'Okay, Beth, I need you to visit Daniel Owen, explain the situation and get a DNA sample.'

Beth checked her watch. 3.45 p.m. 'I'll go after I've interviewed Jordan Quinn.'

'Excellent. Right, that's it, everyone.'

Beth closed her notebook and was gathering her belongings when Freeman called her and Nick back.

'Meet me in my office in five minutes, will you? There's something I need to tell you.'

8

Beth tugged on her collar. Freeman's office was at the opposite end of the corridor from the conference room, a pokey box that always felt stuffy, no matter the time of year. She glanced out of his window at the sports field beyond. Late afternoon clouds were drawing in, bringing with them an early dusk.

'The superintendent wants a reshuffle,' Freeman said after he'd invited them to sit on the plastic chairs opposite his desk. 'You know the score. Her workload's increased and she's delegating more and more down to the team. And I'm sure you are both aware we're losing our DI.'

'Andrea got the Met promotion?' Nick said. 'She hasn't mentioned it.'

'Not exactly. Andrea Leary didn't pass the Met assessment day but she is leaving us. She's going to be the chief constable's aide, starting tomorrow,' Freeman said, his mouth twitching with the edge of a suppressed smile. 'She's taken today to clear out her office.'

Beth shared his elation. She'd rubbed shoulders with the acting DI on their last case when Andrea, a former family liaison officer herself, had made it quite clear she disapproved of Beth's policing methods and accused her of becoming biased and too close to the families she supported. The chief constable's aide, or 'staff officer' as it was generically referred to, was a position sought by those keen to move up the ladder, providing the opportunity to learn the strategic side of policing, a position that would suit Andrea Leary perfectly. Her not leaving Northamptonshire force was a blow, although a move away from homicide would at least afford them all welcome breathing space.

'Which leaves us with a shortfall on the team,' Freeman continued. 'Nick, the superintendent wants to temporarily promote you to acting detective inspector. I'm going to need all the help I can get with this Operation Aspen – we're reviving the original operation name, by the way – and Beth, I understand you've put in your promotion papers?'

'Yes. The interview board isn't until next year.'

'No problem. We'll act you up to DS and review it after your board. You'll continue with your family liaison duties, but we'll also need you in the office more to allocate jobs and hold everything together.' Freeman's face broke into a rare smile that exposed a wide gap between his two front teeth. 'I take it that's acceptable to you both?'

'Err... yes,' Nick said. He looked gobsmacked.

Beth nodded her thanks. But it was what Freeman said next that really caught her.

He moved around the desk as they rose, leaned forward and tapped the top of Nick's arm. 'Need to make the most of you before the National Crime Agency snap you up.'

Beth passed a confused glance from one to the other. She had absolutely no idea what they talking about. Nick averted his gaze and laughed off the comment, as if it was a private joke.

'The temporary promotion will mean long hours,' Freeman said. 'Operation Aspen already attracts attention at the highest levels. I don't think there are many coppers in the force that wouldn't be thrilled to finally see a result on this one. And there'll be a lot of pressure. Nothing you're not used to though.'

He clapped them both on the back and guided them to the door. 'Right, congratulations. Now let's get back to work. I've a meeting with the superintendent and the assistant chief constable.'

'I wasn't expecting that,' Nick said, as they made their way back down the corridor.

Beth was slow to answer. While she was flattered at being offered the temporary sergeant's role, any joy she felt was tempered with discomfort. Whatever Nick said about the force's tolerance of couples working together, she doubted Freeman would invite them both onto his management team if he knew they were in a relationship. But that was the least of her concerns right now.

'Me neither,' she said. 'What did Freeman mean about the National Crime Agency?'

'Oh, that was nothing.'

Beth grabbed at his arm, stopping him in his tracks. 'It didn't sound like nothing.'

Nick took a long breath and spoke through his exhalation. 'I applied for a job there, a while ago.'

Beth stiffened. How long ago was a while? They were living together, working together, sharing the same bed. Yet he hadn't once mentioned he was looking to leave homicide or had applied for a position elsewhere. 'What job?'

'On the Child Exploitation and Online Protection

Team.' He walked on, dismissing the words, as if they were unimportant.

Beth continued alongside. 'You want to leave homicide?'

'I don't know, I've been here over six years. They're desperate for investigators on the NCA. I used to work in child protection.'

'Sounds like a good move.' Beth fought to keep her voice even. She'd thought they were close. It riled her that he wouldn't discuss a decision like this.

He shrugged a single shoulder in response.

'Why didn't you mention it?'

They'd reached the doors of the incident room now. Nick paused. 'We were separated when I applied. Things were…' He dropped his eyes to the floor. '… Awkward. Anyway, I didn't hear back, so it doesn't matter anymore.'

He grabbed the door handle, but before he was able to pull it, the door opened, and Pete stepped out. 'I've been looking for you,' he said to Nick. 'I've got press liaison on the phone. They've received an enquiry from *Northants News* and need to speak with a senior officer urgently.'

'Tell them I'll be right over.' He waited for Pete to retreat into the office, and then turned to Beth. 'I'll get someone to accompany you to Daniel Owen's later.'

'That's not necessary.'

'You know Freeman's line: pair up when out and about.'

Beth rolled her eyes. Since the escape of Dale Yates, the serial killer on their last case, Nick had barely left her side. He was lodging in her house, driving her to the supermarket. She couldn't even go to the loo when they were out, without him standing close to the door. At work, they carried out enquiries together. She understood his concern – during the course of the enquiry, photos of her had been found in Dale Yates's possession – but she'd had a frontline role as the liaison officer on that case, supporting the families, and Yates had merely followed the police investigation closely while stalking his victims. In the six weeks that had passed, nobody had seen or heard from Yates and security on the victims' families had been relaxed. She couldn't see any reason why he'd target her now and there was no way she was going to be babysat indefinitely.

'I'm sure I can take DNA from a bereaved father on my own.'

He checked the empty corridor, his eyes softening. 'You need to take this seriously, Beth. I don't want anything happening to you.'

Beth lowered her voice. 'I'm fine. If I'm to be the DS on this team and liaison officer to the family, you're going to have to give me some space.'

He held her gaze a moment, unsure. 'Okay. Make sure you keep your phone with you.'

9

Fifteen-year-old Jordan Quinn wound her gold neck chain around her fingers, again and again, bulging eyes buried in the floor. She was a small girl, with mouse-like features and sheets of copper hair that hung like curtains either side of her face.

They were sitting in one of the more comfortable interview rooms, with a sofa and coffee table, specially reserved for vulnerable witnesses and, at fifteen, Jordan fell into that category. A social worker shifted in her seat beside her.

Jordan's mother had been waiting outside the room when Beth entered earlier, an intense woman who shared her daughter's red hair and nervously pinched at her neck. Beth guessed it was probably their first brush with law enforcement and asked one of the staff to make her a cup of tea. Kids tended to be more open without a parent in the room – which is why they engaged a neutral contact when questioning – but it would be stressful enough to deal with what Jordan had seen, without bringing her in for a witness interview at which her mother couldn't be present.

'Let's go through this again,' Beth said. 'What time did you enter the construction site this morning?' They were almost twenty minutes into questioning and Jordan was waning.

'Shortly after 8.30. School had just begun.'

'Did you see anyone on the site?'

Jordan cast a brief look at the camera in the corner. 'No. It was empty.'

'What about nearby? You said you slipped inside through a gap in the barrier,' Beth checked her notes, 'close to the end of Boughton Green Road.'

'There wasn't anyone around. Not that I noticed anyway.'

'Have you visited that spot before?'

Jordan scratched her parting. She was a pretty girl, her face lightly made up – a touch of mascara, the amber glow of blusher – and framed with striking pencilled-in eyebrows. 'Yes. I go there when I need to clear my head. I found a gap in the railings, tucked away from the main road, down the side passage of Guilding's Factory.'

'And that's what you were doing there today, clearing your head?'

Jordan's eyes widened as she met Beth's gaze.

'You're not in any trouble, Jordan,' Beth reassured in her most soothing tone. 'We do need you to be as accurate as you can in your account though. The ground is currently being examined.'

'I… um. I had a cigarette.'

'Okay. How many times have you been there?'

She cleared her throat. 'A few.'

Beth watched her pick at the skin around her thumbnail. She suspected it was more than a few but didn't say so. There was little point lingering on Jordan's smoking, she'd receive enough grief from her mother afterwards and the last thing she needed was for her to clam up. 'How many exactly, over the past couple of weeks?'

'Three, I think.'

'Do you always visit the same spot?'

'Yes. It's usually quiet there.'

Beth took her time working through dates and times and jotted them down.

'Have you ever taken anyone with you?' she asked when they'd finished.

'No.'

'Jordan.' Beth sat forward. 'Think carefully before you answer the next question. Have you ever seen anyone else there?'

'No. Never.' The teenager wound her ankles around each other at this remark, lifting her toes and pointing them towards the door. It was difficult to ascertain whether she was agitated because she'd been trespassing or was actually hiding something.

'How long were you there this morning?'

'I don't know. A few minutes maybe. I left when I saw the builder.'

Beth asked her to describe what she'd seen. When she reached the part about the bracelet on the infant's wrist, her face tightened. 'It smelt weird there today.'

'What do you mean, weird?'

'It's hard to explain. A horrible sickening smell.' She wrinkled her nose. 'I've never noticed it before.'

Beth recalled the feedback from the autopsy. The body had been sealed for some time, possibly years. As soon as it was disturbed it would decompose rapidly. That smell would hang in the air awhile. 'Why did you run away?' she asked.

'I shouldn't have been there. I thought I'd be in trouble.' She described how she'd walked the streets afterwards and sat in a nearby park until the school contacted her mother about her absence.

'What happened to it?' Jordan asked, her voice barely a whisper. She looked like she was about to cry.

'To what?'

'The child.'

'We don't know yet, we're still examining everything. Try to put it out of your mind, if you can. You've done a grand job, passing on these details. We'll take over from here.'

10

Beth tapped the front door of number 691 Chalcombe Avenue and waited. A chorus of high-pitched barks sounded from inside, then fell silent.

She pictured Jordan Quinn's face in the interview earlier. The awkward fifteen-year-old who lived alone with her mother, her face like a deer in headlights. Beth had taken a moment to speak with her mother afterwards, recommending she take her to her GP, passing on details for Victim Support. A close eye needed to be kept on the girl for the next few days; she could only imagine how finding a child's remains might affect a teenage mind. They'd carry out the usual checks but, if she was to be believed, she didn't have much to offer.

She glanced at the road. A lorry was parked outside. A light was switched on in a room on the first floor of the house. She strained her ears and could make out the babble of voices inside. She knocked again. More barking. High-pitched. Continuous this time. The upstairs curtain twitched.

The sound of heavy feet on stairs. The door juddered open. Daniel Owen was a tall spindly man with sunken cheeks. Clumps of wet fair hair stuck to his forehead. He tugged the charcoal robe he was wearing around him tighter.

Beth held up her card and introduced herself.

'Sorry, I got back later than expected,' he said, standing aside for her to enter. 'I was in the shower.' A thick Liverpudlian accent coated his words. He motioned for her to follow him into the front room and gestured for her to sit on the sofa opposite a television, blaring out a game show. 'I'll just go and get some clothes on.'

Beth nodded. As soon as he disappeared, she reached for the remote and turned the television down.

The room was clean and tidy and furnished with a brown leather suite, decorated with beige cushions that matched the curtains. A soft pile rug lay across the wooden floor. According to his employer, Daniel had lived there for a year. Her eyes were drawn to a photo on the wall behind the sofa of Daniel and a woman with long blonde hair, having a meal in a restaurant. A few paintings of landscapes adorned the other walls.

A collection of gilt frames on the mantel caught Beth's eye. She crossed the room to take a closer look. Two black and white baby pictures, side by side, shared a frame, and were surrounded by three other photos taken of a young child in its early months of growth. Beth hadn't found anything to suggest Daniel had more children and was beginning to wonder if they were nieces or nephews when she noticed something in one of the photos. A silver bangle laced around the child's wrist.

Footsteps on the stairs drew her hastily back to the sofa. By the time Daniel re-emerged she was sitting down, retrieving her notebook from her bag.

He was carrying a small Jack Russell terrier underneath his arm – the source of the earlier barking. He placed the dog down on the armchair beside the window.

'Hello!' Beth said. She held out her hand to the dog.

'Say hello to the detective, Bailey.'

The dog gave her hand a brief sniff, then turned away and curled into the arm of the chair.

'Sorry, she's not keen on strangers in the house,' Daniel said. 'Different dog altogether when you take her for a walk. Wants to meet everyone.' He rubbed the terrier's head. 'Can I get you anything? Tea, or coffee maybe?'

'I'm fine, thanks. Why don't you take a seat?' Beth's eyes briefly flicked to the baby photos.

He followed her gaze to the mantel. 'You've seen my Alicia then. She's a strapping young 'un.'

Beth smiled kindly. 'Mr Owen, please sit down.'

He squeezed in beside the dog. As soon as he was settled, his knee began to judder.

'Mr Owen—'

'Daniel, please.'

'Daniel. Do you know why I'm here?'

'Not really. The other detective said there were some more questions about our Alicia.'

Beth took a breath. Pete would have given Daniel an inkling, but it was always preferable to deliver bad news face to face. To safeguard and also watch for any reaction. 'I'm here this evening to tell you that the body of a young child was found on the building site at the end of Boughton Green Road this morning. We have to carry out more tests, to be sure, but we have reason to believe the body might belong to your daughter, Alicia.'

The knee juddered faster.

'I'm so sorry.'

'What happened to her?'

'Again, we're not completely sure as yet. She's still being examined.'

Beth went on to explain the circumstances surrounding the find in as much detail as she was able, mindful of Freeman's caution. 'I'm going to have to ask you to keep this confidential, for now,' she said. 'We won't be releasing details to the press until we are positive of her identity.'

His knee continued to tremor. 'Obviously you can't be sure, not until your tests are complete. I mean it could be another child.'

'It could. But the baby wore a bangle like Alicia's,' Beth said. 'And the clothing matches what Alicia was wearing when she disappeared. I'm so sorry.'

He looked like he was going to be sick.

'Can I ask a question?' he said.

'Of course.'

'Was there any sign of... well, you know.' He tilted his head awkwardly. 'Was she abused?'

'Again, I can't tell you. We're still trying to establish exactly what happened. The child's remains will be subject to a full examination.'

His heel hit the floor. The knee stilled. He gulped a breath. 'Have you spoken to Marie?'

'Yes, I was with her earlier.'

'How's she doing?'

'She's shocked, naturally.'

They were interrupted by the sound of a key turning in

a lock and the front door opening. A woman's voice called out, 'Only me!'

Bailey leapt off the chair and met a blonde woman at the front room doorway.

'Hello, darling,' she said, crouching down and scooping the dog up in her arms.

Beth recognised her as the woman in the photo with Daniel Owen on the wall. She'd had a fringe cut into her hair since it was taken, but it was definitely her.

'Oh, sorry. I didn't know you had a visitor,' she said to Daniel. The same Liverpudlian twang danced in her words. The woman looked from one to another.

When nobody spoke, Beth introduced herself.

'This is my sister, Cara,' Daniel said.

'Do you live here together?'

'No, I live up the road,' Cara said to Beth, then turned to her brother. 'What's going on?'

'They've found a child. They think it might be Alicia.'

'What?'

'The remains of a young child were found on a building site this morning,' Beth said.

Cara's face drained of colour. 'I saw that on the news. What do you mean, you *think* it's her?'

'The body has been there for some time,' Beth said, mustering every ounce of diplomacy. 'We need to carry out extensive tests to be sure.'

'Alicia was taken fifteen years ago. There can't be much left of her now, poor thing.'

'As I say, we need to carry out tests, but early indications are it could well be Alicia,' Beth said gently. 'I'm very sorry.'

She turned to Daniel. 'Would you consent to a DNA sample? It would certainly speed up the identification process.'

'Why do you need a DNA sample, if it's Alicia?' Cara asked.

'We need to be sure.'

'Yeah,' Daniel said. 'Course.'

Beth could feel Cara's eyes on her as she removed the pack from her bag and swabbed his mouth.

'I can't believe it,' she said. 'After all this time. I mean we always hoped, but… What happened to her?'

'We're not completely sure, as yet,' Beth said.

'You're not sure of much.'

'Cara!' Daniel's face pained.

'It's okay,' Beth said. 'It's a shock for everyone. It's been a long time.'

Cara huffed. 'You can say that again. Do you know how many false hopes we've been given? The sightings in the early days. People calling up, saying they've seen a baby that fits her description. Journalists knocking on our doors.' She placed the dog down, crossed the room and lowered herself onto the arm of her brother's chair, sliding her arm protectively around his shoulder. 'Dan didn't just lose his daughter when Alicia disappeared, he lost his wife, his marriage, everything. So, when you come round here telling us you *think* you've found our Alicia and don't know how she died or anything about the body, forgive me for being sceptical. My brother's been through enough.'

Daniel put his head in his hands.

'I understand your concerns and can assure you we'll do everything we can to keep you informed. I'll be your family liaison officer, here to support you.' Beth took a card out of her bag. 'Daniel?'

He looked up as she passed the card across.

'Does this mean you're re-opening the old case?' Cara asked.

'The case has never been closed.' Beth kept her eyes on Daniel as she spoke. 'But yes, we will be re-examining the evidence. That's my direct line. Call me if you need anything.'

'What about reporters?' Daniel said quietly.

'We will do everything in our power to keep you informed before anything is released to the press. In the meantime, you have my card.' Beth paused as she stood. 'I must ask you both to keep this to yourselves for now. As I said, we've only released general details about the discovery to the media at this stage. It's important any information feed or updates come from us.'

Silence descended on the room. Bailey curled up in front of the fireplace, oblivious to the tension.

'When will you know for definite?' Daniel said.

Beth's gaze flicked to the photos above the fireplace once more. The juxtaposition between the lives of Alicia's parents struck her. She hadn't seen any photos of Alicia in the Russells' home, yet here, the mantel was littered with them. According to their records, Daniel Owen had never remarried, never had any more children. He was living in the past, holding on to the ghost of his daughter.

'As soon as the DNA results come back, I'll be in touch. It's likely to be a few days. We'll get them processed as quickly as we can.' Beth stepped towards the door. 'Oh, one more question. I understand you have a brother, Scott?'

'That's right,' Cara said.

'Do you have his contact details? If we receive a positive identification, we'll need to speak with him.'

Cara's face puckered. 'Why do you need to speak with Scott? He was at work when Alicia was taken.'

'We'll be talking to everyone who saw Alicia in the days up to she died. It's standard practice. Do you know where we can reach him?'

'No.'

Beth looked from one to another, unspeaking.

'Our brother moved away to London,' Cara said. 'Years ago.'

'You don't have a forwarding address?'

'We haven't seen or heard from him since he left, have we, Dan?'

Daniel shook his head. 'We've no idea where he is.'

11

Marie glanced at the bedside clock. It was nearly 6.30 a.m. She shifted onto her back and stared into the darkness. The house was quiet and still, the rise and fall of Vic's resting breaths beside her, the only sound to be heard.

It amazed her how he slept so easily. Even after yesterday's news, upsetting the balance of lives they'd worked so hard to re-build, he'd still fallen into an exhausted slumber as soon as his head hit the pillow. Sleep was his body's subconscious answer to stress, and she envied him the escape it provided, the respite from the menacing worries that kept her awake during the long hours of darkness.

Marie rubbed her dry eyes. Her limbs were aching and weary, but her brain still refused to give up, continuing to churn over the information they received yesterday and intersperse it with memories dredged up from the past. What happened to Alicia on that fateful day she disappeared? Who took her? She remembered looking over her shoulder, checking the pram when she entered the store. Peering around the end of the aisle while she shopped. Minutes later, leaving the supermarket and finding it gone. She'd replayed that moment umpteen times, searching for answers that failed to reveal themselves.

The detectives weren't sure, but she knew, deep down, that this was her girl. Aside from the police interest and the location, close to their old home and to where Alicia was taken, there was something else. For the first time in fifteen years her daughter was close, she felt it in every fibre of her body. And the sheer suggestion of her baby – with her spidery eyelashes, stubby nose, fluffy dark hair and flawless skin – buried beneath the soil and rubble of a building site, her remains tossed around by the diggers, made her throat constrict.

Very soon they'd find out how she died. It wouldn't be long now.

Another glance at the clock. A minute had passed. It was too early to start the day. At the same time, she couldn't bear to lay there any longer, torturing herself with memories.

She slid out of bed, checked back to ensure Vic's breaths were still even and pulled her robe around her shoulders. It was darker on the landing. She tiptoed past Zac's room, past the bathroom and into the spare bedroom at the back of the house.

Marie closed the door, switched on the lamp beside the bed and crossed to a fitted cupboard in the corner where they stored old toys, Vic's guitar and music books, and other discarded paraphernalia. A couple of board games rocked on the top shelf as she opened the door. Marie unhooked the stepladder at the side, folded it out and climbed up to reach the top shelf. Counters rattled about inside the boxes as she pulled out the games and lowered them to the floor. She pushed aside a pile of soft toys, lifted out a wide box with no lid and carried it across to the bed. A child's painting sat astride the top. Photos of Zac at various stages of growth and early birthday cards slipped about below.

Back at the cupboard, she reached to the rear of the shelf, pawing at another box. A shoebox, smaller than the first one, the lid firmly shut. Dust motes flew off the top and scattered through the air as she lifted it down and carried it across to the bed.

She removed the lid and immediately faced a photograph of baby Liam dressed in a fluffy white Babygro. Alicia's twin, so tiny and frail. She ran her finger around the outline of his face. Beneath were handprints and footprints the nurses had taken, along with his hospital wrist band.

Alicia's wrist band was also there, clearly marked with her name and date of birth. Beside them their hospital cot cards listed the date, time of birth and weight. At 5lb 2oz, Alicia was almost a pound heavier than her brother.

Marie inhaled deeply, closing her eyes. Whenever she opened this box, the fresh aroma of a newborn touched her senses. She'd only had the twins as babies. The first booties, the newborn cards, and that familiar baby talcum powder smell was all she had left to remind her of their presence in her life.

Various photos of Alicia were scattered in the bottom of the box: in her Moses basket, having her first bath, sleeping in her car seat. She'd always settled better in the car seat than the pram. Daniel rocking her in his arms, a goofy smile on his face. A lock of wispy hair slipped out from behind a picture. It belonged to Liam. She leafed through, desperately looking for another. But there were only more photos.

Tears spilled down her cheeks. The nurses at the hospital

had been generous, capturing memories of Liam, giving her plenty of keepsakes because they only had a short time together before he was taken away. She'd always planned to cut a piece of Alicia's hair when it grew, when she lost her baby tufts. They had all the time in the world. Or so they thought.

Marie placed a hand over her mouth to muffle the sob that escaped. Oh, how she wished she'd cut Alicia's hair and taken her handprints while she'd had the opportunity.

Her eyes combed Zac's box. When he came along, she'd been frightened. Frightened that after what she'd been through, losing two babies in such extraordinary circumstances, she wouldn't be able to cope. Terrified they wouldn't bond. Thankfully, she'd felt an affinity with him straight away. The early weeks weren't easy, he struggled to feed, but they soon found their path and fell into a routine.

With Alicia, things were never easy. Marie had tried to make it better. Oh, how she'd tried. Something was always missing.

She studied the photos of her baby girl, now scattered across the bed. Perhaps if she'd tried harder, Alicia would still be with them now.

What would you have been like? Marie wondered. A lump formed in her throat. Alicia would have been a teenager now, studying for her GCSEs, a young woman preparing to make her own way in the world. *Would you have looked like me, or your father?*

She gathered up the photos, shoving them back in the box, fresh tears flooding her eyes. She was about to place the lid on when something caught her eye at the side. She reached down and curled her fingers around the small condolence card with a teddy bear on the front. *How did that get in there?* The condolence cards for Liam caused her so much distress that Daniel had thrown them away soon after his funeral. 'We don't need any more reminders,' he'd said. Yet this one lingered.

Marie opened the card and instantly a spasm of terror shot through her. Of all the cards… She tore it in half and in half again, continuing to rip it until tiny pieces of cardboard began falling through her fingers and floating onto the duvet. Then she scooped them up, checking she'd retrieved every last piece and carried them downstairs.

The kitchen bin was half full. She pushed aside a banana skin and a crisp packet and tucked the torn pieces underneath. Out of sight, out of mind.

12

Beth edged forwards in the traffic and braked. The roads were more congested than usual on her route into work that Wednesday. Nick had arrived home late last night. She'd felt the bedclothes displace as he climbed in, heard his breaths slow as he immediately slipped into a slumber. He'd left before her that morning, leaning over to plant a soft kiss on her cheek as the alarm sounded. In many ways it was understandable – the early days of a case were demanding, especially at senior level, and this was his first shot at inspector rank. He'd want to make an impression.

The exchange in the office yesterday still niggled her. They'd recently got back together. Work was such a fundamental part of their lives and the idea of him considering a change of job and making applications elsewhere without mentioning it felt odd. Although it was only one application and they were on a break at the time…

The radio DJ's smooth voice filled the car, talking about a local Christmas Fayre at the weekend. Beth grabbed her coffee out of the holder, took a sip and was reminded of the photos of Alicia on display at Daniel Owen's house yesterday evening. Alicia had been missing for fifteen years, yet Daniel kept the photographs of her out, a shrine to his lost daughter.

The ringtone of her mobile distracted her.

Nick's voice filled the car. 'Morning. Where are you?'

Beth frowned. It was still only 7.30 a.m. She wasn't late. 'I'm on my way in. Why? Has something happened?'

'*Northants News* have reported a potential connection with the child's body and the Russells. It's all over their website this morning.'

'What? How?' The car in front of her inched forwards.

'Apparently, they interviewed the builder who reported the body. Just in time for a front-page piece on their weekly paper copy. Freeman's going ballistic.'

'What does the article say?'

'It mentions where the remains were found, talks about the hand and arm of a young child, and refers to the bangle. Freeman's going to ring you shortly. He wants you to head straight over to see Marie Russell and let her know.'

Beth adjusted her earpiece. 'Okay, what about the father?'

'He's already at work, his phone is on voicemail. We've left him a message to call us, but given how we struggled to find him, it's less likely the reporters will descend on him straight away.' The line crackled. She heard a voice in the background. 'Sorry, I have to go. I'll catch up with you later.'

The call cut. Beth chewed the side of her mouth, then indicated and pulled over. She was only ten minutes or so from Marie Russell's home in Kingsthorpe, though it was still possible the press would beat her there. She scrolled through her phone, dialled. Marie answered on the second ring.

'Hello.' She sounded wary.

'Marie, hi, it's DC Beth Chamberlain here. How are you this morning?' she said, trying to gauge whether or not they'd heard the news.

'Okay. Why?'

'I need to speak with you.' The line stayed silent. 'It appears the media have made the connection with the child's body being linked to an historical case and put two and two together. You might get some calls.'

'You're too late. They're already outside.'

Beth's stomach plummeted. 'Ah. Are you all at home?'

'Yes. Vic's getting ready to take Zac to school.'

'I'm so sorry. We're trying to determine what's happened.'

'Somebody's written a newspaper article, that's what's happened.' Marie's tone was chipped.

'Could I please ask you both not to speak with the reporters? I'm coming straight over. Should be with you in about ten minutes.'

As soon as Beth ended the call, her mobile rang again. 'Freeman' flashed up on the screen.

'Beth, you've heard about the leak?' She flinched as his voice blared through her earpiece and turned the volume down.

'Nick just called to tell me. What happened?'

'It seems our builder witness was contacted by Pip Edwards last night and couldn't keep his mouth shut. I've sent someone out there to have words.'

'Isn't that the journalist who Daniel Owen took out an injunction against?'

'It is. It seems Mr Edwards is a little obsessed with the case. Reported on it from the initial abduction and as soon as he heard a child's remains had been found, close to where Alicia went missing, he made the connection. Not unexpected, especially now they know about the bangle. I'm trying to work out how he managed to get the details of the builder. Didn't even bloody warn us he was going to run the piece.'

'I've spoken to Marie Russell,' Beth said. 'Apparently members of the media are already gathering outside their house, vying for information. I'm on my way there now.'

'Good. Vic Russell rang earlier and chewed my ear off, so expect emotions to be running high. We've got Judy in the press office organising an urgent conference later this morning. We need to manage this carefully, Beth. Make sure it doesn't escalate. Any enquiries or questions, I don't care what it is, direct them straight to the press office.'

13

Vic Russell was kneeling in the hallway when Beth arrived, fastening his son's school shoes. Beth greeted Marie at the door and wandered in, passing him a brief, 'Morning.'

He ignored her. The Velcro ripped as he tore away the strap and reapplied, then sent his son to collect his book bag.

'What went wrong?' he said to Beth when his son's small frame had disappeared up the stairs.

'We're trying to establish—'

'Yesterday, we were specifically told not to say anything to anybody,' he interrupted. 'Then we wake up this morning with the press on our doorstep. I've seen the article online. It sounds to me like you guys can't keep your mouth shut. Or don't bloody know what you're doing.' He sunk his hands deep into his pockets and stared at her defiantly. 'It wouldn't be a first.'

'It wasn't us,' Beth said, keeping her voice calm. 'A reporter spoke to someone at the building site. We've already visited the individual, reminded them it's a police matter and asked them to keep their account to themselves.'

'It's a bit late for that. And now we have to endure all

this—' he waved an arm at the door '—until you can be sure whether or not the child found is Alicia. I take it you still don't know?'

Beth sighed inwardly. Even she had been shocked at the horde of reporters filling the pavement outside the Russells' house when she arrived. Word had certainly spread fast.

'Not absolutely,' she replied. 'But we have arranged for a press conference later this morning to update the media and will be asking them to respect your privacy.'

He scoffed. Zac trudged down the stairs, wrestling with the strap on his book bag. 'Come on, lad,' he said. 'Let's go and face the circus.'

He stomped past Beth, one arm looped around his son. The door slammed behind them.

'He doesn't like any upset around Zac,' Marie said. 'We haven't told him about Alicia.' She swiped a hand across her forehead. 'God knows what we are going to say to the poor child. We've told him we don't know why the reporters are out there at the moment, that it might be something to do with one of the neighbours, but he's not going to believe that for long.'

Beth followed Marie into the kitchen. Cereal bowls and mugs littered the table from breakfast. The aroma of fresh coffee was pungent in the air. Beth's eyes flitted to the clock as Marie collected the crockery and opened the dishwasher. It wasn't yet 8 a.m. Surely school hadn't started yet. 'Do they always leave this early?' she asked.

'Zac has football training before school on a Wednesday morning. Vic likes to watch when he can. I'm not changing his routine,' she added defensively.

'We wouldn't expect you to.' Beth placed her bag on the

table. 'Can you describe exactly what Alicia was wearing on the day she disappeared?' she asked, changing the subject.

Marie snapped the dishwasher closed. 'I've gone through this a million times. A towelling vest, my mother-in-law was crazy about them, bought me a dozen when she was born.'

'Only a vest?'

'It was a hot day. She'd been sick in the morning. I'd stripped her back to her vest and nappy, with a sheet over her. It made sense to leave her like that, keep her cool.'

'And did she have anything else with her?'

'A cream shawl in her changing bag.' She moved across to the kettle and flicked the switch. 'You need to check the files.'

'A crocheted cream shawl.'

Marie stopped in her tracks and turned, the colour draining from her face. 'It is her, isn't it?'

'We can't be absolutely sure until we get the DNA test results. But the description certainly matches.'

Marie clamped a hand across her mouth, smothering a squeal.

Beth pulled out a chair. It rattled as Marie slid into it.

Beth busied herself with making tea. She closed the door to block out the reporters' voices filtering through from the street outside and searched the cupboards for mugs, tea bags, milk.

It was a while before Marie spoke. 'You must have known this yesterday.'

'Only an arm and hand were visible initially,' Beth said. 'It took a while to uncover her.' She didn't go into specifics. It didn't seem prudent to release information about the gruesome circumstances until identity was confirmed and even then, it was only worth telling the family if it was relevant. There was no point adding yet more grief to a pile already brimming.

'Do we know how she died yet?' Her voice was barely a whisper.

'Not yet. I'm sorry.'

A yell cried from outside, penetrating the closed kitchen door. It grew louder as Beth opened it. She moved into the front room and looked out of the window. A Mercedes was passing through the crowd outside on its way down the street, the angry driver leaning out of the window shouting a string of expletives at the reporters as he told them to move out of his way. She watched it disappear.

Back in the kitchen, Marie was still at the table, staring into space, her face taut.

'I do have some more questions,' Beth said.

A low-bellied roar sounded from outside.

Marie ran another weary hand across her forehead. 'We'll go into Vic's cinema room. He had it soundproofed so he could watch his films at full volume without upsetting the neighbours.'

Beth grabbed the mugs of tea and followed Marie into a large room at the back of the house. Daylight streamed in from patio doors at the end, bouncing off the white walls, giving it a bright and airy feel. A synthetic floral scent met her, like that of a plug-in air freshener. Marie invited Beth to sit on one of the three grey sofas, arranged around an oversized television on the wall. A thick-pile grey rug covered the wooden flooring.

Beth felt an urge to probe Marie more, ask her about her relationship with Vic and how they met, but now wasn't the time. The early days of an investigation were tricky. She needed to build a rapport with Marie and gain her trust.

She settled into her seat and surveyed their wedding photo on the side wall, beside a collection of photos of Zac, taken at various stages of growth. A family liaison officer was trained to filter through the content of everyday life, to fade into the background and observe. In a cold case, with the passing of time, this was extra difficult.

The detective in her was also bitterly aware that most people were killed by someone close to them; the loss, the grief, the doctor's reports on file that confirmed Marie was suffering with depression, and the numerous trips to her GP and health visitor all bothered Beth.

She pressed her lips together. 'Do you feel up to talking to me about the time that Alicia disappeared?'

Marie averted her gaze. She looked tired, weary. 'What can you do that hasn't been tried already?'

'There's a strong possibility we have Alicia now. Which means we have forensics, the chance of new evidence.'

'I'm not coming back down to the police station.' Her shoulders quaked. 'Even the smell of that place makes me sick.'

Beth was taking a risk here. The DCI hadn't asked her to take another account; there were no tape recorders, no cameras here to record it. If they proved the child was Alicia and concerns were raised about Marie's original evidence, the woman would need to be interviewed again formally at the station. But Beth was struggling to get a feel for the case. Fifteen years ago, Marie was distraught, grieving and suffering from post-natal depression. Perhaps now she was better placed to make sense of what happened. She needed to wind the clock back, though it was a fine line, a delicate path, to be navigated carefully. 'I'm not asking you to. We can talk here, now. You and me. What do you say?'

A glance at the door.

Vic would be back from the school shortly. He was protective of his wife and clearly didn't want her unduly upset. From the look in his eyes earlier and his reaction to the press presence, Beth suspected he would resist her questions. 'Why don't you tell me about what happened after Liam died?' she asked.

'Why?'

'I'm trying to understand. If we're to review the case, the more I can learn about what happened, the more I can help.'

Marie stared at the floor. She seemed hollow, empty, the years of unexplained loss draining every ounce of strength from her. 'I don't remember much, it's all a bit foggy. It was difficult. I was feeding and caring for a new baby, while grieving for another.'

Beth pulled the notebook from her bag and turned to a fresh page. 'Go on.'

'The depression was tough. All I wanted was to be left alone and given time to come to terms with everything. But that wasn't an option. Every time I looked at Alicia, I could see Liam.'

'Did they look alike?'

Marie gave a single nod. 'Daniel and his mum organised Liam's funeral, insisting on a Catholic service, even though they'd never been particularly religious. I didn't want it.' She closed her eyes, shuddering at the memories. 'I was raised as a Catholic but later gave up the church. They wouldn't listen though. Kept saying, "It's important to give him a proper send-off." I've got patchy memories of a tiny white coffin with silver handles. Most of the day passed in a blur. Daniel went back to work a week or so afterwards. I didn't want him to, but we had a pile of bills to pay and funerals don't come cheap.' She gazed into space. 'That first morning was the worst. When he left the house and his car pulled off the drive, I'd never felt so alone.' A tear slipped down her cheek. 'I tried to get on; Alicia took her feed and immediately fell back to sleep. But the house was so quiet. It's hard for a new mum, you know. I was scheduled in for a Caesarean but went into labour earlier than expected and left work suddenly. I missed the hustle and bustle of the sales office where I used to work. There were always phones ringing, colleagues chatting. To go from that to being at home alone with a baby is difficult. The emptiness and silence. I couldn't stop thinking about little Liam.'

'What about friends and family? Did they help?'

'People visited at first, especially after the birth. Friends from work, family. Nobody really knew what to say. I was tearful. I knew I was suffering from depression and couldn't take anything because I was breastfeeding. Then, when Daniel returned to work, they stopped coming. Looking back, I guess I probably made them uncomfortable.'

She pulled a tissue from the box beside her and wiped her nose. 'We were young, Daniel and I, only just twenty-two. We'd been together since school. I was delighted when I got pregnant, couldn't wait. When I found out it was twins it was the icing on the cake, a ready-made family. But I struggled to cope with losing Liam, couldn't get my head around the grief. My mum came over for a while. She couldn't stay for long though.'

'How long have your family lived in Australia?' Beth asked. She'd read the case file, already knew the answer, but wanted to keep Marie talking.

'They moved out there when I was nineteen. I had a job here, a steady boyfriend, and didn't want to go. I lived with my gran until she passed away, eighteen months before the twins were born, and stayed on in Gran's house after she died. I had no other family nearby. Most of my friends were at work.' She looked away. 'We had a few...' Her face folded. 'A few problems at the beginning. I didn't produce enough milk. And the bottle gave her colic.'

'What about Daniel's family?'

She huffed. 'His mum was next to useless. I'd never been good enough for him in her eyes and when I lost Liam... I don't know. She seemed to disapprove of everything I did. "You're young and strong, you don't need pills," she said when I was diagnosed with depression. "Breast is best," when I struggled to feed. She wasn't a fan of powdered milk.'

'You didn't get along?'

'Daniel's mum was... different. His mum and dad separated when he was four. None of the kids remember their dad. Apparently, he was a drinker, prone to gambling. She moved them down here from Liverpool after Scott was born and raised them all singlehandedly.' She shook her head. 'They lived in her shadow. Hated upsetting her. All apart from Scottie, the younger one. Nothing ever seemed to bother him. I used to wind Daniel up, call his mum a matriarch. Not to her face, mind you. Wouldn't dare.' She turned to the glass doors and stared out at the lawn beyond. 'Doesn't matter now. She passed away fourteen years ago.'

'Was there no one else?'

'My sister-in-law, Daniel's twin, visited. She was constantly buying Alicia gifts – dresses, hats, baby shoes. I wouldn't care, it was such a hot summer she hardly had a chance to wear them. Spent most of the time in a vest. The shawl in Alicia's changing bag, the one she disappeared with, was bought by Cara. Oh, and Scottie called in occasionally. He loved Alicia.'

Beth recalled Cara and Daniel's comments about their elusive brother. She was tempted to press Marie, but now wasn't the time. She needed to keep her on track, note every detail of her account and check it back with the case file at the office for consistency. 'How did you manage after Daniel went back to work?' she asked.

Marie shifted uncomfortably in her seat. 'Alicia would feed and then cry until she wore herself out. She cried so much I thought she was ill. I took her to see the doctor and they said there was nothing wrong with her. "She just needs to find a routine," the health visitor said. "It's quite normal for a new mother to be concerned." Nothing I could do made it easier. Daniel and I barely saw each other. I was so exhausted I followed Alicia's sleep pattern and slept when she did, which was usually in the evenings. Most of the time I didn't know what time of day it was, let alone what day of the week.

'Daniel reacted by working longer hours. When I was pregnant, we'd decided to extend the house to give us three bedrooms. We wanted the kids to have one each. Daniel decided to do it himself, to keep the costs down. He'd already started on the foundations before I gave birth. When he went back to work, he said he was putting in the overtime to pay for the extension. I think he stayed away because he didn't know how to deal with me. We only had one car which he used, so I was stranded at home with an unsettled baby.'

'That must have been difficult.'

'It was. For a while I felt like I didn't belong to this world anymore. I didn't realise it at the time, but I was heading for a breakdown. Then I discovered walking.'

She looked across at Beth, almost as if this was a revelation. 'I'd put the baby in the pram. Well, the car seat – she preferred to sleep in there. We had one of those modern travel systems, you know, where the car seat attaches to the top of the pram. People used to tell me off, say she should be lying flat, but, honestly, in those early days anything that got her off to sleep was a godsend. And she slept flat in her cot at night. Anyway, I'd click it on, stroll down to the shops, walk into town, or wander out to the country. It was summertime and the fresh air was like an injection of adrenalin, sending Alicia off as we trundled along. If I was tired, I walked around the block, then came back and caught up with my sleep. I started to feel better, more like my old self. Caught up on the washing, unpacked the dishwasher, emptied the ironing basket – all jobs I'd been leaving for Daniel.'

'So, things were improving?'

'That's what I don't understand. The walking was helping Alicia and me. We were finally finding a routine. She was crying less, sleeping more. I walked to the shops the morning she disappeared to get provisions for dinner. I wanted to make something for Daniel. Was planning for us to eat together after I put Alicia down in the evening, like old times.'

Beth gave a sympathetic smile. 'Would you be comfortable talking me through the day Alicia disappeared?'

Marie glanced again at the door. 'I don't know, I've been through this so many times.'

Beth held her ground. The transcripts from Marie's initial interview had focused on how often she visited the shops where the incident occurred, and whether she always took the same route. Marie had said her movements were erratic; she took different paths to the shops and with a newborn there was no regularity or routine to her day. But Beth wanted more. She wanted to be transported back there. To see the event unfold through Marie's eyes. 'There's a possibility we've now found your daughter,' she reiterated. 'She'll be examined thoroughly, her clothes tested for fibres and particles. This gives us the best opportunity to find out who took her and what happened. To do that, we need to go back to the beginning and re-examine all the evidence, all the accounts, afresh.'

14

There was something about the smell of a kill, that pungent aroma of a dead body that awakened the senses. He pulled up at the traffic lights and braked. The crime scene yesterday was the trigger he'd been waiting for; justice was so close now he could almost smell it.

The lights changed, he continued down the road, taking a left at the next roundabout. He was in the heart of Kingsthorpe now; a stone's throw away from the building site. The news last night had been surprisingly vague: a child's remains had been found by a contractor working on the new housing estate on the edge of Kingsthorpe. No specific details. No information about the body. No identity. It was time to re-visit the crowds at the crime scene, listen to the reporters' chatter, find out what else they'd gleaned.

A sandwich board at the side of the road titled *Northants News* caught his eye. The headline, *Is it Alicia?*

The sound of his brakes squeaking filled the air as he pulled onto the curb and climbed out.

A bell rang over the door as he entered the shop. A bored-looking assistant behind the counter flipped through a magazine while twiddling strands of burgundy hair between the thumb and forefinger of her free hand. An Asian man was on his knees at the end of an aisle, filling shelves. The voices of Bon Jovi sang merrily in the background, a song he couldn't place.

He wandered past the assistant to the other side of the counter. Ignored the lines of chocolate and confectionary and made for the news stand.

The shop's fluorescent lighting bounced off the glossy magazines. He bypassed the covers featuring celebrity photos, Royals on engagements and brushed the newspapers, flicking across the headlines until he found the pile of *Northants News*, and then pulled out a copy.

The page was creased, the corners dog-eared where it had been bunched up in the middle of a pile. He smoothed out the front page and stared at a black and white photo of an empty pram beside another picture of a forensic tent, close to the edge of the building site where he had been yesterday.

The line beneath it read, *Have they found baby Alicia?*

Blood fizzed in his veins.

Yesterday, the remains of a young child were found on the building site at the end of Boughton Green Road. Detective Chief Inspector Lee Freeman confirmed they are of a young child, possibly a baby.

Forty-three-year-old builder Aaron Dawson was working on the building site yesterday morning when he noticed an arm among the rubble...

Engrossed in the article, he didn't see the man approach. Didn't hear him speak. A prod on his shoulder made him start.

'Are you going to buy that?' It was the Asian man who'd been re-stocking the shelves when he walked in.

He glared down at his skinny frame, unspeaking. How dare he?

The shop assistant shrunk back at the intensity of his gaze.

The bell over the door tinkled. A shopper entered, her eyes falling straight on them. It wouldn't do to cause a scene. Not yet. The timing wasn't right.

He pushed past the assistant, approached the till, pulled a few pound coins out of his pocket and dropped them onto the counter.

He was out of the store and back in his car, making a U-turn in the road, before they could offer him change.

15

The grey mood of the garden crept into the cinema room. 'Before we start, can I ask you to close your eyes?' Beth asked.

Marie stiffened. It was one thing, talking through the account of losing her daughter, reiterating her story, but quite another doing it with her eyes closed. With her eyes closed she couldn't gauge the reaction of her interviewer and she felt bare, vulnerable.

The detective seemed to sense her uneasiness. 'I know this might seem unusual but it blocks out distractions, helps to concentrate the mind. It can sharpen the memory too, especially when an incident happened some time ago.'

Marie squirmed. The sofa suddenly felt uncomfortable. 'Where do you want me to start?'

'The beginning of the day would be useful.'

'Oh, I don't know.' She wriggled again. Reluctantly closing her eyes, tucking her hands in her lap. 'The morning was quiet. Vic came round to deliver some new hubcaps for Daniel's car.'

'Vic?'

'Yes. He used to deliver car parts for a living. That was his first job from school.' She pictured a younger skinnier version of her husband, the slick dark hair, the bony face. 'He moved through the business. Now owns a company supplying car parts.'

'What time did he arrive?'

Marie could see the grandfather clock in her late gran's front room, with the chime that no longer worked. 'Around eleven. He didn't stay long. Dropped them off and left almost immediately. I was just putting Alicia down.'

'What about afterwards?'

Marie's heart pitted. It wasn't as if she had to dig deep. She'd relived this day, over and over, so many times in her mind. 'I walked up to the bank of shops on Link Road and stopped at the butcher's to get some gammon. Gammon was Daniel's favourite.' She could see it all now. The empty street, the warmth of the sun on her arms. It was all uphill, she was out of breath by the time she got there. 'Alicia was quiet in her car seat when we arrived.'

'Fixed to the pram,' Beth checked.

'Yes. I didn't want to disturb her, she looked peaceful. So, I left her outside asleep. I could easily see the pram from the counter, was only gone for a minute. It was the middle of August, the school opposite the shops was on holiday and the whole place was sleepy.'

'What happened next?'

Marie placed a hand to her forehead. The heat of her skin soothed her tense muscles and shielding her closed eyes somehow made her feel less exposed. 'I left the butcher's, wandered further along to the supermarket at the end. Inside the door they had a bucket of Jersey new potatoes. Daniel liked new potatoes, especially when they were in season.' The bucket was green, inviting. She'd wrestled with her conscience. 'Alicia was still asleep. I thought about snapping the car seat off, taking her inside, but she was getting heavy and I'd struggle with a basket and the seat. And there was no one around.' A blanket of sadness wrapped itself around her at the memory of Alicia's pink face, her pursed lips. This was the last time she'd seen her baby, the last time she'd stroked her soft cheek. 'I figured I'd only be gone for a couple of minutes.'

Tears burned her eyes, forcing them open. She dropped her hand to her lap. 'I shovelled the potatoes into a bag, looking back towards the door, checking on the pram. Checking again from the next aisle. It was one of those shops with adverts across the windows, I had to peer around the edge to see her clearly. When I reached the till, my view of the street outside was obscured by a stand filled with greetings cards. The assistant was struggling with a new receipt roll. I stepped back, looked around the end of the stand. The sun was strong that day. I'd pulled up the hood on the car seat. I remember thinking I must bring out the parasol next time.'

She recalled a brief discussion with a shop assistant called Carol about the fresh flavour of produce in season. One of those fleeting moments you share with strangers, a pleasantry to make you smile, quickly forgotten. Only this time it wasn't forgotten. She could still repeat every word of the exchange, feel every beat of the seconds that passed.

'When did you discover the pram was missing?' Beth asked.

'After I paid, I went straight outside.' She met Beth's gaze. 'I couldn't believe it. Questioned myself at first. Thought maybe I'd parked her around the corner or wheeled her into the shop. Or that someone had moved her out of the sun.'

Heat rose in her chest, creeping up her neck as she was transported back. Running up and down like a screaming banshee. Frantically checking the other shops. Assistants spilling out of the stores. A few residents emerging from houses nearby. It was like a whirlwind, a swirling vortex of voices and bodies charging about, merging together in din.

The uniformed officer arriving. The discovery of the pram. And then she knew. She knew she'd lost her.

Tears dripped down Marie's face. She grabbed another tissue, pressed it to her cheeks. 'It's not true what they said, you know, in the papers. About me not bonding with Alicia, not wanting her. It was tough, a difficult time. But I didn't neglect Alicia. If anything, I neglected myself.'

Marie wiped her face, her chest tensing. This wasn't only about her and her family. There was someone else involved. Someone who'd been searching, seeking answers from the day Alicia disappeared. 'Have you spoken with Daniel yet?' His name stuck like a fish bone in the back of her throat. So many years had passed since they'd spoken, so much heartache.

'I saw him yesterday evening,' the detective said. 'Explained the situation and took a DNA sample.'

Marie's heart thumped. 'Why did you need his sample if you already have mine?'

'It's routine, in cases such as these, to take a sample from both parents.'

'How was he?'

'As well as can be expected. Cara was with him.'

An engine pulled up on the drive, a car door banged shut. Marie wiped her face again and sniffed, shoving the damp tissue up her sleeve. By the time Vic marched into the room, she seemed brighter.

'Those journalists have got a bloody death wish,' he said as he collected their empty mugs. 'Nearly knocked one of them over as I pulled onto the drive.' He stopped in his tracks and passed suspicious glances between the two women. 'What's going on? Is there some news?'

'No,' Beth said. 'We've been talking things through.' She snapped her notebook shut and stood. 'I need to get back and check on the press conference,' she said to Marie. 'Thank you for your help. I'll be in touch as soon as I have more information.'

She gave Vic a swift smile as she passed and looked back at Marie. 'Call me if you need anything. I'm always at the end of the phone.'

The reporters lurched forward as the detective emerged from 146 Redland Drive. Shouting questions, holding out microphones in the hope for a snippet of information, a sound bite for their next news piece. Camera flashes filled the air.

He stayed at the back of the crowd and watched the woman take her time on the doorstep, scrolling through her phone, ignoring the voices at the end of the driveway, the pushes and shoves in her peripheral vision. She wore a black suit. A crisp white shirt stretched across her chest. Wispy dark curls escaped from the hair tie at the nape of her neck, fluttering around a petite face with razor-sharp cheekbones. Everything about her – her composure, her calm demeanour, the way she stood, military-style – screamed of police.

As soon as he'd read the article earlier, he'd about-turned and headed to the Russells', guessing this would be the central focus of the enquiry for now. And he'd been right. It had been so easy to trace their address online. Everything was out there these days, if you knew where to look for it.

He watched her hold out her phone at an angle, as if she was struggling to get signal, and a smile curled the edge of his lip.

It was common practice for the police to photograph crowds gathered at crime scenes, and people outside addresses of interest. Photos would be taken at the building site too and, since this was an old crime, a cold case now re-ignited, they'd feel the need to record who was nearby at every stage of the investigation. Compare the crowds, check to see if any faces without a professional interest cropped up.

Did they really think he was stupid enough to get caught in a photo?

He ducked down, just before the click.

As usual, he was one step ahead.

16

The bank of shops was ghostly quiet that morning. They were situated on a slope, rising up Link Road. Acre Lane with its boxes of 1970s-style semi-detached houses ran along the bottom. Whitehills residential estate, with its mix of terraced housing and bungalows at the top. Set back from the road with a car park out front, the shops faced the playground of Whitehills Primary School opposite. A row of flats above was accessed by a stone staircase at the side. It was in the well of this staircase that Alicia Owen's pram had been found.

Beth took in the Chinese takeaway, the beauty salon, the pizzeria and grill, the supermarket at the bottom, on the corner. A small arrangement of stores to provide essentials to the nearby houses, saving them from travelling out to the larger shops in Kingsthorpe centre, or beyond. The name over the door of the supermarket had changed, the staff inside were different, but the shop was still located in the same place where Marie claimed her baby, Alicia, had been left on the day she was taken.

Apart from a white van, the car park outside the front of the shops was empty. Beth left her car and wandered across the tarmac. Suddenly her ears were assaulted by the shrieking sounds of children. She turned and watched a group of infants spilling out of the school opposite, gearing up for playtime. She tore her gaze away. The incident happened in August; there wouldn't have been any children around because the school was closed for the holidays.

Ash Grove, a small side close, led off Link Road along the top end of the shops, a cul-de-sac of modern terraces and semi-detached houses, the end dwellings having a clear view of the car park. The bottom of Link Road fed into Acre Lane, a horseshoe-shaped thoroughfare, running through the estate and linking it with the A5199 at the bottom. Once again, Acre Lane was lined with houses, yet door-to-door questioning had yielded no witnesses to the event. Perhaps they were out at work or away on holiday when Alicia disappeared. The area was practically deserted today; a sleepy bank of shops nestled in the centre of a housing estate.

Beth walked towards the supermarket on the end and imagined Marie arriving, pressing her foot on the pram's brake and wandering inside. She hovered outside the entrance for several seconds, then walked along the front of the shops towards Ash Grove, taking the route it was assumed Alicia's abductor had taken.

This exercise had been done countless times before: when the case first broke and when a review team arrived to re-examine the evidence, not to mention at the official reconstruction. But, after poring over the case file and listening to Marie Russell's account, Beth felt compelled to start from scratch. This was a part of Kingsthorpe she didn't know well. She'd grown up on the other side of the suburb, and she wanted to get a feel for the area and piece it together with Marie's account.

The other stores looked empty as she wandered past. At the end, she turned the corner and paused beneath the winding stone staircase leading to the flats above. This is where the pram was found, tucked in the stairwell beneath, out of view of the shopfronts. A stray crisp packet in the corner crackled in the light breeze.

Where did her abductor go next?

She climbed the stairs. A landing at the top ran along the front of the flats. It wouldn't have been difficult to wheel the pram to the bottom of the staircase and carry the child upstairs. Though there was only one way in, one out. It would have been too risky to take the child there and, anyway, according to the file, every resident of the flats had substantiated alibis for the morning Alicia disappeared.

Beth wandered back downstairs. There was another short series of steps at the bottom, the pedestrian access to Ash Grove. She navigated them. At the top, a Volvo, a Fiesta and a BMW were parked kerbside. She worked through the offender's potential escape routes.

Turn right at the end of Ash Grove and you'd head through the residential estate of Whitehills towards the A508, which presented the choice of driving into or out of town. Turn left and Acre Lane at the bottom reached down to the A5199 which again offered the same options. Both directions were close to the country and both routes could feasibly be taken to Boughton Green Road. Beth narrowed her eyes. To take a child in broad daylight seemed a drastic move. The car seat, with the child sleeping inside, had been lifted off the pram, taken with her and never been found, along with Alicia's changing bag. Keeping her would have been a huge risk too. Within hours of her disappearance, photos of the child appeared on every news channel. Everyone was on hyper alert. Anyone noticing a neighbour or someone nearby suddenly acquiring a young child would be suspicious. Which meant they had to kill her and dispose of the body quickly.

She couldn't imagine anyone carrying a child in a car seat along any of those routes on foot. No, the risk of being seen by a passing motorist or resident would be too high. The original investigation worked on the assumption that the abductor had a motor vehicle, parked nearby, and made off with the child in the car. Ash Grove was where detectives hypothesised Alicia's abductor had parked. It made sense really. It would have taken seconds to wheel the pram away, tuck it beneath the stairwell, snap off the car seat and climb the steps to a car at the top.

The incident occurred at 11.30 a.m. on a Tuesday morning, only an hour or so later than today. A car whizzed past, along Acre Lane at the bottom. But apart from that, and the sound of the children playing which had merged into a dull chatter, all was quiet. A couple of drivers at the time, who'd seen the pram parked outside the supermarket, had come forward reporting a fleeting glance; they hadn't spotted anyone moving the child though.

Beth looked up at the CCTV cameras, beacons above the shop entrances. The advent of cameras made police work so much easier. They didn't lie, were free from emotion in the midst of a melee, a third eye capturing the scene with remarkable accuracy: the edge of a number plate nearby, the man at the back of the crowd. All potential evidence passing witnesses might miss.

If only there'd been cameras there fifteen years ago.

The investigation team had interviewed witnesses who'd seen Marie Russell with the pram, walking up to the shops, yet none of them had spoken to her. She was another mother out doing her shopping, part of the street scene of the morning. Nobody noticed anyone acting suspiciously nearby.

Marie Russell claimed she hadn't planned to walk out that morning and visit those shops. She hadn't told anyone where she was going, not even her husband, because she wanted to cook him a surprise dinner. Unless somebody had been watching her for days and weeks, following her movements, it made a planned abduction unlikely.

The dearth of information and witness statements in the file troubled Beth. It seemed the only person in their sights so far with means to kill Alicia was the child's mother. But, after hearing her account, something about Marie killing her daughter didn't quite sit with Beth. She switched back to their conversation earlier. This was a painful case, spanning several years. Marie's initial reluctance to talk about it, to dredge up the painful details was to be expected. Though there was – Beth couldn't put her finger on it – a strange uneasiness about her. Was she uneasy about going through the details again, the wider effect on her family, or was there something else bothering her?

17

An ailing light bulb beside the door flickered in the conference room. Beth ignored it, instead focusing on the map of Kingsthorpe displayed on their board.

She traced the route from where Alicia disappeared to the building site at the end of Boughton Green Road, less than two miles as the crow flies.

Beth had driven to the other side of Kingsthorpe after leaving the shops earlier and cruised to the end of Boughton Green Road. Surveying the bystanders and reporters huddled beside the police tape as she slowed to pass the crime scene, she was relieved to see the high banner advertising new executive homes that blocked their view into the building site and prevented them photographing and filming the area on their phones. The last thing Alicia's parents needed was to see footage of their child's crime scene playing out on social media.

The child's body had been removed, although the police tent would still be in position, preserving the area where she was found. CSIs would continue to examine the surrounding area for several days.

She scoured the map. The building site ran for several acres, butting the edge of Guilding's shoe factory grounds, the last unit on Boughton Green Road, running to the roundabout at the bottom, and the open countryside beyond, and reaching back half a mile to the tennis centre at the back end of Kingsthorpe.

Hunter confirmed the size and state of the body resembled that of a three-month-old child, which meant if it was Alicia, she was killed around the time she went missing. Until tests were completed on the residue on the concrete, and soil samples tested from nearby, they had no idea how long Alicia had been in that spot. If she was buried fifteen years ago, whoever hid her knew the area, had local knowledge of where the walkways were, and placed her where she was unlikely to be found.

A flap of the door turned her head. Nick Geary walked in. 'I was told I'd find you in here,' he said.

'I've allocated all the tasks in the office,' she said, aware of her additional responsibilities. 'Given everyone enquiries to follow up on.' As soon as she'd walked into the office earlier, she'd been swamped by questions from the team. Taking on a management role and being FLO on the case was certainly going to prove a challenge.

'So, I see. I've got the address of Tanner, the retired superintendent who was the senior investigating officer on the original investigation. Wondered if you'd like to come out and see him with me?'

Beth nodded and looked back at the map. 'A baby is kidnapped beside a bank of shops on a residential housing estate on a Tuesday morning and nobody sees anything. It doesn't make sense.'

'Nothing about this case makes sense,' Nick said, digging his hands into his pockets. 'I mean look at the mother.

Remarried, playing happy families with her ex-husband's best friend.'

'There's no crime in piecing your life back together.'

He lifted a single shoulder, let it drop. 'Maybe she planned this herself, killed the child and took out an empty pram. Nobody actually saw the baby.'

Beth glanced at the contents of the file, strewn across the desk behind her. She'd read the senior investigating officer's reports, followed the discussions with Marie Russell. 'It was a theory in the original investigation,' she said, 'but the car seat was fixed to the top of the pram. Surely someone would have noticed if the baby was absent.'

'Would they though? Really? The hood was up.'

'To shield the child from the sun.'

'Oh, come on. You heard Marie Russell say it was a difficult time for her. A new baby she struggled with. Grappling with the grief of losing its twin. Reports from her health visitor expressed concern for Marie's well-being. The statement from her doctor confirmed he'd recommended bereavement counselling, and there's no record of her seeing a counsellor.'

'They didn't mark the child at risk.'

'People make mistakes. She had means,' Nick continued. 'They were having an extension built on the side of the house. There were probably plenty of bags of concrete around. She had opportunity. Her husband was at work, out of the way.'

'Why take the trouble to bury the child in concrete?'

'Makes it more difficult to find. If it wasn't for the excavators, the child might never have been discovered.'

Beth switched her mind back to her discussions with

Marie Russell. She'd said herself her memory of the time was foggy. Although, she appeared to recall the day of Alicia's disappearance and the events leading up to it with surprising clarity.

'I don't know,' Beth said. 'Who moved the pram when she was in the supermarket? And a concrete block that size would have weighed a ton. How would she have carried it by herself?'

'Perhaps she had help.'

18

Former Superintendent Mark Tanner greeted Beth and Nick warmly when they arrived at his home at just after 2 p.m., his face lit with anticipation. He'd followed the findings on the news and when Nick called to arrange the visit, he'd invited them straight over, clearly keen to assist in any way.

Beth remembered Tanner from her early days in the force. He was a bear of a man at 6 foot 6 inches, with a quick wit and a tenacious hands-on approach to investigating, a trait rarely seen in his rank these days. Stories of him crawling through undergrowth to assist with surveillance and wading through a river on a search team were still banded around the station. It was a much-changed Tanner they saw today though. The Parkinson's disease that had dogged him since his retirement, three years earlier, had taken a hold. His cheeks were sunken, his clothes hung off him and Beth noticed a tremor in his hands as he greeted them.

Tanner led them to a spacious summer room, at the rear of the property, that overlooked a sloping manicured garden, edged with a low fence. Beyond, a patchwork of fields and rolling countryside stretched to the Welland Valley on the horizon. Nick and Beth sipped coffees, freshly brewed by Tanner's bustling wife, Emma, while Nick gave him the rundown on the case. He waited for Nick to finish before he spoke. 'You're sure it's Alicia Owen?'

'We're awaiting the parental DNA match, but everything points to her – the clothing, the age, the bangle.'

'What state is she in?'

'The body has been preserved enough for pathology to extract DNA. Cause of death hasn't been established yet, she's still being examined.'

Tanner's face softened, hope blooming at the prospect of a result. Unsolved cases wormed under every copper's skin and none more so than those who'd worked on homicide and serious crime, when every waking hour was consumed with the drive to unearth a guilty party and achieve a sense of justice for loved ones left behind.

'The reporter on the news said the child was found by a schoolgirl,' he said.

'Yes. Goes to the nearby girls' school.'

'What was she doing there?'

'Having a cheeky fag before school, by all accounts.'

'I seem to remember I liked a smoke, back in the day.'

'Didn't we all?' Nick said.

Tanner chuckled. When he spoke again, his eyes grew sombre. 'That child.' He shook his head. 'We had half of Northamptonshire out looking for her. Babies don't disappear. As time passed, we all feared the worst. You know the score: the longer they're gone, the less chance we have of finding them alive. And the circumstances surrounding this one, the lack of witness sightings and no body. It was incredibly frustrating.'

'We're wading through the case material. Was there

anything that stood out to you from the original enquiry?'
Beth asked. 'Might give us some focus.'

Tanner stroked his beard. 'If Marie Russell was to be
believed, it was an opportunist kidnapping. But it was also
difficult to believe a stranger would take a child from a
shopping area in broad daylight, especially a baby.

'We called in an expert on those prams, or travel systems,
as they're called,' he continued, cocking a brow. 'Wasn't like
that when we had our kids. Technology had moved on –
mothers were buying complete systems: car seats and prams
that clicked together, so they could move their baby from one
place to another with minimum disturbance. In Alicia's case
this was a huge factor because the abductor hadn't taken
the whole unit. They'd removed the car seat and made off
with the baby sleeping inside, leaving the pram behind. Like
any other product, these travel systems differed from one
company to another. This one wasn't difficult to master, just
a couple of clicks and a lever. But an opportunist would be
in a hurry and it was hard to believe someone would wheel
the pram around the corner and even attempt to remove the
seat if they hadn't used that particular system before.

'We interviewed all the family and close friends that
knew Alicia, or had allegedly been in contact with her –
you'll find the transcripts on file. The liaison officers were
concerned about Marie Russell. She had to be sedated in the
beginning which made interviews difficult, and faced a lot
of criticism from the local community for leaving the baby
outside the shop. We had to persuade her to take part in
public appeals. It was difficult to tell whether her reluctance
was driven by guilt or grief.'

'So, Marie Russell was your prime suspect?' Nick asked.

'I'm sure you've read my notes,' he said. 'I can't deny, Marie Russell was in our sights. She was Alicia's principle carer and home alone with the child that morning. The last person on record to see Alicia. A couple of witnesses saw her walking to the shops with the car seat fixed to the top of the system, but nobody got close enough to see the baby inside. We explored several different scenarios. Arguably she had means and opportunity to kill the child before she left, and then make up a mock bundle in the travel system. A shop assistant saw her park up outside the supermarket. No one saw the pram being moved or the car seat being taken. It couldn't have been her that wheeled the pram away because she was in the shop at the time.'

'You think she had help?'

'It was an avenue we considered. In the event she was guilty, it seemed the only explanation.' He shrugged. 'Our main problem was that the liaison officers couldn't get close to her. When she discovered we were examining her phone records for secret messages or associations, she refused to have officers in the house. Without a body and any evidence, there was very little to go on. And… I don't know. I always struggled with a motive for Marie. To lose one child at birth is tragic. She was suffering from depression and with good reason. Baby Alicia was regularly examined by their local GP and health visitor and they hadn't flagged up any concerns of abuse or neglect. If anything, her GP said she was more akin to an over-protective mother.'

'Beth's doing the liaison job with the family now,' Nick said.

Tanner shot Beth a look. 'How are you finding her?'

'On the whole, cooperative and helpful. It's her husband who seems the more reluctant of the two.'

'Vic Russell.' Tanner nodded knowingly. 'I remember when she married him. They kept it low-profile until a local journalist turned up at the reception and took surreptitious photos. She went crackers when it was reported in the newspaper.' A phone rang in another room. He looked momentarily perplexed, the sound appearing to dislodge his thoughts. 'How are you finding Daniel Owen?' he asked eventually.

'He's a totally different kettle of fish. Talks about Alicia in the present tense, as if she's still around. Has photos of her out in his front room. It's like he can't let go.' A brief silence fell upon them. 'Do you know anything about Daniel's brother, Scott?' Beth asked. 'We're re-tracing everyone Alicia was in contact with before she died but can't seem to locate him.'

'Not much more than you, I would think. He had an alibi and wasn't a suspect in the enquiry. As far as I recall, he was a low-level crim. We'd picked him up for joyriding in his teens. I'm told there was some kind of family argument, shortly after Alicia went missing, and he left home. Nothing unusual there. The Owens were always falling out. Scott often left home and returned later. He was a young lad, late teens. Accustomed to going out with his mates, drinking too much and getting into fights from what we could make out. His mother died of a stroke some time afterwards. Last I heard, Daniel and Cara blamed him for sending their mother to an early grave and disowned him.'

The door opened and Emma appeared. 'That was

the dispensary on the phone,' she said to Tanner. 'Your prescription is ready.' She looked across at Beth and Nick. 'Can I get you another drink?'

Nick and Beth declined the offer and thanked her.

She patted her husband's shoulder affectionately. 'How about you?' she asked. 'You must be parched with all this police-talk.'

'I'm fine.'

An affectionate smile tickled her lips. 'I bet.' She turned to the others. 'He won't have a drink in front of visitors. Hands shake too much.'

He threw her a frown, drawing his thick eyebrows together. 'Emma!'

'What? It's nothing to be ashamed of.'

'It isn't,' Nick said. He gave a gentle smile and stood. 'We need to get back anyway.'

Tanner hauled himself up and placed a brief hand on Nick's forearm. 'Keep me updated, won't you? It would be good to finally see this one through.'

19

Beth and Nick strode into the incident room later that afternoon to find the DCI beside Pete's desk, scrutinising the latest batch of photos sent across from the autopsy. Empty pizza boxes were laying open across the top of the filing cabinets.

'You could have saved some for the management,' Nick said, glancing toward the food boxes with a sarcastic smile.

Freeman laughed. 'Ah, yes. I almost forgot. Everybody, meet your DS and DI for this case. Better take note of their preferences. We know Nick's a Margarita fan. What about you, Beth?'

Heads turned. Beth felt her cheeks heat up. She had less than a year's homicide experience under her belt and, while everyone knew she'd passed her sergeant's exam and was awaiting interview, there were many there that had worked on the murder squad since before she made detective. The last thing she needed was hostility from members of the team who felt they were better qualified. But if the warm smiles and nods of congratulations greeting her were anything to go by, she needn't have worried. Nick gave her a wink from the side of the room.

'Pepperoni with extra sausage,' she said, not wishing to let the moment linger.

'Good choice.' Freeman nodded. 'Okay, gather around everybody,' he said, beckoning his team forward. 'You all need to hear this.'

Beth and Nick passed on Tanner's account.

'So, Tanner ruled out the mother?' Freeman asked when they'd finished.

'He didn't say that exactly,' Nick said. 'More he struggled to find her motive. If she's to be believed, nobody else knew where she was going that day.'

Beth scanned the latest post-mortem photos on Pete's desk. The child's body was completely removed from the concrete now, a tiny frame laid out on a metal gurney. The torso blackened, the skin sinking into every natural recess. Her eyes rested on the bracelet, still laced around her wrist.

'Why leave her bracelet on?' she said. The presence of it niggled her. 'When you've gone to such great lengths to hide a body, bury it in such a way that it might never be found, it's odd they didn't strip her down and remove personal items.'

'Yes, we've been pondering that,' Freeman said.

'Maybe it was a shrine,' Nick said.

'Underground? In concrete?' Beth shook her head in disbelief.

'People resort to all sorts of strange methods when they panic.'

'This looks more calculated,' Beth said.

Pete nodded in agreement. 'Farmers bury all sorts in their fields,' he said. 'Broken, old machinery, you name it…

The block was found close to the ruins of the barn. If the concrete hadn't been chipped, it's likely the remains would have been discarded into land waste with the barn base and never discovered. It's possible whoever buried her thought ahead and considered that.'

Four pairs of eyes stared at the photos as they mulled this over.

'Hunter's confirmed there is an injury to the back of the head,' Freeman said, bringing them back on track.

Beth stopped short. At three months the child's head would have still needed some support. 'How could that happen?'

He pulled a face. 'Difficult to say, apparently. A blow to the back of the head, or maybe her head was cracked against something.' They all winced, horrified at the notion that a young child might have been subjected to such cruel trauma.

'Any chance it could have been caused accidentally?' Nick asked.

'Hunter can't be sure at this stage. There's no sign of sexual interference though.'

Beth recalled the tears in Daniel Owen's eyes when he'd asked the question, the evening before. The gruesome thought that your child was sexually abused was every parent's worst nightmare. At least she could reassure him on that point. It also ruled out another motivating factor.

Freeman placed his hands on his hips. 'What do you think about the mother, Beth? You've been spending time with the family.'

Beth took her time to answer. 'If she was involved, she'd have needed help. We know the pram was wheeled away while she was in the supermarket and the shop assistant witnessed her presence. And even with a young child inside, that concrete would have weighed a ton. Marie Russell's a petite woman, I can't see how she'd manage to transport it and bury it alone.' She looked towards the window, working it through in her mind and grimaced.

'What is it?'

'I don't know, sir. I just don't buy it. I mean, I know she was depressed and grief-stricken after the loss of her son but Marie Russell talks about the incident with such clarity of mind, such depth of emotion. If she's to be believed, it broke her.'

'Maybe she's a good liar,' Nick said. 'She's certainly had plenty of years to practise.'

'What about the workers from the former farm?' Beth asked.

'Old man Moreton's given me a list of labourers spanning the past twenty years,' Pete said. 'It's steep. Since we are reasonably sure it's Alicia, I've prioritised those who worked for him around the time she went missing. We're interviewing them individually, checking their movements at the time and any connection with the Owens. I took a statement from Mr Moreton when I was there.'

'And?'

'Now that we are focused on August 2002, he was able to check his records. He grew oilseed rape that year, harvested it during the middle of July and then cultivated the soil, ready to plant winter wheat mid-September. The field would have been standing dormant for some weeks after Alicia's disappearance on the 13th of August.'

'A labourer would know that.'

'Exactly. It's difficult with the time lapse. Old man Moreton believes he was working on the 13th. They'd finished harvesting and cultivation early that year. He was feeding cattle, doing his normal rounds. His wife was at home; she doesn't work. His son was away, travelling around the US at the time. They don't appear to have any connection with the Owens.'

'Okay, good work. Keep me updated on the labourers,' Freeman said, 'and make sure all the statements are recorded on the Holmes computer system and cross referenced for consistency. We don't want anything missed.'

20

Marie Russell's heart thumped as she placed the cutlery around the table mats. A frying pan filled with chicken breasts sizzled away on the stove. She was going through the motions, trying to keep the routine of a family evening dinner, desperately trying to hold everything together when all she wanted to do was to crawl into a box and hide away, alone. Almost two days had passed since the child's body had been found and there was still no confirmation it was Alicia. It was torturous.

She looked up to find Vic in the hallway, standing at the doorway to the front room, his back to her. Vic, the perfect partner who radiated kindness and treated her with kid gloves. The man who'd helped her rebuild her life after losing Alicia and made it quite clear that she was all he ever wanted. But – her heart thumped louder – there were things about Marie that Vic didn't know, that she'd hoped nobody would never know. And now with the possibility of Alicia's case unravelling, and DNA testing, she wasn't sure how she could avoid him finding out.

She buried her anxiety, pushing it deep inside, then wandered out and stood beside him. Zac was sitting on the sofa working the controls of his games console. Vic wasn't watching the game on the television screen, he was watching his son.

She touched Vic's arm. 'You okay?'

He tugged his gaze away, tilted his head to the hall, indicating for her to follow him.

'What is it?' she asked when they were back in the kitchen.

He pushed the door to. 'We need to speak to Zac about Alicia.'

Heat rose in Marie's head. She wasn't ready for this. Zac was so little. So innocent. 'He's too young.'

'We have to tell him something, Marie. Sooner or later he'll hear it from elsewhere. What did you tell him about the reporters outside?'

'That I thought they were there because they think Elsie's son might be visiting her next door, the one who won some money on the lottery.'

'What? Our next-door neighbour's son won some cash on the postcode lottery, it's very different.'

'He doesn't know that.'

'I can't believe you lied to him.'

She had to admit, guilt had pinched at her at Zac's little face when she'd shared the news. His eyes widening to plates. He was such an easy-going child, so accepting.

'What if he hears about Alicia at school?' Vic said. 'It's all over the news.'

'He's in year one. Who's going to say anything to him?'

'I don't know. One of the other kids maybe.'

'They're five and six-year-olds. They don't watch the news.' Though butterflies were now dancing about in her stomach. She'd shared his concern when they'd seen the news article that morning. Zac was always her first priority; she hated him being upset. Vic and she had discussed it, arranged for him to speak with Zac's teacher when he dropped the boy off, and make sure she kept an eye on him. Surely that was enough for now. 'Didn't you speak with Miss Marsh?' she asked.

'I did. She was very helpful; said she'd keep an eye out.'

'There we are then.'

'No, you don't understand. He needs to hear it from us first. In our words.'

'So, what do we tell him? That he has a sister he doesn't know about who was kidnapped as a baby? And we don't know where she is. It'll scare the living daylights out of him.' This was a conversation she knew she'd have to have with him one day, when he was older, more mature. More able to understand. She'd always planned to tell him the truth eventually. Not when he was six years old.

'There's no need to be so blunt.'

'We can't be absolutely sure it is Alicia until the results of the DNA test come back.' She was putting off the inevitable, she knew that. But she couldn't think of another way of dealing with it right now. 'If it is her, then we'll sit him down together and find a way to explain. If it isn't, the reporters will disappear, this will all go away and we'll continue as before. It's only going to be another day or two.'

Vic looked unsure.

'He's settled at school,' Marie continued. 'Happy. Even the presence of the reporters outside hasn't bothered him. Let's leave it for now. I don't want to distress him unless we have to.'

The babble of a low television filled Daniel Owen's living room: a weather forecaster in a red dress brushed her hand across Northamptonshire on a map and warned of impending snowfall. Beth tried to ignore her.

She'd spent the last ten minutes relaying the post-mortem findings to Daniel in as much detail as she was able. He'd flinched when she mentioned how the child was dressed and the injuries she sustained, appeared mildly relieved at the confirmation of no sexual abuse. His nostrils flared when she mentioned the newspaper article. *He already knows.* Another glance at the television. But if he had read the article or seen any mention of the case on the news, he didn't say.

'I'm so sorry. I have been trying to reach you,' she said. After leaving messages throughout the day, she'd decided to call in after work and was relieved to find him at home. This wasn't the kind of news that should be delivered over the phone.

'I don't answer my phone when I'm working. I haven't checked the messages yet.'

Not surprising, Beth thought, after being plagued by reporters for years.

Bailey was curled up beside him. He reached out, stroked the dog's head. 'Do you know how she died?'

'There's an injury to the back of her head. The pathologist believes it was the main cause of death. There are no immediate signs of any other injuries.'

Daniels eyes watered. 'You still can't be sure it's her though, right? I mean without the DNA match...'

'Not as yet,' Beth said. She was beginning to feel weary. It was important to keep families up to date, so they didn't hear information elsewhere, and when parents or family members lived separately this was even more of a challenge, especially at the end of a long day. Another reason why liaison officers generally worked in pairs.

'Are you sure you don't have contact details for your brother?' Beth asked when she finished up. 'Even a mobile number would help.'

'No.'

'Did something happen between you two?'

'I don't want to talk about it.'

'When did you last see him?'

'I don't know. Years ago. Look, it was a family issue. Nothing to do with Alicia's disappearance.' He sat forward. 'I'm away for the next few days. On a long-haul job to Poland. My phone will be off, I don't like using it in Europe, so you'll need to contact Cara if you want anything. I'll be checking in with her.'

The drone of a car engine filled the room as a car passed outside. Bailey lifted her head and growled.

Beth's eyes rested on the dog. She seemed infinitely comfortable there, lying beside her owner. 'What do you do with Bailey when you go away on a job?' she asked in an effort to loosen the tension in the room.

'Cara takes care of her. Bailey's happy there. Always glad to come home though, aren't you?' He scratched behind the dog's ear and she gazed up at him adoringly.

'How old is she?'

'We're not sure exactly. The vet reckons she's probably about fourteen.'

'You re-homed her?'

'Not exactly. Found her wandering around the estate one evening. No collar. No tag. She came over and followed me back here. When I took her to the vet, they couldn't find a chip and suggested re-homing, but I couldn't let her go. Look at her, she's such lovely company.' A fleeting glance at the baby photos on the mantel. 'Loves children too. Makes a beeline for them when we go to the park.'

'Okay.' Beth gathered her bag. 'I just wanted to keep you updated on our findings and to warn you about the press interest.'

He closed his eyes a second, squeezing his eyelids together. When he opened them, his gaze rested on the baby photos. 'I'd prefer to keep an open mind. Until we know for definite.'

21

It was after eight by the time Beth pulled onto her empty driveway. Nick was still out. She let herself in and no sooner had she shrugged off her coat than she heard a low mewl and Myrtle, her tabby cat, appeared.

'Hello, darling,' Beth said, kicking off her shoes. 'Have you missed me?'

Myrtle mewled again.

Beth bent down and fondled the cat's head. They were interrupted by the trill of Beth's phone. It was her sister, Eden.

'Hey,' Beth said. 'How are you?'

'Good, thanks. Are you still okay for tomorrow evening?'

Beth checked the date on her watch. Tomorrow was the 14th, her niece, Lily's, birthday and Eden was throwing her a party at home. 'Of course,' she said. 'What time do you want me?'

'We're starting at 5.30 p.m. As near to that as possible would be great. I've twenty kids coming.'

'Wow!' With Lily as her only experience of kids, Beth couldn't begin to imagine what was involved in an eight-year-old's birthday party. 'I'll see what I can do. Do you need anything?'

'No, I'm all sorted. I picked up the cake today and Chloe's mum's coming to help me decorate the house while they're at school.'

'Okay. Is Lily alright? I felt awful having to drop her off early yesterday.'

'She's fine. Oh, and make sure Nick's knows he's invited tomorrow. We'd love to see him.'

Beth rang off and stared at the ceiling. A birthday party was all she needed in the midst of a fresh investigation. But it was important to Eden and, after losing their mother last year, there were only three of them left now: Beth, Eden and Lily. She owed it to them both to make the effort to be there.

She cast her phone aside, refilled Myrtle's food bowl and was refreshing her water when she heard a noise. A faint knocking.

Beth turned off the tap. The only sound was Myrtle softly crunching her cat biscuit. She was placing the water bowl down when she heard the noise again. Knock... no, more of a tap. It was coming from outside.

She switched on the outside light, illuminating the middle of her lawn in a tunnel of light. The garden looked empty.

Tap. Tap. Tap.

Beth grabbed a torch from the drawer, unlocked the back door and stepped out into the garden. All was quiet. She spanned the torch around the edges of the lawn in a semi-circle, then walked down the side of the house. The gate was open, hanging on its hinges.

She never left the gate open.

'Who's there?' she called. No answer.

Another tap.

It was the gate. Blowing back and tapping on the wall in the wind.

She hadn't noticed it open when she'd pulled into the driveway earlier, although it was set back, down the side entrance slightly, easy to miss if you weren't looking. She walked down the side of the house to the front, squinted down the road, both ways. All was still.

Beth wandered back to the gate and checked the latch, wondering if perhaps Nick had left it open when she realised her heart was thumping in her chest, her palms clammy. Six weeks had passed since Dale Yates had broken into her house and he'd gained access by the very same gate. Six weeks in which Nick hadn't left her side and as soon as she secured herself some independence, some breathing space, she jumped at the slightest sound.

She cursed her frayed nerves, loosened her grip on the torch. Made to fasten the gate, when another sound caught her. Footsteps. They drew closer. She moved tentatively to the front of the house. A shadow flicked across.

'Hello! Is that you, Beth?'

Beth's shoulders dipped. It was her neighbour, walking their spaniel.

'Hi. You startled me,' she said, bending down to stroke the dog who was leaping about her feet. 'Hello, Benji.' The dog wagged his tail and pressed his nose into her calf.

'What are you doing slinking around in the dark?' he said.

'I heard a noise, came to investigate.'

'Ever the cop, eh?'

'Something like that. Have you seen anyone around? I found my gate open. It's usually bolted.'

'A chap was knocking doors this afternoon, offering to

clean windows and clear guttering. I think he put a flyer through.'

She didn't recall seeing anything on her doormat. 'What did he look like?'

'I can't remember. Average height. Stocky. Seemed genuine.'

'Okay, thanks.' She gave a reassuring smile. 'I'm sure it's nothing.'

'I'm working from home again tomorrow. I'll let you know if I spot anything.'

Beth thanked her neighbour again and closed the gate, checking the latch had caught, then slid the bolt across before she walked back inside. Her phone was trilling when she reached the kitchen. She checked the screen, didn't recognise the number and clicked to answer.

'Detective Chamberlain?' The voice was cultured, deep.

'Who is this?'

'It's Pip Edwards from *Northants News*.'

Beth started. It was the journalist who'd been following Alicia's case, the one who'd written the article that had caused so much bother. 'How did you get this number?'

He ignored her question. 'You're the liaison officer on the case of the murdered child, right?'

'Yes,' she said warily.

'I have some information that might be useful.'

'What is it?'

'I'd rather not talk over the phone.'

'I'm sure you know you can make an appointment with the incident room to come into the office,' she said.

'I'd rather meet you at a neutral location. Do you know Kingsthorpe Cemetery?'

'I do.'

'There's a road opposite the main entrance called Birch Barn Way. Meet me there at 2 p.m. tomorrow afternoon. I'll be in a navy Saab.'

The line went dead. She leaned up against the kitchen surface, phone still in her hand. It was common knowledge Pip Edwards had been investigating the family for years and the idea of him phoning her, at this time of night, and requesting a meeting out of the office filled her with disquiet. Unless it was a tactic and he'd targeted her, fishing for information. It wouldn't have been too difficult for an investigative journalist to trace her mobile number; it was all there if you dug deep enough and knew where to look. He'd prised information out of the builder informant to publish it. Beth gritted her teeth. If he thought she was a soft touch, he was in for a shock.

She couldn't afford to ignore his request though. If he'd spent years delving into the family backgrounds, there was always the outside chance he did have something fresh to add.

Nick's earlier comments about Marie wriggled back into her head.

Beth had dealt with a wide mixture of criminals during her time in the force, from sociopaths to cold-blooded killers, enough to know that people were often not what they initially appeared. Assume nothing. Believe no one. Challenge everything. Those phrases formed the cement, the very basis of the building blocks of any enquiry.

She closed her eyes, replayed Marie Russell's account of the day Alicia disappeared in her mind, pausing when she parked the pram outside the supermarket, again when she wandered up and down the aisles. And as much as she tried to deconstruct the account, it shed no new light. She fast-forwarded to the part when Marie approached the till, paid the assistant, left the supermarket and replayed those seconds in slow motion. It was like a scene from a movie that starts with a happy premise, a special dinner party planned for her husband, and ends with the devastation of her child kidnapped from under her nose.

Within minutes their lives were turned upside down.

Beth imagined the events afterwards. Shop assistants and pedestrians scurrying around, searching for the child. The police cars with their blues and twos, the traffic checkpoints. She scrutinised Marie's reaction as she gave her account earlier that day, considering her body language, searching for any signs of uneasiness or guilt. Outwardly she'd displayed sadness and regret. Sadness that derived from a prolonged police investigation, a cold case destined to remain unsolved. Regret that she'd left her little one in her blind spot, unguarded for the shortest of minutes. But there was a sense of fidgety uneasiness too. Was that because she was reliving the traumatic events, over again, or was there another reason for her agitation?

The lack of witnesses needled her. Surely somebody would have seen something.

Alicia's body was found less than two miles from her parents' home in Kingsthorpe, an area on the northern tip of Northampton. Kingsthorpe was also where most of the extended family lived.

A key was inserted into a lock, the front door pushed open. 'Hello!' Nick called. He dropped a holdall in the hallway and crossed to the kitchen, planting a kiss on Beth's cheek.

'You're working late,' Beth said.

'Not really. I've been in the gym. Got to look after these.' He raised his arm, folded his fist to his shoulder and patted the bicep with his other hand.

Beth snorted at his sarcasm. Although Nick was sleek, he could never be described as a muscle man.

'What's up with you? You look like you've seen a ghost?'

She stared at him, about to ask him about the open side gate then stopped herself at the last minute. She didn't want him to know she'd been out there, checking the garden, or that someone might have entered unannounced. It would only make him jumpy and risk him becoming unduly protective, just when she'd persuaded him to give her space.

'I had a phone call from Pip Edwards,' she said flicking the switch on the kettle.

Nick's forehead creased. 'He called you direct. Why?'

'I'm not sure. He's heard I'm the family liaison officer on the case. Wants to meet me tomorrow, near Kingsthorpe Cemetery.' Beth turned to make them tea.

'Hm.'

'That's what I thought.'

'What did you say to him?'

'I agreed to meet him. Didn't have a reason not to. There's a chance he could add something.'

'Or he's fishing. We'll speak with Freeman in the morning, see how he wants to play it.'

She finished making the tea, passed him a steaming mug across and they leaned up against the kitchen side, supping their drinks, comfortable in their silence. Beth gave him a sideways glance, taking in his dark lashes, the lock of dark hair that flopped down to his brow. Suddenly a wave of desire hit her. It had been good to get out on her own these past couple of days, spread her wings and carry out her enquiries alone. But they'd spent practically every minute of the past six weeks together, breathing the same air, and she couldn't deny a very small part of her was glad to have him back, all to herself.

At work they made a concerted effort not to discuss home, not to speak too personally in company. Did their best to avoid those looks, winks and nudges that might betray their true feelings. Even when they were out on a job together, she did her best to avoid talking about home life. Here, it was different. Here, she could let down her guard, and enjoy him.

He caught her eye, placed down his mug, reached out an arm and pulled her to him. The familiar smell of his sporty shower gel tickled her senses.

'I've missed you,' he said. So close she could taste his breath.

Her mug hit the side. His lips touched hers, parting them with his tongue. Gentle. Warm. He grew hungrier, slipping his tongue in. Moved his hands up her spine, caressing her neck, weaving his fingers through her hair. Every fibre in her body ached for him. Beth arched her back, all thoughts of the case floating away.

Slowly, tenderly, he released her, cupping her chin with both hands, his eyes soft. 'I've waited all day to do that,' he said. The intensity of his gaze was overwhelming.

Beth smiled as he took her hand, threaded his fingers through hers, and they walked, side by side, towards the stairs.

22

The number of reporters outside the Russells' house on Redland Drive had multiplied the following morning. They filled the pavement in their overcoats, their breaths making puffballs in the cool December air. Some clasped coffees, others spilled out onto the road, waving their arms about to keep warm. Beth was forced to drive almost fifty yards up from the house to find a parking space. She spotted two vehicles emblazoned with national media emblems as she exited her car and her stomach clenched for Marie Russell. She'd be feeling bad enough without the weight of the press breathing down her neck.

Beth made her way through the throng, ignoring the microphones shoved in her face, passing 'no comment' to the questions fired at her from all directions. Freeman had made it quite clear he wanted to control the flow of information from headquarters and she wasn't about to do anything to jeopardise that, especially with the leak they'd already faced.

Pleased to see the driveway of number 146 empty, Beth trudged up the pathway to the door. She'd deliberately timed her visit to coincide with Zac's school run. No sense in disrupting the family's morning routine. Plus, she rather hoped it meant she would catch Marie at home alone again. Marie's references to her late mother-in-law and her relationship with Daniel's once best friend intrigued Beth. If Marie wasn't responsible for Alicia's death, she was beginning to wonder if the key to unravelling Alicia's mysterious disappearance lay close by. It would be easier to probe her about the family and their interrelationships without her overprotective husband present. Plus, she wanted to dig deeper into the root of her anxiety yesterday.

She fisted her hand, tapped the hardwood door. Within seconds a chain rattled and the door opened to a narrow crack. A thin line of Marie appeared.

'Morning,' Beth said.

Marie gazed past her at the huddle at the end of the drive, released the chain and ushered Beth inside.

'How are you doing today?' Beth asked. Dark rings hung beneath the woman's eyes; she looked as though she hadn't slept in a week.

'As well as can be expected.' She motioned for Beth to follow her into the kitchen and switched on the kettle.

'Where's Vic?' Beth asked.

'He's taken Zac to school, then he's off to the garage. He noticed a slow puncture on the car when they left earlier. Needs to get it checked.'

Good, that means we'll have more time.

The kettle coughed and sputtered as it heated. 'Do you have some news?' Marie looked desperate.

'We're still waiting for the DNA test results, if that's what you mean. I'm sorry. It can take a few days.'

Marie's face fell, her shoulders slumping under the strain.

'I know this is hard,' Beth said. 'It shouldn't be too much longer.'

'What does she look like?' Her voice was low, barely a whisper and as she spoke her face contorted, as if she wasn't sure she really wanted to know the answer. 'All we've been told is that remains were found.'

Beth needed to be careful here. The finer details of how Alicia was buried hadn't been released to the press. Even the builder that had found the body and spoken to the papers wasn't aware about her being entombed in concrete. 'She was laid on her back, a shawl wrapped around her.'

'Are you saying she was killed quite soon after she was taken?'

'Tests are ongoing, but it certainly looks that way from what she was wearing, yes.' She passed on the details about the injury to the back of the child's head, the possible cause of death. 'I'm so sorry.'

Marie slid into a seat, her eyes filling.

'Let me get the drinks,' Beth said. She crossed to the side, opened the cupboard above the kettle and busied herself with making tea; piling sugar in Marie's tea to calm the shock. It wasn't long before she carried the steaming mugs over to the table.

'I feel like I'm in limbo,' Marie said. 'I can't work, can't sleep. Vic's barely working because he's worried about me. We're only keeping going for Zac.'

'I'm sorry. I know this is hard. We've asked the labs to prioritise the DNA tests.'

Marie pinched the bridge of her nose with her thumb and forefinger. 'My boss has given me the week off, special leave. I don't think he wants the adverse publicity.' She let her hand fall. 'Did you see Daniel again yesterday?'

Beth nodded. 'I passed along the same information I gave to you.'

'Is he okay?'

Beth recalled Daniel's tight voice, the way he sat beside his dog, petting her as if it was a normal evening. Denying the possibilities that lay ahead. 'I think so. He's trying to be strong.'

'I'm worried about him.'

'That's understandable. You were together a long time.'

'I'm really worried about him.' There was a tremor in her voice.

Beth sat forward. Perhaps this explained some of her uneasiness. 'What do you mean?'

Marie placed her hands around her mug and looked away. 'Losing Liam then Alicia tore us apart, but I still care for him, even after all these years. I was fourteen when we got together. He was a big part of my life for a long time.'

'It must have been tough when you separated.'

'It was.'

Beth took a sip of tea and placed the mug down in front of her. 'How did you get along with his family?' she asked.

'The Owens? They're an interesting bunch.'

'In what way?'

'Like I said yesterday, they lived in the shadow of their mother. Had their own rules.'

'What do you mean?'

'Silly things. Like Daniel. Everyone called him by his full name, even me. He hated it when anyone shortened it to

Dan. But Cara and his mother, it was alright for them to call him Dan. It was almost a control thing.'

The secrecy about the Owens and their missing brother was becoming an irritating itch she couldn't scratch. 'What about Cara?' Beth said carefully.

Marie gave a wistful smile. 'Cara was Cara. She barely spoke to me the first couple of years we were together. Left the room when I was there, ignored me if I stayed to dinner. I think she thought I was taking her precious brother away from her.' She snorted. 'The way she used to look at me.' A headshake. 'I was never good enough for Daniel. I don't think anyone ever would be in her eyes. She did relax a bit after she met John though, seemed to accept me being around.'

'John was her partner,' Beth checked.

'Yes. Twenty years older than her. They met when she was seventeen and he was thirty-seven. She kept it quiet for weeks, didn't even tell her mum. I don't know why, because her mother took to him straight away. I couldn't understand why they never married; I know Cara wanted to. John was good for her though, a calming influence. For a while she seemed genuinely happy.'

'For a while?'

'Well, there were always arguments in the Owen family, most of them instigated by Cara. She was scratchy. She argued with her mother, with Scottie, and then Daniel would be dragged in.'

'What about?'

'Family stuff. I stayed out of it mostly.'

'What about after Alicia was born?'

'Cara helped a bit. I don't think she understood my

depression though. Not fully. She popped in, offered to babysit, occasionally got us shopping. After we lost Alicia, she seemed to change. Regress. She seemed to blame me for what happened, wouldn't look me in the face. When Daniel and I separated, everyone tried to talk me out of it. Daniel. His mum. Everyone but Cara really. I got the impression she was relieved to be rid of me.' She stared out of the window, down the lawn. It had started to snow, soft feathers falling from the sky.

'It was John who really upset me. We weren't close, but we'd always got along. Being the outsiders gave us something in common, I guess. We joked about the family when they were out of earshot. Called Daniel's mother "Livia" after the mother in the TV show, *The Sopranos*. Rolled our eyes at their intensity and their arguments. I barely saw him after Alicia disappeared.' Her face fell. 'I was really upset when I heard he died. So young too.'

Beth had read he'd died suddenly, six years after Alicia's disappearance: he'd got drunk one night and choked on his own vomit. It seemed the family had been struck by tragedy, with Scott disappearing, their mother dying and Cara's partner passing away, all in the spate of six years. She swirled the last of the tea in her mug. 'How well did you know Scott, Daniel's brother?'

Marie's eyes softened. 'Scottie? As well as anyone. We all grew up together. Scottie was the baby of the family, a few years below us at school. He was born with a harelip, had to have an operation as a baby. And he was a sickly child growing up. A fussy eater, a skinny scrap of a boy when he was young. It was obvious their mother worried about him. He always got the breast when they had chicken for dinner. It wasn't unusual for the twins to have burgers and Scottie to have steak. He struggled with school, had to move class, found it hard to make friends and when he did find someone, his mother would make a fuss and invite them back for tea and sleepovers. A bit unfair really, the twins were rarely allowed friends to the house. Cara and Daniel clearly resented her treatment of him, especially when he fell in with the wrong crowd.'

'What do you mean?'

'He was caught shoplifting before he left school, arrested for stealing cars shortly afterwards. Daniel suspected he was into drugs at one stage but could never prove it. Once when I was there, the next-door neighbour came to the door, claiming he'd seen Scott trying to break the lock on his shed. The poor man was being neighbourly, he could have gone straight to the police. Judy, their mother, slammed the door in his face. She seemed to fight relentlessly for Scott, whereas if the others got into trouble, she punished them hard.'

'Did you spend much time with Scott?'

'Not really. By the time Daniel and I were married, he was at the age when he went out on the town with his mates. Invariably came back battered and bruised from some fight he'd been in.' A faraway look filled her face. 'He came over sometimes, usually when Daniel was out. Never much one for conversation. He genuinely adored Alicia though. Was a natural with her. He'd change her nappies, rock her to sleep. She settled so much better with him than she did with me. It wasn't Scottie's fault he was the apple of his mother's eye. It's not like he asked for it and I think it made him feisty. It was like he constantly had to prove himself, hence all the fights.'

'We need to trace everyone that was in contact with Alicia before she disappeared. Do you have any idea where we can reach him?'

'No. I heard he left home not long after Alicia disappeared. Ran off to London. We didn't keep in contact.' Her face pained. 'Sad, really. I often wonder what he's up to.'

23

The snow was starting to settle, veiling the garden in a thin sprinkle of white.

'Yesterday, you talked me through the day Alicia disappeared,' Beth said. 'Do you feel up to talking about what happened afterwards?'

A shiver ran through Marie. They'd retreated into the cinema room and the large area felt cold this morning, despite the central heating. She leaned across and placed her empty mug on a small coffee table beside her. 'I don't see how it will help.'

'I've been reading the case file,' Beth said. 'Sometimes it's better to hear things first-hand.'

Marie glanced back out of the window. A robin was hopping around the edge of the birdbath; she really ought to put some food out for him, poor soul.

'Marie?'

She turned back to the detective, her stomach clenching. The prospect of going through the event and the aftermath again was draining. She wanted to push it away, to erase the days and months surrounding Alicia's disappearance, to pretend they'd never happened. Though, now she was facing the reality of it, there were other parts of her life she wanted to erase too. Dark, scary areas she wanted to strike a line through and start afresh. 'I don't remember much about afterwards. The first few days were a blur. I spent most of it in my bedroom. When I did venture downstairs, I jumped at every phone call, expecting news.'

Marie could feel the detective's eyes on her. She'd been here before, so many times. Sitting in rooms with detectives, silence screaming at her until she could bear it no longer.

'Look, Daniel dealt with everything. Answered every phone call, spoke with every caller that came to the door. Switched off the television when the news was on in case it upset me. The only people I spoke to were the police. He was trying to protect me.' She swallowed back the acid taste in her mouth. 'Alicia was everywhere I looked. Her bouncy chair, her changing mat, her soft padded toys. Her steriliser on the kitchen side; her bottles in the fridge. Reminders of her little life waving at me from every room in the house. In our bedroom her cot sat at my side of the bed with the same bedclothes she had woken in, the day she disappeared.'

'That must have been difficult to cope with.'

'I don't think I was totally with it, to be honest.' She clamped her eyes together, trying to block out the images rising within. 'I became aware of other people in the house. Daniel's sister doing the cooking. His mother's voice in the front room. With hindsight, I suppose his strength was waning; he needed help, time to work through the emotions too.'

Her eyes watered as she opened them. 'The guilt was the worst part. I lost count of the number of times I went over the account of Alicia's disappearance with the police.

Nobody said a word, no one apportioned blame, but they didn't need to. As far as everyone was concerned, I was unstable, depressed. If I hadn't left her outside alone, she wouldn't have been taken.' She recalled the knowing looks on faces around her, the whispers from friends and family, barely out of earshot, and clasped her hands together in her lap.

'The days tumbled into weeks. My mother came over and went home. I rarely left the bedroom. I was aware of Daniel going back to work, more from his absence. His mother started popping in and out with cups of tea, plates of food during the day.'

She was transported back to the emptiness of her bedroom, the stillness in the house. Lying on her bed with the curtains drawn, desperately trying to shut everything out; the wrenching heartache. They'd gone through so much losing Liam but, as cruel as it was, they were given information: reasoning, medical explanation. With Alicia, they had nothing. No idea where she was, who had her or even whether she was still alive.

'Daniel tried. I know he did. He tried hard to talk to me. To pull me out of my depression. I just wanted to be alone with my memories. I remember asking him to move into the spare room. It must have been two, maybe three months afterwards.'

'When did you separate?'

'I'm not sure exactly. Maybe five or six months after Alicia's disappearance. The police visits had dried up. Everyone had moved on. His mother had taken to letting herself in and cleaning the house. I ignored them all. Then, one day, I walked into the bedroom to find she'd stripped the cot. All the beautiful pink covers on Alicia's bed, the ones that were there on the day she was taken, had been removed.' She lifted her eyes to meet the detective's gaze, tightening her hands. 'She hadn't even asked.'

'It was all I had left of our last day together. Suddenly, I wanted them gone. The lot of them. With their sympathy glares and their lectures about moving forward, getting on with things. I ordered them all out, asked his mother for her key back. And when Daniel came home, I told him to go too.'

The faces swam in front her. Pained, sympathetic faces. 'They all thought I'd lost it. Daniel must have phoned my mum because days later Mum turned up on my doorstep, without warning. She stayed a week and tried to persuade me to go back to Australia with her, to take a break, but I couldn't leave. I mean, what if they found Alicia and I wasn't here? I'd abandoned her once; I wasn't going to do it again.

'And then there was Vic. The only person who treated me normally. He used to come around two or three times a week when Daniel was here, for coffee, or maybe they'd watch football together. After Daniel left, he kept coming. To see me.'

Vivid memories danced before her. Of a tiny light of happiness at the end of a long dark tunnel. 'It was awkward at first. Sometimes he'd bring groceries and cook, although I barely touched the food. I was living on cornflakes and porridge. And he listened. I'll never forget that. Daniel couldn't bear to talk about Alicia – every time I mentioned her, the pain was visible on his face. So, I tiptoed around the subject. Vic was the one person who I could say anything to.' She could see Vic's face now, the caring creases in his forehead as he sat for hours listening to her talk, question, speculate, cry. She'd cried heaps. Wept until the tears dried up and her lungs were spent.

'When the press wrote nasty articles, implying I'd neglected my baby, or the television programmes aired, discussing what happened to Alicia, Vic didn't ignore them, or pretend they weren't there. He'd watch them with me. And hold me and tell me it wasn't my fault. Daniel kept me from everything. But I needed to see it, to feel it. Because it's all I had, and I was desperately holding on to the tiny thread of what was left.' She released her hands, opening them to find an arc of nails imprinted on her right palm.

'Vic and I became close. I don't think either one of us ever expected it to lead to this.' She rubbed the little dents in the skin and looked around at their comfortable room, the photographs of them together on the wall, of Zac, their son, smiling. 'We were friends. He was Daniel's best friend. In the beginning, he was our go between. As time progressed, I stopped asking about Daniel and he saw less of him.'

She remembered him encouraging her to go back to work, driving her there on that first day to quell her nerves. Playing tracks from Oasis on the stereo, her favourite band, to distract her. 'Suddenly the mist started to clear. There were always foggy patches, darkness around the edges. But I started to interact with others and feel human.'

'What about Daniel?' Beth asked.

'He called by occasionally. I think he still expected us to reconcile. But there was too much sadness, too much pain between us. In the end I asked him to stop coming. His mother became angry, warning me not to cut him out.

Marriage was a sacred oath. But it was the only way I could cope.

'Vic and I no longer talked about Daniel. He would tell me about his work, his business and I would talk him through my day. I suppose that's how it all started. And when the house was sold, Vic suggested I stay at his until I got sorted. Over time, one thing led to another. It wasn't sudden, didn't happen overnight. We slowly realised we had feelings for each other. Eventually, I moved out of the spare room and into his.'

'How did Daniel feel about you living there?'

'I didn't hear much from Daniel. Vic and he had drifted. I assumed he knew about us, with me living there and all. But when I went to see him, about eighteen months after Alicia disappeared, to tell him I wanted a divorce, he asked me to give it another go. I'll never forget his face when I told him I had feelings for Vic. It froze so hard it was like looking at a statue. He asked me to leave. I didn't realise how upset he was until afterwards.'

'What do you mean?'

'He took an overdose the following day. Cara found him at home. They reckoned he'd taken several boxes of paracetamol.' She shook her head. 'I tried to visit him in the hospital. Cara wouldn't let me in. Called me every name under the sun, said it was all my fault. I haven't seen Daniel since. I stalled on the divorce afterwards, afraid of upsetting him further. When I did finally apply, he signed the papers straight away but refused to have anything to do with either of us.

'I sometimes think Daniel thought we were having an affair, Vic and I, while we were still married. We weren't though. I never saw Vic in that way. Not until afterwards. He was a family friend.' Another gaze into the garden, a quiet moment as the guilt clawed its way back to the surface. There were so many things Daniel didn't know. And if they came out now, she couldn't bear to think what they would do to him. 'I know it was a long time ago, but someone needs to look out for Daniel. I'm worried how this news of Alicia might affect him.'

24

Beth pressed a button on her computer and slowly scrolled through the statements from the original investigation, re-reading everything that mentioned Daniel Owen. It was as she thought, his suicide attempt wasn't mentioned in the case records. But then, if it happened some time after Alicia's disappearance, the police might not have been informed. She flagged it up on the file records. Thirteen and a half years was quite a time lapse but if Daniel had been vulnerable once, he might still suffer from bouts of depression and be at risk. She needed to ensure he had support close by when they shared news with him in future.

Beth finished writing up her notes on her meeting with Marie Russell. Pete had worked his way through the farm labourers employed around the time when Alicia went missing and hadn't found anything so far to suggest they were involved. Now it seemed they were no further forward than the original investigation.

She opened her pad and scribbled down the names, Daniel, Marie and Vic. The love triangle. If their accounts were to be believed, they were three people who'd certainly experienced more than their fair share of heartache. But Beth had been in law enforcement long enough to know people weren't always completely truthful: sometimes they lied, or adjusted their version of events to suit their own needs.

What did each of them have to gain from Alicia's disappearance?

Daniel appeared the doting father and was at work on the day Alicia disappeared.

The aftermath of Alicia's disappearance had caused a rift between the Owens, leaving it open for Vic to marry his best friend's wife. He had called in to see Marie on the day Alicia disappeared and was the last person to see them at home. But he was back at work, covering the counter with a colleague, by the time Alicia was taken.

And then there was Marie.

She tapped the pen against the side of the pad, the tendrils of her mind stretching further afield, to Cara, Scott... The clue to solving this murder lay close to the family, she was convinced of it.

A tap on her shoulder. She looked up, surprised to find Nick and Freeman beside her. They'd been absent awhile and, engrossed in her work, she hadn't heard them enter the room.

'We've been discussing your meeting with Edwards this afternoon,' Nick said. 'Might be an idea if I accompany you.'

Beth frowned. 'I don't think that's a good idea,' she said. 'We're unlikely to get anything out of him if we go mob-handed.'

'Where are you meeting him?' Freeman asked.

'2 p.m. Outside Kingsthorpe Cemetery.'

'Strange location.'

Beth shrugged. The same thought had crossed her mind.

'Okay, we're going to need to play this one carefully,' Freeman said. 'Either he's fishing, or he's got a bloody good reason why he hasn't come to the office.'

'I don't trust him,' Nick said. 'Especially after that newspaper article. He must have dug deep to get the details of the builder.'

'That's his job,' Freeman said. 'Ours is to make sure we glean whatever he has. Be careful, Beth. He was just starting out in my early days in the force. Always cropping up in difficult situations. Sometimes, he even got to jobs before we arrived. Never known a reporter with a nose for a fresh crime like him. Take a note of his information but don't engage in conversation. It's surprising how easy something can slip.'

Beth passed on her latest discussions with Marie and glanced down at her pad. 'I'd like to take a closer look at the family members and their movements after Alicia's disappearance,' she said.

Freeman turned down the corners of his mouth. 'What are you suggesting?'

'I'm not sure exactly. The original case focused on the movements at the time. I'd like to explore their behaviour before and afterwards. Like Scott, the younger brother.'

'He was at work when Alicia was taken,' Nick said. 'There's nothing to suggest he was involved.'

'I realise that. I don't know… I can't put my finger on it. The family seem uncomfortable when his name is mentioned. He left under a cloud soon after Alicia disappeared. The family think he's in London but none of our usual checks have located him.'

Freeman placed his hands on his hips, an action that pulled his shirt across his stomach, straining the buttons. 'What exactly are you saying?'

'I'm not really sure. He was close to the child.'

Freeman held her gaze for several seconds. 'Okay. I'm happy for you to dig deeper into the family as long as you are discreet.'

'What about Scott?'

'How long's he been missing?'

'Almost fifteen years now.'

Freeman chewed the side of his mouth, percolating the information. 'We could do an anniversary appeal for any sightings of him on the force Facebook page. If he's living with anyone locally, or even if he's moved away, someone might have his contact details. Let's leave it until we have the child's identity confirmed. Otherwise, the press will jump on it, make assumptions.'

Beth thanked him and Freeman headed back to his office. A phone rang, pulling Nick back to his own desk. Beth watched him go and set about thinking how to prepare a Facebook appeal, when Pete called her from across the office.

'Have you got a minute?' he said, eyes fixed on his computer screen.

'Sure, what is it?' She zigzagged through the other desks to reach him.

'I've been examining the photos of the crowd you took outside the Russells',' Pete said. 'Most of them can be identified as reporters, working for the news channels. There are a few faces in the group that don't look familiar – might be they're nosey locals – plus some that aren't clear.' He brought up the picture of the group on his screen and pointed out a bunch of individuals at the back where only shoulders or the sides of heads were visible. 'No distinguishing features; nothing that could identify them. It's the same with those taken at the building site.' He pressed a button and another photo graced the screen. The photo had been taken secretly from the side. 'Nothing stands out.'

'Okay, thanks,' Beth said. 'Run it by intelligence, will you? See if anyone there recognises anything.'

'Sure.'

Her eyes rested on a fuzzy figure at the crime scene, partially hidden at the back far right. The man was thick set and wearing a baseball cap, the image too blurred to give anything else away.

Faces around him were blurred too. 'Any chance you can enhance that area?' she said, encircling it with her finger.

'I'll give it a go.'

'Great, thanks. Let me know how you get on.'

25

There was something calming about walking among the dead. Wandering across the damp cemetery grass. Weaving in and out of the graves. Those with cut flowers, plants and ornaments adorning their little patch. The bare graves with tufts of weeds reaching up the headstones; the freshly laid mounds with wooden crosses marking their spot. Beth took her time, pausing to read the sentiments, 'in loving memory' and 'always in our hearts'; words lovingly chosen by friends and families harbouring an aching emptiness within.

Every one of them belonged to someone. Every one of them missed. The thought of a baby girl buried among the stone and soil of a building site, with no crafted headstone or flowers to mark her short life, made Beth's throat constrict. She really hoped for a positive DNA result so the child could finally be reunited with her family and laid to rest properly, with the dignity she deserved.

The earlier snow had melted, and a frail afternoon sun hung in the sky. A brutal wind whipped the trees. Beth tugged her coat across her chest. Getting to know the family meant all the family, even the deceased.

She paused at a small grave and crouched down. Little

Liam Owen had died in the same week as her godmother; they were buried a few plots apart. Beth remembered walking past the tiny grave at her godmother's funeral. The train made from yellow and white carnations laid atop the small mound of earth catching her eye while the vicar uttered his final prayer. It hadn't meant much at the time, a young child passed before he'd had time to blossom; a family laying him to rest. They had no idea that, months later, he was to become known as the twin brother of missing Alicia Owen; a notorious case that shook the residents of Northamptonshire to the core.

Liam's grave was tidy, the grass neat and free of weeds. A white headstone engraved with gold letters, *Liam, forever in our hearts.* A vase of old yellow carnations, past their prime, stood beside a plastic toy train, the red and yellow carriages faded by years of sunlight.

Beth dug her hands in her pockets and scanned the surrounding area. Was Daniel's mother close by? She hadn't seen the headstone when she'd walked in.

She moved up a few spaces and wiped dust from the letters on her godmother's grave. Stalks of flowers, long past their best poked from a weathered vase. Beth knelt, replaced them with a bunch of fresh orange roses, taking a moment to arrange them before sitting back on her heels. She could still picture her late mother, her sister and her sitting around her godmother's dining table eating dinner, a half-finished jigsaw puzzle covering the other end. Her godmother's smiley face and rosy cheeks; the yeasty warm smell of her house. It seemed such a long time ago, almost a different lifetime.

Her phone beeped in her pocket, pulling her back to the

present. Almost 2 p.m. Edwards would be there soon. She needed to make a move.

He peered around the edge of the chapel, watched the detective gather up the dead flowers, place them in a bin nearby and make her way out of the cemetery. Pressing his back to the rough sandstone to stay out of sight while she passed. Strange that they'd both chosen today to visit little Liam's grave; their minds were so attuned. Some might say it was poetic. He viewed the graves around him, marvelling at the loss of so many.

And soon there would be more.

The wind picked up. He pressed a palm to his head to keep his baseball cap from flying off. He was rearranging it, pulling the peak low, when another figure appeared. Hair tucked into a black beret, red duffle coat fastened firmly across her chest, dark glasses covering her eyes. She was clutching a bunch of yellow and white carnations in her gloved hand. He slid around the chapel, mesmerised by the grace with which her svelte figure moved in and out of the graves. Held his breath when she stopped at little Liam Owen's, knelt and traced the words on the headstone with her finger.

A glance back at the entrance. The detective was long gone. Interesting, he thought. Liam's grave was particularly busy today.

26

Beth left the wrought iron gates of Kingsthorpe Cemetery behind her, crossed the main road and continued down a side road opposite, scanning the cars parked kerbside for Pip Edwards' navy Saab. Freeman was right, it was an odd place to meet.

She walked down the road to the first turn, checked her watch. 2.01 p.m. Surely, she hadn't missed him? She pulled her phone out of her pocket, about to check the messages, when an engine filled her ears. A Saab passed and pulled into a space at the top of the road, facing towards the cemetery gates.

The passenger side window lowered as she approached.

Pip Edwards was a scrawny man with bushy dark hair, peppered with grey, and wire-rimmed glasses that perched on the bridge on his nose. Close up he looked significantly older than his byline photo.

'Afternoon, Detective.' They'd never met and the fact that he recognised her was slightly disconcerting. He leaned across, opened the door. 'Hop in.'

Freeman's earlier warning flitted in and out of her head as she climbed into the car. Even the odd expression or comment could be misconstrued, taken out of context. No pressure there then.

'You said you have some information for me,' she said, closing the door.

'How's the case going?'

Alicia's identity still wasn't confirmed. The clothing found with her hadn't been released to the public. As far as Edwards was aware, they were currently investigating an unnamed child. But he clearly knew Beth was on the team, supporting members of Alicia's family, should the body turn out to be hers.

Beth raised a brow and said nothing.

Unfazed, Edwards stared out of the windscreen. The driver in front unlocked his car and climbed in. Within seconds he revved his engine and drove off. They now had an unhindered view of the graveyard entrance, less than thirty yards ahead.

'Are the child's remains Alicia Owen?' he asked, gaze fixed ahead.

'We don't know yet. As we've already said, it's a possibility.'

'Then I have some information on the Owen family that might be useful.'

'Okay.' Beth shifted in her seat. The sooner this conversation was over, the better.

Instead of imparting his news, Edwards stayed silent. He seemed focused on something in the distance.

Beth followed his eyeline and spotted a figure in a red duffle coat leaving the cemetery in the distance. A very familiar figure. Marie Russell wore dark glasses and had tucked her hair into a beret, but Beth could see enough to be sure it was her.

'She comes here every Thursday at five minutes to two,' he said, guessing Beth's thoughts, 'with carnations for baby Liam's grave. It's her day off work. Yellow and white, always the same. Sometimes she brings her little boy with her.'

Instinct tempted Beth to duck down. Edwards had been reporting on Alicia's case since her disappearance. There was little doubt Marie would know who he was, and it wouldn't look good for Marie to see her family liaison officer with him, especially after the article he wrote yesterday. She rounded on the reporter. 'What's going on?'

'I thought you guys would know. You're the detectives.'

'What's that supposed to mean?' She had a hundred and one jobs she could be doing rather than sitting in a car with an annoying journalist talking in riddles, not to mention the precarious situation it would put her in with the family if they noticed her with a pain-in-the-arse local reporter.

'Just making you aware of her habits. In case you didn't know. And it seems you didn't.'

The evenness of his tone was galling. 'What are you trying to tell me?' Beth said.

Marie Russell climbed into her car at the front of the cemetery. She was fiddling with her phone, distracted. If she had noticed them, it didn't show.

He gave a hollow sigh. 'You're re-opening Alicia's case, right?'

'It was never closed.'

He sniffed, ignoring her remark. 'The family are not what they seem.'

'The Russells?'

'The Russells. The Owens. You need to take a closer look at all of them. Especially the brother, Scott.'

Beth narrowed her eyes. The secrecy surrounding the location of Scott Owen was picking away at her, along with Marie's description of their family dynamic and the twins' hostility towards him. 'Why?'

'Because he was different to the others. The outcast. The most dangerous one.' He enunciated every syllable of the final sentence.

Beth wracked her brains. Scott was at work when Alicia was taken. There were witnesses on file. And Superintendent Tanner hadn't expressed any particular interest in him. 'What do you mean?'

'Scott was a great disappointment to his mother, a difficult child to raise. I'm sure you've seen his history. In his late teens, he got hooked onto the hard stuff.'

'Drugs?'

'Gambling. Playing the slot machines.'

Beth looked out of the side window. She couldn't see what relevance Scott Owen being a small-time gambler had to the case of a murdered child.

'I'm not talking pub machines here. Fixed odds betting machines. Virtual games terminals where you can play roulette, blackjack, poker, you name it, all in one place – a casino at your fingertips – £50 to £100 a stake. Can't do it now of course, the government have limited them. But the machines are still in betting shops. Scott got himself in deep back in the early noughties. Rumour had it he moved on to poker, the big money card games…'

'What are you saying?'

'He was an addict. Drained his bank account, maxed out his credit cards, and when there was nothing left, he borrowed from, shall we say, disreputable sources.'

'How do you know this?'

'Just doing my job.'

'And your sources are…?'

Edwards looked away. 'I'm not prepared to disclose them.'

Beth huffed. Either he didn't have any or he was saving them for his bloody book. 'So, you're speculating?'

'Not at all. Scott even stole from his mother. Cleaned out her bank account. Why do you think she threw him out?'

Beth fixed him a sideways glare. 'What's all this got to do with Alicia's disappearance?'

'Despite their differences, the Owen family were tight. People knew that. The kind of people Scott was in debt to will have known that too.'

'Are you saying, you think whoever he borrowed from took Alicia? There was no ransom request, I don't see what they'd gain.'

His face hardened. 'I'm suggesting you dig a bit deeper, that's all. Speak to Scott. I know he spent a lot of time at Barton's Snooker Hall around the millennium. When it was run by the McNamara brothers.'

Beth didn't react. She'd heard stories about the McNamara brothers, a couple of local gangsters who ran Barton's and controlled the doors of pubs and clubs in the town in the early noughties. Stories that marked them as a nasty pair, suggesting they were involved in drug trafficking, prostitution and loansharking, although they'd never been arrested or charged. Too clever to be caught within a whiff of anything sinister. CID had been tracking them for years and building up a file of intelligence when they were killed suddenly in a car accident, the year after she joined. She remembered their deaths vividly because she'd worked overtime to staff the funeral.

'No one involved with Barton's at the time will speak to me,' Edwards continued. 'As much as I hate to admit it, you've got more resources than I have. The family think Scott's living rough in London.' The hairs sticking out of his nose fluttered as he snorted. 'He's actually only in Kettering.'

Kettering was a small town on the north of the county. It was also the nearest town to Beth's home in Mawsley Village. 'How do you know?'

'I stumbled across him a year or so back, when I was researching another job. Caught someone call him by his full name. He denied the connection, of course. I'm sure it was him though. It makes sense really. Far enough away that he wouldn't run into his family, but still close by. Can be found sleeping behind the billboard on Northampton Road most nights.'

Beth turned to face him. 'Why are you telling me this?'

Seconds passed. 'I've been working on this story for years.'

'I heard it was a book.'

He cast his eyes skyward. 'I have a draft with a publisher. They want input from the families, an endorsement, before they'll progress. The family should know I've spoken with you.'

So that's it. 'You want me to get you an audience with the family?' Beth was incredulous. 'You must be kidding!'

'I'm not asking you to broker a meeting. You could put in a word, let them know I'm helping.'

Beth wasn't unaccustomed to the tactics the media used to gain information. She'd guarded enough crime scenes and worked enough cases to be mindful of the differing agendas between the press and the police. Reporters looking for a sensational headline, something to sell their newspapers and articles. The police holding back information, only releasing what was essential to drive an investigation forward. But this was the first time she'd had an audience with a reporter who arranged to meet to ostensibly pass on information in exchange for personal gain and the sheer audacity of the man clawed at her.

She fought to keep her words even. 'I'm not here to *put in words*.' She almost added, 'I'm here to solve a murder', and stopped herself at the last minute. A statement like that gave an indication the body was Alicia. She wasn't about to play his games and she certainly wasn't going to let anything slip. 'I'm surprised you haven't been to see Scott yourself,' she said.

'I have. I went over on Wednesday evening, after the news broke. He was gone from his usual spot. I spoke to the others sleeping there and nobody has seen him since last weekend. It seems he's disappeared.'

Beth gritted her teeth as she walked back to the car. The cheek of the man irked her, although she couldn't deny the information on Scott Owen was interesting. To connect it with the child's murder seemed a leap though. He'd implied both the Russells and the Owens had secrets, yet wouldn't go into detail and refused to disclose his sources. Was that because he was speculating or because he didn't have hard evidence? She needed to unpick the family history. And she needed to trace Scott Owen. She was almost at the car when her mobile buzzed, breaking her thought process. It was Nick.

'Where are you?'

'In Kingsthorpe. Just finished with Edwards.' She relayed their conversation.

'That's interesting,' Nick said. 'Scott Owen hasn't been flagged up as living rough locally.'

'If he's been living on the streets for the past fourteen or so years, under the radar, our usual checks wouldn't pick him up,' Beth said. 'Edwards suggested he might have been using loan sharks. I'd be interested in any connection he might have had with organised crime.'

'I'll double check with intelligence, see what they had on him and the McNamara brothers when Alicia disappeared,' Nick said. He lowered his voice. 'Freeman wants to see you when you get back.'

'Why?'

'Somebody's contacted the chief constable about the case. It sounds like a member of the family has expressed concern. I don't know the specifics, I overheard a conversation in the corridor outside Freeman's office.'

It wasn't unusual for victim's families to be frustrated with how an investigation was progressing. It was a desperate time in their lives and police work was time consuming. Often answers didn't come quick enough. But this was an old case revived and she'd spoken to everyone involved, kept them updated. Why hadn't they come to her?

'Overheard from who?' she said.

'Freeman and Andrea Leary. It sounds like the chief's tasked her with sorting it. She's still in with Freeman now.'

Beth ground her teeth. She'd rather hoped she'd be shot

of Andrea after she'd left the team to support the chief, and here she was, returning like a bad smell that refused to go away. 'What did they say exactly?'

'I only heard bits before they closed the door, enough to know it's to do with Alicia Owen. A member of the family isn't happy.'

'Okay. I'm on my way in now.'

Who'd complained? Surely not Daniel, he'd seemed okay when she left him yesterday evening and was now away on a long-haul delivery. Marie? She'd appeared open and frank this morning. Maybe she'd given away more than she planned? Or perhaps she'd spotted Beth at the cemetery. Or Vic. He was agitated, aggrieved at the press leak yesterday.

Beth was back at her car now. She climbed in, turned over the engine and sighed. It didn't matter who'd complained, there was bound to be drama if Andrea Leary was dealing with it.

27

Marie Russell pulled down the sun visor, checked her beret in the mirror and tucked away a few strands of stray hair before she flipped the visor back up and checked the clock on the dash. Almost 3.15 p.m. The mothers were gathering at the school gates in little groups. Shoulders hunched, faces pinched against the vicious December wind.

Usually she'd be standing there on the periphery, listening to their chatter, having dashed back from work to collect Zac. But not today. Today, she clung to the safety of her car like a baby's comforter. Parking close enough to view the gates and be ready to jump out and collect Zac when he came out, and far enough away that her presence wouldn't be noticed.

The mothers would have seen the news coverage and read the speculation over whether it was Alicia. She couldn't face the head tilts, the sorry eyes, the inquisitive questions. And she didn't want those questions near her son.

It had taken years to get past the subject of her missing daughter in company. In the early days, whenever she met someone new, their eyes would flick to the blonde streak in her hair, hear the mention of her name and their faces would tense. Some asked her about her daughter, others looked on awkwardly, unsure what to say. It eased when she married Vic and took his surname, though, occasionally, when she met someone new, they would still squint and glance at her hair uncomfortably.

A few of the mums had eyed her with that same look when Zac started school. Others talked in low voices, behind the backs of their hands, passing pitiful expressions in her direction. Marie was raised in Kingsthorpe. Even if people didn't know of her, the press coverage around the time of Alicia's disappearance branded her image on their brains. Marie didn't react. She'd learned to ignore the gossip, sit it out, wait for it to pass as it inevitably did. She didn't want their sympathy. She wanted to live a normal life, support her family and raise her son, just like them.

She checked the clock on the dash. Whereas her boss had told her to take a week's leave, to sort things out with the police and her family, Vic was self-employed and didn't enjoy the luxury of paid holiday. He'd worked from home as much as possible during the last forty-eight hours. Today he had a meeting with a potential new supplier that had been arranged for weeks. He'd wanted to postpone; she'd persuaded him not to. 'I'll get Freddie's mum to bring Zac home,' he'd said when they'd discussed it that morning. Looking out for her, as always.

'No, I can collect him. I'll be fine,' she'd said. Life had to continue. Only now she was here at the school she could feel her pulse start to accelerate.

This was her first trip out since the news of the discovery of the child's remains broke and she'd planned the mission as if it was a military operation. Dug out her old beret and sunglasses. Donning them and driving straight out of the garage, despite the gloomy day. 'You can drive my old convertible,' Vic had said. 'People are less likely to recognise you at the school in that.' And he was right. But it was one thing staring at a sea of faces from the safety of her front room. Quite another passing through them to get out of her road and it didn't stop the reporters rushing to her side, pressing their faces to her window, the camera flashes as she drove through the crowd outside their house.

Another glance at the clock. 3.20 p.m. Zac would be out soon.

She looked past the waiting mothers to the playground: the climbing frame, the hopscotch area, the worn red and blue steps of the slide. Since she'd had Zac, these were happy places. An outdoors child, Zac loved to run and play and was like a spider on a climbing frame. In the early years, after Alicia and Liam, it was a different story. She'd found herself lost in the presence of children yet drawn to them like a magnet. Spending endless hours sitting on park benches, watching them play, a longing clanging like a bell inside her chest.

And over the last couple of days, she'd felt that clanging return. She couldn't sleep and could barely eat, waiting to see what each day would bring.

A movement in her peripheral vision. A flash of green book-bags. The reception year children were trailing out of school in a line, headed by their teacher. Zac's class would be next. She pulled on her sunglasses, took one last look to ensure her hair was tucked into the cap and was about to climb out of the car when someone tapped the passenger window.

Marie jumped. It was Mrs Tilbury, the headmistress.

Marie slid out of the car, pulled off her sunglasses and viewed her across the roof. The wind was lifting her grey bob and flapping it about. The woman pulled her cardigan across her chest.

'Is everything okay?' Marie asked, glancing about. She was expecting Zac to appear, his mousy hair spiking his crown.

'Zac's inside,' the teacher said, guessing her thoughts. 'Could you come and join us in my office for a minute?'

'Has something happened?'

'We just need to have a chat. We'll talk about it inside.'

Marie had only ever been in the head's office once before, when they'd looked around the school. It was located at the back of the building, overlooking the sports field, and she was relieved when Mrs Tilbury unlocked the side gate and led her down the side passage to the rear. At least she didn't have to pass through the mothers gathered at the gate who were now craning their necks to watch.

'Zac is with Miss Marsh,' Mrs Tilbury said as they entered the building. Miss Marsh was his classroom teacher, a pretty blonde woman, barely out of training. She had a gentle manner with little children and Zac had taken to her almost immediately. Marie was just speculating whether something had happened in class when the headmistress led Marie into an empty classroom with desks and chairs at one end and a play area with a children's kitchen and tent at the other. Splodgy paintings were pegged to a string hung like a washing line that spanned the width of the room. 'I thought we'd have a quick chat before we join the others,' she said.

This sounded serious.

Mrs Tilbury's face was impassive and staunchly professional – she wasn't giving anything away. Marie wondered how many other parents had been led into the school like a pupil for one of her *chats*.

'Thank you for asking your husband to speak with us yesterday about the recent findings. I wanted to say how sorry I am. We all are. It must be such a difficult time for you.'

It didn't sound like a sympathy call. The tone of her speech suggested a 'but'. 'Thank you,' Marie said, cautiously.

'Have the police confirmed whether or not it is your daughter?'

'We're awaiting DNA test results. They should be available soon.'

The woman pinched her lips together. 'That's good.'

'How has Zac been?' Marie asked, her gaze flicking to the door and the corridor beyond. She'd never been in the school when it was empty and it struck her how quiet it was in the classroom now the children had left.

'Miss Marsh has been keeping an eye on him, as you know. Have you spoken with him about Alicia?'

The mention of her missing daughter's name caught Marie. 'No. We'd planned to sit him down after the results come back. We still can't be sure it's her. I don't want to upset him unduly.'

'Ah.'

Marie searched the contours of the woman's face. 'What is it?'

'You asked me how Zac has been. Yesterday, according

to Miss Marsh, he was fine, his usual sociable self. There was an incident today though, at afternoon play.'

'What kind of incident?'

'Zac got into a fight with another child.'

'What?' Marie felt her jaw drop. Her son was the most placid creature she'd ever encountered. They'd had to encourage him to tackle the ball off an opponent in football. 'Who?'

'Ben Knight. I believe they had an argument in the playground. Zac punched him in the face and pushed him to the ground.'

No! Ben was in Zac's class, they were friends. He'd been to their house several times to play on Zac's trampoline in the garden. She recalled him distinctly because of his white-blond hair, his cheeky smile. The same white-blond hair sported by his elder brother when he called round to collect him. 'There must be some mistake.'

'I'm afraid there isn't. Miss Marsh was on playground duty. She broke up the scuffle.'

'Was anyone hurt?'

'Zac has a couple of scratches on his face. He's fine otherwise. Ben's mother has taken him to hospital. There's a cut on his crown, it looks like he'll need a couple of stitches.'

Marie gasped. 'Why didn't you call me?'

'We tried your phone and there was no answer. We left you a voicemail.'

Marie pulled out her phone and checked the screen. Sure enough, a missed call flashed up at 2.05 p.m. It must have been when she was at the graveyard. 'I'm sorry. What happened?'

'We don't know exactly. Neither boy has said much. Some of the other children said they were talking about the child's body that was found.'

Dread seeped into Marie's veins. 'H-how did they know?'

The headteacher's face was full of empathy. 'People watch the news. They talk.'

'Around their children?'

'Sadly, not everyone is as careful as they should be. With the internet these days and older siblings in the house, it's difficult.' She shrugged a single shoulder.

Marie hitched a breath. She'd naively thought people would go to great lengths to protect their young children from the sickening news of child murder. She was wrong. And now the spindly fingers of gossip had reached Zac too. Why, oh why hadn't she listened to Vic and spoken with him earlier?

'We can arrange for a counsellor if you think it will help.'

'No. Thank you. I'll speak with him myself. Can I see him now?'

Zac was sitting on a chair in front of the headteacher's desk studying his feet when they entered her office. He didn't look up, although Marie did notice his legs flinch. He was small for his age, but he seemed tiny squashed into the arm of the large chair. Miss Marsh was standing beside him. She shot Marie a kind smile.

Mrs Tilbury gestured for Marie to take a seat beside her son and moved around the desk to a leather chair behind. Marie glanced through the window at the sports field beyond, the goalposts of the football pitch. They'd been one of the things that caught his eye when they viewed the school. St Andrews wasn't the closest primary school to them, a good fifteen-minute car drive away. They'd chosen it because of its excellent reputation and, after seeing that pitch, Zac had nagged and nagged to go there.

'I've told your mum about the fight in the playground this afternoon, Zac,' Mrs Tilbury said, leaning forward and squaring her hands on the desk. She'd kept her tone soft, but her voice sounded loud and authoritarian, pulling Marie back to her old school days. It seemed too much for a six-year-old, especially considering the circumstances.

'Are you sure there's no mistake?' Marie said.

'I'm afraid not,' Miss Marsh interjected. 'I saw it happen.' Zac didn't move, didn't budge an inch as she ran through the events again.

'Zac?' Marie said to her son when the teacher finished her account.

Zac kept his head down, as still as a statue. A scratch like a sleep crease ran down his tomato-red cheek.

'Are you going to tell us what happened?' she asked, eyes glued to her son, imploring him to respond.

Nothing.

Mrs Tilbury laced her fingers together. 'I realise this is completely out of character for Zac, but you must know we can't tolerate this behaviour. Zac knows that, don't you, Zac?'

He gave a quick nod, refusing to make eye contact.

'I'm so sorry.' Marie looked at her son. 'We both are, aren't we, Zac?' Still no response.

Marie made her apologies again and led her son out of the office, her mind working overtime. She cursed the press. This could have all played out so differently, quietly waiting to see if there was a match, preparing each other. If they hadn't printed the story, if the builder hadn't leaked the findings, her son wouldn't be in this position now.

Thankfully, the playground and road outside were empty, parents and children now on their way home. The wind swirled around them as they crossed the tarmac, his tiny hand clamped in hers, and climbed into the car.

Marie placed her key in the ignition and turned to face her son in the back, his car seat elevating his face to her level. 'You do know you can talk to me, don't you, darling?'

He met her gaze for a split second and looked away.

The sight of his crimson cheeks plucked a heart string. She wrestled with her seatbelt and pulled off down the road.

The purr of the engine was the only sound to fill the car on the way home. Marie navigated through the traffic, checking the rear-view mirror intermittently, only to find Zac staring out of the window. By the time they arrived home, frustration was gnawing away at her. She wanted to know what had happened in the playground, what he'd been through.

Marie ignored the reporters, driving straight into the garage, pressing the button to close the electric door behind them. When they reached the hallway, she could bear it no longer. She crouched down to her son's level, made to undo his coat. He pulled away, unzipping it himself.

'Why, Zac?' Marie said. 'Why would you fight with Ben? You're friends.'

His chin quivered.

'What is it?'

A tear slid down the side of his nose. He wiped it away

with the inside of his cuff. 'Ben said you had another baby. A girl. He said you killed her and buried her in the ground.'

Marie's heart shrivelled to a tiny crisp. Was that what people thought? That she'd killed her own child and buried her beneath the cold earth.

She cast her mind back fifteen years. The appeals, the interviews were draining, every one zapping another drop of energy from a tank already close to empty. Until there was no more to give, and she retreated into herself. It was then that the press turned on her. Interviewing friends and associates from her past. Snapping photos of her whenever she was out. Speculating over her mental health. Raising ugly questions. What kind of person doesn't watch their child? Who would leave a child alone outside a supermarket?

Marie faced her son. 'What did you say to him?'

'I told him I didn't have a sister. He laughed at me; said he couldn't come to my house anymore because you were a killer mum.'

Vic was right yesterday. They should have prepared him. Given him half a chance to cope with the questions, the allegations. She'd considered Zac safe. That his tender age would protect him from the gossip and the conjecture. She was wrong.

Her pulse raced, she found it hard to catch her breath. She needed to explain but her tongue had expanded, filling her mouth and she couldn't form the words.

'You're not a killer, are you, Mum?' Tears glistened in Zac's eyes.

'No, darling. I'm not.' She squeezed the ailing words out.

He wrapped his arms around her, digging his head into

her neck. Marie was dumbfounded. The idea of her son standing up for her was too much. It should never have come to this.

'Can I go and play my Xbox now?' he said when he pulled away.

She nodded and watched him wander into the front room, leaving her to sit back on her heels, alone.

28

Beth jogged up the back stairs of the station, nodding to a couple of passing colleagues. On the drive back, the issue of family concern had rolled around and around her head. What could it be and, more importantly, who'd raised it? She bypassed the entrance to the incident room, heading straight down the corridor. There was only one person she wanted to speak to right now.

Freeman's door clicked open as she approached, and Beth was surprised to see Andrea Leary emerge. Her hair looked freshly cut, a sharp fringe pointing down towards dark eagle eyes. Her brown trouser suit nipped in at the waist and was, as usual, immaculate.

It must have taken Beth almost twenty minutes to drive back to the station. What had she been doing in there all that time?

'Thank you for your understanding, Lee,' Andrea said, using his first name and ignoring Beth's presence beside her. 'Keep me updated.' She turned, viewed Beth a second, gave a sharp nod and moved off down the corridor.

'Sir,' Beth said to Freeman when she'd gone.

'Come on in, Beth.' He signalled for her to enter and take a seat. 'How did you get on with Pip Edwards?'

Beth waited until they were settled in their chairs, facing each other across Freeman's desk, and conveyed her meeting with the journalist.

'Well done,' he said. 'I'm sure that can't have been easy.' He eased back in his chair. 'Scott didn't feature much in the original enquiry. I take it Edwards won't disclose his sources?'

Beth shook her head. 'I guess he wants to save it all for his precious book.'

Freeman rolled his eyes. 'We'll get a court order and force his arm if we have to.'

'That's pretty much what I told him.'

'Good. First, we need to establish a connection.'

'Nick's checking with intelligence. I'm not sure what they'll have with the time lapse though, fifteen years is a long time.'

As if on cue, Nick's head appeared around the door frame. 'Thought I heard your voice,' he said, smiling at Beth.

'You might as well join us,' Freeman said, beckoning him in. 'Close the door, will you? There's something I need to say to both of you.'

Freeman's phone rang. He cast it an annoyed glance. 'I'll just get this.'

'Anything on Scott?' Beth asked Nick as he pulled out a chair and lowered himself into it.

'I've left it with intelligence. They haven't come back yet. I've also tracked down the local community officer for Kettering town centre. He's off duty today, I couldn't reach him, but I've left a message for him to call us. If Scott Owen is sleeping rough, there's a good chance he might recognise him or know where he is.'

Freeman ended his call and replaced the receiver, eyeing them both, his face sombre. 'Cara Owen's been in touch.'

Beth stared at him. 'Daniel's sister?' She was the last person Beth expected.

'She phoned the chief constable. Apparently, he was a member of the same golf club as her late partner, many years ago. They met at a few functions. She's concerned about her brother.'

Beth recollected Daniel Owen's twin with the blunt fringe and the taut face, sitting on the arm of his chair. 'She's certainly protective of him.'

'The reporters have started contacting him again.'

'That's to be expected. I tried to prepare him. Followed all the protocols, kept him updated.'

'She reckons he's vulnerable.'

Beth didn't like the way this conversation was going. 'We talked about this at the briefing,' she said. 'I alerted the right channels, put a marker on his file so he's not alone when we visit with sensitive information.'

'I remember.'

Nick's earlier comments, the voices he'd overheard in the corridor outside Freeman's office pressed on her. Andrea and the DCI. 'A member of the family isn't happy,' he'd said. She looked Freeman in the eye. 'Has Cara complained about me?'

'No. No complaints were made. No names were mentioned. She's just concerned about her brother.'

The short silence that followed was tense. 'You're not removing me as FLO?' Beth asked.

'The chief wants some changes.'

Beth was indignant. 'What? I've done nothing wrong.'

'I know. Which is why I'm not removing you as FLO. We will have to play this carefully though. And we have your sergeant duties to think of. This is a high-profile case.'

'That's not a problem,' Nick said, before she had a chance to respond. 'Beth's allocating the jobs before she goes out on her liaison visits, and I'm usually here or at the end of the phone if needs be. We can manage the team between us.'

Freeman's expression eased. 'Okay. If things step up, we'll have to review the situation. In the meantime, you'll continue as FLO, but as and when we have information, or the DNA results are back, I'll liaise with Daniel myself.'

Beth couldn't believe her ears. She'd started building up a rapport with Daniel, he trusted her. She opened her mouth to retort.

Nick beat her to it. 'Might make sense actually,' he said to her. 'And it'll free you up to spend time with the Russells. It's difficult enough shouldering the liaison burden alone, especially when there are two families involved.'

Anger fizzled within Beth. She opened her mouth again to respond and caught a warning glare from Nick. What was going on here? When she looked back at Freeman, his face was firm, the decision already made. She pulled back, fought to keep her voice even. No sense in quibbling until she knew more. 'He's away the next couple of days,' she said, 'on a long haul to Poland. He switches off his phone when he's in Europe. That should afford him a break from the press.'

'When is he back?' Freeman asked.

'Saturday.'

'Okay. We should hopefully have the DNA results back by then.'

'I'd like to visit Cara Owen,' Beth said, 'follow up on her phone call and get more of an idea of Daniel's needs.' Contacting the chief was a giant step, it made sense to check on her motive. Might afford the opportunity to press her about her younger brother again too. There had to be some reason why Daniel and Cara were uncomfortable talking about Scott.

Freeman surveyed her a second. 'Okay, take it gently. Dress it up as a reassurance exercise, a welfare visit. She's been told I'll be speaking directly with her brother from now on.' He passed his gaze from one to another. 'You can go together.'

Beth closed Freeman's door behind them and stomped back to the incident room at breakneck speed, the anger she'd held at bay re-surfacing.

'Hey!' Nick caught her arm to slow her.

'What's his problem?' she said, pausing and pointing her forehead towards Freeman's office. 'I can't believe he's allowed Andrea Leary to muscle in and remove me.'

'You're not removed.'

'I might as well be.'

'Look, he could easily pull in someone else, a liaison officer from another force even, to take over. He hasn't because he trusts you. He just has to be seen to be doing something.'

29

Zac was perched on the edge of the sofa, playing his games console, eyes fastened to the screen in the corner, when Marie entered the front room with a tray. Half an hour had passed. Half an hour in which she'd turned the afternoon's incident over and over in her mind. She needed to phone Ben's mother, to check on him. But first she needed to talk to Zac about his sister. She knelt and laid the tray on the floor.

'Daddy's going to be home late,' she said. 'I thought we'd have tea here together this evening. A carpet picnic.'

He eyed her suspiciously and turned back to the screen. They rarely ate in the front room.

While he finished his game, she placed the plate of sandwich triangles on the rug, a collection of cupcakes beside it. 'Why don't you put that down now?' she said. 'I've made cheese and pickle. Your favourite.'

He cast the handset aside, slid down onto the floor beside her and eyed the cakes. 'Can I have that one?' he asked, pointing to one with a Smartie atop a swirl of chocolate icing.

'You can. After you've eaten your sandwiches.'

Marie switched the television to the children's channel

and lifted a sandwich to her lips. The idea of eating made her heave, she had to force the food down, but this was a real treat for Zac. Tea was usually a family affair at the table; television wasn't allowed.

'This is nice, isn't it?' she said, leaning her back into the base of the sofa.

Zac nodded and grabbed a cake.

When he'd finished the last crumb, she leaned forward, wiped a smear of chocolate from his face with her finger and passed him a wet wipe. He scrubbed the wipe across his hands.

'There's something I need to talk to you about,' she said eventually. Discarding the wipe and moving a little closer, she wrapped an arm around him. He rested his head on her shoulder, watching the television.

'You remember you have a brother, Liam?'

'The one with the train?'

He was referring to the toy train on Liam's grave. Many a time he'd played with when they'd visited. The lump returned to Marie's throat. This was going to be even harder than she imagined. 'Yes. He was poorly when he was born and went to live in heaven. Well, I've never told you this before, but Liam had a twin sister called Alicia.'

Zac gazed up at her, his eyes like pools. 'Did she die too?'

Marie paused, still unsure of how to find the right words. 'Yes. She died after her brother.'

'Were you sad?'

'Yes. Very sad. Then you came along and made me happy again.' She kissed the side of his forehead.

Zac was quiet a moment. She could almost see the cogs in his young mind working.

'Where is she?' he said.

'We don't know, darling.' She battled to find the right words. 'Someone did a bad thing. They took Alicia from us and buried her somewhere secret.'

'Who?'

'We don't know.'

'A bad man?'

'Yes. That's why we don't speak to strangers.'

He swallowed. 'Where?'

'What?'

'Where did they bury her?'

'We don't know that either, darling. We were never told. The police have been helping us and now they think they might have found her. That's why people have been coming to the house. They're detectives, checking to see if the baby they've found is our Alicia.'

Zac was quiet a moment. 'If it's her, will they give her back to us?'

'They will. And we'll be able to bury her with her brother.' The drone of a car engine passing outside filled the room. 'I think that's what Ben was talking about at school today,' she continued gently. Her son's face tightened, recognition darkening his eyes. Once again, she cursed her naivety at not telling him earlier, at thinking his age afforded him some safety, some innocence. 'Daddy and I were going to tell you about it when the police had finished their enquiries and could tell us whether or not the baby was your sister. We didn't want to frighten you otherwise.'

'What if it isn't her?'

'Then we'll keep looking and hoping that she'll be found and returned to us.'

Zac's face scrunched. A tear welled in his eye. He lifted a fist, swiped it away. 'You didn't kill her, did you?' The words were barely a whimper.

'No, darling. I didn't.'

Another tear dripped down his face. He nuzzled his head into her chest.

Marie's heart cratered as she held him close and kissed the wispy hair around his crown. She should have protected him from this. 'I'm sorry. I should have told you earlier.'

Time ticked by. The programme finished; the credits rolling up the screen to a jaunty tune.

Eventually Zac's breaths evened and he pulled back, wiping his face with his sleeve. 'Is Ben going to be okay?' he asked.

'I think so. I'm about to ring his mum and check on him. Would you like to talk to him if he's there?'

Zac stared at her. He seemed unsure.

'Well, see how you feel.'

The plates clattered together as she gathered them up and placed them on the tray. She made to stand when she felt his hand tug at her sleeve.

'Mum?'

'Yes?'

'Will I ever get a brother or a sister? I mean one that's here, not in heaven.'

Marie felt a griping pain in her stomach, as if she'd been winded. She met his gaze. 'Maybe one day, darling. Maybe one day.'

30

Beth checked the clock on the dashboard as she pulled up outside Cara Owen's semi-detached house on Chalcombe Avenue. It was almost 4.30 p.m. An hour until Lily's party was due to begin. Time pressed on her as she climbed out of the car.

Christmas tree lights winked on and off the tree in the window of the house next door. There were no decorations in the window of number 843. Instead the dull hue of lamplight emitted from the front room, enough to show the silhouette of a woman sitting in an armchair, watching television.

Nick and Beth walked in single file down the driveway, past a white Toyota van emblazoned with 'Garden Pretty' in green letters, a large sunflower symbol beside – Cara's work van, Beth assumed. Surprisingly, for a landscape gardener, Cara's own front garden was plain with a square lawn, a narrow border to the side, a short privet hedge at the front.

A short bark sounded when they rang the doorbell. Cara answered the door seconds later. She was dressed in a white towelling robe; wet hair clumping on her shoulders. Obviously, early evening showers were popular in the Owen family. She was cradling a sleepy Bailey in her arms.

'What is it?' Cara asked, looking from one detective to another.

Beth introduced Nick and didn't miss Cara raise a brow at Nick's title. 'Can we come in, Cara?' she asked. 'We're here on behalf of our detective chief inspector, to follow up on your phone call to the chief constable this afternoon. We want to make sure you're comfortable with the new arrangements,' she added, taking care to keep her voice light. With the proposed changes, she was aware this could be her one chance to probe Cara more about her family and in particular her younger brother, and she needed to keep her engaged.

'How are you doing?' Beth asked when Cara had led them through into the front room.

'I'm okay. It's my brother I'm concerned about.' Cara flicked the light switch as she spoke, illuminating the room in a blinding light that forced Beth to blink several times.

'How was he when you last saw him?'

'He dropped Bailey off this morning, before he left for Poland. He was okay, a bit withdrawn. I know he's trying to keep an open mind, but the investigation... It's chewing him up inside.'

'I understand.' Beth glanced at the window. The road outside was quiet. 'Has anybody from the media been in touch with either of you?'

'Dan's turned off his phone. I haven't taken any calls yet. I'm guessing it's only a matter of time though. I saw the news footage earlier; they're practically camped outside Marie's house.' She closed her eyes. 'God only knows what that will do to Dan.'

Dan. The shortened version of her twin's name struck a

chord and Beth was reminded of Marie's account: only his mother and his sister got to call him Dan.

'As I said earlier, I want them kept away from my brother,' Cara added. She lowered herself into the armchair, placing the dog beside her.

'Legally, we can't prevent reporters from contacting him unless they are on his property or causing harassment,' Beth said. 'But I can assure you, if any announcement is made, we'll do our best to update Daniel, then speak with the editors and reiterate the appeal to respect the family's privacy.'

'Like that'll do any good.' She gave a derisory snort.

'I'm sorry. I know this is difficult for you all.'

'You seem pretty sure it's Alicia,' Cara said.

'The DNA sample will provide confirmation though, from what we've found, we do believe it's her. I'm so sorry.'

Cara clamped her hand over her mouth.

A beat passed. 'Can I get you a glass of water?' Beth said eventually. She didn't answer. Beth gave Nick a nod anyway and he disappeared out of the room in search of the kitchen. One of the things she liked most about working with Nick was that he respected the liaison role and was happy for her to take the lead with families. An attribute she'd miss if he left the team.

'We are aware of your concerns for your brother's health,' Beth said, 'and I can assure you we will do everything in our power to ensure he's safeguarded.'

Nick wandered in with the water and passed the glass across.

'May we sit down?' Beth asked. She'd been standing, hovering in the front room until that point and was now towering over Cara. If they were to extract any information, she needed to calm things down, put them all on an even keel.

Cara gave a brief nod.

Beth waited until they were settled before she spoke again. 'We will be reaching out to everyone who was in contact with Alicia before she disappeared to request a DNA sample,' she said casually.

'Why?'

'There may be fibres or particles on her. If we can take DNA from people who visited her it will help us to eliminate them from our enquiries. Would you be willing to give a sample?'

'I didn't see her on the day she went missing. I was on a job on the other side of town. 'Landscaping a garden, Beth thought. She'd scrutinised the old file, was familiar with the family's movements. 'I realise that. When did you last see her?'

'I called around to see them all the evening before.'

'It's still possible there may be threads or particles.' Beth angled her head to get Cara's attention.

Slowly, Cara looked up, her eyes wide. 'Okay, if you think it'll help. I can't believe you've actually found her after all this time.'

Beth thanked her and removed the kit from her bag, talking Cara through the process as she took the sample. When she finished, she screwed the lid on the tube and thanked her again. 'Would you be willing to talk us through your last meeting with Alicia?' she asked gently.

'I gave a statement to the police at the time.'

'I know, and we appreciate that. But in the light of the

recent discovery, we're reviewing the case. It would be really helpful if you could run through it again in as much detail as you can remember.' Beth could feel Nick's quizzical gaze on her. Once again, she was going out on a limb. She'd read the statements in the case and they were factual, perfunctory. Dates and times. She needed to gain a better understanding of the family dynamics from those who were there. And often things slipped into personal accounts – attitudes, body language – that gave a greater indication of who got along with who, and how relationships played out. But she needed to be careful.

'It was so long ago.'

Beth smiled kindly, letting the silence linger.

Eventually a woebegone expression spread across Cara's face. 'I went to see them after work on the Monday.' She screwed up her eyes, thinking hard. 'It must have been around seven or so. Dan was in the kitchen trying to cook dinner with Alicia in his arms. She was crying. She cried a lot, especially in the evenings. They blamed it on colic. He passed her over to me. I stayed until he finished cooking, then put Alicia down.'

'Where was Marie?'

'I didn't see her that night.'

'Oh?'

'That wasn't unusual. She was probably upstairs, lying down. As soon as Dan came home from work, Marie handed over the baby and went to her bedroom.'

'How was Daniel?'

'He was okay, under the circumstances. It was all a bit hectic.'

'How do you mean?'

'Well, he was struggling with losing Liam. We all were. And he had Marie to deal with too. The depression. The tantrums. It wasn't easy.'

'A difficult time for everybody.'

'Yes. We could all see Marie wasn't coping. She wouldn't accept help unless it was from Dan. We tried to pull her out of it, to encourage her to concentrate on the healthy baby she had, but... oh, I don't know. There was no warmth, no bond between them.'

Beth edged forward. 'I'm not sure I understand you.'

'It's like all the beautiful clothes we bought. That baby wanted for nothing. Yet every time we saw her, she was in a vest and nappy and asleep in that bloody car seat. My mother spent a fortune on a Moses basket for their front room. I'd be surprised if Marie ever used it.'

'I'm told it was a hot summer.'

'Yeah. Marie would say that.'

Beth didn't respond. The health visitor's reports at the time didn't consider the child at risk, yet Cara's attitude towards Marie intrigued her. Marie had been neutral in her descriptions of their relationship, hinting that Cara was hot-headed, possessive of her twin. Was Cara's bitterness down to jealousy, the separation, or was there another reason? Cara scratched her forehead. Stubbly nails coursed back and forth across the pallid skin of a face that showed signs of former prettiness and now sagged with stress. 'Look, I might not have had children myself,' she said, 'but I know babies aren't easy to raise, especially during the early months. Alicia was no exception. They couldn't find a routine that suited her. Took her back and forth to the doctors.' She drew an audible breath, spoke through her exhalation. 'Part of me thinks if they'd all settled down, then she would have too. Marie was so consumed with her own grief, she couldn't see what was under her nose: a good man, a healthy baby, a nice home. I hardly ever saw her hug that child. She spent more time in my arms than her mother's. I'm not saying I blame Marie, I know she was struggling, but it was like someone had switched off the light behind her eyes. We tried to persuade her to go back to the doctor, to get help. She wouldn't listen. If she had, then maybe she wouldn't have left the child outside a shop, alone. I mean, what kind of mother does that?'

Beth searched Cara's face. Her depiction of Marie as detached in the hours leading up to Alicia's disappearance didn't correlate with Marie's account of things improving. If Cara was to be believed, she was sinking deeper into a well of depression. Marie had described her former sister-in-law and the rest of the family as overbearing. Perhaps her behaviour was a reaction to their dysfunctional relationship.

'It would be helpful to trace other members of the family,' Beth said gingerly. 'I know we've touched on this before… do you have any idea at all where we might reach your brother, Scott?'

Cara looked up abruptly. 'No.'

'When did you last see him?'

'I can't remember. As I said, he moved away years ago. We didn't keep in touch.'

'Can you tell me why you and your brother don't have a forwarding address? Did you argue with him?' Beth was careful not to share any details she'd already been told. Keeping other accounts confidential would enable them to highlight any potential inconsistencies.

'I don't want to talk about it, and I don't see how this is relevant to Alicia. Scott left after she disappeared.'

'On the contrary, it may be very relevant. If Scott was involved in something, or with somebody untoward, it may have an impact on the case.'

Cara huffed. 'I doubt it. Christ, this is a family issue. Is there nothing sacred?'

'Not in a murder investigation, no.'

She was quiet a moment. 'Scott stole money off our mother, okay?'

'How much money?'

'About a grand. All she had in savings at the time.'

'What did he use the money for?'

'No idea. Scott was secretive. Always out and about. It was only a week or so after Alicia disappeared. We were all in shock. Scott pinched Mum's cash card and withdrew the money in small amounts every day for almost a week. None of us had a clue until the bank grew suspicious over the number of withdrawals and contacted her.'

Beth recalled Edwards mentioning Scott had stolen from his mother. 'What happened?' she asked.

'Mum confronted him.' Cara shook her head, sadly. 'He was all charm and apologies, as usual. Said he was having trouble with his car and needed some parts. Didn't want to bother her with everything else that was going on. Promised to pay it back. That night he left.'

'How do you mean?'

'I mean, he was there in the evening and gone by the morning. No warning, no forwarding address, nothing. He'd taken a rucksack and some clothes. His toothbrush. But it wasn't the first time. He often came and went. My mother thought he'd gone to lick his wounds and he'd be back when he was ready.'

'Did you hear from him afterwards?'

'No. After about a week, Dan spoke to one of Scott's work colleagues who said Scott had phoned and told them he'd been offered a job in London. That was the last we heard. My mother deteriorated afterwards. Wouldn't go out, refused to see people. Kept watching the door, expecting him to walk through any minute. Apologise. Say it was all a big mistake. And we were looking after Marie, waiting on news about Alicia. It was a difficult time.' She paused, staring into space. 'Mum was less than seven stone when she died, a year later.' Tears welled in Cara's eyes. 'I think, after losing Liam, and then Alicia, then Dan and Marie separating, Scott was the last straw. There was too much sadness for her to cope with.'

'I'm so sorry,' Beth said. 'Did anyone come to the house asking for Scott, perhaps someone he owed money to?'

'Not that I know of.'

A tear slipped down Cara's cheek. She wiped it away with the back of her hand. 'That's why Dan and I stick together,' she said. 'We've only got each other now.'

31

The light was on in her sister's front room when Beth pulled up outside later that evening, the curtains undrawn. She smiled as she watched children marching around a line of chairs in the middle. A tune she didn't recognise played faintly in the background. They'd played musical chairs in her mother's front room as kids, hurtling around until the last chair was occupied, the smell of freshly baked cake thick in the air. And now Eden was doing it with her daughter. She felt a pang. It was such a shame her mother wasn't there to see it.

Beth made her way around the back. The sound of children's chatter and laughter slapped her in the face as soon as she opened the kitchen door. Eden's table was set with pink and grey serviettes, paper plates and trays of sausage rolls, sandwiches and cakes.

She was about to pinch a sandwich when a tall woman in tailored jeans and a loose denim shirt wandered in.

'Oh, hi Beth. When did you get here?'

It was Alex, Chloe's mum. Chloe was in Lily's class at school and lived up the road. Beth had dropped Lily off there for play dates a few times.

'Just now. How's it going?' Beth said, jutting her chin towards the hallway.

A roaring cheer emitted from the front room.

Alex laughed. 'I think everyone's enjoying themselves.'

No sooner had she spoken than Lily came rushing in.

'Auntie Beth!' The child flung her arms around her.

Beth rocked on her heels. 'Happy birthday, pumpkin,' she said, patting her niece's blonde curls with her free hand. 'Do you want your presents now or after tea?'

'Now!'

Beth laughed and handed them over. Within seconds the paper was ripped off the two packages and cast aside.

'Oh, wow!' Lily said, holding up the pink digital camera. Gasps followed as friends rushed in and crowded around them.

'It's waterproof,' Beth said to Lily, 'so you can take photos underwater.'

'Thank you.' Lily placed the camera down carefully and turned over the case in her hands.

'The camera is from me and the case from Nick.'

'Is Nick here?' A pink-faced Eden brought up the rear of the group of children, gently herding them into the kitchen.

Beth threw her an affectionate smile. 'Afraid not. He had to work.' The relief on Nick's face was amusing when she'd dropped him at the station to book in the DNA sample and check on intelligence earlier. Somehow the laborious task of searching for Scott Owen was more palatable than entertaining a bunch of eight-years-olds, however fond he was of Lily. 'But he's expecting to see lots of photos,' Beth said to her niece. The child beamed back at her.

'Right, everyone to the table,' Eden said, clapping her hands.

The next hour passed in a whirl of sandwiches, crisps and trifle, the din of excited chatter only broken momentarily when Eden brought out the birthday cake. It was designed like an Olympic swimming pool complete with lanes and the head and goggles of a swimmer in one of them. Everyone gaped. Beth's heart warmed at her niece's wonderment. Like Beth, Lily had taken up competitive swimming before she started school. Always at her happiest in water.

Beth occupied herself with cutting and wrapping slices of cake in small serviettes and very soon parents were calling to pick up their little ones. 'Shame Chris couldn't make it,' she said to Eden as she waved off Chloe and Alex.

'He's working,' Eden said, her face souring at the mention of her husband; their messy separation, only months earlier, still fresh in her mind. 'He came over this morning, gave her a card and a present. They're going bowling tomorrow evening together to celebrate.'

'You two finally seem to be sorting everything out.'

'We're agreeing on custody, keeping it simple for Lily, if that's what you mean.'

Beth touched her arm. 'I'm pleased.' The breakup hadn't been without its sticky moments and it was reassuring to see Eden so buoyant.

Eden grabbed a bin liner and started sweeping the contents of the table into it. 'Are you still okay to drive us to the airport on Monday?' she asked.

Beth collected a cloth and wiped the tabletop. 'Yeah, sure.'

'You've forgotten.'

'I haven't. It's your trip to...'

'Lapland! Lily's really looking forward to it.'

'I bet. You'll have a lovely time.'

'I will if my lift arrives to take me to the airport. 6 p.m., okay?'

Beth laughed. '6 p.m. on Monday evening. I'll be there.'

Lily wandered in, camera in hand, and clicked a photo of them both.

'Someone's going to be busy,' Beth said grabbing her jacket.

Eden thanked her for coming. Beth hugged them both and lifted the rubbish bags. 'I'll put these in the bin on my way out.'

A bustling wind hit Beth as she stepped outside, billowing her jacket as she moved down the side of the house and placed the bin bags in the wheelie bin. She was still battling with her jacket, pulling it across her chest when a figure emerged from a car parked at the end of the driveway. A very familiar figure.

Beth halted and watched Kyle Thompson approach. 'What are you doing here?' she said.

His hair was shorter than she remembered, razored to number two, and he'd grown a goatee beard. A silver stud glistened in his ear. More than ever, his dark features resembled the mugshot taken of him when he was charged for aggravated burglary in his early twenties, the most recent of a string of offences on his police file.

After he was released from prison, he'd taken a job managing Starling's Bar in town, although station intelligence suggested it was a front to a drugs ring he was involved with, and he was flexing his muscles, moving up the chain.

He was also Eden's ex-boyfriend, the man who broke up her marriage.

Kyle slowed in front of her. 'Now that's not a very nice welcome, is it?'

Beth gritted her teeth. When the relationship was outed, Beth had faced an internal investigation over a potentially compromising association, and Chris, Eden's ex-husband, also a cop, threatened to fight for full custody of Lily. Eden was forced into a corner and claimed she'd given Kyle up. But within weeks he'd moved across town, buying a house in their village to be closer to her and Beth was pretty sure they had continued to see each other behind closed doors, however much Eden denied it.

And his presence here today did nothing to curb that presumption.

'I asked you a question,' she said.

He held up the present in his hand and Beth pressed her teeth together harder, the *Finding Nemo* wrapping paper irking her all the more. 'The same as you, I guess.'

'You're not welcome, Kyle.'

'Just being neighbourly. No crime in that is there.'

They stood for several seconds, Beth blocking his path – standing so close she was breathing in the sickly-sweet smell of his aftershave – until the back door opened.

'Kyle!' Eden cried. 'Didn't know you were coming.'

'You know me, not one to miss a party,' he said, eyes still on Beth.

Eden glanced at the present in his hand. 'I'm about to put Lily to bed. If you're quick, you'll catch her.'

He nodded. Gave Beth one last stare and pushed past her into the house.

'What's going on?' Beth said to her sister. 'I thought—'

'Leave it.'

'How many times have we been here?'

'We're friends.'

'Great company for Lily to keep.' Anger boiled in Beth's veins as she made off towards her car. Two years younger than her, Eden had never been easy. Always drawn to anything with an inherent risk. She'd settled with Chris, but it wasn't long before Kyle caught her eye and turned everything upside down. Only a couple of months earlier, she'd said they were finished. And here they were again.

'Beth, please!' her sister called after her.

'I can't do this,' she said, holding up a flat hand.

Eden was still in the driveway, watching as she pulled off and drove out of the close. Beth imagined Kyle inside, chatting with Lily and her anger tightened a notch. He knew she couldn't be associated with him, yet he wouldn't leave her sister alone. It was almost as if he was playing some kind of game, goading her. The organised crime unit had opened a file, looking into his earnings at her request, checking to see if his legitimate income supported his outgoings. If they could prove he was living off the proceeds of crime, they could slap a charge on him. That had been weeks ago. Initially DS Osborne at organised crime had been giving her daily updates. But it wasn't long before they'd fallen on a big drugs bust and his attention was taken elsewhere.

Financial investigations took ages to conduct, they had to follow the paper trail on every purchase. She made a mental note to contact DS Osborne tomorrow and check on the status of their case. Anything to remove him until Eden found a fresh focus.

32

Beth glanced up at the low clouds as she pulled onto her driveway. It was almost 7.30 p.m. She checked her messages. The local community officer for Kettering still hadn't got back to her and Pip Edwards' earlier words about Scott were dancing a jig in her mind. Where was he?

She sat in the car, mulling this over, when the kernel of an idea formed in her mind. Kettering was only ten minutes' drive from Mawsley. Maybe she could take a look herself.

Her mobile trilled, distracting her. 'Nick' flashed up on the screen.

'Hi,' she breathed. 'You okay?'

'Yes.' He sounded weary. 'I've been working on a case to secure more staff for the investigation. Just about to leave. Do you want me to pick up a takeaway?'

'Um... I'm heading out actually,' she said, her idea developing.

'Going anywhere interesting?'

'Thought I might visit the billboards on Northampton Road in Kettering. See who's there this evening.'

'Beth!' His tone raised a decibel. 'We got uniform to check out the area earlier. There was no one there.'

'It was probably too early. They'll be bedding down for the night now.'

'We can get a patrol car to check. The community officer will be able to tell us more when he's back in the morning.'

She paused. She'd soaked up the energy from the kids and suddenly a couple of hours of old-fashioned police work, trudging the streets, questioning the local homeless community for any sightings in the fresh air seemed appealing. It couldn't be noisier than a bunch of eight-year-olds.

'The patrol cars are busy enough. I might have a wander, speak to a few people. Get a feel for whether he's been around.'

'Right. I'll meet you there.'

'There's no need.'

'I'm already on my way.'

The air was thick with the promise of rain by the time Beth arrived in Kettering. She parked up in the town centre, in the empty bays opposite the library, and checked her watch. Nick wouldn't be there to meet her for at least another twenty minutes. Maybe she should make a start before the heavens opened.

She climbed out of the car and turned the corner. Northampton Road was quiet, devoid of the daytime congestion. The wind picked up as she traipsed down the road. By the time she'd reached the bottom, a soft rain was peppering her shoulders.

The billboards loomed in front. Two of them, forming

a corner to the roundabout. One advertising dog food, the other a tribute band playing at a nearby theatre. The lights beneath each, creating an iridescent glow stretching up to the sky.

Beneath them, crisp packets and empty takeaway cartons littered the pavement. Behind, trees and shrubbery covered the bank to the railway line at the top.

Beth snuck behind the billboards.

It was darker back there, the boards providing the perfect barrier to the lights outside. She could just about make out a narrow strip of scrub ground before the bank rose to a steep incline. Tree branches hung over the area, creating a natural canopy and, even at this time of year, it was surprisingly dry beneath. More takeaway boxes, plastics bags and used cans were scattered around the area, punctuated by a couple of makeshift shelters.

Beth pulled out her torch and switched it on, illuminating the area in a tunnel of light.

'Hey!' a voice called out.

'Cut that out,' grunted another. A hand flashed out from a tube of cardboard, covering the face.

Beth angled the beam away enough to be able to see clearly without blinding the two faces now in front of her. One was peering at her from a roll of cardboard, covered with bin liners. The other looking up from a square-ish den, made from pieces of wood with carrier bags shoved in the corners and tarpaulin covering the back. She could see the edge of a sleeping bag inside.

The sweet aroma of alcohol mingled with the smell of urine and damp air, cloyed her nostrils.

Beth introduced herself to a chorus of groans. 'Where else are we supposed to go on a night like this?' one of them asked.

'I'm not here to move you on,' she said. 'I'm looking for some help, to locate someone.'

'Yeah, right.' The man in the cardboard turned away.

'Do either of you know a Scott Owen?' Beth continued.

No response. The man in the shelter was sitting up now, taking a swig from a bottle.

'He's not in any trouble, we just need to reach him. We have some news about a member of his family.'

Shelter man placed down the bottle and pulled his sleeping bag up to his chin. 'Never heard of him.'

'Do you sleep here often?' she asked.

He shrugged.

'We've been told Scott slept here until recently.' She described his appearance, aware her description referred to a man fifteen years ago.

'I told you, I've never heard of him.' The man stared at her. 'Now if you're not going to move us on, can you at least let us get some sleep while it's quiet? The London train'll be along soon. Could do with some shut eye before it shakes us awake.'

Beth tried to press further, asking them for names and details of others that slept there, to no avail.

She was walking back up Northampton Road when a car pulled over beside her. It was Nick in his Toyota.

Beth climbed in and wrestled with the seatbelt. He'd rented this vehicle after his beloved vintage Alfa Romeo Spider was written off on a chase on their last job. He'd always driven old quirky cars and it seemed odd to see him in this new model. 'Isn't it about time you started looking for a new car?' she asked.

'I am looking. Just haven't found the right one yet. He steered around the corner and parked up beside her Mini. 'What were you doing back there?' he asked.

'I made a start behind the billboards.'

Nick's face clouded. 'I thought you were going to wait for me.'

'I was early.' She didn't miss him cuss under his breath, but he swallowed his anger, clearly not wishing to fight. 'And?'

'A couple of guys are sleeping rough there. If they do know Scott, they're not talking.'

'Okay, where now?'

'The churchyard. My sister mentioned seeing a few tents pitched there last week.'

The rain grew heavy, dropping in sheets as they exited the car and crossed the road. The church of St Peter and St Paul was set back from the road in the centre of town, a fifteenth-century, sandstone affair with a tall steeple that towered over the surrounding buildings. A small churchyard attached. Beth pulled up her hood as they strode around the edge of the wrought iron fence containing the churchyard and entered at the gate. They switched on their torches and walked around the graves. It was empty.

'Let's try around the back,' Beth said, raising her voice over the rain. Nick tugged up his collar, his face pinched against the inclement weather. They walked around the church, past the lime trees that marked its perimeter, about to give up when they saw a few tents pitched close to each other, beneath a yew tree at the far end.

'Police,' Nick called out as they approached. 'Anyone there?'

No answer from the first tent.

Beth noticed a slight movement in the second. 'Hey!' she said and introduced them again. 'We're trying to locate someone urgently. Can you help?'

'No.'

'Please, it's important. We need to give them some information about their family.'

A rustle. The tent was unzipped slightly, just enough for a face to appear. Dark eyes glared up at her.

She gave the name and a brief description. The rain was getting worse, penetrating her jacket now. She hunched her shoulders. While the tents enjoyed the shelter of the low hanging Yew, they were both still exposed to the elements.

'Never heard of them.'

Nick shook his head. This was going nowhere. 'Let's leave it until the morning,' he said to Beth. 'The local officer probably has some contacts.'

Beth shared his frustration but she couldn't bear to leave with nothing. She gave one last shout to the final tent.

Another zip unfastened. A wizened face popped out, topped with a mop of matted curls flecked with grey. Beth angled her torch beam away from the woman's eyes. She was gaunt, with sunken pockmarked cheekbones, red-rimmed eyes and appeared older than the others. 'Oh, man! Look at the rain.' Her face puckered.

'I'm not here to move you on,' Beth repeated. 'I'm asking for some help, to locate someone.'

'Who?'

'Scott. Scott Owen.'

If she'd blinked at that moment, she'd have missed the hint of recognition in the woman's eyes. 'Do you know him?'

'Can't help you.'

'But you do know him?'

'I didn't say that.'

Nick made to move on but Beth didn't budge. 'It's important. He's not in any trouble. I need to speak with him. I have some news about his family. Please. Anything you can tell me will help.'

33

Beth was soaked to the skin by the time she walked back to her car. The woman, who'd given her name as Lisa Roberts, hadn't been able to tell her much, apart from the fact that she knew of a Scott who'd been sleeping rough in various places around the town for several years. He came and went. Even slept out in minus temperatures because he didn't like to use the shelters. Lisa described him as a drug-dependent loner who didn't talk about himself much. When Beth asked for a description, she'd said he had dark hair and a bushy beard. No chance of checking on the harelip surgery scar then. And, crucially, she hadn't seen him for some days and had no idea where he might be now.

Nick was a few steps behind her, his phone pressed to his ear, relaying their findings back to the office. Beth gave him a wave, motioned for them to meet at home, then climbed into her car. What she needed now was a warm shower and her bed.

The wind whistled around the car as she reversed out of the bay. She was glad to be in the dry at last. If she put her foot down, she'd be home in ten minutes.

The roads were quiet out of Kettering, residents seeking shelter from the inclement weather. The rain turned to hail, icy pellets pounding her windscreen. She slowed and switched up the front and rear wipers.

There was only one car behind her as she drove past the billboards, under the railway bridge and onto the A6013. It stayed with her as she navigated the road out of town and tailed her over the roundabouts. It looked dark, possibly black, too close to make out the number plate. Nick's Toyota hire car? Maybe he'd put his foot down to catch her up.

She left Kettering behind her now, the town's street lights like tiny dots in the distance. At the next roundabout, she slowed for a lorry. The car was still behind her. It was a saloon, not a hatchback. Not Nick's Toyota then. And it was hanging a little too close for her liking. She drove straight over at the roundabout, glanced in her rear-view mirror. Headlights flashed up, almost blinding her as it followed.

The road was slick. Traffic lights in front flashed up green. She slammed the brakes anyway, in an effort to give her tailgater a shock. If it hadn't been such a wet evening, she'd have pulled them over, given them a piece of her mind. But she was wet and tired and all she wanted right now was to get home.

Her car slid as she braked, though it was a planned manoeuvre; she'd left herself plenty of room. The brakes of the car behind screeched as it skidded to a stop, narrowly missing her. Probably some idiot racer. Perhaps that would teach them a lesson. All she could see in her rear-view was the silhouette of the driver. The sun visor was pulled down, obscuring their face.

She accelerated onto the A43, surprised to find the car

still there. There was nothing else on the road. They were deliberately tailgating her.

A sudden acceleration. She checked her rear-view mirror, desperately trying to catch the number plate. They were annoying her now. If this was bloody Pip Edwards or one of the other reporters, they'd be in trouble.

She raced forward, far enough to take a better look at the car. It was a black BMW. She read the number plate quickly, before it caught her up and sat on her tail. Definitely not Edwards in his Saab then.

They raced down the A43 and Beth turned off towards Mawsley Village, watching in her wing mirror as it continued to follow. She steered into her village at the far entrance, checked her rear-view again. The road behind her was empty. A breath of relief, another repeat of the number plate. She'd be sure to report the incident, check the plates on the PNC tomorrow and make sure an officer went round and gave the driver certain words of advice.

Myrtle was sitting in the kitchen beside her empty food bowl, mewling when Beth crossed her threshold. She dropped her bags, shrugged off her wet jacket and rushed through to the kitchen, grabbing a pen and pad from the kitchen side to scribble down the number plate.

It wasn't until she finished that something felt wrong. She walked back into the hallway. The air was displaced in the small area, as if someone had been inside recently. Nick was with her in Kettering, there wouldn't have been time for him to call in home on his way over from headquarters. The doors to the front room and dining room were pulled to. They usually left them open to give Myrtle the free run of the house when they weren't home.

Myrtle's mewling grew louder, but Beth ignored her. She clutched her phone in her hand, pushed open the front room door and flicked the light switch. It was empty. She did the same with the dining room, then took to the stairs, checking each of the first-floor rooms, one by one.

Finally, satisfied the house was empty, she dropped onto the edge of her bed, cursing her frayed nerves. Nobody was there. The doors and windows showed no sign of a break-in. Only Nick and she had keys. She recalled the open gate yesterday. It must be the break-in during their last investigation playing on her mind. She needed to get a grip.

The sound of an engine filled the room. Headlights flashed outside. Nick. He couldn't see her like this. At best, he'd follow her around like a shadow again. At worst, he'd persuade her to take time off work, seek counselling. She didn't fancy either option, especially when she'd been given a shot at acting sergeant.

Another cry filtered up the stairs. Myrtle needed feeding.

Beth stole a breath and wandered back down the stairs. Her nerves had been rattled by the tailgater. Tomorrow morning she'd check that number plate and make them pay for their dangerous games.

Marie Russell sat under the dull hue of the Christmas tree lights in her front room, twirling the crimson wine around her glass. It was less than two weeks until Christmas; Zac broke up from school for the holidays in a few days. She usually relished this time of year: watching him run downstairs and open his advent calendar in his pyjamas in the mornings; the trips to see Santa; soaking up his excitement in the run up to the big day. Yet the news on Tuesday had pressed the pause button. She could see the festivities going on around her, was aware of them on television, on the radio, in the handmade decorations Zac brought home from school, but they no longer seemed real. Not in her world.

A tear dropped off her chin, landing on the side of her glass with a plink. She thought of Zac's little face earlier. It was bad enough that her discussions with the police raked up uncomfortable memories for her. Now the incident had infiltrated all their lives.

It had been difficult filling Vic in on Zac's actions at school. His face had fallen, distraught. To his credit, he hadn't grown angry and blamed Marie. Not once had he said, I told you so when, really, he had every right to do so.

After their earlier discussion Zac had settled remarkably well. Better than his father who she'd found sitting on the sofa when she'd come downstairs from putting their son to bed, staring at the blank television screen, an untouched mug of coffee in his hand. It was his darts evening, the one night of the week he usually went out. Ordinarily, he'd had have left straight after dinner and come rolling in about ten-thirty, stinking of lager. Yet after the incident with Zac, he'd brushed it aside. He didn't want to leave her alone, but she'd insisted. The break would do him good and, anyway, she needed some time to herself. Time to process.

She took a sip of wine and listened to the soft sounds of Zac's breaths as he slept. Vic kept pressuring her to get rid of the monitor. 'You're babying him,' he said. 'Give him some space.' She knew Zac hadn't been a baby for years, though at times like this, when uncertainty rained down, threatening to swamp her, Marie found the ebb and flow of her son's breaths calming. And he had no idea she was listening, the monitor was hidden behind a book, high up on the bookshelf in his room, so there was no harm done really.

Marie gulped the wine, finishing the glass, relishing the bitter tang it left on her tongue, the warm fuzziness it brought to her head. Talking through Alicia's disappearance beckoned all the old anxieties and fears to the fore. The ones she'd buried deep in the dark depths of her mind. The dark sickening notions of what her daughter had gone through after she was taken. The police were pretty sure she'd died of a trauma to her head. There was no sexual interference – a blessing. But what had gone through that tiny child's mind? She was old enough to know her mother, to recognise her family and those close to her. Was she frightened? Did she suffer?

She poured herself another glass, blinking out the fresh tears brimming in her eyes, sending them cascading down her face. She'd become obsessed with missing children after Alicia was kidnapped. Child abduction was rare and when it did occur, it was usually between families or separated partners, or part of a kidnapping with a ransom call. Stranger abduction, especially of children, was rarer still. She'd read an article about a woman in Canada whose sleeping toddler disappeared from her car while she paid for her petrol. The child was later found dead in a shallow ditch nearby. Another family in New Zealand whose five-year-old daughter disappeared from a playground when the mother's attention was turned elsewhere. Years later, she was found in a cellar where she'd been kept captive. Marie's mind had raced, her thoughts colliding with the possibilities of what might have happened to her girl. And when Madeleine McCann's disappearance hit the headlines in 2007, she'd resolved to stay away from the news. It was too painful.

Who would take a child, a baby, hit them on the head and murder them?

She recalled the police questions at the time: Have you had any disagreements or arguments with anyone? Can you think of anyone who might want to hurt your daughter or your family? She'd racked her brains. But there was no one. No one she knew would commit such a heinous crime, would they?

The DNA test results would be back soon. Trepidation rushed through her. Trepidation at the confirmation it was her daughter, but also at what the results could uncover. The can of worms it could open. Another tear fell. She was watching it disperse into the wine when the door creaked open.

Marie jerked forwards. The freshly poured wine sloshed over the lip of the glass. 'I didn't hear you come in,' she said to her husband, pressing her free hand to her chest.

'I came in the back way. Didn't want to disturb Zac. Is he alright?'

'He's sleeping.'

'Good.' He glanced around the room. 'You okay?' he asked, 'sitting here in the dark?'

Marie tried to brush the wine droplets from her shirt. 'I think so.'

34

The atmosphere in the incident room the following morning was tense with frustration. Officers sat huddled over computer screens with handsets glued to their ears, following up on the dregs of enquiries. There was no doubt about it, leads were dwindling and even though they'd recovered a body, Beth had to face facts: they'd made no more headway in solving the abduction and murder of Alicia Owen than Tanner's team, fifteen years earlier.

Rain pounded the windows. Freeman had been called to a meeting with the chief superintendent, delaying their morning briefing, although there wasn't much to report. They'd worked through the results of the public appeal and, apart from the usual crank callers, no one had reported any sightings of activity in the field at the end of Boughton Green Road.

Beth had scrutinised Marie, Vic, Daniel and Cara's bank accounts after the abduction, and searched their phone records, but couldn't find anything untoward. Three days had passed since the child had been found. Three days in which the family were left on tenterhooks. 'Any news on the DNA tests?' Beth shouted across to Nick who was standing at a desk in the corner, speaking with one of the analysts.

'I'll ring the labs,' he said making his way over and pausing beside her.

He turned to go when Pete strode across to her desk. 'I ran a trace on the plates you reported last night.'

Nick stopped in his tracks. 'What's that?'

'Oh, some idiot racer I encountered on my way home last night.' Beth waved her hand in the air dismissively. 'Needs a few words of advice on their driving habits.'

She waited until Nick had moved off to a desk in the corner before she looked back at Pete. 'What have you got?'

'That's the thing, I don't have anything.'

'I'm not with you.'

'The plates are cloned. Borrowed off a BMW previously registered in Rugby.'

'Previously registered?'

'It was involved in a collision on the M6, recorded as a write-off last year.'

Beth frowned. 'Are you sure?'

'Absolutely.'

She hadn't scribbled down the number until she'd got home. Could she have mistaken a digit? It was doubtful, she'd repeated it to herself numerous times. Though she couldn't be positive. What a shame, she was looking forward to wiping the smile off the driver's face. All they could do now was log it as intelligence and get the ANPR police cameras to watch out for it in the county. But she couldn't help wondering what the driver had been up to last night. Their intention appeared to be to intimidate. Surely somebody wasn't trying to distract her, or warn her off the investigation? Once again, she cursed her paranoia. There was still the chance the car had been sold on, and this was a joyrider. Though the incident left her uneasy.

'Okay, Pete. Thanks for trying.'

Her mobile buzzed with an unknown number. Beth drew it to her ear.

'Beth, it's Martin Callaghan here, the community beat officer for Kettering town centre. I've just received your messages. I think I can help.'

Beth felt a frisson of excitement. 'You know where Scott Owen is?'

'I've a good idea if it's the same guy. I only know him as Scott. Are you able to come over? I'll take you straight to him.'

35

PC Martin Callaghan was a short man with thinning blond hair, a pale complexion and an overhanging girth to rival Freeman's. He greeted Beth with a wide smile, exposing a row of uneven, nicotine-stained teeth and a firm handshake. He was carrying a takeaway coffee in his other hand.

They met in the car park beside the swimming baths in Kettering, as neutral a location as any she guessed for the town centre, and in the time it had taken them to wander down to Northampton Road the rain stopped and she learned that Martin had served three years in the police, a late joiner, and had been covering this area as the community officer for past six months.

'It's mostly shoplifters and residents complaining about dog muck on the pavement,' he said, 'but once you get to know everyone, it's not so bad.'

'What do you know about Scott Owen?' she asked.

He passed her a sideways glance, the untouched coffee carton in his hand held out at an angle. 'Not much. We've moved him on for begging a few times. Don't normally bother if they're discreet and outside the town centre, but he's usually off his head on heroin.'

'What about his background?'

'Only as much as you, I guess. I looked him up this morning. He's very different to the photo, he's got a beard and a moustache and is pretty unkempt compared to the manicured mugshot on our files. I can tell you he's been around here for most of the six months I've been policing the area and I'm not aware of any feuds, or people trying to trace him.'

They reached the billboards at the bottom of the road. Beth followed Martin as he slipped behind the boards, the untouched coffee still in his hand.

The area was markedly different with the dappled daylight seeping through the overhanging canopy of branches. Beth imagined it would be completely covered in summer, when the trees were in bloom. A sleeping bag was clumped in the corner of the makeshift shelter Beth had seen the night before, although, in daylight, it looked precarious, like it would fall at the slightest gust of wind. The edge of the roll of cardboard poked out from beneath several torn bin liners in the corner.

The stench of urine was stronger today, mingling with the damp air, and she had to resist the temptation to cover her nose.

A man sat beside a makeshift shelter, a lit roll-up hanging out of his mouth. He had short dark hair, in dire need of a wash, and was wrapped in a tatty grey blanket.

'Alright, Harry?' Martin said. 'How's it going?'

Beth immediately realised the reason for the coffee as he passed it across. 'Where is everyone?'

Harry thanked him for the drink, resting a suspicious gaze on Beth.

'You the cop that came here last night?' he asked.

Beth nodded.

'Bet you got soaked.'

'We're looking for Scott,' Martin said casually, changing the subject. 'Hoping he can help us with something.' He eyed the other pile of bedding as he spoke. 'Don't suppose you've seen him recently?'

'What do you want to speak to him about?'

'It's a family matter.'

'Yeah. That's what the journalist said.'

Beth caught Martin's eye. Did he mean Pip Edwards?

'What journalist?' Martin said.

'The once with the bird's nest hair. Nosey bugger. He's been back again since. Don't know what he said to Scott, but it really spooked him. Haven't seen him for a while.'

Martin took down dates and times when they'd last seen him. 'Do you have any idea where he might have gone?'

'Nah. You got any cigs?' He'd finished the roll up now, chucked it down and stamped it out with the toe of his boot.

Martin pulled a packet out of his pocket, flipped the lid and offered it across. Harry's eyes shone as he took one. He lit up and took a long drag, closing his eyes, savouring the moment.

'What about Pete?' Martin asked, jutting his chin towards the empty bundles.

'He's popped out to the High Street. He hasn't seen him either though. He'd have said.'

They waited a while longer, making light conversation while Martin probed Harry further. Scott had camped with them on and off for years. He often took himself off on his own. When he'd exhausted his questions, Martin bade his farewells and indicated for Beth to follow.

'That would have been my first choice,' Martin said as they started up Northampton Road back to the car.

'Yes, it was Pip Edwards who told me Scott Owen was there,' Beth said. 'I tried those people camping in the churchyard too.' She passed on her conversation with Lisa Roberts.

A wry smile curled the officer's lip. 'Ah. I doubt you'll find Scott there.'

'What do you mean?'

'The church doesn't want the homeless there, but they don't like to move them on, it's not very Christian-like. It's an exposed area, very central. Lisa's militant. Gives her a chance to make her point. I doubt your guy will be there if he's lying low. She's deliberately drawing attention to their plight.'

'Why?'

'Kettering doesn't have a shelter. Well, not until the extreme weather kicks in. Extreme heat or cold. The council are obliged by law to set up a temporary shelter then. Otherwise, there's nothing.' He turned his eyes skyward. 'In a town of 56,000 people, that's saying something.'

Beth raised a brow.

'According to the local council, we don't have homeless people. They rely on the police to move them along, hide the problem. Which is why those are camping in the churchyard. It's private property and they are visible, making their point that there are plenty of vagrants in Kettering. They need help.'

'Is there anywhere else we can try?'

'There are lots of potentials. Isolated spots. We could try the waste ground beside the rugby pitch on London Road. Occasionally, someone pitches a tent there, especially when they want to be alone.'

Edwards said Scott had disappeared. Did he think the reporter was onto him and decide to hide away? 'Great, we'll go in my car.'

By the time they'd navigated through the traffic, it was almost 1 p.m. Martin motioned for Beth to pull into a layby on London Road, close to a cut through to the housing estate beyond.

'This runs alongside the rugby ground to Windmill Avenue,' he said as they climbed out of Beth's car. 'People use it to walk their dogs.'

She followed him along a tarmacked pathway that punctuated the scrubland. Through gaps in the branches she could see the rugby ground to her left. Bare tree branches reached across and entwined at the top and Beth could see it would make for a pleasant walk, especially in summer. The wire fencing around the ground was broken in places and Martin led her in and out of it, checking for sightings of anyone sleeping rough on the bank, but the area was empty and surprisingly clear of litter.

Martin walked up a little further. They were fifty yards or so from the road, when he nudged Beth and pointed. She squinted through the scrub to see a tiny brown tent pitched in a clearing, beneath a circle of sycamores and oaks.

An icy gust of wind hit them as they approached, taking Beth's breath away. She shivered. It was hard to imagine how people managed to live under a thin piece of canvas, with no bricks and mortar for shelter, in these wintry temperatures.

The tent was zipped to the floor.

'Scott!' Martin called. He waited a couple of seconds. There was a rustle inside and then it went quiet. 'Scott, it's Martin here, PC Callaghan. I know you're in there. I need to ask you some questions.'

'Not interested,' a voice croaked.

'At least he's compos mentis,' Martin said in a low voice. 'Always a good start.'

'Don't make me come in there.'

With the stench of urine and whisky emitting from the tent, Beth was hoping he was coming out because there was no way she fancied going in.

Martin reached forward, about to tug the zip when it was pulled down and a pair of eyes looked out. Thick wedges of dark hair poked out of the sides of a navy beanie hat. He blinked at the daylight, still covering his mouth with the tent. 'What time is it?'

'Half ten, give or take.'

Another groan.

'How long have you been here, Scott?' Martin asked.

'Is that what you came to ask?'

'No, we have some questions.'

'Are you Scott Owen?' Beth said.

The man looked across at her shiftily. 'Why? Who wants to know?'

'Because if you are, we have some news about your family.'

'Oh, not this again. I already told that bloody journo. I'm nothing to do with Alicia Owen.'

'Pardon?'

'He thinks I'm the uncle of the kid that went missing. Keeps tracking me down, offering me money to answer questions for his damn book.'

'Did you take his money?' Martin asked.

'I might have done. The first time. Biggest mistake I ever made, mind you. Can't get rid of the bugger now.'

'But you are Scott Owen?'

The man rolled his eyes. 'It's the name I've been using for a few years, yeah. The second biggest mistake.'

'What does that mean?'

'It means, I don't give out my real name. Look, I chose this life. I don't claim benefits, don't bother anyone. Why can't you all leave me alone?'

'What's your date of birth?' Beth asked.

'I'm not giving it to you. And, since I've done nothing wrong, you've no reason to ask for it.' He glared across at her defiantly.

'Scott, I understand you don't want to be found,' Beth said. 'If you are related to Alicia though, we need to talk to you about the case. It's important.'

'I just told you, didn't I? It's not me.' At that moment, he shifted position and the zip slipped down a few inches, exposing more of his face

Beth stared at his upper lip. It was bare, the beard and moustache recently removed. There was a little regrowth, but certainly no sign of the harelip scar. It couldn't be the same guy.

'Now, I'd like to get some kip,' he said. And with that he zipped up his tent.

Beth and Martin were quiet on the way back up the track. Could this be a coincidence? That this man had taken Scott's name to protect his own identity? And, if that was the case, where was the real Scott Owen? Beth was pondering this, and almost at the car when Nick called. He didn't bother with preamble. 'The labs have got the DNA report on the test with Marie Russell,' he said. 'They've had it since yesterday. Apparently, it's been sitting on someone's desk.'

'And?'

'It's a match. Looks like our child belonged to Marie Russell.'

'Right,' Beth said. She passed along her search results. 'I'm heading back now,' she said. 'I might as well call in and see the Russells on my way. I'll call you when I'm done.'

He listened to the rain drops pitter patter on the roof. Watched them gather on the portholes and trail down the glass, harmonising with the trickling notes of Wagner playing in the background.

The boat rocked gently as it pulled and tugged on the mooring ropes.

He'd sat back and watched the police investigation unfurl, following their movements. Giving them a chance to interview witnesses, review the old file, do their legwork. Once again, the police were losing touch, letting it slip through their fingers.

The leather sofa squeaked as he rested back, took a sip of whisky and surveyed his surroundings. It was nice here. Not a sound apart from the occasional boat passing, the rain, the crows cawing above. He had food, shelter: a bedroom and a separate bathroom, his own kitchen, a comfortable lounge area. More than he'd ever had. It was the kind of home he'd choose. Transient, mobile. Different views every day. Shame things were about to change.

The music rose to a crescendo, filling the boat in a dramatic tidal wave of instruments. He drew a deep breath and swirled the whisky in his glass. Twisted his neck out to the side until the cartilage gave a loud crack. He needed to relish his final days of luxury. Because very soon it would be time to shake things up. And shake things up he would. Good and proper.

36

Marie was in the kitchen, scrubbing the red wine stain out of her white shirt when the doorbell sounded. She glanced at the clock. Almost 2 p.m. Vic was at the school with Zac. She'd considered keeping her son at home today, to give the gossip a chance to die down, but Zac insisted on going. He was playing football against Brixworth School, a special seasonal match this afternoon he'd been looking forward to for ages. The altercation yesterday, long since forgotten in his youthful mind. Vic was vehement in his support and this was one issue on which Marie didn't have the strength to argue. 'Kids have arguments,' he'd said. 'Zac's not one for grudges. The longer he leaves it, the worse it'll be.' She'd reluctantly acquiesced, but it didn't stop her worrying about how her son's day was going. Ordinarily, she'd be there too, cheering Zac on from the sideline, but after the events of the past few days they'd agreed it would be better if she stayed home.

The doorbell sounded again. She dried her hands, desperately hoping this wasn't another problem at school. She was surprised to find the detective at the door – she hadn't phoned to say she was coming.

Beth gave her a gentle smile as she invited her in and enquired how she was feeling today. Her cheeks were reddened from the wind that had picked up outside and was now whistling down the side of the house. She took off her jacket, followed Marie through to the kitchen. 'Is Vic home?' she asked, her eyes darting to the ceiling.

'No, he's watching Zac play football.' Marie held her gaze. She seemed more formal this afternoon. None of the easy warmth she usually exuded. 'There's some news, isn't there?' she asked.

'I do have something to tell you. I'd rather wait until your husband's home.'

Apprehension gripped Marie. 'Tell me now.'

'I think it would be better—'

'Please?' The word escaped breathlessly. She'd waited so long for this moment, there was no sense in prolonging the agony.

The detective gestured towards the table and pulled out a chair. 'Shall we sit down?'

Marie sunk into the chair opposite. The cold wood seeped through her denims. 'What is it?'

'We've received the results of the DNA test. I can confirm that there is a match between the baby and your sample.'

'It's definitely Alicia?'

'It certainly appears so.'

A sharp intake of breath. The room blurred around her. She blinked twice, steadying her vision. For so many years she'd longed for news and now it came, now she had confirmation, her brain refused to process the words. It was as if they'd been spoken in a foreign language. 'Are you sure?'

'I'm afraid so. I'm sorry.'

She covered her face, shoulders trembling as the tears came, bleeding through her fingers, spotting the table in front. An arm was placed around her shoulder. Soothing words uttered. But she couldn't decipher them, drowned out as they were by the intermittent hum of a drill nearby. The drill continued, the sound rising and falling as she wept. It wasn't until she removed her hands from her face and paused that she realised it wasn't a drill at all; the hum was coming from her.

Running water. A glass placed on the table in front of her. She gulped it down, the cold liquid cascading through Marie's insides, sharpening her senses. Grabbed a tissue from the box that appeared in front of her and blew her nose. For so many years she'd been on tenterhooks, awaiting news of her baby. Speculated over how she would feel – if Alicia was still alive; if they found her dead. Relief? Anger at what her child had been through? Yet, right now all she felt was a displacement in her chest, as if something had chipped off inside.

'What about Daniel's results?' she asked tentatively.

The detective gave her an odd look. 'They're not through yet. We'll speak with him later. What time is Vic due back?'

'Not for a while.' She dabbed her eyes with the tissue.

'I'll stay with you until he gets here.'

Beth switched on the light. Half an hour had passed since she'd delivered the news to Marie. The room was dimming, the murky clouds outside making for a gloomy afternoon.

She needed to get back and check on things at the office, but Marie was in no condition to be left alone. She was just thinking about asking if there was anyone else who could sit with her, her neighbour maybe – she had mentioned an elderly neighbour once or twice, they sounded close – when her phone rang. It was Nick.

'Do you mind if I take this?' she asked, angling her head towards the back door. Marie gave a nod of approval and Beth slung her jacket over her shoulders, moved outside and closed the door behind her.

'Everything okay?' she said to Nick in a low voice. 'I'm with Marie Russell.'

'How did she take the news?'

Beth glanced through the window at the woman's hunched frame, elbows on the table, staring at the fresh tissue in her hands. 'I think she'll be okay. I'm waiting for her husband to come home, then I'll head back to the office.'

'We've received Daniel Owen's DNA results.'

'Oh, right.' Beth took another look through the window. Marie was wringing the tissue in her hands, over and over. She didn't want to leave her for long.

'There's no match.'

'What?' She dragged her gaze away.

'The DNA doesn't match.'

'Could there be a mistake?'

'I'm told not. Daniel Owen isn't Alicia's father.' She could hear a distant voice calling him. 'Listen, I have to go. See what you can find out from Marie Russell, and tread carefully. This opens up a whole new line of enquiry.'

Beth ended the call and shivered. The temperature was

dropping rapidly, mirroring the ailing light. She stared down the bare garden. If Daniel Owen wasn't Alicia's father, then who was? There was never any question over paternity in the original investigation, although that was before they had a body to test against. She ran through her early conversations with Marie. The fidgets. The unease. The way she'd pressed for someone to look out for Daniel. She'd assumed she was concerned for her family, her former partner. And she was, but for a whole different reason. No wonder she'd been jittery. No wonder she'd shown so much interest in Daniel's DNA results. If she'd slept with someone else around the time the twins were conceived, she must have had doubts about paternity. Why hadn't she mentioned it earlier?

Back in the kitchen, Marie was still at the table. Her face was puffy, eyes fixed in space.

Beth slipped off her jacket and hung it over the back of the chair. Gently does it. She needed to play this one carefully. Even if Marie knew or suspected Daniel wasn't the twins' father, she'd kept it to herself and let everybody assume he was.

'Can I get you a tea or coffee?' Beth asked.

Marie shook her head. The glass in front of her was empty. Beth refilled it, placed it back on the table and slid into the seat opposite.

'Do you feel up to talking?' Beth asked. 'I have some more questions for you.'

Marie stared ahead and said nothing.

'As you are aware, we took a DNA sample from Daniel the other day, to test against Alicia,' Beth said slowly. Marie froze.

She knows, thought Beth. 'The results have just come back. And they didn't match with the child.'

Marie's eyes widened. She looked like she was going to be sick. 'What?'

'There was a direct match with your DNA. This is your baby. But it isn't Daniel's. Daniel isn't the child's father.'

Her eyes bulged, though her gaze was still averted. She wouldn't meet Beth's eye. 'That's impossible.'

'Is it?'

'Yes. He's a twin. She's a twin. I don't have any twins in my family.'

'That doesn't prove paternity. I'm sorry, Marie, I have to ask you who Alicia's biological father is?'

Marie's jaw tightened. There were so many parts of this case, tiny areas, that couldn't be explained or didn't make sense. Like the ease with which a stranger had clicked the car seat off the pram. Surely, you'd only attempt something like that if you had a pretty good idea how it worked. Which raised the dirty question again: had she killed her own daughter and tried to cover her tracks and, if so, who helped her? Who hid the pram that day while she was in the supermarket? Had she been play acting all along, fooling them?

'Who else did you have relations with when Liam and Alicia were conceived?' Beth asked.

The silence lingered long enough for a cloud to flicker over Marie's face. A hint of terror behind her eyes. 'I don't believe this,' she said eventually.

'What is it?' Beth wasn't leaving until she had an answer to her question. 'Was it Vic?'

'No! I told you, we didn't have an affair. Not while I was still with Daniel.'

'I'll need to take down names,' Beth said. 'Contact details of everyone you had sex with around the time the twins were conceived.

Tears glazed Marie's eyes. 'There's only one.'

37

Marie struggled to control the tremor in her hands as she lifted the mug. After all these years, she should feel relieved that she had some answers. But instead her worst fears were being fired at her, one by one, and she had no idea how to deal with them. 'I don't know where to start.'

She'd felt faint after the DNA revelation, her head woozy and the tea the detective had made her did nothing to calm her shattered nerves. How could this come back to haunt her after all this time?

'Why don't you start by telling me how you met?' Beth asked.

Tea sloshed around in the mug, her hands continuing to shake as she took another sip and placed it back down, casting her mind back. 'Daniel and I got married before Mum left for Australia, while all the family were still together, and Daniel moved into Gran's with me. Somewhere to stay while we saved for a house.' A brief smile touched her lip as she pictured her gran, tiny and mouse-like, white hair clipped back from her face, making them eggs and bacon before work. She loved having them there: laundering their clothes, cooking them a meal when they came home from work.

'Gran was a staunch Catholic. I was raised as a Catholic, but Mum wasn't really interested. We only went to services at Christmas, Easter; the occasional wedding. Gran went to church every Sunday; Father Bryan, the priest, was like family to her. He often came for dinner, much to Daniel's annoyance – he wasn't particularly religious back then, it was difficult enough for him to suffer a full Catholic wedding ceremony.' A cold stone wedged itself in her chest. 'Father Bryan was charismatic and loyal to his parishioners. Always on the end of the phone. Popped around at the drop of a hat if they needed him. Gran and he, they were always trying to encourage me to "join the church family". Daniel played football on a Sunday morning, so I started going along with Gran during that last year of her life.' She could almost feel her gran's arm slip through hers as they walked up the pathway to the church, see her chest puffed with pride. 'It made her happy, showing me off to all her friends.'

She paused, the memories dislodging the lid on her well of grief.

'Gran died eighteen months after we married.' Marie met Beth's gaze. 'I remember it like it was yesterday: her standing in the hallway on the phone, talking to Mum, their usual weekly catch up. We didn't do FaceTime back then and she refused to have "one of those hands-free instruments", as she called them, convinced that others would be able to listen to her conversations. Daniel was watching television in the front room. I was in kitchen, making coffee. One minute she was standing there, chatting about Mrs Gibbs from over the road and her new granddaughter, the next I heard a thud, rushed into the hall and she was on the floor.'

Sadness trickled through her afresh. '"A massive heart attack," the doctors said.'

'I'm sorry.'

'It was awful afterwards. There was so much to sort out. Daniel and me, we were just kids. Gran had taken us under her wing. She left us the house, so we had somewhere to live. I struggled though, what with all the paperwork and organising the funeral... Mum was an only child and with her being so far away, it was difficult.

'Father Bryan stepped in almost immediately. I suppose he'd helped lots of families in those circumstances. He made phone calls, came to meetings with us – at the funeral parlour, the bank. And we became friends. Or so I thought.'

'What do you mean?'

A lump formed in Marie's throat. 'Mum came over for the funeral. After she went back and we'd sorted all the paperwork, he continued coming around. Daniel hated his visits. Didn't like the guy, said there was something odd about him, but I was so grateful for his help and he'd been such a good friend to Gran. I think he guessed Daniel wasn't keen because he started coming on a Wednesday, when Daniel was at football training. Sometimes we'd share a glass of wine and talk about Gran. I didn't have any other family here. It was good to have someone to talk to. Until...' the words cut.

'Did you have relations with him?'

A derisory snort. 'Daniel said I was sweet on him. Kept teasing me about fancying older men, said I flirted with him, laughed at his silly jokes. Honestly, Father Bryan was old enough to be my dad. I thought he was being supportive. And he was genuinely funny and nice to have around.'

'Are you saying you saw him as a father figure?'

'I suppose. I never knew my own dad. Mum remarried when I was fourteen.' She felt her shoulder rise and fall, almost of its own accord.

'What exactly happened?'

'He came around one Wednesday. Daniel was particularly difficult that night. It was six months to the day that Gran had passed away. He bought me flowers, said he wanted us to get on with our lives, live with our memories. He couldn't see why the priest was still visiting, went on about me prolonging my grief, wallowing in self-pity, said I should cut him out. I brushed off his comments. Daniel hated not being centre of attention. I guess it was something to do with the way his mother was.' She paused again. The priest had arrived minutes after Daniel left, waving a bottle of wine from side to side as she opened the door. They'd both laughed. 'Father Bryan bought a bottle of Chardonnay. Said it was his favourite. It was the first time I drank white wine. And the last.'

Silence hung in the room for several seconds.

'We were drinking, chatting about a church sale, the usual stuff, when he moved to kiss me. I mean, right out of the blue. I pulled away, confused. Marriage is sacrament in the eyes of the church. He apologised, said he didn't know what had come over him. I remember being uncomfortable, awkward, not quite sure how to react. I was so young. Accepting his apology, letting him fill my glass seemed the easiest option. We sat there a few minutes, forcing conversation. Him drinking his wine. But I was uneasy. I asked him to leave, to give me a chance to process what had happened. That's when his face changed. He took the wine out of my hand. And then he was on top of me. Pressing me into the sofa. I struggled, tried to push him off. I was terrified.'

Suddenly she was there again, pinned to the sofa. Tasting his breath – rancid, in her mouth. Feeling like a child in an adult's world.

'Afterwards, he zipped up his trousers and finished his wine, then said he'd see me in church. So matter of fact. Almost as if he'd talked me through confession.'

'Did you call the police or tell anyone about the attack?'

Attack. The word made it sound even more sordid. 'No, I was ashamed. I kept thinking of Daniel's chiding remarks, convincing myself it was my fault, that I'd led him on.'

'You're saying you were raped.'

Marie nodded.

'He was a priest, a trusted member of society,' Beth said. 'Even if you'd advanced on him, he should have turned you down. It's not your fault.'

Marie swallowed, desperately trying to suppress the fear groping her insides. 'I cleaned up, had a shower. I was just drying off when Scott called in for a late coffee. I was all over the place. My face puffy from crying. I put him off, said I was tired. I was in bed when Daniel came home. The next day, I told Daniel he was right, and we should put the past behind us. I stopped going to church. Daniel seemed pleased.'

'Did you see Father Bryan afterwards?'

'Only once. We were invited to a christening a month later. I felt sick from the minute we got the invitation, almost didn't go, but I didn't want Daniel to be suspicious. And he was all charm, with both of us, said he'd missed me at church and hoped to see me soon. As if nothing had happened. When I think of him that night, the darkness in his face…' Fresh tears burned her eyes. 'How does someone flip like that?'

The detective gave an empathetic smile.

'He came to the house after Liam died, you know. I was upstairs with Alicia. Told Daniel to send him away. He left a card, said if he could do anything to help, to give him a call.' The card with the teddy on it she'd found in Alicia's memory box the other day made her shudder. How could his card, of all of them, still be there? It was like a sign, an omen that the past was coming back to haunt her. 'I heard he moved away afterwards to Leicester and became a bishop. I put it behind me. I've never been to church since he left Kingsthorpe, not even for a wedding. Can't face it.'

'I'm sorry, I have to ask you this. Was Bishop Bryan the only man you had intercourse with, apart from Daniel?'

'Yes!' Marie's head ached.

'Did Scott have any inkling that something had happened when he came around that evening?'

'He could see I'd been crying. I said I'd had a row with Daniel. We quarrelled a lot in those days.'

'Did Scott ask you about it again?'

'He called in later in the week when Daniel wasn't home, asked if I was okay. Like I said, they didn't get along.'

'Do you know why?'

The criss-cross questions were starting to irk. 'No. Daniel wouldn't talk about it. But I liked Scottie, he was always nice to me. And he adored Alicia when she arrived.'

'When did you last see Scott?'

'I can't remember. Sometime after Alicia died, I think. Does it matter?'

Beth sat back in her seat, ignoring her question. 'When did the attack occur?' she asked. 'I'll need the date.'

Marie worked it through in her mind. 'It was the middle of September, the 12th. I did think of it when I found out I was pregnant. Was scared for a while. Then, at the twelve-week scan they told me I was carrying twins and I convinced myself it was karma. Daniel had to be the father because twins run in his family.'

'But you always wondered.'

Marie bowed her head and gave a nod.

'Why didn't you say anything when Alicia was taken?'

'Because it wouldn't have changed anything. All it would have done is cause upset and hurt to everyone.'

'I'm going to need to take a statement,' the detective said. She opened her iPad, tapped a key.

Fear pinched at Marie. After all this time... 'Do we need to do that? I mean, can't we keep this to ourselves?'

'I'm obliged to feed it back,' Beth said. 'It could have a bearing on the enquiry.'

Marie clutched her throat. 'You're not suggesting Father Bryan came back and killed Alicia? He wouldn't.'

'Fathering a child wouldn't do his career in the church any good,' Beth said. 'We certainly need to speak with him.'

Marie gulped, the air wedging in her windpipe. Of all the things Father Bryan was, she couldn't see him as a potential child murderer. The thought hadn't even entered into her mind. Not now and certainly not when she was taken.

The keys on Beth's laptop clicked as she started to type. She checked back dates and times as they continued.

'Can we keep this confidential?' Marie asked forlornly. 'It's not just me... It would be awful for my family if this came out. And Daniel.'

'I'll see what I can do. We will have to keep it to ourselves for the next couple of days in any case, Daniel is away and uncontactable. I need to ask you to keep the paternal DNA results to yourself too, it's important he hears it from us first.'

'Please.' Her voice was barely a whisper.

'Let me speak with my boss,' Beth said. 'I can't make any promises.'

'I don't want Vic to know.'

'Don't want Vic to know what?'

Marie jumped as the door swung open and Vic entered. He seemed harassed. Zac was beside him.

'Didn't hear you guys come in,' she said to her husband and son, quickly recovering herself. 'You're early.' She stood and enveloped the boy in a hug.

'They let the kids with parents go as soon as the match finished.' Vic's face tightened. 'Don't want Vic to know what?' he repeated.

'Nothing.' She released Zac and forced a weak smile. 'Did you have a good day?' she said to her son.

'We beat Brixworth, 3-0.' Zac's face lit up as he spoke, oblivious to the tightening tension in the room. 'I scored a goal!'

She brushed his fringe back. 'That's brilliant, darling. Well done.'

'Take your bag upstairs, Zac,' Vic said.

He ruffled his son's hair as he passed and waited until he disappeared before he spoke again. 'You look awful,' he said to Marie. 'Has something happened?'

'I need to go,' Beth said. 'Call me if you need anything.'

The sound of the front door closing reverberated through the house.

Vic rounded on Marie. 'Don't want Vic to know what?'

Marie recoiled. She couldn't tell him now. She didn't have the strength. 'We'll discuss it later.'

'I don't see why—'

'When Zac's in bed. Did they say anything at the school when you picked him up?'

Vic shifted uncomfortably. 'No. His friend wasn't at school today. Miss Marsh said his mother was keeping him at home in case there was any sign of concussion. Just a precaution. Zac seemed fine. Played his socks off at the match.'

Feet thumped the stairs and Zac appeared in the front room. Marie smiled at him. 'We've got syrup cake for pudding tonight. Your favourite.'

38

'She's alleging rape,' Nick said. The three of them were in Freeman's office. Nick leaning up against the radiator, arms folded across his chest. Beth sitting on a chair opposite Freeman.

Beth nodded.

'Okay,' Freeman said. 'I take it you've got the bishop's latest address?'

Beth had done her homework and phoned through for Pete to complete the checks on her drive back to the station. 'Yes. He lives across the border in Leicestershire.'

'And there's no intelligence on him, no security markers?'

Markers indicated associations or a propensity to hold firearms or weapons. A little unlikely with a priest, but it was always worth checking. 'He's clear.'

'What about on the original investigation?'

'His name doesn't crop up. I guess if Marie was no longer going to church or in touch with him, and they didn't know about the alleged attack, he wouldn't have been a person of interest.'

Father – now Bishop – Bryan, was a prominent member of the church, someone with a reputation to uphold. They needed to address the rape allegation and couldn't ignore the fact that if he'd discovered she was pregnant and suspected the child may be his, he had a lot to lose, perhaps enough to drive him to commit abduction and murder. It was the closest they'd come to a viable motive yet and the excitement in the office was palpable.

'Right. Go and visit him together. Let's see what he's got to say for himself.'

Beth nodded. 'Have you managed to get hold of Daniel Owen yet?' she asked. Now that the DNA results were back the need to speak with him, to update him before he discovered the news elsewhere weighed heavily.

'I've left two voicemails. He hasn't come back to me.'

'Right.' Daniel's unavailability made her nervous. 'Marie has agreed to keep the test results to herself for the moment.'

'Okay, I'll keep trying.'

Beth braked at the lights. Bishop Bryan lived in Market Harborough, a small market town just across the border in neighbouring Leicestershire, almost an hour's drive from headquarters. Shops, coffee houses and quaint old buildings lined the streets of the town centre. They passed a gothic sandstone church, its steeple reaching up to the sky.

Nick had drifted off to sleep beside her, the long days on the investigation taking its toll.

It was almost 4 p.m. Daniel Owen hadn't returned their calls and his lack of contact continued to bother her. He said he switched off his phone on long hauls. Surely, he had to check in occasionally with his boss. An idea struck her. She selected a number on her car phone and placed her microphone on her ear. DC Pete Wilson answered on the second ring, his dulcet tone filling the car.

'How're you doing, Beth?'

'Good, thanks. We're five minutes away from Bishop Bryan's house. Can you do me a favour? Can you check with the haulage company Daniel Owen works for and find out if he's made his drop, or if there's a collection he still needs to make? Perhaps one of the depos can give him a message to call us urgently.' She paused. Freeman had made it clear he was to deal with Daniel direct. She didn't want to step on his toes. 'Let the DCI know what you find, will you?'

The lights changed and Beth continued up the road.

'Sure. I'll get onto it now. What about his sister?'

'I've tried her. She said he hasn't been in touch and she'll pass on the message if he calls.'

Nick stirred. He sat forward, rubbed the back of his neck. 'Who's that?'

'Pete,' she mouthed back.

'There's something else,' Pete said. 'I've been doing some digging—'

'Hold on.' Beth clicked the control panel and slipped off her earpiece. 'You're on speaker.'

'There's still nothing back on Scott Owen,' Pete said. 'I've looked into the McNamara brothers' operation. They ran the local clubs, controlled the doors on Barton's Snooker Hall and Ruby's Casino in town until they were killed in that car accident in 2008.

'Intelligence suggests they were the biggest gang leaders during the early noughties with links to drugs, prostitution, money laundering. Their names even came up in connection with a human trafficking ring that broke in 2005, but they were far too removed to be caught near any of it.'

'Who took over after they were killed?' Nick asked.

'Nigel Sherwood.'

Beth looked at Nick. They'd arrested Sherwood earlier in the year for assault and money laundering; he was currently on remand, awaiting trial. She recalled his belligerence at the time of the arrest, his 'no comment' interviews. If he took over from the McNamara brothers, it was likely he'd worked for them for some years and moved up the chain of command. If Scott Owen was associated with them, he'd be well versed to advise, although he wouldn't speak with them. Reams of intelligence indicated he was still pulling the strings, managing the gang from the inside.

'Some of the senior boys in Sherwood's circle might know about Scott's relationship with them,' Beth said.

'If they do, they're not talking. We sent the source handlers out to speak with their intelligence contacts in the field. Everyone's shut down, spooked by Sherwood's recent arrest.'

Nick rolled his eyes. 'That's all we need.'

Beth gripped the steering wheel tight for a completely different reason. Rumour had it, a local heavy named Kev Richardson had stepped into Sherwood's shoes after his arrest. And his sidekick was Kyle Thompson, her sister's recent love interest.

Even though Kyle would have been in his early teens when Alicia disappeared and was unlikely to be involved, the connection was too close for comfort. She'd already been taken off one case and subjected to an internal investigation because of her sister's association with him. His arrogance at Eden's the other night, his smarmy smile still riled her. She reminded herself to call DS Osborne when she was back in the office and chase the financial investigation.

'I have found one person of interest,' Pete said, jolting Beth back to the present case. 'Jimmy Carvel. He was one of their henchmen, enforcing their debts in the early noughties, around the time Scott disappeared. Might be of interest if we can get him to talk. He's stewing in Bedford Prison now, was put away for GBH in 2006 – apparently he set about a man with a baseball bat and cracked his skull.'

Nick snorted. 'Nice.'

'That's not all. Two years after his conviction he threw boiling water in an inmate's face in prison and picked up another six years. He's got a string of convictions on file for affray, manslaughter, aggravated burglary.'

'When can we see him?' Beth asked. Tracing Scott didn't seem such high priority with the new information about Bishop Bryan – it wasn't a crime for an adult to disappear without trace – but, still, there was always a chance the bishop was innocent, and it was a lead that needed bottoming out.

'I've organised prison passes for you both to Bedford Prison tomorrow. There's something else you should know.' He cleared his throat. 'You'll be seeing him in the hospital wing. He's got lung cancer, only a few weeks left.'

39

Beth steered onto the gravel driveway of an attractive Georgian house, with a square frontage, set among manicured gardens. Fingers of ivy climbed around the large sash windows. She parked beside a shiny black Audi A6.

'Looks like our Bishop is doing alright for himself,' Nick said as they climbed out of the car.

The door was answered by a small woman dressed in a pale-pink jumper, and navy trousers. Short grey hair was styled away from her face in soft waves.

Beth held up her badge and introduced them both. 'Is Bishop Bryan home?' she asked.

'Yes, but I'm afraid he's with someone.' She spoke slowly, carefully crafting each word, as if a boiled sweet was lodged in the side of her mouth.

'And you are?'

'Emily Peters. I'm his help.'

'Fine. We can wait,' Beth said stepping forward. They hadn't phoned ahead. The last thing they wanted was to warn the bishop of their visit and give him time to concoct a story. Plus, she wanted to watch his body language unfold as she delivered the news. There was often a lot more given away in the non-verbal communication.

The entrance lobby was an old-fashioned affair with black and white tiled flooring, a coat stand to their right. An oak staircase rose up from the centre, sweeping to a landing on the first floor. Around the edge of the lobby, doors leading to different rooms were closed.

Beth and Nick shrugged off their coats and Emily led them into a large room at the back of the property, with patio doors overlooking a long lawned garden. In the centre of the room, two leather sofas faced each other beside the fireplace, a colourful Persian rug covering the parquet floor between them.

Emily indicated for them to sit and clasped her hands together. 'Can I get you some tea?' She was clearly accustomed to greeting the bishop's visitors.

'Tea would be lovely, thank you,' Nick said.

'Could you let the bishop know we're here please?' Beth said. She watched the woman leave the room and raised a brow at Nick.

'I'm gasping,' he said, grinning. He sat back into the sofa. 'This is plush.'

The room was large, light and airy. A wall to ceiling bookcase covered the far wall, filled with faded hardbacks that looked ancient. A painting of the Virgin Mary surveyed them from its position above the open fireplace. A corner dresser caught Beth's eye. It was packed with bottles of wine and spirits. Her eyes lingered on an unopened bottle of white Chardonnay and she was reminded of Marie Russell's admission.

The door juddered open. Emily re-entered with a circular silver tray mounted with floral cups and saucers, complete with matching teapot and milk jug. It reminded Beth of a tea set displayed in a glass cabinet in her godmother's house when she was young. Her 'wedding set' she called it. Only used for 'particular guests'. They must have been very particular because Beth never saw the set outside the cabinet.

'Bishop won't keep you long,' Emily said as she set down the tray and left the room.

Nick sat forward and poured the tea and the milk, stirring it with a tiny silver spoon that chinked against the china, before passing it across to Beth and pouring himself another. Beth smiled to herself at the delicacy he lent to the task. If he made a cuppa at home it was usually strong tea in oversized mugs, it amused her to watch him take such care. The drink slipped down easily. Beth was about to ask for another when she heard voices in the hallway. Seconds later, a face appeared around the door.

Bishop Bryan was a tall man, with a thick head of grey hair and a Richard Gere type handsome face that seemed a lot younger than his sixty years. The dark shirt and trousers he wore, flattered his slender frame. His white clerical collar accentuated his naturally olive skin.

'I'm so sorry to keep you waiting,' he said, taking time to greet them individually with a warm smile and a handshake. Marie Russell had mentioned his charisma and Beth couldn't help but agree. He'd been in the room less than a minute, yet he oozed natural, easy charm.

'What can I do for you?' he said, settling into the sofa opposite.

Beth took a breath. This was an historic allegation. They had no evidence and no witnesses, bar Marie's account. She needed to word it carefully to gauge his reaction. 'Do you keep a diary?' she asked.

He looked taken aback. 'Yes, of course. I couldn't manage my day, let alone my working week without one. It's on my computer.' He flashed another dazzling smile. No questions. No probing.

'We need to ask you some questions about an incident that occurred sixteen years ago. Would you still have a diary for that time?'

'I don't understand.'

'Perhaps I should re-phrase the question. Can you tell me where you were on the 12th of September 2001?'

'I'm afraid my memory isn't that good. I'd need to look in the diary archives. I'm not sure if we go that far back, mind you. Why do you need to know?'

Beth ignored his answer. 'Do you, or did you, know a Marie Owen?'

He paused a moment, his forehead furrowing. 'Marie? Ah, yes. She was Annie McPherson's granddaughter. Annie was one of my parishioners.' A brief smile. 'Lovely lady.'

'Did you visit Marie during the month of September 2001?'

'I'll need to check. I think that's the year Annie died. If so, then, yes.'

'Were you alone when you visited?'

'I believe sometimes we were alone. Her husband wasn't religious.'

'Can you explain to me what your relationship with Marie Owen was?'

'I was her priest. I visited her after her grandmother died, helped her to make the funeral arrangements and counselled her in her time of grief. Same as I would for any of my parishioners.' His expression was relaxed, open. No tics or awkwardness. Not an ounce of guilt.

'Did you have sex with Marie Owen?'

'What?' For the shortest of seconds his mouth gaped, incredulous. He quickly recovered. 'This is preposterous.' The word was tough but spoken calmly. 'Who said that? Marie?'

'If you could answer the question please.'

'No, I did not have sex with Marie or anyone else.' He was careful to keep his voice calm, even. His face slackened. 'Detective, women sometimes form bonds with priests and manufacture things in their mind. They're only human, after all.'

The gentleness of his voice, so practised, so controlled, rankled her. She flicked her gaze to the drinks cabinet, the bottle of Chardonnay. 'Marie Owen was a married woman.'

'I'm aware of that.'

'I need to ask you to supply a DNA sample.'

'You're not serious?'

Beth raised a brow. 'I have the pack here. It won't take a minute. Do you consent?'

'No, I don't consent. And I really can't see why you would ask me to.'

The measure of his tone was starting to grate. He must have heard about the discovery of the child's body, the speculation about it being Alicia Owen. It was all over the news. Found in the neighbouring county of Northamptonshire, a child of one of his own parishioners when she disappeared. If Marie Russell was telling the truth, there could only be one reason why he'd refuse to offer a DNA sample.

Beth stood. 'Bishop Bryan O'Connor, I'm arresting you on suspicion of rape.'

40

The interview room light glistened on Bishop Bryan's forehead. Gone was the smiley face that welcomed them at his home earlier, the shiny eyes, the warm tone in his voice. It had taken almost an hour to transport him back to the custody block and take the prints and DNA samples – a mandatory process now that he'd been arrested. They then had to wait for his solicitor to arrive and, while still outwardly composed, it was obvious from his icy glare that resentment at how he was being treated now simmered beneath the surface.

It was nearly 6.15 p.m. They were three quarters of an hour into the interview with Beth leading the questioning, Pete beside her. Nick and Freeman were in the room next door, watching remotely. He'd confirmed he was at Marie Owen's home in Gorse Close on the evening in question. He'd admitted they were alone. Nothing untoward there, he'd visited most Wednesdays during the months after Marie's gran's death. Not unexpectedly, he'd denied the rape allegation. But there was something about his demeanour that put her on edge. Why had he refused to give a DNA sample at the house? She couldn't help wondering if the shame of fathering Alicia, the potential damage to his career, presented him with a motive for her murder.

It was also possible someone else knew about Bishop Bryan and Marie, and they'd done the maths and made the connection with Alicia's birth. If so, it gave them cause to blackmail him.

'How well do you know the Owens?' she asked.

'I met Daniel a few times at their house. Can't say I know the others.'

Beth narrowed her eyes. 'What about Scott?'

'The younger brother? I don't think I met him.'

'Bishop Bryan, can you tell me where you were on the 13th of August 2002.'

His solicitor lurched forward. 'What is this? My client's been arrested for an alleged incident in September 2001.'

Beth ignored him, watching recognition dawn on the priest's face. He'd done the maths too. Knew the police had re-ignited the investigation into Alicia's disappearance. Guessed they'd requested his DNA to check with hers.

The solicitor tapped his pen on the table to get Beth's attention. 'Detective, will you—'

The bishop placed a hand on his solicitor's arm, silencing him. 'You're talking about the day Alicia Owen disappeared,' he said softly.

'You remember,' Beth said.

'Who doesn't? Most folk who lived in Kingsthorpe, or the whole of Northamptonshire at the time for that matter, know the date. Not to mention, it's all over the news now, with the discovery of a child's body.' He closed his eyes briefly, shook his head. 'Dreadful affair.'

Beth watched him carefully. They still hadn't released the child's identity to the press, although there'd been enough talk about the possibility of it being Alicia these past few days. 'You were based in Kingsthorpe when she disappeared, were you not?'

'I was.'

'And?'

'I'm sorry?'

Beth resisted the temptation to tut. Was he being deliberately obtuse? 'Where were you on the 13th of August 2002?'

'Oh, that's easy. I don't even need to check my diary. I go away for the middle two weeks of every August. To Caldey Island, off the Pembrokeshire Coast. It's a regular retreat. Have done for the last twenty years. There'll be records, even after all this time, I'm sure.'

The room fell quiet. Beth listened to Pete's pen scratching the pad beside her as he made his notes.

'Did you drink any alcohol with Marie Russell on the 12th of September 2001?' she asked eventually.

If he was taken aback that she'd returned to the rape allegation, it didn't show. 'Quite possibly. I'm afraid I can't remember.'

'Possibly,' she repeated. 'Can you remember what you drank?'

'No. But it isn't a crime to drink a glass of wine.'

Beth ignored his statement. 'A glass of wine. Like Chardonnay. That's your tipple of choice, isn't it?'

A light flashed behind his eyes. 'You've been in my sitting room, Detective, and seen my drinks cabinet. You'll know I keep Chardonnay.'

'Did you drink more than you intended on that evening?'

'No. I would have driven home. I'm sure I'd only have one glass.'

'Bishop, I repeat, did you have sex with Marie Russell?'

'And I repeat, I did not.'

Beth hooked his gaze, holding it for several seconds. The rape allegation was his word against Marie's. He would be aware of that, and with a historical allegation they had no evidence to put to the bishop. No witnesses. He also knew they'd be checking his DNA against Alicia Owen's. Was he hedging his bets, hoping Marie had slept around, that perhaps there was a chance there wouldn't be a match? He certainly seemed confident, self-assured.

'Okay, interview terminated—' she checked her watch '—at 6.26 p.m. She slid back her chair. 'Bishop, we'll need a note of all your associations at the time. You'll then be released tonight pending further enquiries.'

He said nothing.

It tormented her to let him go, but she had no valid reason to keep him. For now. 'I need to remind you to stay away from Marie Russell,' she added. 'You are not to contact her, telephone her or visit her while the investigation is ongoing. Is that understood?'

Suddenly, Beth sensed a change. The bishop's face hardened. He stood, lifting his chest, flexing his hands. Eyes like bullets. Being told what to do, wasn't something he took kindly to.

Beth stilled, chin high, waiting for the explosion. Instead, he braced his hands against the desk and stayed quiet. Controlled to the end.

Beth yawned and checked the time in the corner of her computer screen. Almost 7.30 p.m.

The bishop had given them an alibi for the period encompassing Alicia's disappearance and a quick phone call to the retreat confirmed he was booked in there for the dates given. It didn't necessarily mean he wasn't involved, but it meant he wasn't personally responsible for taking her. Bishop Bryan had a clean record, they were no other allegations on file. They could only hold him in custody for twenty-four hours, and only then if they were carrying out relevant inquiries, and here there was nothing imminent. All they had was Marie's account which he refuted.

If he'd fathered Alicia and worked through the dates, it might suit him to put her out of the way.

But Marie and Daniel had played happy families, and they clearly believed they were the child's parents. The question of paternity had never been raised. They were going to have to dig a lot deeper into his background, his associations at the time, to find any potential evidence of guilt. They'd sent a team to search his house and seize his devices, belt and braces really, she didn't expect to find much. People changed their computers every few years, phones more regularly. The chances of finding anything relating to Alicia or Marie after all this time were slim. Their best bet was to check his bank accounts for the period, to see if there were any improprieties that might suggest blackmail, which would take time, and with nothing else improper on his file, they had to let him go.

But Beth wasn't about to let him waltz back into his old

life without alerting the right people. If he was guilty, others might be at risk. And if he was Alicia's father, Bishop Bryan had broken his vows and lied.

As soon as they'd finished interviewing, Nick spoke with the bishop's cardinal, making the church aware that an allegation had been made, and requested Bishop Bryan was either chaperoned or removed from frontline duties while under investigation.

He also requested details of his postings since he'd joined the priesthood in his early twenties and sat with Freeman to establish a strategy forward. Their team would look into the priest's associations around the time Alicia disappeared, check his bank accounts and ensure he wasn't being blackmailed and there wasn't an impropriety that put him in the frame for Alicia's murder. Investigating him – talking to the people he'd come into contact with, checking his conduct during his career to make sure other women weren't attacked – was a larger and more time-consuming task. Too big for a homicide team with a case on; their focus remained on whether he'd fathered Alicia. Freeman was now liaising with colleagues to set up a sub team to look into the priest's background.

Beth finished her report and shut down her laptop. Tomorrow she'd phone Marie Russell and update her.

41

Marie Russell took her time to feed her son and put him to bed that evening. She wanted to make sure he was okay after the altercation at school yesterday, though she needn't have worried. He might be mild-mannered, but he showed a remarkable resilience for one so young. But there was another reason for drawing out Zac's bedtime routine, giving him a long bath and reading him an extra bedtime story. It bought her time, giving her longer to work out what the hell she was going to say to Vic.

Should she tell him about Father Bryan? The detective said not, although Marie couldn't see a way of avoiding it. He was her husband. If it came out later and he didn't know, he'd never forgive her. He was also Daniel's best friend. He'd adored Alicia, was there for them both when she went missing. All those late nights consoling her. The visits he'd made after the separation. The unyielding support. And all the time, Alicia belonged to another man.

She'd trusted Father Bryan implicitly and he'd abused her trust. Rape. The word made her shiver. It sounded so horrid, so heinous. And it was horrid... Daniel's old remarks floated into her head. Bishop Bryan was charming. She'd been flattered by his interest, grateful for his support.

Had she flirted with the priest? If Daniel thought so, maybe others did too. They'd certainly spent a lot of time together after her gran died.

She finished the book and looked across at her son. His eyes were closed, his head gently resting to the side. Her gut knotted as she tucked the duvet around him and turned off the light. They'd all grown up together: Daniel, Vic, Cara and Scottie. Gone through the same schools. Vic had rescued her after Alicia's disappearance, given her support and friendship when she needed it most. Taught her how to love again. He believed she'd only ever had one partner other than him, her childhood sweetheart. How the hell could she shatter his illusions of her now?

By the time she'd descended the stairs, Vic was draining a pan of pasta over the sink. The soft under-cupboard lighting created a dull hue in the room. A candle burned on the table. The curtains were undrawn, darkness peering in from outside. It was a family scene, a couple having their dinner together after they'd put their young son to bed. The knot in her gut tightened.

The minute she entered the kitchen, he cast the pan aside and encased her in a hug. He pulled back, cupped her chin in his hand, kissed the end of her nose. The tenderness of the gesture brought a tear to her eye.

'It's going to be okay,' he said, his eyes searching hers. 'I know you've had a tough day. We will get through this. Together.'

The knot tightened again, this time suffocating her breaths.

He made to guide her to a chair, but she freed herself up, waved him away. His attentiveness, his care was too much.

She didn't deserve it. For years, she'd kept a secret from him, buried it deep. It wasn't fair.

She pulled out a chair and watched him mix the drained pasta with vegetables in a pan, add sauce and slowly stir, every minute or so eyes flitting to her, checking she was okay. It was heart-wrenching.

When he finally served up the food and sat opposite, acid swirled in her mouth. The last thing she wanted was to eat anything right now.

'You seemed tense when the detective was here earlier,' he said.

Marie picked up her fork and pushed the food around her plate. 'They've confirmed the DNA match. It is Alicia's body.'

'I'm so sorry, love.' He dropped his fork, reached across and took her free hand, weaving his fingers into hers. A comforting gesture he'd adopted a million times over the years. A tear splashed into her pasta.

She looked up and through her bleary eyes she suddenly saw the young boy in him again. The lanky teenager with the cow's lick framing his face. Daniel's quiet mate who always hung behind, one of the wallflowers of their friendship group. Everyone liked Vic, though few people got more than a few words out of him, apart from Daniel. Not bad-looking either when he filled out in his early twenties. Daniel had the charm and the lip, and Vic was the silent one, always in his shadow. Rarely with a girl in tow and when he did have a girlfriend it was always a passing fling, over in a few weeks. Never a long-term relationship.

It wasn't until after Alicia's disappearance, after her separation with Daniel, that she'd broken beneath the surface with Vic and realised what a thoughtful man he'd become, and how deep and interesting he was. She had no idea he painted watercolours, or was learning to play the saxophone, or, like her, read Jeffery Deaver novels.

It seemed the more they talked, the more they had to talk about, flitting from one subject to another, often changing mid-sentence. Vic seemed more relaxed when it was just the two of them and opened up. They chatted and chatted, as if time was coming to an end and they'd never have the chance to discuss everything.

After she'd agreed to marry him, he owned up to having harboured a crush on her since her early teens. She'd always been his best mate's girlfriend and for that reason he'd kept his distance. No wonder his other relationships were so short-lived.

'No secrets,' he said on their wedding day. 'That's the key to a successful relationship. We tell each other everything.'

Except she hadn't told him everything…

Losing Liam had changed Daniel. He'd sailed through life until then, getting what he wanted with a wink of those blue eyes, that lopsided smile. The twins' birth and Liam's death morphed him from a laid-back twenty-two-year-old to a ready-made adult, bearing the stresses and strains of the world. And if Liam's death cast a cloud over them, losing Alicia only served to thicken it, immersing them in a fog of sorrow until they couldn't see anything before them. Gone was the perennial twinkle in Daniel's eye, the forever optimism. Replaced with sunken cheeks and the greying pallor of worry.

There were few who could have coped with the inevitabilities of losing their best friend and half their friendship group by declaring their love publicly. Vic had put everything on the line for her and they'd been as close to happy as Marie could have hoped for. Until now.

'What can I do to help?' he asked.

Marie pulled her hand away. 'There's something I need to tell you,' she said. 'And I want you to know how sorry I am, and to know I really had no idea.' Her words became muffled by the sobs that followed. She covered her face with her hands.

A chair scraped the floor. And he was there, at her side, stretching his strong arms around her. The action, touching as it was, made her feel even more wretched. She dug her head in his shoulder, took a deep gulp and eased her breaths.

Vic filled a glass with water and handed it to her. Their carefully prepared dinners sat on the table untouched.

'I need to tell you,' Marie said. 'and ask you not to judge, to bear in mind how young we all were.'

His face contorted. 'I don't understand what you are saying.'

She met his gaze. His eyes wide like pools. Suddenly, she realised she couldn't do it. *Not here, not now.*

'I'm so sorry for everything that's happened, everything I've put you through.' Her chest heaved and she sobbed again.

'Are you okay?' Vic asked. 'I mean, I know you're not okay, but can I do anything to help?' Half an hour had passed. Half an hour in which they'd eaten their food in relative silence and moved into the front room. Vic had switched on the television. A comedy panel show filled the screen, although neither of them were watching it. 'I know this is hard. You can talk to me, you know?'

The elephant in the room was so large it was suffocating. Marie turned to him. 'The DNA test showed Daniel wasn't Alicia's father.' There, it was out there. She'd said it.

'What?' He jolted back, surveying her from afar. 'Are you saying what I think you are saying?'

Marie cleared her throat. She wasn't sure how to craft the words. 'Daniel isn't her father she repeated. There was someone else.'

'And you only thought to tell me this now?'

'I didn't want to upset anyone.'

'Marie!' His voice hiked up a notch. 'You've had the police running around in circles, brought heartbreak to a family, broken a man who grieved for a son who wasn't his and believed his daughter had been kidnapped... and you never told anyone. How could you?'

'Vic, listen. We can't tell anyone. The police have to—'

Well, that won't be difficult for you, will it?'

'Please! Let me explain?'

'Explain? You've had fifteen years to explain. All those long discussions, those intimate moments. You cheated on your husband and let us all suffer. How could you?'

'Vic, please.'

'No. This time it isn't about you, Marie. This is too much, too heavy for me to process.' He stood.

'Don't.'

He paused for the shortest of seconds. 'I don't believe it. I mean, if you can lie about this...'

'It's not what you think.'

'How do I know when you're being honest? I mean, what

other lies have you told me?' He held up his hand, moved towards the door. 'I need some time out.'

She knew she had to tell him the truth. But the truth was so horrific, she grappled for the right words. She followed him into the hallway, opening and closing her mouth, rooted to the spot as he stalked out of the front door.

42

Marie slumped in the kitchen chair and hung her head. She'd wanted to tell Vic about the priest so many times, but there was always a niggling voice buried deep preventing her. What if he didn't believe her? What if he thought she'd brought it on herself? Fifteen years ago, everyone knew Father Bryan. He was an upstanding individual, well respected; his face occasionally gracing the pages of the local newspaper for the charity fundraising he did in the community.

And then there was the problem with Alicia. What if Vic had put two and two together and questioned her paternity back then? He was her one constant. Daniel and he were best friends at school. He'd given up his closest mate to be with her. How would he feel if he knew she'd lied about something so fundamental?

And she had lied.

Tears burned her eyes. Father Bryan had been all smiles and attentiveness. Attentiveness she'd mistaken for care. She shuddered, thinking of his condolence card with the teddy bear sleeping on the front. The card she'd found in Alicia's memory box. The card he'd delivered after Liam had died.

An icy shiver slipped down her back. Father Bryan was

now a bishop, rising high in the senior echelons of the Catholic Church. On the rare occasions he came back to Kingsthorpe, he was treated like royalty. Nobody would believe he would attack anyone.

She'd told no one at the time. Stood under the shower until her back ached and her legs were raw. Kept the secret. It was his word against hers. Convinced herself that Daniel was the twins' father. Of course he was. Twins ran in his family. Yet many a time, she'd wondered, worried, pondered about whether to share the burden. What if he forced himself on someone else? But she'd kept it under wraps, unable to deal with the fallout and the shame.

She switched back to that fateful evening. Sitting at either end of the sofa; her squished into the corner with her feet tucked beneath her. White wine sloshing in their glasses as they chatted. The low clouds outside heralding an early dusk. She'd switched on her grandmother's corner lamp to brighten the room, the shadows creating a silhouette of him on the wall behind as he lifted his glass. Their usual Wednesday evening chat.

He'd caught her completely off guard. One minute, she was asking him to leave. The next he'd placed his glass down and was there, on top of her. She remembered the confusion, the panic; his weight bearing down. Pleading with him to stop. He'd seemed in a trance, oblivious to her calls. When she'd screamed, he'd pushed her face to the side, a hefty hand pressed against her cheek, holding it there. Frozen in a paralysis of fear. Pain tearing through her.

Just when she thought she could no longer bear the pain, he climbed off. She didn't notice him pulling up his trousers. All she could recall was the rip of the metal as he zipped up.

And she'd laid there, not daring to move. Her pants around her ankles. It was as much as she could do to wriggle down her skirt.

The sofa had shifted as he'd moved back to his seat and ran a hand through his hair. 'Now Marie,' he'd said in the calmest voice. 'I think we both know that shouldn't have happened. I'm not sure what God's plan is, but I expect to see you at confession. This is between you, me and God. He will be our judge. It won't help the situation to involve anyone else. We need to deal with this properly. Like adults.'

With that, he'd rearranged his clothing and she'd wriggled back, her breaths hitching, not daring to speak. 'Think on what I said now, Marie. This is between you, me and God.'

She didn't remember him leaving. Didn't even recall the front door close as he let himself out. Stayed hunched on the sofa, listening to the sound of his car engine disappear into the distance. Knees pressed to her chest. Feeling wretched. Violated. Desperately trying to make sense of what had happened. Daniel was her first boyfriend; the only man she'd ever slept with. They'd been together since she was fourteen. Had she encouraged Father Bryan without realising?

Deep down she knew it was wrong. He'd broken his vows and taken advantage of a young woman he was counselling. A woman who'd recently lost the only family she had close by. She should call the police, report him. He might do this to someone else. But so many things had stopped her. Would people blame her for leading him on? And his words, 'God's plan'. What did that mean?

She thought about the days and weeks afterwards. Of walking around in a stupor. Daniel didn't question the change in her mood, putting it down to her continuing grief over losing her gran. He liked the way she stuck to him like glue, going along to his football matches, watching him at practice, because she didn't want to be in the house alone.

Then the pregnancy... She knew she was pregnant, even before she saw the blue line in the window of the pregnancy test. She'd noticed the changes in her body. The nausea, the fatigue. And the inevitable question reared its ugly head. All those weeks panicking, worrying, standing beside a beaming Daniel while he told everyone their news. Marie swiped another tear from her eye. The relief at finding she was carrying twins, convincing herself they were Daniel's.

Did the police really think Father Bryan might be responsible for Alicia's death? Surely not. Although, he'd already broken his vows and found a way to justify a rape. A shiver rushed through her. She'd kept the rape a secret afterwards, turned her back on the church. Continued to keep the secret throughout the pregnancy and after the birth. So that when Alicia disappeared it was so dark, so dirty that she couldn't bring herself to tell anyone. She'd persuaded herself she was doing the right thing; Father Bryan couldn't have been involved in Alicia's abduction, all she'd do was pour more anguish on an already brimming pile for the family. But now... now that everything was out there, she was beginning to wonder at the ramifications of her decision. At the people she'd let down.

A car engine sounded outside. Vic. Marie jumped up, rushed to the front room window, peered around the curtain's edge. And watched her neighbour opposite climb out of their car. Her heart deflated. She stepped away from the window, lowered herself into the armchair. The sound of Zac's breaths brought her back to the present, to reality.

The attack wasn't her fault. She'd been raped.

She needed to find a way to tell Vic, to explain, and soon. She couldn't bear to lose him too.

43

Beth was awoken by the sound of a mobile phone ringing. Darkness filled her bedroom.

Nick stirred beside her. 'Yours or mine?' he mumbled.

'I think it's mine.' She reached out and patted the bedside table until she found it, blinking at the brightness of the screen as she swiped to answer.

'Hello!'

'Beth, I'm sorry to bother you so early.'

The urgency in the voice at the other end of the line made her sit upright. 'Who is this?'

'I'm sorry, it's Marie Russell. I didn't know who else to call.'

A fleeting glance at the clock. 6.28 a.m. 'Has something happened?' Beth asked, her voice full of sleep.

'It's Vic. We had a… disagreement last night. He stormed out. Didn't come home. I've tried his mobile and it goes to voicemail. I don't where he is.'

'What kind of disagreement?'

'That's what I need to speak to you about. Can you come over?'

Beth rubbed her forehead. 'Okay, I'll be there in half an hour.'

★

Redland Drive was quiet when Beth arrived. Apart from a dull light in the Russells' window, the neighbouring houses were immersed in darkness, curtains tightly drawn, residents inside enjoying the final minutes of night before their day began.

Marie was at the door before Beth exited the car. Limp hair hanging loose around a sallow and drawn face.

'What happened?' Beth asked in a low voice, stepping inside.

'It's complicated.' She motioned for Beth to follow her into the kitchen and closed the door behind them.

Beth pictured Vic, the attentive husband. It seemed odd for him to go AWOL at such a crucial time for Marie. Unless there was more to it... 'Is your son with him?' she asked.

'No. Zac's asleep upstairs. Vic didn't leave until after he'd gone to bed.'

'Where was he going?'

'I don't know.'

'You don't know?'

'He didn't say.'

'Has he ever stayed out before?'

'No. Never.'

'What exactly happened, Marie? You said you had a disagreement.'

Marie's face fell. She indicated for Beth to sit, pulled out a chair for herself and explained her conversation with Vic, the evening before. When she got to the part about Vic's anger over Alicia's paternity Beth held her breath. They still hadn't been able to speak with Daniel and he wasn't due back until lunchtime. She thought of the cherished photos on his mantelpiece, the determination in his face, the refusal to accept the suggestion this body might be Alicia. The thread of hope in his eyes that they might have found another child and his daughter might still return one day. Problem was, she wasn't his daughter and the last thing Beth needed was for Vic to spill the beans and word get out before the police were able to alert him themselves and check he was safe.

'I presume Vic knows to keep this to himself?'

'I did tell him, but—'

'What?'

'He was angry. I'm not sure it went in.'

The air in the room thickened.

'Why didn't you tell him you were attacked?' Beth asked.

Marie looked down and touched her wedding ring. 'I don't know. I wanted to. I tried to. I just couldn't find the words. It was difficult enough having to admit it to you yesterday.' She lifted her gaze, nervously twirling her wedding ring between her thumb and forefinger. 'Did you speak with Father Bryan?'

'Yes. He came to the station and gave a DNA sample.'

'What did he say?'

It wasn't usual practice to share information about an interview unless it benefited the case. She did need to update Marie though. 'He denied the rape. He was away on a retreat in Wales when Alicia was taken. We've released him pending further inquiries.'

Marie blanched. She twisted the ring faster. It was a moment before she spoke. 'I'm worried about Vic.'

Beth took a breath. Usually a man of Vic's age and

position, staying out all night after an argument with his wife wouldn't be high priority for the police. She wasn't aware of any health issues or history of depression that made him vulnerable. But Beth was curious. If there was something else at play, something Marie wasn't sharing with her, finding Vic might prove the catalyst to uncovering it.

'Okay, think carefully. Where would Vic be likely to go? Does he have any friends nearby he might stay with, or family?'

'His mum and dad passed away some years ago. He has a sister who lives in Newcastle.'

'What about friends?'

'I'm not sure. I didn't want to start calling anyone this early, especially after the news of the last few days.'

'Think carefully.'

'He plays darts once a week but doesn't really socialise with the guys outside their meetings. Vic's more of a family man. He does like a drink though. Usually I go with him if we can get a sitter and drive him home. Is it too early to try the local pubs?'

'Which ones?'

'He plays darts at the Old Five Bells in Kingsthorpe centre and occasionally watches the football down at The Windmill nearby. We generally go out to quieter places together. He likes the country pubs best.'

Beth jotted down his favourites, asked what he was wearing and requested a recent photo. It was almost 7.30 a.m. 'Right,' Beth said. I'll drive around to the pubs nearby and see if I can get any response. You ring Vic's sister and his friends to see if anyone has seen or heard from him.' She held up her phone. 'If he gets in touch, call me immediately.'

44

Reporters were starting to gather by the time Beth left the Russells'. They rushed forward, clearly wondering if her early visit heralded news, and called out. Beth ignored their questions, relieved she'd parked on the driveway, and revved her engine, crawling forward for them to part to allow her to pass through. There wasn't much chance of poor Zac sleeping in with that din outside.

Around the corner and suitably out of sight of the press, she pulled over, grabbed her phone and dialled Daniel Owen herself. Sighing when his voicemail clicked in, then tried Nick.

'Everything okay with the family?' Nick said. 'You dashed off quickly this morning.'

'The Russells had an argument last night.' Beth explained Vic's absence. 'Can you get someone to check the ANPR cameras and put a message out to the patrol cars, get them to look out for his Volvo?' she asked. She passed along the number plate. 'How are things there?'

'Just gearing up for briefing. I'll let Freeman know where you are.'

'Okay. I'm going to drive around here and see if I can locate Vic. Could you do me a favour? I'm concerned about

Daniel Owen. We still haven't reached him. Can you check with Pete and maybe try Cara again to see if she's heard from him?'

Beth rang off, continued out of the estate and made a left onto the main road at the bottom, heading for the first pub on her list: The Windmill. It was 7.39 a.m. Kingsthorpe was sleepily coming to life. There were few cars on the road, and she was able to take it slowly, glancing about as she drove. The Windmill was closed, the car park empty.

She turned off into a recreational field nearby called The Pastures. Vic grew up near here. The Pastures would have likely been one of his regular haunts as a kid. The car park was empty and apart from a couple of dog walkers the park appeared clear too. She drove around Acre Lane and up to the shops. A couple of people milled in and out of the supermarket, but there was still no sign of the Vic or his Volvo.

Beth was about to head into the centre of Kingsthorpe, to the Old Five Bells, the next pub on her list, when a comment Marie made, nudged her. *Vic prefers the quiet county pubs.* She made a right at the junction and headed out of town, past a long line of houses until she was surrounded by green fields.

The Windhover was a gastro pub on the very fringe of Kingsthorpe's border with the countryside. Beth steered into another empty car park and climbed out of the car. Maybe the manager was here and would remember if Vic had been in. She was crossing the car park when she caught a movement around the back of the building. She paused. A man was facing the wall, taking a piss.

Beth approached him, more to ask how long he'd been

there and whether he'd seen Vic than to warn him about the laws on public urination, when she noticed his denim jacket, dark jeans, athletic stance. It couldn't be…

'Vic?' she called out.

Vic Russell jumped and hastily zipped up. 'What are you doing here?'

Dark circles hung under his eyes. His usually groomed hair was lank and dishevelled, his clothes creased into deep grooves.

'Looking for you. Marie called me. She was worried.'

He hung his head back, muttered something inaudible under his breath.

'Where's your car?'

'Parked around the back.' His face turned sheepish. 'Didn't want anyone to spot it.'

'You slept here last night?'

'Tried to. It was bloody freezing.'

'Marie's really upset.'

'She ought to be.'

Beth imagined the conversation the night before. Marie telling him the DNA confirmed a match with Alicia. Then sharing that Daniel wasn't her father. He still looked angry, tense.

'She's had a tough time.'

'Haven't we all.'

'I don't think you completely understand, Vic. Let me explain.' He levelled Beth's gaze, almost as if he wasn't sure whether he could trust her. Rain started to fall, spotting Beth's shoulders, sending a shiver down her back. She inwardly cursed herself for not putting on her jacket. 'Why don't we sit in my car a minute?'

Vic stood rooted to the spot for several seconds, surveying her warily. The rain picked up.

'Come on.'

Reluctantly, he followed her.

It was warmer in her Mini and in the confined space the scent of alcohol emanating from Vic was stronger. 'What did Marie tell you about Alicia's father?' Beth asked.

He glanced at her askance. 'What? I know it wasn't Daniel, if that's what you're asking.'

'She didn't give you any more details?'

'No.' He stiffened. 'I'm not interested in the gory details of her love life.'

'Then you won't know, she alleges she was attacked.'

'What? And you believe her?'

'We're investigating it, yes.' Steam crept up the window as she filled him in on the basics of Marie's attack, careful to leave out names. When she finished, nobody spoke for a while.

'She was raped,' Vic said eventually.

Beth nodded. 'That's the allegation she's made.'

'Why didn't she tell anyone at the time? Or at least when Alicia disappeared.'

'People experience a range of emotions after a rape. Sometimes they feel guilty, worry they sent out the wrong signals and blame themselves. Sometimes they can't face reporting it and relaying the whole episode again. Sometimes they put it out of their mind, try to pretend it never happened.'

'She could have told me.'

'I believe she wanted to. Tried to even. But it was something she buried years ago. It's very difficult for her to talk about.'

'What about the father. I mean if he's connected to Alicia—'

Beth raised a flat hand. 'We're looking into it.'

His jaw hung a second. 'She really said she was attacked?'

'She did. And explained the incident in detail.'

'Christ.' He covered his face with his hands. 'Who was it?'

'I'm not at liberty to share that, I'm afraid.'

Raindrops tapped the windscreen, the only sound to break the steely silence in the car. Beth gave him a minute to churn over the revelation. It wasn't easy to hear your partner, the mother of your child had been attacked, even if the incident occurred before they were together. It was a part of her life, a part of her memories, a deeply embedded scar he wasn't aware of.

The issue of Daniel Owen's paternity slipped into Beth's mind. She nodded towards the pub. 'Were you here all night?'

'Yes. I came straight here. Sat at the bar.'

'On your own?'

A single nod. 'There was only one company I was looking for last night.' He swiped a hand down the front of his face, the calluses scratching and scraping against his stubble. 'I've no idea how much I drank. A shot with every pint. One after another.'

'What time did you leave?'

'Don't know. Must have been late. I started walking home, but I could barely see the road and there's no pathway for the first stretch.' He stared ahead, into the mist on the windscreen.

'Was it busy here last night?'

'I couldn't tell you,' he said. 'There were a few cars in the car park when I arrived. No one at the bar inside, I think they must have belonged to diners in the restaurant. Why do you ask?'

'Did you speak with anyone, or see anyone you know?'

'I don't think so.'

'Vic, this is important. We haven't been able to reach Daniel Owen about the issue of Alicia's paternity. Marie was told to keep it to herself. Did you tell anyone?'

He frowned. 'I don't know. I don't think so. But there's so much of the evening I can't remember, I couldn't be sure.'

He wiped the cloth against the window, taking his time to work it into the corners of the glass, to eradicate the smears, before he turned and cast a fleeting glance at the house opposite. A woman stood at the window, anxiously looking out. It was the detective's sister waiting for her daughter to arrive home from music school. He went back to his work, the cloth squeaking as he rubbed it up and down, the glass gleaming back at him. Music school was held at the village school around the corner on a Saturday morning. It finished at 10.30. Lily arrived home at 10.40. She'd left at 8.50 that morning, her rucksack bouncing against her back, waving at her mother until she reached the corner, just as she did during the week.

Another furtive glance. The child was running late.

He could see Eden in the window opposite now, leaning on the ledge, craning her neck to peer further down the street.

He pulled the peak of his baseball cap down, took another

cloth and was running it along the window ledge when he noticed the reflection of a young girl in the glass. Lily was dawdling, humming a jaunty tune to herself, tousled wisps of blonde hair flying around her cheeks, her red coat billowing in the gentle breeze. She liked to sing and dance.

He'd watched her from afar as she'd danced around the room at her birthday party the other night, playing musical chairs with her friends. Her mother, Eden, had her hands full there. But she'd had help that evening – Auntie Beth was on hand to lend her support. Shame she wasn't there more often.

He'd watched Beth leave the Russells' earlier. Striding to her car. So confident, so self-assured, yet she was missing what was under her nose. She had no idea he was close by, watching the case and following her family. Waiting for the right time to strike.

She had no idea her world was about to upend.

He dropped the cloth in the bucket, gathered everything together and made for the car. It was time to make the detective sit up and take notice.

45

'Damn traffic,' Nick said. The road out of Northamptonshire to Bedford Prison was slow moving. Christmas was quickly approaching and shoppers were out in their hordes, visiting festive fayres and picking up last minute presents.

Beth stared out of the side window at the gloomy countryside. The car inched forward and juddered to a stop. Again. 'How long did Jimmy Carvel work for the McNamara brothers?' she asked.

The traffic moved again. Nick paused while he pulled out to overtake a lorry. 'We're not sure exactly,' he said when they were safely back on their side of the road. 'The intelligence archives indicate about seven years, before he was locked up again in 2006. Officially, he was working at Barton's Snooker Hall, though reams of intelligence had him down as one of their senior enforcers.'

'It's a wonder he wasn't picked up earlier.'

'There were several allegations and a couple of arrests for assault. But it was the usual – witnesses withdrew, lack of evidence. He's a nasty piece of work, by all accounts.'

'Does he know we're coming to see him?'

'He's been told. Whether or not he'll speak to us is another matter.'

Beth rested her head back. Even after the McNamara's deaths, the bubble of secrecy around them was tight. It seemed unlikely they'd get anything valid about Scott out of Carvel this afternoon.

Her mind switched back to the Russells earlier. She'd persuaded Vic to leave his car at the pub and collect it later, convinced he'd still be well over the limit to drive, and taken him home. He'd kept his head down when they'd steered through the reporters, moved into the house quickly when she'd parked up.

Marie was standing at the kitchen sink when they entered the house, Zac upstairs.

Vic didn't bother shedding his jacket, his shoes. Instead he strode down the hallway, pulling his wife into his arms, holding her tight for several seconds. Neither of them uttered a word. Eventually, he'd kissed her hair and rested his chin on the top of her head. It was a touching moment and for some reason Beth was reminded of her and Nick. She'd made her excuses soon afterwards and left. They had much to talk about and she had a prison visit to prepare for.

Beth looked across at Nick. He was staring ahead, eyes on the road.

'Any news on the job front?' she asked, forcing a smile. The fact they hadn't spoken about his job search since their discussion outside Freeman's office seemed odd. He'd been in homicide six years and had hinted it was time for a change.

'What?' He glanced fleetingly in her direction, forehead scrunched, as if he'd been deep in thought.

'The National Crime Agency?'

'I told you, I haven't heard anything back. It's probably long gone now.'

'Nothing else?'

'No. Why?'

'I wanted you to know that I'll support you if you want to move from homicide.'

'Anyone would think you were trying to get rid of me.' He passed her a wry smile and indicated to take the next turn.

'Just saying.'

'Well, there's no need now. I mean once you get your promotion and I revert back, we'll be the same rank. They'll be nothing to stop us going public then.'

A car cut in front of them. Nick banged on the horn, swore under his breath and they pulled off towards the dual carriageway. And the moment was gone.

46

Beth's stomach growled as the prison guard searched through his keys for the hospital wing. It had taken over an hour to navigate the traffic to Bedford Prison and pass through security. It was now almost 1 p.m., and having dashed out without breakfast that morning, her body was protesting.

The guard unlocked the door and led them through into a small hospital ward where patients lay in two rows of metal beds, facing each other. Several pairs of eyes followed them as they strode past and entered a private room at the end.

The difference between the image of Jimmy Carvel on their records and the man that lay before them now was striking. Gone was the puffed chest, the thick neck, square head and dark intimidating eyes of the once forty-something henchman. In front of them was a scrawny man, with pasty, paper-like skin and sunken cheeks. The hard man bones of his once thick skull jutted out of his bald head. He had no eyebrows or lashes, a legacy of the chemotherapy she guessed, which only accentuated the dark shadows beneath eyes that seemed to have faded, the colour drained out of them.

He lifted a sinewy arm, made to push himself up the bed, and the tube from the canula at his wrist to the drip beside juddered.

Beth and Nick introduced themselves. 'Thank you for agreeing to see us today,' Nick said. 'How are you feeling?'

Jimmy eyed them suspiciously and said nothing.

'We're investigating the murder of Alicia Owen,' Nick said shuffling into a chair. 'The baby that disappeared in Northampton, fifteen years ago.'

'I know it.' His words were slow, breathless.

'We're trying to locate all the family members still living. Do you know Scott Owen?'

Jimmy gave a single nod.

'Do you have any idea where we might find him?'

'No.' He stared back at them and blinked.

'When was the last time you heard from Scott?'

'Couldn't say.'

Nick exchanged a deflated glance with Beth. Their journey was beginning to feel wasted.

Beth sat forward in her chair. 'Please, Mr Carvel. It's important we trace everyone who had contact with baby Alicia. The family have been through so much.'

A raspy cough. A gaze at the ceiling. 'I had a daughter born the same year as that kid that disappeared.'

'Then you'll appreciate what the family are going through.'

'Hannah, we called her. Lovely little thing, a wisp of a girl.' His eyes were still averted.

'That's nice.'

He met Beth's eyeline. 'Haven't seen her for ten years.'

'I'm sorry. We've recovered Alicia's body,' she said

trying to move the conversation back on track. 'As you can imagine, the family—'

'Maybe we can help each other.'

Beth didn't falter at the interruption. 'I'm not with you.'

He eyed her a moment. 'Can you get a message to my Hannah? Tell her I'm ill. Her mother hasn't brought her to visit me in years. Doesn't even write anymore. I'd like to see her. One last time, you know?'

Beth could feel Nick shuffle uncomfortably beside her. They weren't here to bargain. Although, there was no harm in passing along the message of a dying man to his next of kin. Especially if it encouraged him to open up and talk. 'I can't make any promises,' she said, 'but if you give me the details, I can certainly try to trace her mother and pass along your request.'

His face brightened slightly. He gave her the contact details for the mother and daughter and she jotted them down. 'Now what about Scott Owen?' Beth said.

'Haven't seen him for years.'

'But you did know him?'

He coughed, wiped his mouth with a tissue. 'He was a gambler. Small-time, we all thought. Borrowed money off Sean to feed his habit. I collected from him a few times... roughed him up once when he was short.'

Beth could only begin to imagine how he'd 'roughed him up'. 'Are you saying he borrowed off Sean McNamara?'

'Yeah.'

'When was this?'

'Must have been... the summer of 2002. I didn't hear the truth of it until afterwards.'

'What do you mean?'

'Scott owed Sean a lot of cash – almost twenty grand. What Sean didn't realise was that he'd borrowed from Richie too.' Another rasp. He cleared his throat.

'The other McNamara brother,' Nick checked.

'Yeah. He played them off against each other.'

'Surely, they knew who their debtors were?'

He lifted a shoulder, let it drop. 'They lent money to a lot of people. Kept their own accounts. Twenty grand wasn't unusual, even in that time.'

'Are you suggesting Scott fled to avoid the debts?' Beth asked.

He ignored her question. 'The brothers were angry. They had a reputation to maintain.'

'I'm not with you.'

'People didn't mess with them, not like this. Scott was different somehow. Nothin' seemed to bother him.'

'What do you mean?'

Another cough. It was several seconds before he continued. 'They had this tactic. If someone failed to pay what they owed, they went after loved ones: partners, siblings, aunties, uncles, friends, even parents. Let's just say, it was effective.'

Nick angled his head. 'Women too?'

Jimmy shrugged.

If this was the case, the individuals affected were unlikely to report the attacks, afraid of repercussions. And witnesses would be frightened about coming forward. Beth narrowed her eyes. 'What about children?'

'Children were supposed to be exempt.' He pushed himself up the bed again, wheezed and took a sip from a water bottle beside him.

'Supposed?'

He looked away, didn't answer.

'What did they do to Scott?' Nick asked.

Carvel shifted uncomfortably. 'Look, I'm no grass but I haven't long to go and, for the record, I didn't agree with them going after folks' nearest and dearest.' He pulled a face. 'Thought they took it too far. Sometimes, the wives, girlfriends, cousins didn't even know their loved ones were in trouble. I wouldn't admit that to the brothers, mind you. Wouldn't dare.'

'Were you involved in executing this?' Nick asked.

'Let's just say, they knew I didn't approve.'

Beth pulled on her knowledge of the Owen family. There were no police reports of violence to family members around the time when Scott went astray. 'Are you saying they abducted Alicia to make a point about Scott's debts?' she asked.

'Not them. They wouldn't get their hands dirty. But someone they hired might. It was no secret that Scott idolised that child. There were rumours... rumours they'd staged her disappearance to flex their muscles, make a point.'

'A baby?' Beth could barely believe her ears.

'Like I said, I can't be sure. They never told me. If they were responsible, they brought help in from elsewhere. But there were whispers they'd taken her to give everyone a fright and meant to give her back. Then with all the fuss it was too risky.'

'Where is Scott now?' Beth asked.

He took a breath. 'You think they'd let him live after all that fuss?' His words cascaded into a flurry of coughing and wheezing.

A nurse put her head around the doorframe, raising a brow. 'Okay, I think that's enough.'

Pete rang as Beth stepped out of the prison entrance. 'Still no news on Daniel Owen,' he said.

'He's not back yet?'

'Hasn't checked his return load in.'

She paused, pressing the phone to her ear. It was now after two. Daniel was due back at lunchtime. 'Lorries don't disappear. Isn't there a tracker on it?'

'Apparently not this one. We're looking out for it on it the ANPR cameras. We'll keep trying.'

Beth thanked him and fed back her meeting with Carvel, along with the request to trace his ex-partner and daughter. Frustration itched at her as she disconnected. 'What do you think?' she asked Nick as they crossed the main road and made their way back to their car. Bedford Prison was located close to the centre of town and with their own car park at capacity, they'd been forced to park in the side streets nearby.

'I don't know. It seems a stretch to abduct a child, a baby at that.'

The supermarket on Link Road skipped into her mind, servicing the local residential estate. 'Might explain why there were so few witnesses. The McNamara brothers were well known.'

'Their death in 2008 was well publicised. If there were witnesses, they could have come forward afterwards.'

'Maybe. Although members of their inner circle are still around, keeping the gang going, like Sherwood. Terror's an interesting deterrent. It's almost more frightening when you don't know who you are fearful of. And if the McNamaras panicked, sought to get rid of the child, it might explain why they'd gone to such extreme measures to conceal her.'

'We're talking about a baby here. I find it hard to believe someone wouldn't let something slip. I mean, this scenario is every parents' worst nightmare. Especially if, as Jimmy suggests, they killed Scott anyway.'

They turned into a side street. An engine revved nearby. 'It's all speculation, isn't it?' Beth said. 'I mean without the McNamara brothers or Scott Owen to question, and with no other evidence, we can't prove anything.'

Nick pulled down the corners of his mouth. 'Perhaps we'll never know.'

47

Nick and Beth were back in Northampton, cruising towards the town centre, on their way back to headquarters, when they heard the sirens. Nick pulled over to allow a police car with lights blazing to pass. It was quickly followed by another, then an ambulance. They watched the brake lights flicker as they navigated a sharp bend in the road, and disappeared. The empty boxes of the takeaway they'd picked up on the way back, shifted along the back seat as he steered back onto the road.

'Looks urgent,' Beth said. She was wondering whether to follow and offer a hand, when Nick's mobile rang. He answered it on open speaker.

Pete didn't bother with preamble. 'Where are you, guys?' He sounded breathless, as if he'd been running.

'On the A428, heading towards the town centre,' Nick said.

'We've got a jumper, off the multi-storey car park beside the theatre. It's Daniel Owen.'

Beth jerked forward. 'What?'

'There's a uniformed officer already on scene. He recognised Daniel from the photos in the news.'

'We're a few streets away,' she said. Nick flatted the

accelerator and she flew back into her seat. 'We'll head straight there.' They steered into Victoria Promenade. 'Oh, and Pete?'

'Yeah?'

'Get someone to pick up Cara and bring her over. If anyone can talk Daniel down, she can.'

Beth cut the line as Nick took a sharp right at the roundabout to a kaleidoscope of flashing lights. Police vehicles were parked at angles, blocking off Swan Street. He parked up at the kerb and they raced through the line of stationary vehicles that had reached the roadblock. Drivers were making U-turns in the road, others getting out of their cars, trying to see what had caused the commotion.

Beth and Nick held up their cards at an officer standing beside the cars. His colleague was unwinding a roll of police tape, setting up a cordon.

The multi-storey car park loomed in front. Beth looked up to see a figure teetering on the edge of what appeared to be the top floor. Faces were pressed to windows on the low building opposite.

'Move these cars back,' Nick said to the officer with the police tape, waving at the vehicles behind them, 'and take the cordon wider. We don't want anyone injured if he decides to jump.'

An officer beside the top entrance to the car park was talking into a radio. Beth recognised him as Sam Bert, or Berty as he was known to colleagues. They'd done their first aid training together only last month. She introduced him to Nick. 'We're working on the Owen case,' she said to Berty. 'What do you know?'

'Not much, we've only been here a few minutes. The first responders are already up there with Mr Owen.'

'You're sure it's Daniel Owen?'

He nodded his head. 'Sure as we can be without checking his ID. We're just trying to get the area emptied. It's a bloody nightmare, the car park has numerous exits and entrances.'

Nick nodded a sympathetic thanks. 'We'll head up, see what we can do.'

'His sister is on her way,' Beth said. 'Can you make sure she's guided through the cordons please.'

Berty's attention was taken by a voice on his radio. He nodded and waved them through.

Beth knew the car park. She'd parked here only last week when she'd brought Lily to the pantomime. It was busy, they'd had to drive up to floor eight. She'd never quite made it to the top though.

Beth dashed up the stairs, one flight after another, her knees burning, the metal rail cold in her hand. She could hear Nick's breaths, thick and fast, as he followed. Did Daniel know about the DNA results, the paternity? They'd only been shared with Bishop Bryan and the Russells, and only then out of necessity to the investigation. She'd sworn them both to secrecy. But while she churned this over, a nasty prospect sunk into her like a stain. Vic had argued with Marie on the night he discovered Daniel wasn't Alicia's father and spent much of the evening in the pub in a drunken haze. What if he'd let something slip? He was drinking at The Windhover in Kingsthorpe, close to where both men were raised. Perhaps someone had heard him and contacted Daniel.

She was Daniel's liaison officer; she'd assured Cara she'd keep him safe.

By the time they burst on to the top floor of the building, Beth's heart was pounding in her chest. She looked this way and that, frantically searching the empty tarmac. Where were they? She dashed to the edge, where she thought she'd seen the figure earlier. It was empty. She peered over. There was a ledge below. It was impossible to jump off here to the ground.

'Down!' she cried to Nick.

They raced down a level, to the floor above where she'd parked last week, and she flashed her badge at an officer she didn't recognise, guarding the exit of the staircase. In the distance, she could see a figure in denims and a hoody, despite the close to minus temperatures, standing on top of the wall. He was facing away from them, a shoulder leaning against a concrete pillar to the side.

'How long has he been there?' she asked, her eyes glued to Daniel. He only needed to slip his footing, lean slightly...

The officer's brow furrowed. 'We're not sure exactly. He was spotted by a passer-by below who called us.' He checked his watch. 'We arrived twelve minutes ago.'

Nick made to move forward, to go and relieve the young officer standing close to Daniel. Beth put out a hand to stop him. 'I'll go. Daniel knows me.'

'You sure?'

Beth nodded. If her actions in any way contributed to this situation, she owed it to Daniel to get him down. And she owed it to herself too.

It was icy cold, the air still.

The other officer was eight metres or so away from

Daniel. She walked over to him and introduced herself. Another face she didn't recognise; there were so many new recruits these days, she was losing touch.

'Has he said anything?' she asked in a low voice.

'Nothing, apart from warning me not to come any closer. We recognised him from the media photos, called it in straight away.'

'Thanks.' Beth gave a sideways nod for him to retreat. She'd only been in this situation once before when a young mother had threatened to throw herself off the top of the shopping centre car park in the middle of town. Beth was a rookie at the time, just out of training. Single-crewed because they were short-staffed. After much to-ing and fro-ing, and much to Beth's relief, the woman stood down before backup arrived. But Beth had never forgotten the drill. Keep it basic. Clear the area. Give the victim one point of contact, one voice. The last thing they needed was for different tones and accents to cause confusion, or, worse, panic.

She waited for the officer to join the others and moved forward. Gently does it. Slow paces. 'Daniel,' she called. 'It's Beth.' First name terms. Keep it personal.

He tossed her a fleeting glance and turned back, unspeaking.

She inched forward. 'Daniel, is it okay if I come a bit closer?'

The air swished around her. If he'd heard her, he didn't respond.

Another tentative step. And another. She was only four metres away now. A few more and she'd be within grabbing distance.

A siren bellowed in the distance. Daniel looked down. She recalled the crowd gathered below, watching with bated breaths.

Beth stilled, waited for the siren to fade, then held out her foot again.

'That's enough.' He was watching her out of the corner of his eye.

'I just want to speak to you, Daniel,' she said gently.

'I don't want to talk.'

'I'd like to help.'

He was quiet a second. Staring out at the tufty clouds filling the sky. It was a surreal picture. The rear view of a man standing with a backdrop of sky behind him. 'You know, don't you?' he said eventually.

'What?'

'About Alicia. You've had the test results back.'

'Daniel, why don't you come down and we can discuss this?'

'Discuss what?'

Beth paused. She needed to tactful here. She couldn't afford to lose him. 'Discuss everything.'

'There's nothing to discuss. I don't want to know.'

Keep him talking. 'What?'

'The test results. I don't what to know whether or not it's Alicia.'

He didn't know. About the DNA results or the paternity. The shot of relief Beth felt was short lived by the pithiness in his voice. He'd made up his mind.

'Daniel, come down. Please. I'll get rid of everybody here and we can talk, just you and me.'

He ignored her question and looked out at the sky. She

tried again to persuade him, plead with him. Every time in the same gentle voice. But he didn't answer.

She was beginning to think she'd lost him when he eventually said, 'I almost stayed there, you know.'

'Where?'

'In Poland. I wondered if I could make a life there. Genuinely considered it. The truth is, I can't make a life anywhere. My life ended fifteen years ago when I lost my kids and my marriage.'

Beth swallowed. She called upon her training. She needed to work harder, find his Achilles heel, bring him back to reality. 'Daniel, Cara needs you.'

'Cara'll be fine. She's independent. Can look after herself.'

'She loves you.'

He shifted position and wobbled, grabbing the pillar to his side to steady himself.

Beth's heart was in her mouth. 'What about Bailey?' she said, picturing the Jack Russell on his lap, staring up at him. 'She adores you.'

'Cara will take care of her.'

Beth wracked her brains. She was digging deep, desperately working through the case file in her head, trying to think of something else when she heard a sharp gasp behind her.

Cara called out, 'Dan!'

The voice of his twin sister caught Daniel's attention. She'd dashed forward and was struggling against the steely arms of Nick, restraining her, twenty metres or so back.

'Please, Dan!' Cara wailed. 'Come down. Talk to me.'

Daniel wavered. He looked back at the sky.

'I can help,' she said. 'I always help you, don't I? We're a team, you and me. From the same mould.'

'I'm beyond help.'

'Don't say that! We can go away someplace. Me, you and Bailey. Away from everyone. You'd like that, wouldn't you? Just the three of us.'

He turned back. Met her gaze and for a moment it seemed like only the two of them were there, immersed in their own world together. His face softened. The corner of his lips curled into an affectionate smile. A longing. Then froze.

His eyes widened as he swayed, leaned back, held out his arms, and fell into the air.

By the time Beth emerged from the car park, a pair of paramedics were beside Daniel Owen, their feet carefully placed to avoid the pool of blood around him. They parted as she approached, giving her a clear view of his body.

Daniel's remains were smaller, concertinaed by the force of the fall. One arm was wedged underneath him, a leg stuck out at an awkward angle. The right side of his face was pressed into the tarmac, his head split open and bits of bone and grey matter were merging with the blood continuing to spill out. But it was the eyes that really caught her. Open wide, glassy.

The same eyes she'd seen only minutes before, when he'd been standing above them, breathing air into his lungs. Alive.

Guilt clawed at her. Was there something else she could have said or done?

Cara's screams rolled around her head like a song on replay; she'd lunged forward when he'd fallen, and it had taken all Nick's might to hold her. That wasn't a lasting image any loved one should be left with. The thump as he hit the ground, surprisingly loud at nine floors up, had brought a rush of bile to Beth's throat.

Beth tore her gaze away from Daniel's broken body and forced herself into work mode, noting down her actions in readiness for the statement she'd have to make later. She could hear Nick talking about CCTV nearby, and witnesses. A paramedic was unravelling a body bag. The scene being processed.

Berty joined her. 'We found his car on the eighth floor,' he said. 'Looks like he drove here.'

Beth looked up at the multi-storey car park. Slats of concrete marked each floor. Stairs at either end paired up with lifts. She imagined Daniel Owen arriving earlier, taking a ticket at the barrier, driving in. A ticket he was never going to redeem. He'd ignored everybody's calls over the last few days: his company, the police, his sister. Had he been planning this? Or did the desperation grow, minute by minute, until he could bear it no longer. He didn't want to know if the child they'd found was Alicia. After all these years, it was easier to live with hope than face the reality. And when he could no longer avoid that reality, he could no longer cope.

A voice behind her broke her abstraction. 'Ma'am?'

Beth turned to see the uniformed officer who'd been guarding the top floor earlier. 'Cara Owen's asking for you,' he said. He pointed at an ambulance parked at the bottom of the road. 'She said it's important.'

Beth nodded her thanks and made her way down to the ambulance. The sound of Daniel's body thumping the ground replayed again in her head. She pushed the image of his broken body out of her mind. *Stay professional.*

A paramedic was standing beside the open doors of the ambulance. Inside Cara sat with a blanket around her shoulders. She'd fainted after her brother's fall. They had to wait until she'd regained consciousness and the paramedics were with her before they'd descended the stairs.

Cara's ghostly face stared up at her. 'Is it true that he's...' Her voice splintered, her lip quivering as a tear dripped to the floor.

Beth nodded. 'I'm so sorry.'

Cara's shoulders jittered under the blanket. 'It's all my fault,' she said.

'No. You mustn't blame yourself.'

'Oh, you're wrong. I am to blame. I'm to blame for everything.'

The intensity of her tone struck a chord inside Beth. 'What do you mean?'

'It was me that took Alicia. I was responsible for her death. If she hadn't died, Dan would still be alive.'

48

Cara's confession floored Beth. She'd been scratchy during questioning, protective over her brother, taken steps to contact the chief constable to express concern for Daniel's welfare. Yet not at any point did Beth think she might be responsible.

Still reeling, she viewed Cara Owen across the Formica table now. The woman had been surprisingly quiet on the short journey across town to the nearest station at Campbell Square, her face taut like a mannequin. They'd had to wait for her to be checked over by the paramedics before they left, then wait another hour for her to be checked over by the force doctor when they arrived. It was almost 5 p.m. by the time they were able to commence interviewing.

'In the ambulance earlier, you confessed to the murder of Alicia Owen,' Beth said.

Cara's face crumpled. 'It wasn't murder. I said I was responsible for her death. That's very different.'

'Okay.' Beth stretched out the syllables and exchanged a sideways glance with Pete who was taking notes beside her. Freeman and Nick would be watching remotely through the camera in the corner of the room. Possibly even the superintendent with them. She needed to take it gently. This was one of the biggest cases Northamptonshire Police had faced; one of their greatest disappointments. With so much time lapse, Cara's account would be crucial. She couldn't afford for her to clam up. 'Can you tell us exactly what happened on the day Alicia disappeared?' she asked.

Cara's eyes shifted from side to side, as if she was sharing a confidence. 'I took her, from outside the supermarket. I took her and she died. But it was an accident. It wasn't meant to happen.' The words were gabbled out so fast they merged together.

'Alright,' Beth said slowly. 'Let's go through this step by step. Why did you take her?'

'I'm not sure exactly. I hadn't planned to, it all happened so quickly.' She shook her head, as if to shake away the bad thoughts. 'I'd been to an appointment at the clinic in Kingsthorpe Hollow, received some bad news.'

'Oh?'

'John, my husband, and me, we were trying for a baby. We'd been trying for some time. And they told me...' her lip quivered. 'They told me our latest attempt at IVF hadn't worked. I was distraught, couldn't get hold of John. I remember driving through Kingsthorpe and stopping at Acre Lane shops – I'm not even sure what I stopped for now – anyway, I saw Alicia's pram outside the supermarket. Recognised it straight away, my mother bought it for her when she was born. She'd chosen it specially because of the burgundy hood and the car seat that fitted into the top.' A tight breath. 'I pulled into the road at the top, parked up.'

'Why didn't you use the car park?' Beth asked, picturing the scene in her mind.

'Oh, there was often broken glass and stuff in there. Kids

hung around the shops in the evenings. John didn't like the car in there. We always parked on the road nearby.'

Beth nodded for her to continue.

'I assumed Marie and Alicia were both in the shop. I wanted to hold the baby. Just for a minute.' She cleared her throat. 'I couldn't believe it when I crossed the road and found Alicia outside.'

She stared at Beth, her eyes imploring a response. Beth said nothing.

'I was worried about Marie. We all were. She hadn't been right since the birth, since she'd lost Liam. We rallied around, trying to help. After the funeral she wanted to be alone. Let herself go. She was losing her grip. You only have to see how little Alicia was dressed that day. She had some beautiful dresses, wanted for nothing, yet she was wearing a towelling vest and a nappy. And she'd left her asleep in the car seat clipped to the top of the pram in full sun! I'd bit my tongue until then, tried to be supportive but, you know, she might have lost one child, but she still had another. It was almost as if she didn't want her.

'I considered going into the supermarket to look for Marie but I didn't want to leave the little one. So, I waited outside and pushed her up the path a bit, to get her out of the sun.' She dropped her eyes. 'And I kept pushing. Before I knew it, we'd reached my car and I'd lifted the baby seat off and fastened it into my passenger seat and placed the changing bag in the back.'

Cara began to wring her hands, one after the other. 'I didn't mean to take her. Not really. I wanted to give Marie a fright. To make her appreciate what she had. I was so thrilled when Marie fell pregnant, so looking forward to having a baby in the family. And she pushed me away. She pushed us all away.' She dropped her hands into her lap.

'What happened then?' Beth asked.

'I left the pram near the shops. I was angry; I wasn't thinking straight.' She raised her eyes, met Beth's gaze. 'You have to believe me, my mind blanked. I didn't think about the fuss it would cause, or what would happen afterwards. I just went through the motions of getting Alicia home. Keeping her safe.'

Silence hung heavy in the room. 'Where did you take her?' Beth asked.

'I drove straight home. We lived on the edge of Kingsthorpe at the time, it only took around ten minutes.' A faraway look filled her face. 'Bless her. She slept the whole time. I meant to phone Dan when I got there but when I walked through the front door, she woke up and started to cry. I changed her nappy and that didn't make a difference. Fed her some milk solution from her changing bag. As soon as she finished her feed she started crying again. I panicked. Didn't want to call Dan while she was distressed. And then John came home.' She paused, looked away, reliving the memory in her mind.

'He assumed I was babysitting at first. Took Alicia off me, winded and rocked her. Time was passing and I was aware Marie would be starting to worry. I hadn't planned this. So, I told him what I'd done. And he went ballistic. Started shouting at me, told me I was wrong in the head and just because we couldn't have our own children, I shouldn't take someone else's. I hadn't taken her though, she was family. I truly believed if Marie missed Alicia for a while, she'd realise how lucky she was; see she needed help. He wouldn't listen. The more he shouted, the more Alicia screamed. He refused to talk it through. Stormed into the kitchen with the baby. I followed, pleading with him to stop shouting. He grabbed his phone. I tried to take her off him. He wouldn't let go. We wrestled. I thought I had her.' Cara's face froze. 'One minute I'd pulled her away, the next she was falling. We both tried to reach for her. Her head cracked as it hit the table edge. She went quiet. And I knew straight away, she was…'

Tears spilled out of Cara's eyes, dribbling down her face. 'And then she was on the floor and there was blood. So much blood. Spilling out of the back of her head. And all I could hear was the breeze outside whooshing through the trees. We both flew to her side. Her little head sat at such an awkward angle. She must have died instantly.'

'Why didn't you call for an ambulance?'

'There was no point. There wasn't anything anyone could do.'

'We sat there on the floor beside her for ages. Then John got up and closed the windows, even though there was nobody nearby – our neighbour was in Spain on holiday. He said we should call the police, hand ourselves in, explain the situation. It was an accident, after all. But would they believe us? I'd been under the doctor, on and off anti-depressants. It was no secret we desperately wanted children of our own. The more we talked about it, the more we realised what we'd done. I'd taken our niece and she'd died in our care. The family would turn against us. We'd be charged with manslaughter, or murder. The pain, the upset it would cause to my mother, my brother, to so many people.' She placed a fist to her mouth and took a breath.

'And that's when John decided we should conceal the body, bury it. I was against the idea at first but what alternative was there?'

'Why did you bury her in concrete?' Beth asked. The question that had been niggling her for so long.

Cara flinched. 'John was... pedantic. Every border perfect, every corner straight, every shrub pruned to perfection. He considered everything in the minutest of detail. Once we'd decided we couldn't own up, he set about planning how to dispose of her. Many bodies turn up days, weeks, months, years after the event. You hear about it in the news, don't you? He said he'd make sure that wasn't going to happen to us. That's why he didn't tell me where she was.'

Beth sat forward. 'Are you saying you didn't know where Alicia was buried?'

Cara nodded. 'I knew she was in a field, somewhere remote. That's all. He buried her alone. Carefully planned it all out beforehand. He said she'd need a deep hole. Deep enough to avoid any machinery so she wouldn't be disturbed. When you dig deep into the subsoil and replace it afterwards it takes a while to compress and settle. That's why you see mounds over new graves. Being landscape gardeners, we knew to avoid that. Someone might notice a mound of earth. He'd have to rearrange some of the soil, to make it flat, and when it compacted a sinkhole would form. He went into so much detail. Decided to put in a structure to avoid this. That's why he used the concrete. It held up the earth above.'

A tight gasp. 'I wasn't keen. The idea of Alicia being covered in concrete...' A strangled sob escaped. 'I couldn't bear it. He said she'd be safe there. No insects would get to her, no animals could dig her up.'

Beth sat back and surveyed her a minute, recollecting Cara's remark about there being nothing left of the body when she first visited Daniel. She'd thought she was safe.

'Before I knew it, he was down the shed making a wooden frame to enclose the block and mixing concrete,' Cara said. 'He told me to clean up, get her ready. I changed her nappy, put on a clean vest. I wanted to dress her up, lay her to rest properly, but there weren't any clothes in the changing bag. I covered her in the shawl, leaving one arm out. That's how she liked to sleep. She was always wriggling that left arm out from the covers.' Another tear meandered down her cheek. 'Poor little soul. I used to worry that she would be cold, stuck in there, underground. Had nightmares for months afterwards, thinking of her tiny body shivering. The shrillness of her cry.'

'When did he bury her?' Beth asked.

'The following night. We had to wait for the concrete to set and—' a ragged breath '—when Dan phoned and told us she was missing, John said people would expect us to join the search.' She closed her eyes a second. 'I felt like a robot. Cleaning up, washing away the blood, changing my clothes. Then walking the streets, knocking on doors, wandering over fields. All the time knowing she was in our shed.'

The dull buzz of the light bulb filled the room.

'What happened the following night?' Beth asked.

'John waited until after dark. The concrete block was already in the barrow. John removed the wooden frame. I helped him wheel it into the back of the van. I remember the low drone of his engine as he left the driveway. Sitting in the front room in darkness, biting my nails, imagining where he'd gone, what was happening. When he came back, he said he'd buried her somewhere she'd never been found.'

'Did you talk about it?'

'I wanted to. John wouldn't have any of it. I was beside myself. Jumped at every phone call, every knock at the door. Was convinced someone had seen something and would call the police. I pleaded with John to tell me where she was so I could visit her. He refused to tell me. Said it was better for me if I didn't know. As time passed, I forced myself to believe he was right. I had to. Otherwise I'd go insane.'

Beth had scrutinised the case notes from the original file. Cara hadn't been a suspect in the original investigation because she had an alibi. 'According to your client, you were on a gardening job on the other side of town on the day Alicia disappeared.'

'I was first thing. I popped out to go to the clinic, then didn't feel like going back to work. I billed the client for the full day, they had no idea.'

Silence lingered for several seconds.

'John started drinking afterwards,' Cara said. 'He always liked his drink, but he hit the bottle hard after Alicia's death. Started having a chaser of spirits with his beer, usually whisky. Then he'd just have a whisky. I didn't notice at first. I guess we both hit the bottle a bit and we were trying to…' Her voice cut. She cleared her throat. 'We were trying to support the family. Dan was in a terrible state. Marie had to be sedated. We were all questioned by the police. My mother was at her wits' end. I managed my drinking. As the days and months passed, John became more and more elusive. I'd come home from work and find him drunk. Sometimes he polished off a whole bottle of whisky in an evening.

'And he was pulling back from the business, leaving the brunt of the work to me. I tried to confront him, but I couldn't get through. I suppose, after what he'd done for me, I deserved it. We carried on like that for years. Him drinking, me working. Neither of us talking. Going through the motions of life. People around us put it down to shock over losing Alicia. It was dreadful. Marie and Dan separated, and my mother died. I was consumed with the family, desperately trying to keep Daniel buoyant. John moved into the spare room and we became strangers, sharing a house. Then one morning, I got up for work and found him on the bathroom floor. He'd choked on his own vomit in the night. And I thought, that's my penance for what happened to baby Alicia.'

She hung her head. 'People rallied around me after he died, and I ignored them. Disappeared into myself, couldn't accept the sympathy. That's why I live alone now. I don't deserve company. I don't deserve to be loved.'

A tear spotted the table as she looked up. 'I wanted to tell Marie so many times, to let her know her baby died instantly. But I couldn't bear to lose Dan. He was everything to me. Always there when I needed him. Now he's gone...' She reached out, grabbed Beth's wrist. Circles of white forming around her fingers. 'You must tell Marie her baby didn't suffer. That I never meant to torment her. You must.'

49

Beth's mind was racing when she arrived at headquarters, shortly after 7 p.m. Cara's glassy eyes while the charge was read out, imprinted on her brain; the woman's zombie feet scraping the floor as she was led to her cell.

The car park was quiet. She reached the back door to the station, rested a fleeting hand on the door handle, then released it and gazed back out into the night.

Cops saw more than their fair share of suffering in their careers. Trauma and tragedy were expected. Beth had attended plenty of incidents and delivered more death messages than she dared remember. Some stayed with her, like the panic-stricken man whose wife and two children died in a house fire while he was working the night shift. 'But I only left them five hours ago,' he'd said. 'They were cuddled up on the sofa watching *Strictly Come Dancing*.'

Empathise and support. Remain objective. Don't take it personally. That's what their police training taught them.

Problem was, no matter how professional and detached you tried to remain, for a liaison officer it became personal. These were people she worked closely with. People she got to know, spending time researching their backgrounds in order to provide much-needed support. Sitting on their sofas, making tea and coffee in their kitchens. They shared personal thoughts, intimate details. And sometimes it was impossible to switch off that investment.

Daniel Owen's face flashed before her. The desperation in his ice-blue eyes. The glimpse of his weak smile, before he fell to his death.

The crippling sadness of his sister's admission of an incident that shredded her immediate family into tiny pieces and ruined the lives of so many.

The wind swirled around Beth. She leaned up against the cold bricks and stared out across the dimly lit car park. They'd found Daniel's lorry parked outside his home. He'd driven back, picked up his car and headed to the car park.

An ambulance blared out as it passed on the nearby dual carriageway. A bird flapped in a tree nearby, momentarily disturbed on its roost. She was beginning to think about going inside when she heard the door click open.

Nick hunched his shoulders as he joined her. 'That wind's a killer.'

Beth felt a chill run through her, noticing the cold for the first time. She folded her arms across her chest, tucking in the final remnants of heat.

'You okay?' His forehead creased in concern.

She'd worked the case like any other, pushing aside her feelings to process the scene and interview her suspect. Now that was over, the horror of the situation hit her like a freight train. Along with a repeat of that ugly question: Could she have said or done anything differently? Could she have stopped Daniel Owen falling to his death...

'I will be.' She looked away.

'It'll be alright,' Nick said gently, reaching out, snaking his arms around her. Drawing her close.

'I know.' Instinctively, Beth checked over her shoulder.

'There's no one here.' He pressed a kiss on her forehead and for once she didn't worry about the public show of affection.

The comfort of his embrace was soothing. She rested her head on his shoulder and relished the gentle tap of his heart against hers. She wasn't sure how long they stood there. The warmth of their two bodies shared.

The sound of a boot on a gritty path filled the air. Beth pulled back. Smoothed her top, re-crossed her arms awkwardly. The footsteps grew louder.

Pete stepped out of the shadows and stubbed a cigarette against the brickwork. How long had he been there?

Nick dug his hands in his pockets. 'You okay, mate?' he said.

Pete's gaze slid from one to another. If he'd seen their embrace, it didn't show in his face.

'Better than the boss right now,' Pete said pulling a face. 'I passed Andrea Leary on my way out. She was heading for his office and she's got a real dog shit face on her.'

Beth and Nick looked at one another and moved inside. They could hear raised voices as soon as they reached the stairs. Freeman's Birmingham accent was stronger when he shouted. Andrea's pitch higher. They were speaking at the same time, drowning each other out.

'Sounds like she's gone off on one,' Pete said, bringing up the rear.

In the corridor, a crowd had gathered outside the incident room.

'Okay, guys,' Nick said. 'Let's give them some space.' The voices cut as he herded the bodies back inside. Freeman's door clicked open. Beth and Nick were still in the corridor, waiting for the last of the homicide team to filter back into the incident room, when Andrea emerged. She slammed the door behind her and marched towards them. Red blotches covered her neck. Her eyes squinting to tiny holes. She ignored them both, strode past and disappeared around the corner.

Beth watched her go, then made for Freeman's room. She could hear Nick's low voice behind her. Warning her to leave it, to give the DCI a moment. Senior management clashed all the time. But Andrea was the chief constable's staff officer. It was her that had delivered the message expressing Cara's concern. Her that had requested changes were made on the team.

They had a result on the case. One of the biggest cases Northamptonshire force had ever faced had been solved. What the hell could be the problem now?

Freeman opened his office door as she arrived. His face flaming red, the skin taut over his cheekbones.

'Ah, Beth. I was coming to get you.' He waited for Nick to join them before inviting them inside and closing the door.

Freeman walked back to his desk, sitting with a 'humph' before he spoke. 'It seems there are some that aren't pleased with how we've handled things.'

'What?' Nick's voice was indignant.

Beth already knew what was coming next. 'Daniel Owen committed suicide after recent contact with the police which means there'll be an investigation.'

'That's routine,' Nick said. The Independent Office for

Police Conduct examined the circumstances when a member of the public died after recent contact with the police to check officers had acted appropriately. 'And given that Cara herself, the guilty party, contacted the chief expressing concern, some might think she was trying to throw us off the scent. I mean, she had no idea whether or not we were close to discovering her secret.'

'I realise that. But it was Beth who dealt with Daniel and since the chief had asked for changes, they weren't expecting Beth to be the officer present with him when he died.'

Nick sat back and crossed his arms. 'That's ridiculous.'

'I know.' Freeman looked across at Beth. 'That's why I've told them I ordered you both to attend the car park as you were nearby. I've also told them I asked you to liaise with Daniel because you'd built up a rapport with him and knew him better than anyone else at the scene. These were emergency circumstances. We pulled on the most skilled person on hand at the time.'

The air in the room was palpable. Not only had Freeman tried to protect her in her liaison role when concerns were raised, he had now falsified an account to say she was at the car park on his orders. How could she ever have doubted him?

'There will be an investigation and I trust you will both concur with my orders in your statements.'

They both nodded. 'Thank you, sir,' was all Beth could muster.

'Thanks aren't needed,' Freeman said.

'What about the chief?' Nick asked.

'This hasn't got anything to do with the chief,' Freeman said. 'I spoke with him after Andrea's visit the other day.

The concern raised was general. Individual names weren't mentioned.'

Beth was astounded. The request to change Beth came from Andrea. This wasn't about policing changes to appease the family. This was about a personal vendetta Andrea couldn't let go of, and the fact that she was continuing it in her new role was galling.

'So, we didn't need to remove Beth as Daniel Owen's contact?' Nick said.

'We needed to show we'd listened and made sure the family were adequately supported, which we did. All relevant agencies were notified of Daniel Owen's potential vulnerability. He was a grown adult, functioning in society. He hadn't been sectioned and hadn't asked for help. It's a sad situation, but we cannot be held responsible for the incident that occurred this afternoon.' He gritted his teeth. 'Let's get our statements in and move on.'

Beth and Nick stood. 'Thank you,' they chimed.

'There's something else.' Freeman's face turned grim. 'I've been alerted to a… rumour, shall we say. That you two are having a relationship.'

Beth's heart cratered. This was the moment she'd dreaded. Had someone seen them outside? Pete wasn't one for gossip. Andrea maybe? Or had someone seen them elsewhere? They were normally so careful, so discrete.

'Sir, I—'

Freeman raised a hand to silence Nick. 'It's only a rumour and given that you're working and living together, not surprising. Frankly I'm not interested in whether or not it's true.' He looked from one to another. 'But you must know that I can't have officers in an intimate relationship on my management team, certainly not with one being the line manager of another. So, I'll say this once. If there is any truth to this, one of you needs to consider a move. Otherwise, squash the gossip.'

Freeman rubbed the back of his neck. 'Okay, I'm expected in the conference room in two minutes,' he said changing the subject. 'We're preparing the press for a conference at 9 p.m. to update them on Cara Owen's charge. There will also be a mention of Daniel's death, I imagine the chief will play it down as a father distressed at losing his daughter. The investigation into his death won't be mentioned. Nick, I'll need you with me.' He turned to Beth. 'How are you feeling? You've had quite a day.'

'I'm fine, sir, thank you.' Right now, she wasn't quite sure how she felt, a maelstrom of emotions rushing through her. But she wasn't about to let him know that.

'Up to visiting the Russells? I can get someone else—'

'No. I'm their liaison officer. The news should come from me.'

'Well, okay. If you're sure. Take it easy and text me when you are done. We won't be releasing anything to the press until the family are informed, no matter how keen the chief constable is to get this news out there.'

50

Marie Russell's eyes were glued to Beth who was sitting in the corner of their sofa. When the detective had phoned and said she was coming over, at nearly 8 p.m. on a Sunday evening, she'd known it was important. Thoughts of Daniel had whirled around her mind. Or Bishop Bryan – maybe they had the test results. Or worse, they hadn't substantiated his alibi. But Cara, guilty? No... That was something she'd never contemplated.

She stayed quiet while Beth relayed Cara's admission, barely believing her ears. Allowed her to explain everything. Every piece of information like tiny glass bullets, piercing the skin.

Her mind switched back to the fateful day she lost her baby. John sitting on the sofa, trying to comfort her while Cara made tea in the kitchen. Her kitchen! All the time knowing they had killed her baby. Joining the search, driving around the estate, desperately searching for Alicia's car seat. A car seat they'd disposed of along with the changing bag.

One sentence. One tiny sentence was all it would have taken to have put her out of her misery. All that angst. All those sleepless nights, wondering if Alicia was still out there, if she was hurt, if whoever had taken her was looking after her. All those years of guilt, an overwhelming guilt, like a scouring pad, tearing at her.

Cara could have negated that. Could have put a stop to the speculation. Yet she said nothing. Did nothing. And watched everyone suffer around her.

'She's been charged with child abduction, concealing a body and murder,' Beth said. 'I'm so sorry.'

'She will be kept in custody?' Vic checked.

Beth nodded. 'She'll appear before Magistrates tomorrow, a formality really. They'll keep her on remand.'

Vic's eyes narrowed. 'There's no chance she could get off, is there?'

Marie grabbed his arm, but he shook her off. 'No, love,' he said. 'I want to make sure. I don't want her anywhere near my family.'

'She's admitted to abduction and concealment of a body. It will be for a judge to decide on her sentence.'

'And the murder?'

'The CPS have authorised a charge of murder for now. An expert will be called in to examine her account and check it against the injuries Alicia sustained. If they are confident it all fits, the charge may be adjusted to manslaughter. She's admitted the offence though, she'll still go to prison.'

'Why now?' Marie said. 'Why not fifteen years ago?'

The questions were rhetorical. She felt a movement beside her. The warmth of Vic's arm sliding around her shoulders.

'I'm afraid there's something else I need to tell you,' the detective said. 'Daniel's dead.'

Suddenly, the walls felt like they were closing in. Marie heard Vic gasp. Saw him press his free hand to his mouth.

Was aware of him asking questions: 'What? When? How?' The detective talking about a car park. The words merging together, until she heard the word 'suicide'.

A strangled scream clawed up from within.

Vic pulled her close. 'What happened?' he asked Beth. Whatever had passed between the three of them, there was a time when Daniel was Vic's best friend and Marie's soulmate. During early adulthood they'd shared a life together, celebrating their successes, consoling each other in times of need. He couldn't be dead.

Beth explained how the police had been called to an incident in town. How he'd jumped off one of the high floors of a car park. It was too much to bear.

'Did he know about Cara?' Vic asked.

The detective was quiet a moment. 'It didn't seem so.'

'Why? I mean, why would he do that now? After all this time.'

'We're not sure. He refused to accept the child's remains might be Alicia. Didn't want to talk about it. Maybe it was too much to deal with.'

Fear clutched at Marie's chest. 'Did he know about Alicia and the rape?' Her words were forced out, barely a whisper.

'No,' Beth said. 'I was with him until the end. I'm certain he died thinking he was Alicia's father.'

Too much death. Too much heartache. Marie covered her face with her hands, hot tears rolling through the gaps in her fingers as she sobbed. Alicia's disappearance was an unanswered question in her and Daniel's shared history, an open wound they could never attend to, a barrier that kept them apart. Now that they had answers he was gone and she'd never have a chance to speak with him, to share her feelings and listen to his; they'd never be able to grieve the loss of their daughter together.

'I'm so sorry,' Beth repeated.

Time passed. Slowly, Marie calmed. She could barely focus, thinking of her sister-in-law and John. 'Both of them turned to drink after Alicia disappeared,' she said, wiping a tissue across her cheeks, bleary eyes staring in space. 'We all thought it was because of the pressure on everyone, the sadness.' She tossed her head, one side to the other. 'How could they?'

'Cara claims it was an accident, she didn't mean to hurt Alicia. She'd just received news her latest attempt at IVF hadn't worked and wasn't thinking straight.'

'But to take her away from me like that. And not say anything...' The room was starting to dance around her. 'All those years of wondering what had happened. Of hoping. All that terror. And all the time she knew.' She squeezed her eyes together tight, trying to erase the images crashing into her head. Of Alicia in her pram. Of Cara cradling her. Of her child, her baby, broken and buried in the ground.

'My detective chief inspector will be giving a statement to the press tonight,' Beth said, 'confirming the charge. He'll reinstate the plea for family privacy.'

Marie wasn't interested in the press or the public. There was only one question plaguing her mind, only one thing she was interested in now. She blinked to clear her vision. 'When can we have Alicia back?' she said. 'I want her buried with Liam.'

'Of course,' Beth said. 'We'll get that organised for you.'

★

A low fog had descended when Beth left the Russells' home, swirling around the cars parked out front. The day's events coupled with her visit to the Russells left her weary and hollow. The result of solving a homicide, catching a killer was always tempered by the sadness of the lives lost and, in this case, any satisfaction she might have felt was marred by the shocking events that led up to it, and the years of pain the family had endured afterwards, only to face the crushing reality the person responsible was one of their own. Cara and Marie were sisters in marriage. They'd been raised in the same circle, spent family occasions in each other's company, celebrated birthdays and weddings together.

She'd avoided sharing the explicit details of Alicia's burial. Hadn't told Marie her daughter was entombed in concrete. She'd have to share it with her, sooner or later, and as tactfully as she was able. Too many people were aware of the circumstances for her not to. But, for now, the family had enough to deal with.

Marie and Vic Russell had looked pale when she left them. Translucent, empty. As if every ounce of colour, of happiness had been squeezed out. They'd experienced more than their fair share of pain and anguish during their marriage, that was for sure.

She paused under a streetlamp, pulled her phone from her pocket and sent a quick text to Freeman confirming she'd delivered the news. The press conference was arranged for 9 p.m.; Freeman would be practising his statement in his best suit, waiting for the all clear from her before he started. Maybe the superintendent would join him, the chief constable too, looking to cash in on the conclusion of a case that had blighted the force for so many years.

She was about to slip her phone into her pocket when it erupted in her hand. It was Eden.

'Hey.' The normality of her sister's voice grounded Beth. Simultaneously, a wave of fatigue hit her and she suddenly felt ridiculously tired. 'How are you doing?' Eden's voice sounded distant, as if she was standing on top of mountain.

'I'm fine, thanks. Just finished work. Where are you, you're sounding fuzzy?'

'Oh, sorry.' A pause was followed by a jolt and footsteps clanking on metal. 'Is that better?'

'Yes. What are you up to?'

'I was in the loft, sorting out the suitcases. Are you still okay to run us to the airport on Monday evening?'

Beth rubbed her forehead, reminding herself of the arrangements. 'Of course. Pick you up at six we said, didn't we?'

'Better make it five-thirty. There are roadworks on the M1. I'd hate to be running late and have to rush at the last minute, especially for Lily's first time on an aeroplane.'

Beth smiled to herself. She could imagine Lily skipping around her bedroom, packing her suitcase, fizzing with excitement for her holiday in Lapland. There wouldn't be much hope of getting her to sleep for the next couple of nights. 'I bet she's really excited.'

'You could say that. We'll finish packing tomorrow, then she's got her last day at school before we go.'

'Good luck. How's she getting on with the camera?'

'Goodness, she won't put it down. Even sleeps with the damn thing. She's snapping pictures of everything.'

Beth laughed. 'Don't forget to take it with you. Is there anything else you need?'

'No, I'm all sorted. I'll see you here at five-thirty on Monday.'

Beth sucked in a lungful of damp air as the phone line cut. All she craved now was a hot drink and a warm bed. She lowered her arm. And noticed a movement in her peripheral vision. A figure standing in the shadows on the other side of the road. Tall. His face obscured by a baseball cap, the peak pulled down low. The thick-set physique, the square head looked vaguely familiar. She squinted through the mist. It couldn't be...

'Hey!' she said, making her way across the road. He didn't budge.

Her phone rang. She pulled it out of her pocket. It was Nick. She clicked it off and looked up again. To find him gone. Footsteps nearby tapped the pavement. She turned both ways, desperately trying to place the sound. The mist was thickening, she could barely see a few metres in front. He was running off. Which way? Beth searched the road, up and down, disorientated by the gathering fog. The footsteps faded. An engine ignited in the distance. He must have parked in one of the side roads nearby. She picked up speed, jogged down to her car. By the time she'd reached it she could no longer hear the engine.

Beth looked back towards the Russells'. It was dark. Misty. The figure had been standing on the other side of the road, away from the streetlights, making it impossible to see him clearly. Why run off like that?

Her mobile rang again. She flicked her thumb across the glass, raised it to her ear without checking the screen, expecting to hear Nick's voice.

'Detective Chamberlain?' The tone at the other end jolted

her. She glanced up and down the road, paranoia eating away at her. 'Are you there, Detective?'

It was the reporter, Pip Edwards. Beth calmed her ragged nerves. 'I can't talk right now,' she said. 'I'm expecting a call.'

She cut the line and climbed into her car. The case was solved, Cara had made an admission and given a detailed account of the circumstances, yet something still felt amiss.

Her mobile buzzed again and she looked down to see a voicemail from Pip Edwards. Damn, he was persistent. She was about to cast her phone aside, listen to the message later when something stopped her. She dialled and put the phone on speaker while she belted up. The message was short.

Detective, I was outside the Russells' when you went in earlier, hoping to catch you for an interview before the press conference, and I saw someone watching the house. I believe it's a person of interest to you. I also saw him at the cemetery when I was waiting for you the other day. I wasn't sure at the time, but I am now because he was wearing the same navy baseball cap. I'll send you a photo in case it's helpful. Do get in touch when you're free, I'd be keen to work with you, and report the case from someone close to the family.

A text beeped. Beth swiped the screen and opened the photo. Only to come face to face with a serial killer.

51

Nick was standing at the entrance to headquarters' car park when Beth drove in twenty minutes later. She'd called ahead, reported Edwards' voicemail to Pete and forwarded the photo.

She steered past Nick and pulled into a bay. He was beside her car when she exited.

'I take it you've heard the news?' she said.

He nodded, his face tight. 'You okay?' His eyes flooded with concern.

'Yes. What was Dale Yates doing outside the Russells' home?' The thought of the escaped brutal murderer from her last case being so close by made the hairs on the tops of her arms upend.

'I'm not sure,' Nick said. He spoke slowly, clearly, his face contorted as if he didn't trust his voice. He guided her towards the staff entrance. 'It's not the first time he's been there.'

'I don't understand.'

'Pete's got the enhanced photos back of the crime scene and the crowd outside the Russells' house on Tuesday. They're still a bit blurred, but there's a figure in both. And that figure wore the same baseball cap.'

She hadn't yet told him about Edwards' sighting at the cemetery. Nick's face hardened as she passed it along. 'I still can't see why Dale Yates would be following our murder investigation,' she said.

'Neither can I. We can't find any connection between him and the families. I've spoken with Freeman. He's renewed the wanted banners for Yates on the police system and updated the intelligence to include the recent sightings.'

They were at the back door of the station now. Beth felt Nick's hand at the small of her back, ushering her inside and suddenly a wave of déjà vu hit her. Yates was back and, now he was alerted, Nick was not going to let her out of his sight until he was confident she was safe.

Barely seven weeks had passed since they'd tracked down Dale Yates, charged him with multiple murders and he'd escaped from police custody. And despite their public appeals, he hadn't surfaced. She'd convinced herself he'd taken himself off somewhere, out of the county, to evade capture. But, it seemed, for the last week at least, he'd been sitting right under their noses.

Memories drifted into her mind. She snagged them: the edginess at home; the side gate left open, the car that tailgated her with the cloned plates. She'd questioned her own sanity, wondered if she was losing her nerve. What if there was more to it? What if Yates, in his own warped sense of reality, wasn't following the case, he was following her? He'd been in prison, serving time for murder when Alicia was kidnapped. He had no links with the family and there was nothing to suggest he was involved in the abduction. She considered his presence at the graveyard, at the Russells', at the crime scene. All places she'd frequented as she'd carried out her duties.

'Come on up,' Nick said as they reached the stairs. 'Freeman's pulled out of the press conference, left the super to cover it, and called an urgent meeting.'

Minutes later, sombre faces focused on a new board at the front of the conference room covered with a map of the area, highlighting the recent sightings of Dale Yates. Freeman, Nick, Beth and Pete sat around the end of the table, listening to Archie Reynolds from intelligence as he talked them through the board.

They should have been down the pub now, celebrating the end of a prolonged cold case with the rest of the team. Instead they were staring at photos of an escaped criminal.

'We all know Yates is a master of disguise,' Reynolds said. 'He's shaved off his beard, taken out his earring, used a baseball cap to obscure his face. His mistake is that he's worn the same navy cap each time. That's what made us look a little closer.'

'Wasn't he wearing a baseball cap on one of the photos we have of him from the last case?' Nick said.

Reynolds nodded.

'Might explain your tailgater the other night,' Pete said to Beth.

Nick rounded on Beth. 'Why wasn't I told about this?'

Beth avoided his eyeline. 'I did mention it. I was on my

way home from Kettering. Thought it was joyriders at the time. We logged it as intelligence.' She recalled playing it down to Nick, not wishing to arouse any suspicion. Perhaps she should have taken it more seriously.

'Was the driver wearing a baseball cap?'

She shrugged. 'It was dark. I couldn't tell.'

'Well, at the very least it needs to be marked as another potential sighting,' Freeman said.

'Where has he been staying?' she said. 'Someone must have been harbouring him.'

'We've already tried everyone we know,' Reynolds said. 'No one's talking.'

'More to the point, what does he want?' Pete chipped in. 'If he relished his freedom, he certainly wouldn't come back to Northamptonshire and risk getting close to an investigation by a team of officers that know him.'

'Okay, let's alert the victims' families from our last case, heighten the security and make sure they're safe,' Freeman said. 'Although I think he would have gone after them by now, if he was minded to.' His gaze rested on Beth. 'Right, I think that's enough for one day. Beth, I want you to take a couple of days off.' Beth opened her mouth to protest, but before she could speak, Freeman held up a hand to silence her. 'You've had a heavy few days. We can keep things ticking over here. Build the file on Cara Owen. Keep searching for Dale Yates. I want someone with you all the time, and I mean all the time, until Yates is either back behind bars, or we are clear of his intentions. I take it Nick is still lodging with you?'

In his office, Freeman had implied he already knew the

answer to that question. He was playing to the audience. Beth played along and gave a single nod.

'Right, I'm giving him time off too.'

He looked across at Nick. 'Think of it as a working holiday.' It would have been funny if they hadn't had the relationship conversation earlier.

52

Beth felt a tugging, as if she was being drawn up from the depths of the ocean floor. She battled to open her eyes, blinking several times to focus. She was in her bedroom. Her shirt pooled on the chair in the corner; her keys rested on the bedside table. She'd tossed and turned for most of the night, tormented by flickering dreams of Daniel Owen teetering on the edge of the car park wall. Watching him lean back, sway, and fall. Reaching forward to grab him. Too late. Again, and again, like a film trailer without the commentary. His crumpled body on the pavement, staring up at her with the sable eyes of Dale Yates, her mind merging the two figures.

The digital numbers of her bedside alarm clock flashed at her. 9.30 a.m. Milky sunlight crept in through a gap in the curtains where they didn't quite meet.

Nick crouched beside the bed, fully dressed, a plaid shirt hanging loose over a pair of navy trousers that clung to his muscular thighs. He tugged her arm again. 'Hey, sleepy head.'

'What is it?'

'It's Monday morning.'

Beth blinked her eyes wide. 'What?' Vague images of Nick bringing her drinks and a sandwich seeped into her mind. She'd thought she was dreaming. Was it possible she'd slept right through?

'You missed Sunday,' he said smiling. 'I guess you needed the sleep.' He held up her phone.

'I only woke you because your mobile keeps buzzing. It's Eden.'

She pulled herself up to a sitting position and dug the pads of her hands into her eyes, then took the phone. Four messages from her sister from earlier that morning flashed up. She dialled Eden without checking them.

'I'll get you a cup of tea,' Nick said.

Eden answered on the second ring. 'Beth, where are you?' Her tone was chipped. Anxious. 'I've been calling and calling.'

Accustomed as she was to her sister's mood swings, Beth rubbed her eyes again with her free hand. 'At home. I was asleep.'

'Lily's missing.'

'What?' Her hand dropped to her side.

'She's gone. I can't find her anywhere.'

'Wait a minute.' Another glance at the clock. At 9.30 a.m. on a Monday morning during term time there was only one place Lily could be. 'Surely she's at school?'

'No. The school secretary phoned me half an hour ago to tell me she hadn't arrived.'

Beth sat forward, the urgency in her sister's voice razor-sharpening her senses. 'Okay, slow down. Tell me exactly when you last saw her.'

'She left home at twenty past eight. She was supposed to walk to school with Chloe, the little girl who lives up the road.'

'I know Chloe.' Chloe was in the same class as Lily. Her mother had been helping at the party the other night.

'I rang Chloe's mother after the school called me. Lily didn't arrive to call for her. They assumed she was taking the day off because of her holiday and made their own way.'

Beth felt the hand of fear clutch her chest. It seemed an odd decision for Eden to allow her daughter to walk to school alone. She rarely let her out of her sight. 'Try not to worry,' she said calmly. 'I'm sure there's a simple explanation. Where are you now?'

'I've just arrived back home. Chloe's mum and I have scoured the village. We've been to the school, the park, everywhere I can think of, looking for her.' The grip on Beth's chest tightened a notch. Mawsley was a modern village with less than 2500 residents and set within rolling countryside. The nearest town, Kettering, was over five miles away. There were very few places for a child to hide, even if they were minded to.

'I'm scared, Beth.' Eden's voice splintered. 'I've called the police.'

'Where are you now?'

'Back at home.'

'I'll be there in five minutes.'

53

The short drive, from one side of the village to the other, took longer than usual that morning. A lorry had broken down, blocking the main route, and Beth had to take the long way around. She was aware of Nick beside her, phone glued to his ear, and shut out his conversation, instead searching the pavements as she navigated the winding roads, desperately searching for Lily's red coat, her blonde curls.

Last week, they'd been investigating the case of a missing child. Today, her own niece had disappeared. It seemed surreal.

Nick ended his call. 'I've spoken to some friends at the office, pulled some strings,' he said, turning to Beth. 'Warren Hill's back from annual leave today. He'll meet us at Eden's, take her account.'

'Thanks.' The child had been missing for less than two hours but given the circumstances – an eight-year-old, ordinarily happy, excited to go on holiday to Lapland that evening, disappearing on her way to school – she'd be treated as vulnerable. She could imagine the scene at the office right now: Freeman would be pulling in his detectives. Sleepy faces recovering from the long hours on the Owen case, engaged in a new enquiry. She gripped the steering wheel.

'They've also ramped it up a gear and despatched uniform to make a start on door to door,' Nick said. He placed a comforting hand on her knee. 'Just precautionary, of course. We'll cancel it when we find her.'

Beth appreciated his tactfulness, though it didn't stop the fear continue to grip her chest. She'd worked a few cases of missing children. Mostly kids from foster homes and children's homes who'd run away. Unhappy kids with issues who were later found and returned. There was one incident of a five-year-old who'd become separated from his mother in a shopping centre. By the time Beth arrived, he was sitting on a desk in security, swinging his legs and waiting for his mother. Very few youngsters disappeared and if her job had taught her anything, it was that time was crucial. The longer Lily was missing, the more sinister the circumstances.

By the time they pulled up outside Eden's house, Beth's heart was chugging in her chest.

Eden was at the door before they reached the step, a tissue pressed to her cheek.

'What happened?' Beth asked, squeezing past the two pink suitcases in the hallway.

'I don't know.' A fresh wave of tears spilled down Eden's cheeks. 'She left here at twenty past eight. I waved at her from the front window, watched her to the corner. It was only another two hundred yards to Chloe's house. I thought she was at school until the secretary phoned me to say she hadn't arrived.'

'What time was that?'

'Just before nine. She was supposed to start at 8.45.'

A slender woman with dark hair pulled back into a high ponytail was beside the fireplace when they entered the front room. Alex, Chloe's mother. She was dressed in a smart black trouser suit.

'I'm so sorry,' Alex said. 'I knew she was going on holiday this evening. When she didn't arrive to walk with Chloe this morning, I thought perhaps she was taking the day off, and took Chloe to school myself. I was leaving the village, on my way to work, when Eden phoned.'

'You didn't see anything unusual on your school route?' Beth asked. 'A car you didn't recognise, any strangers hanging around?'

Eden gasped. 'You think someone's taken her?'

Beth exchanged a flickered glance with Nick. 'No, of course not, darling,' she forced the words out, looking back at her sister, her face impassive. 'These are routine questions. We're checking for witnesses who might have seen her.'

Alex paled. 'I didn't see anyone unusual.'

'What about the school?' Beth said to Eden. 'Could she be in a different class today, or have missed registration?' The questions were futile, Beth knew that. The school would have already made these checks before they alerted Eden, but they needed to be positive.

'The secretary has done a thorough search. You know how small the school is, there's only one class per year. Lily's never off. Even when she's ill, she insists on going. That's why they called me so quickly. The teacher asked the kids in her class and nobody has seen Lily this morning.' She dabbed her eye with the soggy tissue.

'Okay. How did she seem when she left home?'

'Fine. Normal. Excited about the holiday, her last day of school.'

'What about her favourite places nearby?' Nick said. 'Is there somewhere she particularly likes to go?'

'We go to the pond to feed the ducks, and the playground, but we've already been there.'

'Anywhere else?'

'She likes to walk down the lane to see the horses. I've checked there too.' Eden drew a ragged breath. 'I'm worried something's happened to her.'

Beth reached out an arm and pulled her sister close.

'Where do you live?' Nick asked Alex.

'Around the corner, at 23 Tennison Road. It's on the way to school.'

'I'm going to head out in the car, take another look for her,' he said. 'Can I borrow a photo?' When Eden looked alarmed, he added, 'Just to show anyone we pass, to check if they've seen her.'

She juddered a nod and passed him one of Lily holding Mickey Mouse's hand on their trip to Disneyland Paris last year. A beaming smile on her young face. She confirmed with Nick exactly what Lily was wearing. 'We'll come with you,' she added.

'No. You need to stay here with Beth,' he said to Eden. 'We don't want Lily to come back to an empty house now, do we?'

'I'll come,' Alex said. 'I can show you where everything is.'

Beth passed Nick a grateful nod and guided her sister to the sofa. Seconds later, the front door closed and Nick strode down the driveway with Alex on his tail.

Eden studied Beth's face. 'Where is she?'

Beth lent her head against her sister's. 'I don't know, darling. Try not to worry.'

'How can I not? She's been gone over an hour.'

Beth didn't answer. There were many other possibilities of where Lily might be and, right now, she didn't want them rolling around inside her head. She preferred to hold onto the thread of hope that Lily had taken off on her own, to feed the horses or go to the shops, and they'd missed her. Because the alternatives were unthinkable.

'Have you spoken to Chris?' she asked.

Eden pulled away, her face clouding at the mention of Lily's father. 'She isn't with him. He's at work. He last saw her on Sunday.'

'Let's call him again, double check.'

'No. I'll message him. He'll only come over, make a fuss about me letting her walk to school on her own. I don't want him here.' Eden glanced at an old school photo of her daughter beside the television. Her hair was tied into pigtails, her mouth parted slightly exposing a thin gap between her front teeth. 'This isn't like her.'

'How long has she been walking to school on her own?' Beth asked.

Eden's chin quivered. 'She's been begging me to let her walk with Chloe since they started year 3. I kept saying not until your birthday. And after last week, well… Chloe's mum and I agreed we'd let them walk together for the last few days of term, to see how they got on. It only takes ten minutes or so. They walked to music school together on Saturday morning too. Oh, why did I say yes?' She dropped her head into her hands.

Beth enveloped her sister in a hug and rubbed her back, fighting to remain calm. But as much as she tried, fresh spikes of fear snuck in. Out of the window, she spotted a police car pull up. Two uniformed officers spilled out. One of them gave Beth a nod as he wandered up the driveway of Eden's next-door neighbour. They'd start house to house in Eden's close, then branch out to the rest of the village. Lily disappeared a few minutes after leaving home, between the corner of her street and Chloe's house up the road. It was a small area. Hopefully one of the residents had spotted something.

Eden choked a sob and Beth kissed the top of her head. The officers wandered down the drive next door and crossed the road. She was reminded of Marie Russell's face when the woman gave her account, only days earlier. The pain of the search for her child. The anxiety of not knowing. She gulped a breath. 'Where's your phone?'

Eden lifted her gaze and jutted her forehead towards the coffee table. 'Why?'

'We need to ring everyone you know, everyone that's met Lily. Parents of kids she's been on play dates with, her swimming tutor, the teacher from her drama class. Everyone. All your contacts.' Eden pulled a perplexed look. 'It's only what the police will ask you to do. Find out when they last saw Lily, when they last heard from her and how she seemed in herself. Perhaps she agreed to help someone—'

'She would have told me.'

'Not if it was on a school day and she thought it might upset you. We need to cover every eventuality. What about Kyle?'

'What do you mean?'

'Well, what if he's upset someone? People know you two used to be involved.'

'No, Beth. You're not putting this on Kyle. He's a friend. He'd never do anything to put Lily in danger.'

Beth held out her hand, unconvinced. 'Okay, give me the phone. I'll make a start.'

54

'Let's go through this again,' Warren said. 'What time did Lily leave here this morning?'

For the past twenty minutes they'd been sitting around Eden's dining room table while DC Warren Hill took an account of the morning's events and scratched notes on the A4 pad in front of him. Beth nudged her chair closer to her sister's, placed an arm around her and looked up at Warren gratefully. His hair had grown into short silver waves on his holiday and with his freshly tanned skin, and super-lean body, he seemed well. It was heartening to have him close by. An experienced liaison officer, he was good at his job, subtle. He'd mentored Beth in her role, and they worked well together. Although this time she was on the receiving end, a member of the family he was supporting.

Warren scribbled down Eden's answer. 'Do you have a recent photo you'd be happy to share?' he asked. His West Country accent was soothing and gentle.

'I gave one to Nick earlier.'

Beth watched her sister's face pain. Nick would have circulated the photo internally. The officers carrying out door to door would have copies.

'Yes, and we're very grateful. We can't have enough

though. Perhaps you've got one in the clothes she was wearing today, or something similar?'

Eden heaved a breath.

Warren smiled kindly. 'I know this is difficult, but every little detail will help.'

Eden waved her hand towards a dresser against the far wall where every shelf was littered with family photos: Lily holding up a medal at a swim gala. Lily and Beth on the beach at Cromer. Endless school portraits and snapshots with friends. Beth released her sister and crossed the room, working through them and returning with her last school photo.

'No! She was in mufti today. Jeans and a pink sweat top. Those shiny trainers. I've got a better one.' Eden grabbed her phone, frantically scrolling through. 'Here,' she said eventually holding it out to Warren. 'This is more like she looked this morning. I tied her hair in the same ponytail. I'll email it to you.'

Warren thanked her and passed across his email address. 'Does Lily have a phone?' he asked when they were done.

'No. She's too young.'

'What about access to a laptop, or a games console?'

Eden nodded.

'I'll need to take them for examination, in case she's been talking with anyone online. It's just a precaution.'

'Oh, and there's her camera too,' Beth said.

'She took that in for show and tell this morning.'

'To school?' Beth turned to her sister aghast. 'Are they allowed to take in valuable items?'

'No, not really.' Eden's face folded. 'She pleaded with me and it was her last day of school before the holiday. I probably shouldn't have let her.' Her eyes glazed. 'Not that it matters now.'

Beth excused herself to go and make tea while Eden took Warren up to see Lily's room and sort through their devices. She switched on the kettle and gripped the kitchen side.

Please let them find her.

The sound of the doorbell made her start. She pulled herself together, made her way to the door. It was Nick and Alex.

Nick shook his head at Beth.

The sound of feet descending the stairs in soft thumps filled the air. Eden rushed forward. 'Any news?' she asked as the pair crossed the threshold.

'Not yet. We're sending out more officers, trying every house,' Nick said.

Eden grabbed her mouth. Nick motioned for Alex to guide her through to the front room, then followed Beth into the kitchen and closed the door.

'What is it?' Beth asked.

'How are *you* doing?'

There really wasn't any news. Nothing. Tears sprang into Beth's eyes. She battled to keep them at bay. They both knew child abduction was incredibly rare. And they also knew, the longer Lily was gone, the more likely it was someone had taken her. 'You don't think it's Yates, do you?' Beth said looking up at Nick. 'I mean, after what we discovered on Saturday, we know he's nearby.'

'I don't know,' Nick said. 'The thought has crossed my mind. But something about it feels wrong. Yates is all about justice. We don't even know if he's targeting you and if he is, I don't see what he could have against your family.'

Beth's throat was raw. She wasn't so sure.

'Freeman's called us all in for a strategy update,' he continued. 'He's setting up a major incident room, organising a search of the surrounding area.' He hugged her, pressing his head to hers. 'We're doing everything we can to find her,' he whispered, his nose in her hair.

The smell of him, the even tone of his voice was comforting. But it didn't stop the sickly acid rising in her mouth. 'I want to be involved,' she said, pulling away and brushing a tear from her cheek.

'You're needed here. With Eden.'

He was right, of course. But the very notion of the search, the investigation going on around her, just out of reach was like someone tightening the buckle on her straitjacket. 'Phone me, please? I want to be updated as soon as you have anything.'

'Of course. Make sure you keep the doors locked and your phone is with you. I'm going to take Alex home to get changed. She wants to be involved in the search.'

55

Beth wandered out of the bathroom and checked her watch. It was almost lunchtime and there was still no word on Lily. Warren had returned to the office for a briefing and Eden had fallen asleep on the sofa, exhausted after the morning's events. She glanced across the landing, her gaze resting on the sign on Lily's door.

PRIVATE
LILY'S ROOM
KNOCK BEFORE YOU ENTER

They'd made that sign together last summer, using the new scented felt tips Beth had bought her. Every one holding a different fruity aroma. A woeful smile twitched the corner of her lips as she re-read the final line. KNOCK BEFORE YOU ENTER. Lily had insisted on using every colour in the pack and the yellow E and pale pink R on the end were barely legible in the dull landing light.

She listened for any sound, any hint of her sister waking. All was quiet. Then she crossed the landing and slipped into the child's room, pushing the door to a gentle close behind her.

The room smelt of the child's violet talc. Lily's pale blue walls, dolphin-covered duvet, fairy lights attached to the white headboard of her bed all looked the same as when Beth was last there. When her niece was with her. White curtains sat open at the window. A matching pink onesie and bathrobe hung on the back of the door. Her bedside table was littered with a collection of odd shaped pebbles Lily had brought back from holidays; a mango lip balm and a few hair bobbles strewn to the side.

Beth opened the wardrobe and brushed the dresses, trousers and tops hanging on a single rail, a rainbow of colours. Eden was an attentive mother, ironing her daughter's clothes as soon as they were dry from the washer, arranging them in her cupboards. Nothing like the tumbling ironing basket in Beth's house. She approached the chest of drawers and worked her way through underwear, tops, socks. Sat on the bed and smoothed the creases around the dolphin's nose on the pillow, then lay down, resting her head to the side and taking in Lily's soft scent. The child had lived in this house since she was born. Many a time Beth had laid here with her niece, reading her a bedtime story. She looked at the plastic stars fixed on the ceiling. Stars that lit up in the dark to resemble a night sky.

Where are you, Lily?

On the wall beside the door, a photograph of Lily's grandmother stared back at her. Beth's mother. What would she make of this?

Beth wasn't sure how long she lay there. Time passed. Eventually she turned her head, made to sit up and felt a hard lump beneath the pillow. She sat forward, reached underneath and pulled out Lily's camera. The child hadn't taken it to school for show and tell, after all. It was right there in her bedroom.

Beth switched it on. It would be useful to check Lily's photos to see if any strange faces cropped up. The power light stayed black. It was out of charge. She pulled open the drawer on the bedside cabinet, sifting through more hair bobbles, a notebook, several pens and felt tips, until she found the charger. Taking time to pull it out, locate a socket and plug it in. It would probably take a few minutes. Rising to look out of the window, she was surprised to see a Range Rover parked on the drive. The doorbell hadn't sounded.

Leaving the camera to charge, Beth slipped out of the room. Muffled voices filled her ears as she crept down the stairs. A male voice with a local twang. It couldn't be…

Beth wandered into the front room to find Kyle Thompson standing beside the fireplace with Eden. He was staring into her sister's eyes, his hands on her shoulders.

'What's he doing here?' Beth struggled to control the barbs in her voice.

Eden jumped. 'Kyle's agreed to help us,' she said recovering herself. 'He's going to put some feelers out. See if anyone knows anything.'

'We don't need those sorts of feelers, Eden.'

Kyle lowered his hands, his face mournful. 'I've spent a lot of time with Lily,' he said to Beth. 'I'm fond of her.'

'This is a family matter.'

He ignored Beth, turning back to Eden. 'I saw the appeal on the lunchtime news. I want to help.' Eden's eyes widened. 'That's how I found out,' he said to her. 'And anything I can do, anything at all, I will.' He looked across at Beth. 'You can't stop me.'

Beth clenched her jaw. The last thing she needed was input from a hardened criminal. A criminal whose association with her sister had already caused her problems in the job. 'Try me.'

'Stop it, both of you! My little girl has been gone over five hours.' Eden glared at her sister. 'Your lot haven't found her yet, have they? The way I see it, we need all the help we can get. I don't care what it takes, I just want Lily back.'

The doorbell sounded. Suspecting it was Warren, Beth made her way out into the hallway and pulled open the door. It wasn't Warren, it was Chris, Eden's ex-husband.

'Beth,' he said. 'What's going on? I hear my daughter's missing.'

'Eden didn't tell you?' Beth was incredulous. Eden had refused to phone Chris first thing, assuring her she'd messaged him. How could Eden not have told Chris?

'She texted me this morning, asked if I'd heard from Lily. Never told me she was missing. I learned that from the guys at work.'

'I'm so sorry, Chris. I had no idea you didn't know.'

'What happened?'

Beth ran him through the morning's events. It was awkward, standing on the doorstep, but she didn't want to invite him inside while Kyle, the man who'd broken up their marriage, was there.

Chris listened intently, his eyes glued to her. By the time she had finished, Beth's heart had shrivelled to a tiny lump. What an awful way to find out your daughter was missing. 'I am sorry, Chris. I thought you knew.'

'You've tried everyone?'

'Everyone we can think of. What about you? Any contacts your end? I know your parents live away.'

'No. I lost our joint friends when we separated. Lily and I usually go out on our own.' He stared at the ground a few seconds, eyes darting about. 'Well, are you going to let me in?' he said eventually.

Beth was torn. The last thing Chris needed right now was to find his wife in the front room of their former family home with her criminal lover, the man she was supposed to have given up.

'It's not a good time,' she said. 'Eden's in pieces.'

'I don't care.'

'She doesn't want to see you.'

Voices trickled through from the front room. Chris looked back at the Range Rover parked at the end of the driveway and recognition flared in his eyes. 'Yeah, and I can see why.' With that, he stepped inside. Beth put a hand to his chest. She'd already argued with Kyle. There was no way she wanted to add salt to Eden's many wounds by letting Chris loose on him. But Chris had already made up his mind and she was no match for his stocky build. He pushed her aside and marched into the house.

'Chris,' Eden said when he entered the front room. 'I didn't know you were coming over.'

'What's going on?' Chris said, looking from Eden to Kyle. 'You didn't think to tell me our daughter was missing?'

'I—'

'Don't even start with the explanations, Eden. I've a right to know. I'm her father.'

Eden's eyes watered afresh.

.

'There's no need to speak to her like that,' Kyle said.

A muscle flexed in Chris's jaw. He ignored Kyle, focusing on Eden. 'What's he doing here?'

'Kyle popped round to offer support.'

'We don't need the support of a convicted criminal.'

The air in the room tightened.

'Chris, please?' Beth said. 'Let's take this outside.'

Chris hooked Kyle's gaze. 'I need to speak with my wife.'

'I'm not going anywhere.' He stared back at him defiantly. 'Not until Eden says so.'

'What did you say?' Chris took a step closer.

'I said, I'm not going anywhere.' Kyle enunciated every syllable, eyes bulging.

'Get out!' Another step closer.

'Stop it,' Eden cried.

Beth was between them in a flash. 'That's enough,' she said. 'Lily's missing. If you want to do something constructive, join the search.' She shoved Kyle towards the hallway.

'So, he gets to stay,' Kyle said.

'No, you just get to go first.'

Kyle scowled at Chris, then shouted to Eden, 'Call me if you need anything.'

Beth shoved him again. They were in the hallway now. She opened the front door. He glared at her a second, then sucked his teeth and made his way back to his car. She waited until he'd pulled off the drive before she turned back. There was no way she was letting them both outside together to fight on the lawn.

'That's not fair!' The high pitch of Eden's voice met Beth as she walked back to the front room. Her shoulders quaked afresh as she pressed another tissue to her eyes.

'Okay, you too, Chris,' Beth said.

'You are joking?'

'Do I look like I'm joking?'

He ignored her, reached out to Eden. 'I'm sorry. I didn't mean—'

'I said, out. This is isn't helping.'

He glared at Beth, face like thunder, then stomped past her.

'I'll call you as soon as I hear anything,' Beth said when they reached the door.

Chris shot her a hard stare. 'This is linked to him; I know it is.' He pointed to the driveway, where Kyle's car had been parked.

'What makes you say that?'

'A man of his nefarious connections. Everyone knows about his relationship with Eden. He's upset someone, is indebted to someone, or someone wants to teach him a lesson.'

'Why target Lily? Chris, she's just a kid. It doesn't make sense.'

'Yet.' He flared his nostrils. 'I don't care what it is, it's something to do with him. And I'm going to find out what.'

Beth watched him climb into his car and press his phone to his ear. She closed the door and rested her forehead on the cold plastic. From the very first moment he'd told an unknowing Beth about Kyle and Eden's relationship, Chris had said he didn't want Lily near Kyle. She couldn't argue with the fact that Kyle was a bad influence: the intelligence system connected him to the senior echelons of the organised crime community. Associations like that were easily upset. Could Lily have been taken as a result of Kyle's connections? Like Chris said, Kyle hadn't taken any steps to hide his relationship with Eden. He'd moved across town to pursue her. She thought back to the McNamara brothers on Operation Aspen and the way they pursued the friends and family of their debtors to teach them a lesson. Scott Owen had royally pissed them off. Jimmy Carvel talked about rumours they were responsible for the abduction of baby Alicia. They weren't responsible, but the speculation hadn't done them any damage at all. And Scott had never been found. Had Kyle upset someone, and they were teaching him a lesson by abducting Lily?

The rumble of an engine overhead. The force helicopter, deployed to conduct an area search of the surrounding fields, its heat sensors seeking out a presence. Or a body. Back at the office, they'd be drawing up a list of convicted paedophiles nearby, in case this was a sexually motivated attack, covering all the bases.

And then there was Yates. The idea that he might be involved made her dizzy.

Beth gripped the door handle, the cold metal cooling her sweaty palms. *No. Not Lily. Please, don't let this happen to Lily.*

She wasn't the type of girl to go astray, but Beth desperately hoped she was wrong. That she had taken herself off somewhere. That any minute she'd turn up at the door, ready for her holiday, wondering what all the fuss was about. Because she'd been missing for over five hours now and there'd been no ransom call, no indication of who had taken her and why.

Beth scrolled through her phone, selected DS Osborne and pressed call. At least that was one area she could chase.

56

'Why isn't there any news?' Eden placed her head in her hands.

Beth was thinking the same. They were sitting on the sofa in her sister's front room. It was almost 3 p.m. Warren hadn't returned from the briefing, instead phoning to say he was joining the search. Either there wasn't any news, or the police were being tight-lipped. Beth knew that feeling of compromise only too well. Only disclosing to the family what was necessary. Keeping things back, watching those close to the victim in case a piece of information inadvertently slipped out in conversation and inferred guilt. Once again, Marie Russell's pallid face flashed up in her mind. She forced it away.

'You should eat something,' Beth said, stroking her sister's hair.

'I can't face anything.'

'A drink then? You need to keep your energy levels up for when she comes back.'

Eden waved her hand in the air despondently. Beth ignored her and made her way into the kitchen.

Frustration gnawed at her. She searched the cupboards, bypassing the boxes of breakfast cereal, the tins of beans.

The bread bin was empty too, and the fridge apart from half a carton of milk. Eden had clearly run down their food rations, ready for her holiday. Eventually she settled on some cup-a-soups and set about boiling the kettle. Later, she'd order a takeaway to be delivered.

Nick hadn't been in touch all afternoon. She was just thinking about calling him for an update when she remembered the camera charging upstairs.

The kettle was still coughing and spluttering. She slid out of the kitchen, past the front room door which was pulled to, and quietly navigated the stairs. She didn't want to alarm Eden, or alert the rest of the police team to the camera's presence until she'd taken a look herself.

Rainclouds had thickened outside, making Lily's bedroom appear darker, gloomier. Beth crossed to her bedside table and checked the camera. A band on the rear screen indicated it was fully charged. She unplugged it and sat back on the bed. Eden was right. Only days had passed since her birthday, yet Lily had already racked up over a hundred photos.

She started scrolling through them. Lily and her friends at her party. Head shots. Side shots. Usually with half a face missing. The table set for tea. A lopsided one of her birthday cake. A child learning to work her new toy. Beth's mobile vibrated in her pocket. She cast the camera aside and pulled it out. It was Nick.

'Hey,' she said. 'Any news?'

'Not much, I'm afraid. I've spent the last hour questioning Kyle Thompson.'

'What?'

'Chris seems to think Lily's disappearance is down to him. He contacted Freeman himself.'

Beth recalled Chris's earlier words. Why was he so convinced Kyle was involved? Was it because of his connections or was there another reason he hadn't shared?

'He stated categorically that Lily's disappearance had nothing to do with him,' Nick continued. 'Was quite indignant.'

'And you believe him?'

'He was cagey about his associations. Wouldn't give anything away. But there's no doubt he loves that child. If he had any reason to believe her disappearance was linked to him, I think he'd have a job to hide it. And he was at work, at the casino, when she disappeared. There are witnesses. I've no reason to suspect him personally.'

'Okay.' When she'd spoken with DS Osborne earlier, he'd assured her they were close to an arrest. He'd promised to put every resource on the case to work through Kyle's recent bank statements. Under the circumstances, Kyle's presence around Eden was one stress they didn't need.

'Anything else?'

Nick was quiet a minute. 'A neighbour claims she saw Lily get in to a silver Audi, minutes after she left home. She gave us a partial on the plates and we picked it up on the A508 on one of the police cameras.'

'And?'

'The plates are cloned from another Audi, registered in Birmingham. We checked and the owner was at work this morning, his car still parked in the company car park. Someone has copied the plates, put them on a similar model.'

A sense of disquiet gripped Beth. So, Lily had been taken. And the person that had taken her had gone to great lengths to cover their tracks.

'Any description of the abductor?'

'No. They didn't get much of a look at them. We're appealing on all the major news sites and Freeman's live on the radio this evening. We'll share the details there.'

It was awful sitting on the side-line, unable to do anything constructive to assist the case. Beth rolled the camera through her hands and flicked across a few more photos when…

Beth sat forward, breathless. 'No!'

'What is it?' Nick asked.

She scrolled to the next photo. It was clearer, less fuzzy. The next was even better, taken on centre. Beth gasped. 'I've found Lily's camera. She has photos of Dale Yates on there.' Beth's mouth dried. In the background she could see Eden's front room window. He'd been to their house.

Eden was beside the window when Beth re-entered the front room with two steaming mugs. Outside rain had started to fall, large droplets showering the road out front from a heavy sky. She could see a little girl with an umbrella walking back from school with her mother. Another child running behind. Lily should have been one of them, skipping through the front door, bubbling with excitement about their upcoming holiday.

'Come and have your soup,' Beth said gently.

It was a while before Eden answered, and when she did her voice tremored. 'Do you think she's warm enough?' She turned to face her sister; her eyes wet. 'She hasn't got her big red coat on, she insisted on wearing that silly denim jacket. I'm worried she's going to be cold.'

Lily being cold was the least of Beth's worries right now. She took a breath, placed the mugs down and guided Eden to the chair.

'What is it?' Eden said.

'There's something I need to tell you.'

Eden doubled over and clutched her stomach when she told her about Lily climbing into a car. Her child had been lured away by a stranger. It was every mother's worse nightmare. She started to shake.

'Breathe,' Beth said. She'd dealt with numerous distressed people over the years, but to see her sister like this… It was too raw. Too close. Tears pricked her eyes. She explained how she'd found Lily's camera in her bedroom. Eden barely listened, too wrapped up in her own agony.

Beth retrieved the camera and flicked to the photo of Yates. 'I'm just working through to make sure there's no one of interest on there. Do you know this man?' she asked gently.

Her sister glanced across. 'He came round the other day, gave me a quote for cleaning the windows. Seemed nice. Laughed when Lily asked if she could take his photo.'

57

Beth sat at the kitchen table cradling her empty coffee mug. It was almost 7.40 a.m. Dawn was starting to break outside, creating a murky half-light in the room.

Eden had been a mess after she'd delivered the news to her yesterday about Lily climbing into a strange car. A car they couldn't trace. She'd played down Yates' photo on Lily's camera to Eden – there was no point in causing further anguish until they knew what they were dealing with – and called in a doctor to sedate her sister, then reported Yates' presence in the vicinity to the office.

Masquerading as a window cleaner. She was reminded of the conversation she'd had with her neighbour about a window cleaner knocking on doors in the village. On the same night her gate was left open. The car that tailgated her the other evening, also with cloned plates...

When she'd spoken with Nick, late last night, he'd said the enquiry was now focused on Yates.

All night Beth had laid beside her sister, listening to her heavy breaths, her mind whirring at the possibilities of what Lily was going through. Was she hurt? Frightened? There'd been no more sightings of the car. Once again, Yates had disappeared into thin air. Had her niece been taken to get back at her? If so, why?

Please, God, let her be okay.

Another glance at the clock. The team would be preparing for morning briefing. She imagined Freeman standing at the front of the conference room, a map of Mawsley Village behind him; Lily's address and her route to school highlighted. Almost twenty-four hours had passed.

She took a sip of her coffee, re-working all the information they had so far, desperately searching for something out of kilter, a hole, a gap, a clue, when a movement flashed in her peripheral vision. She looked at the window. It was a misty, grey day outside; the garden was empty. A scratching followed. Then a shadow through the misted glass of the back door. The handle rattled, but stayed firm.

The shadow disappeared.

'Who's there?' Beth called out. It was too early for Warren and, in any case, he'd use the front door.

Beth grabbed her phone, fingers working the keys as she approached the door. The garden was still clear. She was about to call Nick, within touching distance of the window, when a face appeared on the other side of the glass.

Beth jumped back. Pressing a hand to her chest.

It was Kyle Thompson.

She unlocked the door. 'What the hell are you doing creeping around?' she hissed. 'You scared the life out of me.'

'Sorry. I tried the back door. It was locked.'

'You didn't think to knock? It's not even 8 a.m.' Beth stared at him aghast. Only close friends and family used

Eden's back door. Eden and Kyle were clearly still a lot closer than she'd hoped.

'I wanted to catch you on your own, before your colleague gets here.' He looked past her towards the kitchen door. 'Where's Eden?'

'Asleep. I had to get in a doctor to sedate her last night.'

'Good.'

Beth narrowed her eyes at his response. Good that she'd been sedated, or good that she was out of the way? 'What's going on, Kyle?' He seemed edgy.

'I think I know where Lily is.'

The hairs on the back of Beth's neck prickled. 'Is she okay?'

'I think so.'

'What do mean, you think so? How do you know?'

'I can't say.'

'Kyle, this is Eden's kid we're talking about! Where is she?'

'We need to be careful.'

Chris's comments, less than twenty-four hours earlier, flew into Beth's mind. He'd been convinced Lily's disappearance was connected to Kyle, yet after the photographs she'd found, she'd fixated on Yates. 'Tell me where she is.' Squeezing the words through teeth tight.

'I can't do that.' Another glance behind him. His eyes were red-rimmed, weary. 'I've got to be careful. I shouldn't even be here.'

'What do you mean? What have you done?'

His face slackened slightly. 'Oh, that's what you think. It's got to be something to do with me, right? That's why you had your colleague interview me yesterday.' He cussed under his breath. 'You've no idea.'

'Then. Tell. Me.'

'I put the word out among associates, that's all. Made it clear I wanted to locate the missing child. People know about me and Eden. Know how fond I am of her child.'

'Who's got her?'

'I don't know him. Not personally. But he's dangerous.'

Beth's chest tightened. He was talking in riddles. 'How did you hear?'

'The boss received a tip-off.'

'The boss?' Beth arched an eyebrow.

'I'm not giving out names.'

She held his gaze. 'A tip-off from who, Kyle?'

'An anonymous text.'

'Oh, come on—'

'No, this is serious. It was sent from someone who saw a man carry a child from a car. A young girl.'

Carry from a car. *Was she still alive?* Her pulse quickened. 'Where?'

'I can't tell you.'

'Oh, for Christ's sake.' Beth rubbed her forehead. 'I want a name.'

He viewed her a second, still unsure. 'Dave Salmons.'

Beth baulked. She was so sure he was going to say Dale Yates. Dave Salmons wasn't a name she was familiar with. 'Why has he taken her?'

'That I don't know.'

'Take me to her. Now.'

'I can't be seen to be assisting the police.'

349

'Then tell me where she is, Kyle, and I'll deal with it.'

'I can't! Listen, I'm told he goes out every morning at 10 a.m. for a run. Even went yesterday when...' He cut off. 'It's some kind of routine. Do you know Moreton Bridge on Bunkers Hill?'

'No.'

'It's off the Laughton Road, near Lutterworth. Meet me there in two hours. I'll take you to her. No police.'

Beth surveyed him cautiously.

'Look, you want Lily back, don't you?' The question didn't warrant an answer. 'Then we do this my way. It's one thing us finding her, bringing her back. Quite another for me to be seen informing a police operation.'

Beth scoffed. 'This isn't about you.'

'Maybe not. But any whiff of assisting cops in my game threatens me and those close to me. And we're not talking a P45. We do this my way.' He shifted his feet. 'It's our best chance of getting her back.'

Beth folded her arms against her chest. She didn't like what she was hearing but there was something else bothering her. Kyle had lost his usual cockiness. He appeared jumpy. 'I don't understand. You said, no police. You know where she is, know their routine. Surely, it's easier for you to rescue Lily, bring her home yourself and earn some Brownie points with Eden.'

'This isn't just about Lily.'

'What then?'

He raised his eyes. 'Eden won't see me. Because you're police. Because you disapprove. Always the same answers. If she sees us work on this together, bring her daughter back...'

Beth felt a ball of anger swirl inside. 'You're playing games? At a time like this. I don't believe it.'

Kyle's face hardened. 'I'm going out on a limb here. Putting myself on the line. You know what happens to informants in my world.'

Beth did know. Only two years earlier, when organised crime had been tracking the crime boss, Nigel Sherwood, one of their sources had been found floating in the River Nene. He'd been shot in the eye, his tongue cut out.

Her internal antennae twitched. Everything about this felt wrong, but this was about getting Lily back and if Kyle knew anything, if his information was sound, this might be her only chance. She thought about Marie Russell and how much she'd have welcomed a chance to save her baby. 'How do I know this isn't a trap?' she said.

'Because I'm coming with you. If anything happens to you or Lily, Eden'll never forgive me.'

Beth's phone rang. She checked the screen. It was Nick. About to give her the post-briefing update she'd insisted upon.

'I've got to go,' Kyle said. 'Meet me at ten at Moreton Bridge. On your own.' He opened the back door.

'Kyle!' Beth made to catch his arm, to stop him. Too late. He slipped her grasp, dashed past the window. And was gone.

Her phone was still ringing in her hand. She stared at it, unsure of what to do. Nick rang off. Seconds later it beeped with a text message.

You okay? Call me as soon as you get this.

Beth drew a long breath, then scrolled through her phone to Nick. Her finger hovered over the call button. She should phone this through to the incident room, have it dealt with properly with a tactical support team present.

But Kyle hadn't told her exactly where Lily was, only that she was to meet him at a specific location. She Googled Bunkers Hill. It was almost twenty miles away, half an hour's drive. She enlarged the map; it was remote, rural. What if this was simply a meeting point and Lily wasn't nearby? He'd said no police. If he noticed their presence, he could refuse to help.

Lily had been gone almost twenty-four hours. Who was Dave Salmons? An associate of Yates? Kyle said he was dangerous. Why? Every fibre of her body wanted to call it in, check the name on the police computer. But if she called it in, she might be risking Lily's life.

The objective in a kidnapping was always the same: preserve life. Pay the ransom, do whatever was reasonably required to get the victim back alive. And, at the moment, as much as she hated to admit it, Kyle was her key to bringing Lily home. Her only key. She had to play this his way. For now.

58

Two hours later, Beth pulled off Laughton Road onto Bunker's Hill. She spotted the small bridge almost immediately, taking the single-track road over Moreton Bridge that ran over the top of the Grand Union Canal. She parked up on the grass verge and checked back and forth. No sign of Kyle's Range Rover. In fact, no sign of anything. It was a sleepy Tuesday morning on a winding country road, surrounded by farmer's fields on both sides. She locked the car, walked up to the bridge and peered over the wall, down into the canal. Two barges were moored upstream, one behind the other. The grass had grown up around the guy ropes. It was a strange location. Unless of course, Lily was on one of those boats.

A gust of wind caught her, blasting her hair into her face. She pulled a tie out of her pocket, roughly tied it back. Eden had still been sleeping when she left; Beth had asked Chloe's mum to sit with her on the pretence that she needed to go to the office and check on things. Where the hell was Kyle? Should she wait, or head down onto the towpath and knock the door of the barges below. She was toying with this when... something didn't feel right. If this did have anything to do with Dale Yates, he was a planner. Which was one of the reasons he'd managed to evade arrest for so long. He stalked his victims, watched their habits. Carefully organised his kills. If he'd organised the abduction of Lily, it meant he or those close to him had been watching her habits for days, maybe weeks. And he was unlikely to keep her near a road, or close to other boats.

She leaned on the bridge, tapping her fingers against the cracked stonework as she waited. Time passed. She checked her watch. 10.10 a.m. Still no sign of Kyle. She pulled her phone out of her pocket, tapped out a message to Nick to say where she was. She was heading back to her car when she heard the low purr of an engine. It grew louder. Eventually a black Discovery appeared over the brow of the bridge. Despite the grey day, the driver's sun visor was low, obscuring their face. They indicated and parked behind her Mini.

Beth slipped her hand in her pocket, still clutching her phone as a man unfolded himself from the car. He was average height and lanky, dressed in baggy jeans and a black hoody. His head was shaved; a dark goatee beard covered his chin.

'Beth?' he asked.

Beth eyed him warily. 'Who are you?'

He looked across at her through hooded eyes. 'Kyle can't make it.'

'What do you mean, he can't make it?'

'He was on his way when the police caught up with him. They've arrested him for some kind of fraud, taken him down to the station.' He turned, pressed a button on his key fob and locked his car. 'I guess you know all about that.'

Beth's heart slid into her boots. This was the phone call

she'd made to organised crime to get Kyle out of the way. Osborne said he'd act quickly. And, after almost seven weeks, he'd finally come up trumps and made an arrest. The timing couldn't have been worse. 'And you are?'

He was quiet a moment. 'Spike.'

'Okay, I guess I'm off.' Beth made to walk back to her car.

Spike grabbed her arm. 'Not so fast.'

'I beg your pardon.' She shook off his hold. 'Do you know where my niece is?'

'I'm here to show you. I promised Kyle. And there's no way I'm going back without seeing it through.'

He seemed desperate. What hold did Kyle have over him to persuade him to do this? 'What's your real name?'

He stared at her. 'My mates call me Spike.'

'You sure you know what you're getting into?'

'Kyle's filled me in.'

Beth squinted, unsure of what she'd been told or whether to trust him. She pulled out her phone again, switched on the screen.

Before she could scroll through her contacts, a hand shot out. 'No phones.'

Beth tightened her grip on the plastic. The screen was still lit. The signal low. Her last message to Nick shown as draft. She hadn't pressed send.

'The boat is owned by someone with very influential friends. If they get a whiff of Old Bill, we'll all be for it.'

'But they're happy for someone to keep a kidnapped child on there.'

Spike ignored the statement. 'A favour will have been asked, down the chain. They probably don't realise what it's being used for. These are high stakes. We get in and get your kid out with minimum fuss, right? You can do whatever you like afterwards.'

Beth didn't answer. She'd take the details of the boat herself, deal with the owner later. Right now, her priority was to get to Lily. 'Which one is it then?'

Stones crunched under her feet as she followed him, scurrying down the footpath at the side of the bridge. At the bottom, Beth looked each way. The two boats bobbed at the side of the canal. A weak winter sun had broken through a narrow gap in the clouds and shimmered on the water; the air was eerily quiet.

'This way.' Spike turned left and strode down the towpath away from the moored boats. She wanted to slow him, question him more – there were no more boats, no houses she could see nearby – but his pace was fast. He marched under the bridge, checking back over his shoulder every few seconds.

They walked about fifty yards or so. Low hanging hawthorn snagged at her jacket. The canal an empty pool of darkness. Irritation scratched at her. 'What do you know about Dave Salmons?' she ventured.

He didn't answer, quickening his step.

She'd had enough of his games. She reached out to grab his elbow, force him to speak, when they turned a corner. A boat sat ahead of them, moored to the bank, forty yards or so away. A blue narrowboat with bunches of bright coloured flowers painted along the side. Round portholes, the name *Rosalie* written in swirly red and white letters.

As they grew closer, she could see the portholes were

blocked out by blinds, masking the view inside. Rippling notes of classical music filled the air.

Spike sped up. For a second, he looked as if he was going to continue along the towpath. At the last minute, he stopped, checked both ways and climbed aboard the boat.

The door was closed. Locked.

'What are you doing?' Beth asked.

'What does it look like?' He dug his hand into his jacket pocket and retrieved two metal objects. A pick gun and tension tool. It was a Yale lock. He planned to break in.

Beth squirmed as he inserted the mechanisms and worked them against each other. 'How can you be sure this is the right place?' she said.

He said nothing. There was nothing obvious to suggest Lily was here and she wasn't about to be party to breaking and entering someone's property. Beth wandered down the side of the boat, searching for a gap at the side of any of the blinds. It seemed deserted. If it wasn't for the music playing...

Was Lily kept here? Or was this a trap, to finish Beth's career good and proper? She only had the word of a friend of a convicted criminal, after all. Not exactly trustworthy. If she was in uniform, she'd have a baton, maybe even pepper spray to defend herself. Here she had nothing. She spun around, searched the bank for a stick, a branch... But it was mid-winter and the hawthorn edging was bare.

Beth doubled back to find Spike crouched down, examining the lock. Again, she grabbed his arm, more firmly this time.

He rounded on her. 'What're you doing?' he hissed. 'We don't have long.'

'I want to know exactly how you know she's in there. Otherwise, I'm out of here.'

His face clouded. 'We don't have time—'

'Who found her?'

'An associate. He walks his dog down the towpath every morning. The boat's been here a couple of weeks. He's watched the guy go out jogging. Yesterday, he spotted him carrying something wrapped in a blanket. He wasn't sure what it was until he saw a clump of blonde hair and realised it was a child, unconscious. Kyle had put the word out about the missing girl. Which is why he alerted us.' He looked sheepish, as if he'd said too much. Turned back to the lock, inserting his tools, working them harder.

An associate. Kyle had said the informant had been anonymous. Doubt whirled inside her. She was about to hop off, to leave when a click filled the air. The door popped open.

Crisp classical notes floated out into the air.

Spike opened the door wider and peered inside. 'It's clear.' He indicated for her to follow. They dropped down the steps into a surprisingly roomy area that was furnished as a lounge with a wooden floor, a leather sofa and a folding table opposite a wood burner. Photographs of birds hung on the wall. A bookshelf beneath. The closed blinds made it feel dingy, but through an opening further down Beth caught the edge of a fridge in a small kitchen, a darker corridor leading to the back of the boat.

Lily was sitting on a stool in the corner, head bowed, face obscured by a curtain of tousled hair.

'Lily!' Beth cried. The child didn't move. Beth rushed to her side, grabbing her wrist. A pulse. She was still alive!

'Lily, it's Auntie Beth. You're safe now, darling.' She folded back her niece's hair, examined her limp face. Her eyes were closed. She must have been drugged.

Spike urged her to hurry. He stayed beside the door, ready to make a quick exit.

Lily's wrists were duct taped together. Her ankles cable-tied to the stool which was bolted to the floor. Beth tugged at the ties. They wouldn't budge. She glanced about, pointed to the kitchen and hissed to Spike to search for a knife or some scissors while she started work on the duct tape.

He seemed uncertain, hovering for the shortest of seconds.

'Come on!' she said, motioning for him to move past her. She smoothed back Lily's hair again, kissed her forehead. Uttered soothing words as she peeled away at the duct tape. It was only a matter of time now...

The sound of a toilet flush filled the room.

Spike jumped back from the kitchen. They weren't alone.

But it was what was behind him that made terror firework in Beth's chest. Dale Yates appeared in the doorway.

Spike saw the look in her eyes, started to turn his head. Too late. A claw hammer thrust out, catching him square on the nose.

'Argh!' The boat rocked as Spike stumbled back, clutching his face. Ribbons of blood splattered the walls. Another blow. Spike lost his footing that time, grabbed at Yates. The boat thudded against the bank, water sloshing up the sides as both men fell back into the sofa.

Still the music of Wagner played in the background, a poignant accompaniment to the violence unfolding.

Beth was scrabbling with the ties on Lily's ankles, keeping

half an eye on the men. If she could just break them... The next blow cracked like a whip.

Instinct made her turn. Spike was on the floor, his body limp. Yates was back on his feet, pulling back a boot. The screaming urge to stay with Lily, to free her, was deafening. But if she didn't stop Yates, he'd kill Spike.

She tore herself away, searched frantically. Grabbed a lantern off a low table and hurled it at Yates. It connected with the side of his temple, startled him enough to make him pause. For a moment, Yates swayed, then froze. Eyes of pure evil staring at Beth.

The music ended abruptly.

A line of red trickled down Yates' temple. 'I've been waiting for you,' he said to Beth.

59

Nick shut down his laptop and rubbed his forehead. Lily had been missing for over twenty-four hours now. Statistics suggested most kidnap victims were kept close to where they were abducted, yet they'd carried out extensive searches of the countryside around Mawsley Village, done a public appeal for any sightings, and exhausted door to door in the vicinity. Apart from a fleeting glance from a neighbour who lived on the corner of Eden's close, nobody had seen the little girl after she left home.

He looked at the pictures of Yates plastered across their murder wall. The photos on Lily's phone confirmed he'd visited their home in the past week.

Every tick of the clock itched.

He swivelled in his chair, his elbow inadvertently catching a pile of papers on the edge of his desk. Statements from Operation Aspen. He watched them drift to the floor, a chill running through him.

Yates was mirroring their last case, the disappearance of a child.

The waif-like Lily with the thin blonde curls, her cheeky sense of humour, filled his mind. So easy. Keen to please. Happy-go-lucky. Even her parents' separation and her mother's occasional bouts of depression failed to bring her down. As he became closer to Beth and got to know her family, he'd grown fonder of Lily. A lump hardened in his chest. They were playing the waiting game. Waiting for sightings. Witnesses. Intelligence. And it was driving him crazy. He couldn't bear to sit here a second longer. He needed to re-join the search. He grabbed his coat and was making his way out of the office when the phone on his desk rang.

'ADI Geary,' he answered.

'Nick, it's Angelo from custody. We've got Kyle Thompson down here. He's asking for you.'

'What's he here for?'

'He was brought in by the organised crime squad on a fraud allegation.'

Nick brushed his free hand down the front of his face. Of all the days to make an arrest… 'What does he want with me?'

'I don't know. He won't tell me. He did say it was to do with Beth's family. Asked to speak with you specifically.'

Nick thanked the custody sergeant, dropped his jacket over the back of his chair and made for the stairs. Was Kyle looking to bargain something crappy against a fraud charge? He hoped not. The last thing he needed right now was a desperate criminal coming up with loose information masked as cooperation. Not when every minute was precious.

He paused at the top of the stairs, scrolled through his phone and dialled DS Osborne in organised crime. Thompson was a tricky customer with a string of previous convictions. Current intelligence indicated he was continuing to cement his reputation as a career criminal. He wasn't about to walk into an interview room with Kyle until he knew what he was dealing with.

Osborne answered on the second ring. 'Nick, good to hear from you. Any news on Beth's niece?'

Word was all over the station. A missing child tugged on every copper's heartstrings, but anyone that had worked with Beth knew how close she was to her niece and how much the child meant to her. 'Nothing yet, I'm afraid. I understand your team have brought Kyle Thompson in,' he said changing the subject.

'You don't think he's involved in her disappearance, do you? I thought you'd already questioned him.'

'I interviewed him yesterday and didn't think so, but he's called me down to the custody suite to talk about Beth's family. Can you fill me in on the details of your case? I won't tread on any toes; I just want to be sure of what I'm dealing with.'

'Of course. He's been arrested for fraud and money laundering. We've been watching him for a while and delving into his finances. Unless he can come up with some pretty quick answers and account for how he's financing his lifestyle, he's got problems. We're waiting for his solicitor to arrive before we start on him.'

Nick thanked Osborne, rang off and called Beth. The phone went to voicemail. He cursed and took the back stairs, two at a time.

'Thanks for coming,' Angelo said as he approached the custody desk.

Nick jutted his head at the door that led to the cells. 'How long's he been here?'

'Twenty minutes. Long enough to be booked in, and to

make a phone call to his solicitor. We're waiting for his brief to arrive.' He directed Nick down to an interview room. 'I'll bring him through.'

Kyle looked pale and gaunt. Nick made no move to sit as he was guided in. He wanted to keep this short. 'What is it, Kyle?' he said, the minute the door closed.

'I'm checking you've heard from Beth.'

'I'm sorry?'

'Just making sure they're all okay.'

Nick sunk his hands into his pockets. 'Is there something you want to tell me?'

Kyle flicked his eyes towards Angelo and then back to Nick. 'Can we do this alone?'

Nick shot him a hard stare. Osborne seemed convinced the evidence they had on Kyle was tight. If that was the case, he could be looking at a reasonable sentence and, with previous convictions for failing to answer bail, he'd be considered a flight risk; there was a good chance he'd be held in custody, on remand until his trial. Kyle would know this. Was he seeking to bargain? And what was Beth's role in all of this?

Kidnapping was a serious crime. If he provided information or intelligence that led to an arrest, a judge might view his cooperation favourably when it came to sentencing.

He nodded to the custody sergeant to leave them, waited for the door to close behind him, then turned back to Kyle. 'This had better be good.'

'When did you last speak with Beth?' Kyle asked.

'Just after nine. Why?'

'Are you sure you haven't spoken to her since?'

'No.'

'Call her.'

The desperation in his voice made Nick's stomach drop. 'I just did. It went to voicemail. What's all this about?'

Kyle closed his eyes and hung his head. 'I don't believe this.'

60

Beth stared into the sable eyes of Dale Yates. She had no weapon to defend herself with. And nobody knew where she was.

'Cat got your tongue?' he said, a pernicious smile curling the edge of his lip.

Beth slid her gaze past him. He was standing between her and the door. Another glance, this time at the kitchen. There must be another exit at the other end of the boat. If she was quick, she might make it out before he grabbed her. But Spike lay still, unmoving. Lily was tied up in the corner. Even if she could get out, in the time it took her to get help, God only knew what might happen to them.

Yates' mouth opened into a menacing grin. 'A dilemma, isn't it? Save them, or yourself?' The cackle of laughter that followed filled her with foreboding. He was playing with her, like a cat with a mouse.

'Those wounds need attention,' she said, nudging her head at Spike who lay limply on the floor. A gash at the side of his nose. Another at the top of his arm. A pool of blood gathering around him.

Yates was unmoved, his eyes still on her. Tapping the claw

hammer gently against his thigh. 'How's the investigation going?'

Beth didn't answer. He must have seen the news footage, know about the charge.

He drew a long breath, spoke through his exhalation. 'I've been watching you play happy families with your detective boyfriend. Waiting for another case to grab your attention. And what a case!' His eyes shone like diamonds. 'So inspiring. In fact, it gave me an idea.' He tipped his head back, jutted his jaw. 'What's it like to be on the receiving end? Of finding someone precious taken from you?'

A quick glance at Lily. So small, tucked up in the corner. Vulnerable. 'Don't do this, Dale.'

'Dale,' he said, the decibels in his voice rising as he repeated the word. 'So, we're on first-name terms now, are we?'

She edged back as he took a step closer. The hammer was still at his side, tapping harder now. 'I must say, you have a very interesting job there, as a liaison officer.' His lip curled.

'I support victims' families.'

'Even if they include the guilty party, I see. Rather a crooked sense of justice, don't you think?'

A murmur from the corner. Beth looked anxiously at Lily. 'I'm doing my job.'

'Oh, I don't think it's only that, is it? Not really. You go above and beyond.' Another step closer. 'Where are your morals? Your ethics?'

'I'm employed to administer the law.' Beth inched back further. Eyes frantically searching for something, anything, to throw at him. But the surfaces were clear. She wasn't close enough to the bookcase and the pictures were fastened to the wall, top and bottom.

'What about true justice? Where does that fit in?'

Beth could smell his rancid breath now. Her phone, still in her pocket, pressed against her thigh. If she could get to it, she could press send on the text to Nick. Give him some idea of their location.

'I didn't get a liaison officer when my girlfriend died.' He snorted. 'You have no idea what it's like for people like us. No family. Raised by the system. My girlfriend was raped, abused, yet nobody did anything. I served eighteen years in prison and left, forced to seek my own justice.'

'You almost killed a man, then attacked another in prison.'

'And why do you think that was? Jess killed herself because no one listened. And when I tried to raise the issue, I was shut down, ignored. Because no one listens to people like us. No one cares.'

So that was it. In his deluded mind he was blaming her for a social system that had let him down.

'I've never had children,' he continued. 'Never had anyone who bothered about where I was, whether I was healthy, happy. When I was in trouble and needed help, nobody listened.' A line of spittle flew out of his mouth. 'But instead of putting things in place, people like you comfort and care for these people.'

Beth looked over her shoulder. And inched to the side, turning her left pocket away. She needed to keep him talking, distract him. 'I support the families of victims. They're not at fault.'

'The families are where they come from! They're the people that produce these vermin.'

'Not everyone you killed was guilty.'

A flippant shrug. 'What can I say? Collateral damage.'

Beth moved a hand back. A quick movement. She could feel the outline of her phone now.

'This here is about showing the world what injustice does to people. How it ruins them.'

Another murmur. Was Lily coming around? 'What have you given her?' Beth said, eyeing her niece.

'Nothing much. It's quite harmless. When used properly.'

Those last words ripped through her insides. Yet again, he was playing games. And she didn't like how this one was going. 'Let her go, please. If you let Lily go, we can talk. Together.'

Yates' face loosened. For a second, he seemed pensive, as if he was considering her request. She watched him turn his head, twist it to the side at an odd angle. Flinched as the cartilage cracked. 'Oh, come on, Beth. You know me better than that.'

Another swallow. Long, dry. 'What do you hope to gain from this?'

'Well, that's easy,' he said, widening those menacing eyes. 'You see, when people don't listen, you have to make them.'

The pithy undertone in his voice was like being plunged into icy cold water. She needed to keep him talking. The longer they were there, the more chance she had of diverting him, or catching the attention of someone. Anyone. Spike had said a dog walker had reported his presence. Sooner or later someone had to pass by, or maybe a boat.

'I don't understand.'

The hammer hung limp at his side. He surveyed her a second. But he was enjoying himself too much to stop. There was nothing Dale Yates enjoyed more than preaching about his twisted sense of justice.

'My girlfriend died because the services failed her. I waited eighteen years to make those responsible pay for what they did. And even then, what happened to her, my motivation, was never given due consideration. Instead of acknowledging the mistakes made, they send out people like you to support and care for the families of those evil bastards.'

'This won't help.'

'Won't it? Oh, I don't think you understand. I'm going to make you suffer.' His pupils dilated. 'So you can see what it's like.'

He was so close she could feel his breath on her. Hot. Sticky. Pungent. Beth shrunk back.

'Your sister is going to find out what it's like to have no one. No daughter. No sister. And you'll die knowing it was all your fault that she lives a life of suffering, because of you.'

A click sliced through the air. The sound of a lock turning. From the other end of the boat.

Yates turned his head. Giving her half a second.

Beth slipped past him and scrabbled up the steps. She was almost at the top when Yates roared. She glanced back to watch him swing the hammer. And ducked.

The hammer came crashing down against the folding table. The boat smashed against the bank, the movement sending Yates off balance. He slid to the right. Grabbed the corner of her jacket, tugging her with him.

Pain rumbled through Beth as she fell to the floor with a thud. Yates was on top of her now. She felt his hands at her throat. Grabbed at them. Tugging, pulling as they tightened their grip.

Struggling for breath.

The boat rocked from side to side. Blurred around her. Voices inside her head. Getting louder. Her tongue filling her mouth.

Then she was wrenched upwards. It was a while before the mist cleared and she realised he'd been pulled off her. And she was coughing, gasping for air.

'Take it easy.'

A familiar voice. Beth blinked several times, her vision slowly clearing to find Nick in front of her. The boat filled with an army of officers in uniform, wrestling handcuffs onto Yates.

'Looks like we arrived just in time,' Nick said.

61

Beth wandered through the children's ward, checking the faces of each of the youngsters sitting up in their beds as she passed. A clock on the far wall read 3.10 p.m.

She could still smell Yates' grubby hands, taste his rancid breath, feel the intensity of his icy glare. She needed to go home, shower, scrub the smell of him from her. But first she needed to check on Lily.

Four hours had passed since they'd left the canal boat. Four hours in which Yates had been taken into custody, Spike and Lily to hospital. Beth had to wait to be checked over by the paramedics and go through the motions of giving her statement to officers at the scene, and debrief Freeman, when all she wanted was to see her niece. They'd told her Lily was responding to treatment. As soon as she'd finished, Beth raced to the hospital, jumping out of the car at the entrance, leaving Nick to find a parking space during peak visiting hours while she rushed up to the ward.

Spike was in the High Dependency Unit on the other side of the hospital. He'd come around in the ambulance. Lost a lot of blood, broken several ribs and suffered concussion but doctors were stitching him up and were confident he'd make a reasonable recovery. And, shocked at the treatment of one of their own, the intelligence sources were talking. Yates had been transporting drugs under the name of Dave Salmons, a former drugs supplier from Manchester. Enquiries revealed Salmons and Yates shared a cell in Gartree Prison and were released around the same time. Salmons had gone to Bulgaria to look up an old flame, allowing Yates to adopt his persona after his recent escape from police custody. Far from going for a run in the mornings, Yates was distributing cocaine from a holding location, setting up the street gangs with their day's supply. And he was working for the crew attached to Kyle.

He'd learned about Kyle's relationship with Eden, infiltrated the network, assumed Dave Salmons' identity to gain their trust. A phone found on the boat confirmed he'd sent the text to Kyle's boss himself to lure Beth in. The manipulative nature of Yates sent a fresh shiver skittering down her spine. It was ironic that Kyle, the man she'd fought to put away, the bad influence on her sister, was the one who alerted Nick and gave away their location. The thought of what would have happened if Nick hadn't reached them in time filled her with dread.

Beth approached the desk.

A blonde nurse with a phone pressed to her ear was tapping a pen against the desk. She appeared to be on hold. 'Can I help?' she said, her eyes drawn to the bruises like rainclouds on Beth's neck.

Beth lifted her hand to shield her neck. 'Yes. I'm looking for Lily Carter.'

'Oh, she's in room three down the corridor.' The nurse pointed to the end of the ward.

Beth thanked her and followed her direction. It was dark

and dingy out of the ward. She passed a room with relatives huddled around a bed, another with a young child sleeping. The door to room three was closed. Beth peered through the small window. Lily was laid as still as stone, her eyes shut.

'Beth?'

Beth turned to find Chris beside her, a plastic cup of coffee in his hand. 'How is she?' she asked, risking another fleeting glance at her niece.

'Headachey, dehydrated and a bit grouchy. The doctors are pretty convinced the drug is out of her system thankfully.'

'What was it?'

'I don't think they're completely sure yet. Tests haven't shown any liver or kidney damage, which is a blessing.'

'Does she remember anything?'

He shook his head. 'I've spoken with her. The last thing she remembers was walking to school.'

Relief flooded her veins. An experience like that could play tricks on the mind, blight a life, especially for someone so young. 'I'm sorry, Chris.' The words felt inadequate.

'The main thing is she's going to be okay.'

They both looked through the window. 'Is she up to visitors?' Beth asked.

'No.' The voice was firm, resolute and came from behind.

Beth turned to face her sister. 'Eden, I can explain—'

As soon as Nick had arrived at their location, he'd ordered paramedic attendance, expecting the worst. The aftermath passed by in a whirl of ambulances, interviews and discussions. Chris notified Eden and took her to the hospital. This was the first time Beth had seen her sister, her first opportunity to speak with her. And Eden couldn't have been frostier.

'I don't want your explanations,' Eden said, her face pinched. 'I don't want you anywhere near her, or me.'

'That's unfair,' Chris said. 'We wouldn't have her back if it wasn't for Beth.'

Eden cussed. Her eyes as black as coal. 'It wasn't Beth. It was Kyle. He told her where Lily was. If it wasn't for him, we might never have found her.'

'He was supposed to meet me—'

Eden rounded on Beth. 'And what did you do? Have him arrested.'

'That's not true.'

'Isn't it?' She levelled Beth's gaze, goading her for more information.

Beth was torn. Eden didn't know it was Dale Yates, the serial killer who'd escaped from their last case, who had taken Lily in a deranged attempt to get back at her. She only knew what Kyle had told her, that it was an opportunist named Dave Salmons. Sooner or later Yates' name would come out along with his connection to Beth and his motive, which would only add salt to her sister's wound. 'Kyle was arrested for money laundering,' Beth said.

'Convenient timing.'

Chris opened the door and stepped inside the room. Placing a placating hand on his wife's forearm, he passed Beth a loaded glance. While Eden might not know who Lily's abductor was, he knew. He was a cop, he had the inside track and was aware of the whole scenario.

Eden shrugged him off. 'Stay away from us,' she said to

Beth, then followed him into the room and closed the door firmly behind them.

A warm hand on her shoulder. Beth turned to find Nick beside her, his eyes soft. 'She's still raw,' he said. 'Give her time.'

Epilogue

The gold handles on the tiny white coffin glistened in the morning sunlight as it was lowered into the ground.

'Earth to earth.'

Finally, little Alicia Owen was re-joining her twin. And, after fifteen years, her mother would be safe in the knowledge that she knew where her daughter was, could visit her, tend her grave, leave her flowers.

'Ashes to ashes.'

Beth looked up to see Marie Russell dab her eyes with a tissue. Vic was beside her, his arm tucked comfortingly around her shoulder.

'Dust to dust.'

Five weeks had passed since Daniel Owen's tragic suicide and Cara's admission. Christmas had come and gone. Marie had graciously delayed organising Alicia's funeral until after Daniel was laid to rest. 'He deserves to have his own service, his own burial, and not to be overshadowed by that of the child he believed was his daughter,' she'd said. Her generosity of spirit was laudable.

Most detectives wouldn't attend a funeral, especially not a cold case, unless they were personally attached to the victim or particularly wanted to pay their respects. Beth's decision to come along today was more about support. She'd spent several difficult weeks working closely with the family and she wanted to be there for them, to the end.

The coffin jolted to a stop. Marie dropped a pink carnation onto it. Vic dropped a yellow one. A beat of silence filled the air. The twins were finally reunited.

The group around the grave was small. Marie and Vic and Marie's mother, who'd flown in especially for the occasion, along with a few close friends. They'd requested privacy for the service. Everyone involved in the arrangements was sworn to secrecy and for once in the Russells' lives, their wish had been granted. There were no reporters hovering, no cameramen with zoom lenses lingering on the edge of the cemetery grounds. No onlookers or rubberneckers holding out phones to catch a snapshot. For once, even Pip Edwards, the reporter who had trailed them throughout the investigation, hadn't received the lowdown.

Her phone had pinged with several messages from Edwards since Cara was taken into custody, asking to meet. He was persistent. She'd ignored his calls but couldn't quite find it in herself to block him from her phone. He was the witness who'd alerted them to Yates' presence. Without him, they wouldn't have known that Yates had resurfaced until she found the photos on Lily's phone.

Beth looked back at the Russells. She'd spent many an hour in their company over the past few weeks, advising on the release of Alicia's body and returning her belongings, and she'd been touched by how they'd pulled together. Even little Zac, who was missing today, seemed stronger, brighter. They'd taken the decision to save their little boy from the burial. In years to come they'd talk him through what had happened to Alicia. For now, it was enough that he knew she was back with them.

The Owens were gone. It was time to lay Alicia to rest and move forward with their lives.

Beth watched the vicar walk over to the pair and address them solemnly. Marie had refused to press charges against Bishop Bryan. Not surprisingly, she'd faced enough adversity in her life and didn't wish to rake up the past. She also didn't want it publicly released that he was Alicia's father. Without her support, they couldn't pursue the rape. But they were obliged to continue their own investigation into the bishop's conduct to ensure others weren't at risk. A small team had been established to work through his postings and speak with people who'd been exposed to him. It was a mammoth task. Bishop Bryan had moved around a lot during his career and there was a wealth of people to work through.

The DNA results proved his paternity. Whether or not he committed rape, he'd broken his vows with the church and lied to the police. They'd alerted his cardinal who'd relieved him from his duties, pending the ongoing police enquiry, and the church put out a press release, saying he was 'taking a sabbatical for personal reasons'. Would the sub team uncover any more allegations? Time would tell.

Beth bade her farewells to the family and moved a few graves along, to her godmother's resting place. She crouched down and surveyed the gold writing on the headstone. Her sister had ignored her calls and messages, and turned her away when she called at the house, still smarting over Kyle's charge and remand in custody. Eden was hot-headed, they'd fallen out before. Though never for this long. Beth stood, fastened the top button of her coat and wandered out of the cemetery.

Beth peered around the edge of the shop wall and watched the child skip along, hand held tightly by her mother. They moved quickly down the street. Only yesterday, at Alicia Owen's funeral, she'd witnessed a family unite in the face of adversity. Today, she watched as hers continued to operate worlds apart. Catching brief glimpses of Lily on the way to school wasn't enough. Missing out on spending quality time with her niece was crippling. Eden would come around eventually like she always did but the waiting was purgatory.

They were in the distance now, Lily's pig tails jogging in the wind. Beth turned back and made for her car.

Dale Yates had pleaded guilty to the abduction and false imprisonment of Lily, and GBH relating to his attack on Spike and Beth. The legal system being what it was, he'd spent the past five weeks in prison while doctors assessed his mental stability and a case file on the abduction and assault were put together, along with his previous murder charges. Yesterday afternoon, she'd watched from the public gallery as he was finally sentenced for his crimes. The judge called him a bitterly dangerous man. Yates didn't flinch when the judge gave him life, with a minimum term of thirty-two years. He'd spent most of his days in prison, after all. Was more used to penal routine than the freedom the outside world offered. Perhaps he preferred it. What terrified her, what set off a fresh round of fireworks in her chest, was the look of contempt Yates gave her when he was led out of the courtroom. In his warped mind, he still considered her at fault, representative of a system that had let him down.

The smell of eggs and bacon filled the air, growing stronger as Beth walked up her driveway and pushed open the front door. Myrtle met her in the hallway, slinking around her ankles. Beth slipped off her jacket, dropped the bag she was carrying and scooped the cat up in her arms, nuzzling her head with her nose.

The sound of Nick's voice, singing along to an old Elton John track induced an inadvertent smile. It was their day off. She'd have preferred to go out for breakfast, but he liked to cook. He spent more time in the kitchen than she did these days.

'Hey!' Nick looked up from the eggs he was stirring in the pan, grinned and planted a kiss on her cheek. The love of a good man. A hearty breakfast awaiting her. In many respects, she was lucky. If she could only resolve her feud with Eden...

'Did you see them?'

She squirmed at his words. The fact that he knew she was slipping out to glimpse her niece, that he was attuned to her desperation, only made matters worse. She nodded, unspeaking.

He placed the spoon down and enveloped her in a hug. The embrace was long, hard and comforting. 'Eden'll come around.'

'When?'

'When she's ready. She can't do without you.'

The eggs and bacon were delicious, slipping down with ease, helped along with a mug of strong coffee. The food worked its magic and suddenly she felt energised. She glanced at the window. It was a clear January day, barely a cloud in the sky. 'I was thinking of taking a walk over the fields to Cransley Village,' she said.

'Sounds like a plan.'

The letterbox clattered. Beth left Nick to collect the morning post while she cleared the plates. She was loading the dishwasher when he sauntered back in, reading a letter.

'Everything alright?'

'It's from the National Crime Agency. They've opened more positions. Invited me to an interview.'

After Freeman's cautionary chat, Nick had offered to be the one to move jobs and thrown himself into searching for other positions. In many ways it made sense; he'd served six years in homicide, she less than twelve months. It was awful watching him try to get excited about the idea when she knew this wasn't a route he'd take by choice. They'd laughed off a few jokes at work and the rumour that they were romantically involved soon fizzled out. Though it was only a matter of time before someone spotted them again. And, with Andrea Leary continuing in her role as the chief's staff officer, another rumour could jeopardise both their positions.

Problem was, there had been a shortage of job vacancies for detective sergeants with Nick's level of experience. Which made this news even sweeter.

She forced a smile. 'That's amazing. When is it?'

'Week after next.'

'I'm pleased for you.'

'Are you?'

'Of course!' She nudged his arm and made to place her plate in the dishwasher. While she couldn't imagine working the homicide team without him by her side, at least it would put an end to all the creeping around behind colleague's backs. A small mercy.

Nick refolded the letter. 'I hate being pressured to move.'

Beth shut the dishwasher and engulfed him in a hug. 'Come on. You said yourself, you were looking for a new challenge. I think you should go to the interview, find out more about the job.'

He paused. 'We could always think about making things a bit more permanent.'

Beth released her hold and stepped back. 'Are you saying what I think you're saying?'

'We'd take it slow. Perhaps look for a place together, when I get settled. Give people a chance to get used to the idea. What do you say?'

'Well, it's not the most romantic proposal I've received!'

He laughed. 'Oh, you've had others.'

'Now, that'd be telling.' She chuckled and kissed him, long and hard on the lips.

'Mm. If you put it like that, I might have to think about this interview.' He tossed the letter on the side, snaked his arms around her waist.

'Hey, watch it, wise guy,' she said, wriggling out of his grip. 'We've got a long walk in front of us.'

Acknowledgements

This has been one of the most labour-intensive novels I've written in terms of research. Thankfully, I've had lots of help!

First, I do hope local readers will forgive me for the liberties I have taken with the Kingsthorpe area. I have rearranged Boughton Green Road, purely in the interests of the story, however many of the other areas mentioned still exist today.

I'd like to thank Linda Ainscough, Senior Forensic Reporting Scientist on Anthropology, Archaeology and Ecology for giving up her valuable time and providing fascinating information about the effects on bodies buried in concrete. Also, to Professor Philip Lumb who gave great advice on pathology. As always, any inconsistencies or errors in the story are purely my own.

I'm incredibly grateful to DC Jamie Edwards for his insight into the workings of prison hospitals, and also to retired DC Garry Liburd for his continued assistance with the role of the family liaison officer.

Also, to Victoria White for providing birthing details relating to twins, and to Kate Galley for information about hairdressing and Mallen streaks.

Gratitude goes to David and Dennie Tanner who provided great background on farming methods (and a lovely evening over a bottle of wine – I still owe you that dinner!), and to Danny and Steve who assisted with details on the local homeless community. Also, to Alison Root for the lovely tour around her canal boat.

To my husband, David, and daughter, Ella, who help relentlessly at every stage in the writing process. On this novel particularly – to David for assisting with my experiment to bury a pig's shoulder in concrete, despite the consequences(!), and to Ella for graciously donating the joint of meat she was planning to cook for Sunday dinner!

Massive thanks go to Rhea Kurien and all the team at Aria Fiction who've been amazing to work with on all the books in this series.

I'm very fortunate to be part of a wonderful online book community and always feel incredibly grateful for their authorial support, in particular Rebecca Bradley and Ian Patrick. Brilliant book clubs too including Anne Cater and all at Book Connectors; Shell Baker and Llainy Swanson at Crime Book Club; Tracy Fenton, Helen Boyce and all the team at The Book Club (TBC), David Gilchrist at UK Crime Book Club and Wendy Clarke and the gang at The Fiction Café Book Club. Also, the amazing reviewers and book bloggers, far too many to mention individually, who work tirelessly to spread the word about new books. I'm truly honoured to be part of such a lovely world.

So many friends have listened to early storylines, helped with cover art, proof read, talked through characters and generally offered a shoulder to lean on, most notably David and Lynne Anderson, Colin Williams, Emma Thompson,

Stephanie Daniels, Martin Sargeant, and Philip and Abi Bouch.

Finally, to my gorgeous Labradors, Bollo and Digity. For without them, I wouldn't be wandering over the fields every day, churning up ideas for more murder and mayhem and would have to get a real job.

About the Author

JANE ISAAC lives with her detective husband and daughter in rural Northamptonshire, UK where she can often be found trudging over the fields with her dogs. Her debut, *An Unfamiliar Murder*, was nominated in the Best Mystery category in the eFestival of Words Best of the Independent eBook Awards 2013. The follow up, *The Truth Will Out*, was selected as the 'Thriller of the Month' by E-Thriller. com in April 2014.

Jane is the author of eight novels. Her latest series is based in Northamptonshire and features Family Liaison Officer, DC Beth Chamberlain.

Jane loves to hear from readers. Contact her via her website at www.janeisaac.co.uk, or join her book club to hear about upcoming titles, take part in competitions, be in with a chance to win giveaways, and receive book recommendations.

Hello from Aria

We hope you enjoyed this book! If you did let us know, we'd love to hear from you.

We are Aria, a dynamic digital-first fiction imprint from award-winning independent publishers Head of Zeus. At heart, we're committed to publishing fantastic commercial fiction – from romance and sagas to crime, thrillers and historical fiction. Visit us online and discover a community of like-minded fiction fans!

We're also on the look out for tomorrow's superstar authors. So, if you're a budding writer looking for a publisher, we'd love to hear from you.
You can submit your book online at ariafiction.com/we-want-read-your-book

You can find us at:
Email: aria@headofzeus.com
Website: www.ariafiction.com
Submissions: www.ariafiction.com/we-want-read-your-book

f @ariafiction
y @Aria_Fiction
⊙ @ariafiction

Printed in Great Britain
by Amazon